Praise for

DRESSED TO DIE

"*Dressed to Die* grabs the reader's attention from the very first page and never lets go until the last paragraph on the last page. Highly recommended."
—*The Bookwatch*

"This book will keep you guessing until the very end."
—*Herald-Whig*, Quincy, Ill.

"The plot is serpentine, the solution ingenious, the academic politics vicious, and Lindsay's appealing. This entertaining mystery is as chock-full of engrossing anthropological and archaeological detail as a newly discovered burial mound." —*Publishers Weekly*

"Delightful." —*Northwest Arkansas Times*, Fayetteville

"Nail-biting suspense." —*State Journal*, Frankfort, Ky.

"A multi-dimensional mystery that deserves comparison with Patricia Cornwell. —*Booklist*

DRESSED TO DIE

A LINDSAY CHAMBERLAIN NOVEL

BEVERLY CONNOR

CUMBERLAND HOUSE
NASHVILLE, TENNESSEE

To my brother, Charlie Heth.
This one's for you.

Copyright © 1998 by Beverly Connor

Published by:
    Cumberland House Publishing, Inc.
    431 Harding Industrial Drive
    Nashville, TN 37211-3160.
    www.cumberlandhouse.com

Cover design by Bruce Gore, Gore Studios
Cover art by Dominic Doyle

Library of Congress Cataloging-in-Publication Data

Connor, Beverly, 1948-
    Dressed to die : a Lindsay Chamberlain novel / Beverly Connor
        p.   cm.
ISBN: 1-58182-246-4
I. Title.
PS3553.05138D74   1998
813'.54--dc21
                                              98-34125
                                                CIP

Printed in Canada
1 2 3 4 5 6 7 8 —05 04 03 02 01

Acknowledgments

Thank you, Charles Connor, Diane Trap, Judy Iakovou, Takis Iakovou, and Harriette Austin, for your untiring support and invaluable criticism.

Thank you, Barbara Gerrard, for answering my questions about Arabian horses.

And thanks to you, too, Robbie.

North Campus

To teach, to serve, and to inquire into the nature of things

UGA Motto

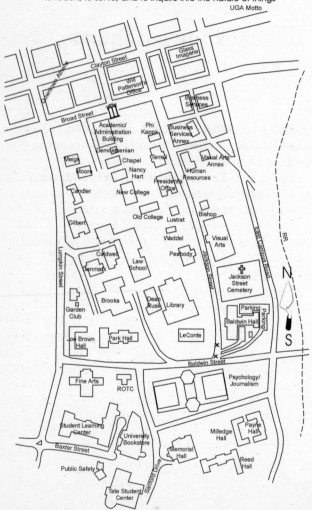

Author's Note

Although this book is set on the campus of the University of Georgia, I have repopulated the university with my own characters—none of whom bear any resemblance to anyone living or dead. If they do, it's a complete coincidence.

Those of you acquainted with the campus will note that I've added a building. Nancy Hart was indeed a Revolutionary War heroine from Georgia, but there is no building on campus bearing her name. Most of Lindsay's campus is the same as the real one, but I did make small changes here and there.

The archaeology lab is no longer in Baldwin Hall and the description of the Archaeology Department is how it appeared before the current renovations. Also, I have split Archaeology and Anthropology into two departments. At the university they are one.

Georgia has 159 counties, and not one of them is named Dover.

DRESSED
TO DIE

Chapter 1

"**W**HY DO YOU believe she's buried here?" Lindsay Chamberlain asked, pushing a strand of wind-whipped hair from her face and shivering in the early morning April air.

Private detective Will Patterson, dressed in jeans and a short-sleeved shirt and oblivious to the gusty air, gave a slight shrug. His tanned, lined face showed no expression. "Anonymous call. Makes sense. The land belongs to the husband's family. Her folks believe the husband killed her. They may be right. It's not easy to get rid of a body . . . and not be seen doing it." He looked around and gestured with a nod. "This place'd be safe."

Lindsay had to strain to hear his husky, low voice over the wind that blew through the trees. Patterson took one more drag on his cigarette, dropped it, and ground it into the gravel drive.

Lindsay and the private detective were standing with the sheriff and two deputies at an abandoned two-story farmhouse that was weathered to a silver gray. Lindsay looked up at a shuttered window to the attic.

"We've searched the house," Will Patterson answered her unasked and, in fact, unthought, question.

Lindsay was trying to imagine this as a family home. It looked haunted. Her gaze fell on a rusted red farm tractor that sat in a ruined heap in front of a falling-down barn, the only outbuilding that remained.

"The place has been tied up in an inheritance mess for years," said the sheriff, following Lindsay's gaze. Sheriff Irene Varnadore was a woman about six inches shorter than Lindsay's five-foot-eleven height, with short-cropped graying hair and a face showing the effects of years of exposure to the sun. She had said little since Lindsay arrived, only acknowledging her with a nod.

"Those pines are overdue for harvesting," said one of the deputies to no one in particular. "The family fighting's costing them plenty. Pine beetles are already spreading." He shook his head and pointed to several trees with dead, rust-colored needles.

"Do you really think you can find anything?" the sheriff asked.

"How many acres?" Lindsay looked out over the meadow to the stand of tall pine trees the deputy had been observing.

"A hundred and fifty," the sheriff answered.

Lindsay raised her eyebrows and looked at Patterson. He took out a pack of cigarettes and started to tear it open, changed his mind, and put it back in his pocket. "It's a long shot. I know. But the person who called said Shirley's body is here—somewhere here on the property. Thought you, being an archaeologist, might be able to find her."

"This person didn't happen to give you any indication where?" the sheriff asked.

"No. Just said she was buried here on the Foster place."

"Humph," snorted the sheriff and looked back at Lindsay, who hadn't yet answered her question.

"She disappeared four years ago?" Lindsay asked, and they nodded. "How much did she weigh?"

"What?" asked the sheriff.

"Her weight," repeated Lindsay. "What was it?" She could feel the subtle beginnings of a headache and didn't want to be here looking for a body that could be buried anywhere on the 150 acres or, more probably, was somewhere else entirely.

The sheriff made a gesture with her hands that said she had no idea and what did that have to do with anything anyway.

"About a hundred and fifteen pounds," said Will Patterson. "Her husband was big and strong enough to carry her over his shoulder." He looked at Sheriff Varnadore as he talked.

"Dead bodies are hard to carry, even for a strong man," Lindsay said. "She will probably be close to a place a vehicle could be driven."

"If she's here at all," said the sheriff, staring hard at Will. "We don't know she's even dead."

"Shirl wouldn't walk out on her parents and certainly not on her children," Patterson said. "You know that, Irene."

"I don't know what she'd do."

"We'll start looking in places accessible to vehicles. If we don't find a grave, then we can do a grid search of the entire farm," Lindsay said as she turned toward the sound of automobiles. Two cars were turning onto the gravel drive. In the first was Sally, her graduate assistant. She pulled a departmental Jeep in beside Lindsay's Rover. The second car, a Mercedes hardtop convertible, pulled up beside her.

Sally got out of the Jeep carrying a backpack and a camera. A large-boned, barrel-chested man, his dark blond hair disheveled and his fair skin flushed with anger, got out of the Mercedes at the same time, eyed her, and yelled.

"Damn you! Get out of here!"

Sally, wide-eyed, jumped back into her Jeep, slapped her hand on the door locks, and waited. Lindsay rushed over to the man, followed by the others.

"And who're you?" he asked Lindsay.

"I'm Dr. Lindsay Chamberlain, and that's my assistant you just yelled at."

"I thought she was a reporter," he said.

"Don't be such a bully, Tom," said Patterson.

"I should've known you'd be behind this, Patterson. You know as well as I do, Shirl's not dead."

"Look, Tom," interrupted the sheriff. "I'm real sorry about this. Will's got himself a court order." She held it out to him, but Tom Foster waved it away.

"Go on and do what you have to do, but this is the end of it," he said to Will Patterson. "Tell her folks that this is the end of it."

Sally got out of the Jeep, retrieved a straight-edged shovel from the rear, and eased her way to Lindsay, all the time giving Tom Foster a reproving stare. Lindsay motioned for Patterson.

"Who is he?" she asked.

"That's Tom Foster. Shirley Foster's husband," he answered without taking his eyes off him.

"Why is the victim's husband here?" Lindsay whispered.

Patterson shrugged. "My guess is Irene called him."

Lindsay watched Tom Foster and the sheriff talking. It was not difficult to see whose side the sheriff was on. Lindsay didn't like having the main suspect here as she searched.

Patterson nodded his head at Foster and the sheriff. "He won't do anything rash," he said. "You and your assistant will be safe. He's not a fool."

Still, thought Lindsay, this was not a good idea. She was about to speak when an old farm truck drove up. What now? she thought. A young man with brown hair got out and walked toward them. Lindsay guessed him to be in his late twenties.

"Chris, what are you doing here?" Sheriff Varnadore asked, her narrowed eyes glaring at Will Patterson.

"Dad wanted one of the family to be here," he said. "She's my sister."

"We don't know she's here," said the sheriff.

"She isn't." Tom Foster spat out the words to Will Patterson.

"She may not be," said Will. "But we'd all be derelict in our duty if we didn't look, after being told she is here."

"Yeah, sure, Will." Tom pointed his finger at Patterson and stabbed the air, punctuating his words. "I don't believe for a second you got an anonymous call."

"Why don't we start?" said Lindsay.

"Lead the way," said Sheriff Varnadore.

Will Patterson briefly introduced Chris Pryor, the missing woman's brother, to Lindsay. His dark brown eyes were set deep in his lean face. He acknowledged her with a nod, muttering that he hoped she could find his sister.

"I'll try," Lindsay said, but gave as little credibility to a vague anonymous call as did the sheriff.

From her vantage point the farm appeared to Lindsay to be half open land and half woods. Someone dumping a body would look for concealment, even on his own land. He—or she—wouldn't want a family member or anyone else to catch them in the act of burying a body. Ruts from an overgrown roadbed led off the main driveway. Lindsay took her straight-edged shovel and backpack and followed the old trail. The others followed her.

She led the strange parade to the stand of beetle-infested pines the deputy had previously pointed out. She turned and looked back at the house and drive. The others stopped and turned, too, looking in unison. If Lindsay's headache had not been getting worse, and if this were not such a grim search, she would have laughed.

The entrance to the house site was still clearly visible, so she proceeded down the narrow road, watching for old wounds on trees or broken branches that might mean a vehicle had passed. She saw nothing, but after four years the signs would be subtle. The wind died down and the air grew warmer, as did the bickering between the private detective, the sheriff, and the husband. Lindsay ignored her entourage as she and Sally scrutinized the ground for signs of disturbance.

When Lindsay was twelve, her mother's horse, Starr, died. Starr was thirty—old for a horse. She simply collapsed in a creekbed one day. The sandy bottom acted like quicksand—caught her and wouldn't let go. Lindsay held Starr's head to keep it above water while her mother, her older brother, home from college for his twenty-first birthday, and the vet dug in the sandy bottom, trying desperately to free the horse that was too weak to free herself.

"It's time," Lindsay's mother had said finally.

"Maybe if we . . . ," her brother began, but Lindsay's mother shook her head.

Lindsay remembered the effort of holding back the tears as the vet administered the overdose. Her mother took her place and held Starr's head during the last minutes, speaking calming words in the horse's ear. It was over soon. Starr died peacefully. Her brother dragged her out of the creek with his truck, and the county brought a bulldozer to dig a hole big enough to bury her. The next day Lindsay went to the stream to mourn privately and was surprised to see that a small pool had formed in the creek where Starr had died.

The struggling horse had dug out the bottom of the creekbed enough to slow the water, and debris had caught in a narrow spot downstream, backing up the creek even farther. A casual observer would have only noticed the pool. Someone familiar with the movement of water might have wondered why it had pooled at that spot. Lindsay had smiled through her tears. The pool was like a small memorial to Starr. Nothing passed without nature taking notice.

No one could have dug a grave and buried the body of Shirley Foster and not leave some trace. The trick was to watch for the signs—small anomalies that would be accounted for if the body was really there.

They traversed the last old roadbeds that crisscrossed the land, taking detours in every place that looked as if it might be good for concealment. Lindsay told them what to look for—depressions, mounds, vegetation out of place—but only the deputies seemed interested. Will Patterson was more concerned with observing Tom Foster than looking for the grave. The sheriff showed practically no interest at all. Chris Pryor walked with his hands in his pockets, looking into the woods, squinting his eyes, as if that would make his sister's grave stand out from its surroundings.

"This must be hard on him," Sally whispered to Lindsay.

"I imagine," she answered.

Will Patterson took out his pack of cigarettes again, tore them open, and bounced the top on his hand, causing one to peek out the top. "Do you mind?" Foster yelled. "The woods are dry. I don't want you burning them down." Will put the pack back in his pocket.

The pine forest had given way to more lush hardwoods as the roadbed terminated at a lake. Lindsay stopped, unconsciously rubbing her head, and watched the breeze make ripples on the surface of the water.

"I guess it's time to do another search pattern," she said to Sally.

"There's nothing here," the sheriff observed. "We're wasting our time."

"I agree," said Tom Foster. "I have a business to run. I can't be tramping around out here all day."

"You are free to go at any time," said Will Patterson. "You shouldn't be here anyway."

"Now you look here—"

"Look, Sheriff," said Chris, "why are you so eager to leave?"

"Just what do you mean by that, Chris?" Sheriff Varnadore asked.

"He means," said Will, "that we haven't nearly covered the property and you are ready to give up. It looks suspicious."

"Here's something," called a deputy, and they all went

over. He had swept away forest litter from the surface of a sizable depression. "Look at this," he said, pointing to a smaller depression in the center.

"That looks like something," said the sheriff. She directed the two deputies to start digging.

Lindsay looked at the depression the deputy had cleared. It was at the bottom of a small rise. What looked to be a narrow path led to it and out the other side, down toward the lake.

Lindsay shook her head. "I think that was made by erosion," she began, and the deputies stopped.

The sheriff looked up at her. "This is the classic shallow grave site. Small depression within a larger one—small one being made when the victim's intestines decompose." Irene Varnadore smiled, clearly wanting Lindsay to understand that she knew how to do this as well as Lindsay.

"Irene!" shouted Will Patterson.

The sheriff glanced at Chris and Tom. "Oh, sorry, I'm not used to having family around."

"I think," Lindsay said, "that the larger depression was actually eroded out by runoff. The depression in the center is where a small tree died, rotted out. The depression is too deep—Mrs. Foster was a slim woman."

"I don't see any evidence of the tree," the sheriff said.

"I'm sure it washed away long ago," answered Lindsay.

"Well, I guess we'll find out," said the sheriff, and she ordered the deputies to continue. They dipped their pointed shovels into the ground and began as if digging a hole.

"Slow down," said Lindsay. "If there is bone, you'll damage it. Let me and Sally do the excavation."

The deputies looked up at the sheriff and she nodded for them to continue. Lindsay looked at the shovelfuls of hard compact soil and let the matter go. She turned to Sally.

"Do you have some aspirin?" she whispered. Sally dug into her pack and came out with a bottle of buffered aspirin and gave Lindsay a couple along with a drink from her canteen.

"There ain't nothing here," grumbled a deputy after a while.

"Wait," said the other one. "I've hit something."

Lindsay didn't even cringe as he reached into the soil and pulled. Nor was she surprised at the rotting tree root in his hand. "Damn," he said, "thought I had something."

"I told you," Sheriff Varnadore said to Will Patterson. "Shirl's not here. This is just a waste of time."

"No," said Lindsay softly. "I told you she wasn't *here.*" She made a slight gesture toward the ground. "We haven't nearly searched the property. Do you want me to continue?"

"Yes," said Patterson.

"By all means," added Tom Foster. "I don't want Will saying we didn't do a proper search. Then I want this over."

"Dammit, Tom, Shirl was your wife, for God's sake!" Chris surprised everyone with his outburst. He said more quietly, "Don't you understand what this has done to our family, to Dad . . . Mom—and me? Nothing's the same, nothing—" He turned and walked into the woods.

Everyone stood quietly for a moment staring at the ground or out into the woods where Chris was leaning against a tree. Lindsay wanted to be anyplace else. During their quarreling her gaze had rested on a small, young, dead hardwood tree several yards away. It showed no signs of disease or attack from insects. She wasn't sure why she noticed it at all, but she walked over to it. Beside the dead tree was a long, almost imperceptible, shallow depression. Beside the depression was a small mound with three young trees growing in a row, straight, tall, budding with green leaves.

"Let's try here," said Lindsay, and she and Sally had cleared away the forest litter before the others noticed that they were digging.

"You've found something?" asked Patterson, coming over, followed by the others.

"I don't see anything," said Tom Foster. "I thought you said there would be a depression."

"There is," said Lindsay, outlining what she thought was the edge with the blade of her shovel. Taking her trowel, she knelt and dug down into soft earth in the center of the depression.

She and Sally then took shallow shovelfuls of dirt, just skimming the surface. Lindsay dug outward until the earth hardened. "This is definitely an edge separating soft fill from compact undisturbed soil. Stay away from the edge," she told Sally. "We can excavate that with a trowel later and it may give an indication of the type of tool used to dig the hole." Sally nodded. It was not unlike excavation techniques she had used at archaeological sites.

"Is it her grave?" asked Chris in a low voice.

"It's a pit that's been dug and filled in. That's all I know now," said Lindsay. They dug down a foot and the ground was still soft. They continued, alternately using their flat-nosed shovels to take shallow scoops of dirt and their trowels to dig deeper, carefully looking for bone. They found nothing. It was a slow process.

"It's an empty hole," said Tom Foster. "I told you she's not dead. You know that, Will Patterson. You know where she is. This is some plan the two of you cooked up together."

"I have something," said Sally.

They all stopped and looked into the hole.

"Probably a dog or cow," said the sheriff.

Lindsay's head throbbed as she leaned over the pit and dug away the dirt with a wooden tongue depressor, revealing a dome-shaped object.

"A human skull," said Lindsay.

"Oh, God," said Chris, dropping to his knees, peering into the grave.

"Shirl," whispered Will. "Is it her?"

"I don't know," said Lindsay. "I just know it's human."

Sally started to dig around the bone. Lindsay put a hand on her arm. "We have to stop now. The sheriff has to notify the coroner."

"Call the coroner," Sheriff Varnadore told one of the deputies. She turned to the other one. "Go ahead and dig her up." The deputy took his shovel and positioned it above the grave, ready to dig.

"It would be better if you allow us to excavate the remains," said Lindsay. "You may lose a lot of evidence digging like that."

"I reckon I know how to do my job. Enough time has been wasted. We need to get this done. We can't wait around here while you dig with that Popsicle stick."

"If that's Shirl, you'll not be digging her up like a dead cow. I won't have it." Tom Foster, ashen faced, spoke for the first time since Lindsay announced the bones were human. Sheriff Varnadore looked as if she had been slapped in the face. Tom Foster turned to Lindsay. "Go ahead. Do it right."

"I have to wait for permission from the coroner." Lindsay's voice was gentle, and for the first time that morning, she felt sorry for Tom Foster.

Chapter 2

"**S**HOULDN'T WE WEAR a mask, you know, for the smell?" Liza, a hazel-eyed, dark-haired graduate student, was dressed in khaki shorts, T-shirt, and sun visor. She stood with her nose wrinkled at an odor that was not yet manifest.

"You can. I have some in the truck, but if you're interested in forensic work, it's better to get used to the smell. This won't be as bad as a body that's partially fleshed out," Lindsay told her and smiled.

"That's a comfort," said Brandon, another of her students, dressed similarly to Liza but without the visor.

"Sally and I will do the excavating. Brandon, you and Liza do the sifting."

Brandon quickly set up the screen used to sift and separate objects from the fill dirt. Earlier, before the students had arrived, Lindsay had set out stakes and string, making a grid of the crime scene. She and Sally walked down the narrow path to the grave. Lindsay had already inspected a swath of ground for evidence and designated it as a safe path. She and Sally sat down on the ground by the grave and laid out their trowels, wooden tongue depressors, spoons, brushes, and dental picks. Beginning at the bone they could see, they began the careful task of removing the soil to expose the bone they couldn't see.

When the coroner arrived, he sent Tom Foster, Chris Pryor, and Will Patterson home. Lindsay had met him at a local symposium and liked him. He was a good-natured elderly man with fine white hair and, though creased with age, the pink skin of a baby. The change of atmosphere from the bickering of that morning was welcome. Sheriff Varnadore, deprived of people to argue with, hung back and watched until a couple more deputies showed up, one with a metal detector. The sheriff and her four deputies began a ground search of the area extending about two hundred feet from the grave site. Her search pattern was less methodical than Lindsay would have done and Varnadore did not lay out a grid to guide the search, but Lindsay knew better than to try to tell her how to do her job.

Lindsay and her crew excavated the skull first, gradually shaving the dirt away with the flat wooden tongue depressors. She preferred wood to metal spoons or grapefruit knives for the delicate work—when the dirt was soft enough—for it lessened the chance of damaging the bone.

"How did you find the grave?" asked Sally. "I didn't see anything that looked like a disturbance."

Lindsay shrugged. "I don't know. I just wondered what killed that tree. It didn't show signs of insects or disease. Root damage seemed the most probable. That's when I noticed the slight mound with the row of saplings—they looked strong and healthy. Then I saw the depression alongside the mound."

"Well, I'm impressed," Sally said.

"It's not an uncommon arrangement. I've seen it before. The digger damages the roots of a tree too young to recover. The dirt he takes out of the hole won't all fit back in, so he leaves a small mound beside the grave. Seedlings grow in the mound and are noticeably healthy because they are fed by the decaying body. Simple as that."

"Yeah, but it's a big forest," Sally said, "and everything looked alike to me."

Lindsay brushed the loose dirt from the skull. It stood

out a mottled cream color against the dark forest soil, stripped of all remnants of skin and hair.

Sally touched the smooth dome of the forehead. "It looks female."

Lindsay nodded in agreement. "What else?"

"Looks like a healed fracture," said Sally, pointing to a line on the face. Brandon and Liza had made their way down the path and looked into the grave over Sally's shoulder.

"What kind?" Lindsay asked, watching Sally wrinkle her brow at the skull.

"Let's see. Is it a LeFort?"

"What type?"

Sally traced the fracture line across the orbits and down the cheeks. "The whole face was broken. Is that a type three?"

"Yes. Anything else?"

"I don't see—wait, the nose is broken, too." Sally looked up at Lindsay and grinned. "It's a combination— types two and three."

"That's right."

"Showoff," said Brandon, grinning. He filled another bucket of dirt and took it to the screen.

"She took a hard blow," the coroner said, motioning for the sheriff to come over. The sheriff disregarded Lindsay's path, walking over unexamined ground, and stepped over the string to the edge of the burial. "Irene, was Shirl in the hospital for any extended period?"

Sheriff Varnadore sat on her haunches beside the grave, knocking clumps of dirt from the edge into the hole, and squinted at the skull. "Let's see . . . yes . . . she had a wreck in that little car of hers about six years ago. Had her jaws wired shut. Is it her, then? Is it Shirl?"

"Maybe," said the coroner. "Won't know until Lindsay does a thorough analysis."

The sheriff stood, still looking down into the grave.

Lindsay watched her as she turned and walked back to continue the search with the metal detector.

"Irene is a good officer," he said. Lindsay looked from the sheriff back to the coroner's liquid blue eyes. "Some people just aren't their best when they're around certain other people," he continued in a low voice.

"You mean Tom Foster," said Lindsay, carefully removing dirt from the first cervical vertebra.

"Yes. I delivered all of them—Tom, Irene, Will, and Shirl, too. I used to be the GP here. They all went to school together, went on to college at UGA, except Shirl; she went to Princeton. At one time they were all friends. Tom and Will played football together. Then . . . well . . . life comes along." He sighed and shook his head. A sudden breeze lifted his thin hair. Lindsay moved a stray strand of her own hair from her face and continued her work.

Lindsay and her crew excavated until late in the afternoon. She and Sally had the entire upper skeleton uncovered. A musky smell of decay rose from the grave. Sally put her hand over her nose for a moment, then let it drop to her side. Liza and Brandon hung back while leaning forward, craning to see the remains. "Look at this," Lindsay said. The coroner and the sheriff came over and looked into the grave at the bones of the rib cage that Lindsay indicated.

"It looks like the thorax has been burned," he said.

"Tried to burn the body to get rid of it," the sheriff said, coming up behind him and removing her gloves. "Wouldn't be the first time someone found out how hard it is to burn a body." Sheriff Irene Varnadore stared at the skeleton for several moments. "I guess it must be Shirl. I didn't really think she was dead." She looked over at Lindsay and asked, "Did you know her?"

"No. Why do you ask?" Lindsay said.

"I just thought since you both worked at UGA—" replied the sheriff.

"I didn't know she worked there. What did she do?"

"She taught art. Textile design. Supposed to be pretty good—"

Liza gasped. "That's Dr. Shirley Foster? I know her. I mean, my brother was her graduate assistant. My parents had her over for dinner once." She started sinking to the ground and Brandon caught her by the arm. Lindsay jumped up and helped her walk over to a rock and sit down. The coroner came over and told her to bend over and keep her head down. "I'm sorry, Dr. Chamberlain," she sobbed. "I didn't know her that well. It's just that I'd met her."

"I understand," said Lindsay. "It's all right. Why don't you let Brandon take you home? You can help us finish up in the morning."

Liza rose with Brandon's help. "What time do you want us here tomorrow, Dr. Chamberlain?" he asked.

"Early . . . as soon as it's light."

Light came too early for Lindsay. She had stayed at the crime scene working late, only going home to her renovated cabin in the woods for a short sleep. Adding to her discomfort, she'd only been able to take a Spartan sponge bath when she got home. When she turned on the shower, it had sputtered and dripped and stopped. She went outside with a flashlight to inspect the well. She pushed the tin roofing atop the low wall of cement blocks around the well, expecting to find that she needed a new water pump. Instead, she discovered she needed a new well. This one was dry. She went back into the cabin, melted some ice in the microwave, gave herself a bath, and went to sleep.

As the sun was just showing itself though the trees, Lindsay was uncovering the grave and beginning work on the bones. The deputies who had guarded the crime scene through the night seemed grateful to have someone to talk to. They were especially grateful to Lindsay for stopping at

Dunkin' Donuts on the way out of Athens and bringing them a box of fresh doughnuts and a couple of Styrofoam cups of hot coffee. Sitting up with the dead was not a pleasant task. Sally arrived, followed shortly by Brandon and Liza.

"I'm really sorry, Dr. Chamberlain," Liza said.

"It's all right. I know it was a shock to think this may have been someone you knew."

"In class it all seems so—so mysterious and, I guess, fun. You kind of forget it's a person."

"I know."

Lindsay and Sally had excavated the entire skeleton by midday. The others joined her as Lindsay stood looking down at their work, fascinated by the remains of death and repulsed by the odor it brought. In this particular case the odor rose from the putrid remains in the pelvic girdle. The full skeleton lay extended in the grave. The tops of the ribs were blackened. The finger bones were mottled a yellow-gray color and had a network of tiny cracks. The tips of the fingers were burned gray or were missing.

"Strange," Lindsay said, shaking her head. "The bone indicates the fire was hot where she is burned on the tips of her fingers, but the bone on the face and legs is hardly burned at all. But what I find just as strange is the careful way she's buried. She was a tall woman, and whoever buried her dug a hole long enough for her to fit. In disposing of a body after a murder, the perpetrator usually does not dig a big enough hole and ends up bending the legs, or quickly digging a place for them to fit, so the hole looks like a keyhole or something odd."

"Not exactly what I'd call a typical shallow grave, either," said the deputy.

"It took somebody a while and a lot of work to dig this hole," said Lindsay. "And they rested her hands across her stomach. This was carefully done."

"I agree." Sheriff Varnadore nodded. "It doesn't quite fit with the rashness of trying to burn the body."

Lindsay looked at her and immediately regretted it, for she did not want to show the surprised look on her face. If the sheriff noticed, she said nothing.

Lindsay pointed to the grave wall. "You can take a cast of these marks. It looks like they were made by a pointed shovel. There are some thin gouges here and there, like the shovel had a burr or a weld mark on it. Liza and Brandon will give you a diagram of the pit's cross-section."

"Anything else you found?" asked the sheriff.

"There's a partially melted plastic zipper on the pelvis. Her shoes are still intact. There are fragments of hose around the shoes and some material left clinging to the left and right tibiae. We found a metal hair clasp near the skull that's in good condition. I'm puzzled by the burn pattern."

"What do you make of it?"

"I don't know, maybe nothing. But if you are trying to burn a body by piling it with brush—" She shook her head. "That kind of fire doesn't get that hot as a rule. Look at the tips of her fingers."

"You don't think she could have been tortured?" The sheriff looked at Lindsay.

"I don't know."

Lindsay conducted her examination in the autopsy room of Clarke General Hospital with Eddie Peck, the medical examiner for Clarke County. The diener, John Booth, had laid out the bones on the table and now stood a few feet away with his arms folded, his dark face solemn. Lindsay had met him before, and not for the first time did he remind her of some mythical person waiting to ferry the dead across the River Styx.

Most of the bones were still held together by hard, yellowed cartilage. In places, there were traces of burned flesh. The voice recorder clicked on as Lindsay recited the preliminary information about the remains.

"Was she a ballet dancer?" asked Eddie, after carefully removing the shoes from her skeletal feet.

Lindsay looked briefly at the healed fractures in the second and third phalanxes on her right foot. "Looks like it, doesn't it?"

"The third phalanx on her left foot has had a fracture, too," he said. "My girlfriend's into ballet. Drop-dead gorgeous girl, ugliest feet you've ever seen."

Lindsay went back to the skull. "The roots of the teeth show signs of stress and Shirley Foster had at least one abscess that required surgery. The teeth are capped, all of them," she said.

"The car wreck?" Eddie asked.

Lindsay looked at the skull x-ray of Shirley Foster and shook her head. "They were capped before the accident. I'd like to see her dental report."

"I've got it right here, but there is no mention of the capping being done. Must have had it done somewhere else," Eddie said.

"They're old," said Lindsay. "I'll bet she used a dentist where she went to college."

Lindsay turned the skull carefully in her gloved hand, looking for signs of trauma other than the LeFort fractures. She found none.

The door opened and Sally came rushing in, out of breath. "Sorry I'm late," she said.

"That's all right. We just started." Lindsay looked at her red-rimmed eyes. "Are you OK?"

"Yeah, I guess. Just as I was about to leave, I checked my e-mail and there was a Dear Jane message from Brian. He wants to date other people—in particular, Gerri Chapman. You remember Gerri, don't you, the redhead with the attitude? I just don't get it. I thought he couldn't stand her."

"I'm sorry, Sally," said Lindsay.

"He e-mailed me—*e-mail,* for heaven's sake. Oh, Lord, is that thing recording me?"

"I can fix you up with a great guy," Eddie said.

"No thanks, Eddie," sniffed Sally. "I'm through with men. Gerri, of all people; she's such a jerk."

Eddie took skin and soil samples from the pelvis, ribs, and vertebrae, bagged and labeled them, and placed them in a box. "There's an IUD in the pelvic cavity," he said and proceeded to bag it as well.

"The olecranon of the left and right ulna, the margins of the spine on each scapula, and the dorsal surfaces of the third and fourth ribs are all charred black and yellow," Lindsay said to the recorder. "The dorsal surfaces of the first, second, third, fourth, and fifth metacarpals on each hand are mottled yellow and gray as are the corresponding phalanxes. Distal phalanxes five and three on the left hand and five, two, and one on the right hand are missing. The others are charred gray and white. It's interesting that the innominate bones show little indication of burning."

"I wonder why?" commented Eddie.

"I'd like to look at the bones cleaned," she said after Eddie had taken all the samples he wanted.

"Sure. Booth'll have them cleaned by next week."

Lindsay looked at the diener briefly and he nodded at her. "I'd like to see some cross sections of her long bones," she said. "We can do that after they're cleaned. I'd also like to see a cross section of her canine teeth."

"We can do that," Eddie said. "It'll take a couple of weeks."

"I have a method of mounting the tooth in plastic resin and making a polished cross section. It works very well and takes half a day. Sally can do it."

"Interesting," Eddie said. "I'd like to see it. Only works with teeth, I suppose."

"And rocks," answered Lindsay.

"Well, what is it, Dr. Chamberlain?" asked Eddie. "What killed this woman?"

Lindsay shook her head. "I don't know. The fire's troublesome. The bones are burned where the skin is the thinnest, that's not surprising. . . . I don't know, there is something that bothers me. The pattern, I suppose."

Eddie shrugged. "Fires can burn hot and just burn out. I've seen it. Fire is a strange animal. The killer could have tried to get rid of the body by burning it, and when that failed . . . buried her."

"But from the pattern, the back was burned just like the front. If the fire was built by piling debris on top of the body and lighting it, as is common, the back of the body wouldn't have been burned."

"You have a point," said Eddie. "Maybe there will be something in the tissue samples that will be enlightening."

"By the way, you guys know who I can get to drill me a well?" Lindsay asked. "Mine went dry on me."

"That happened to Dr. Cassidine just last week," Eddie said. "Expensive. You need to move to the city so you'll have city water."

"Yeah," said Sally, "with all the additives."

"My cousin drills wells," said John Booth. "You want me to put in a good word for you?"

"Would you do that? Is he reasonable?"

"No. He's the orneriest man I ever met, but he knows how to drill wells."

Instead of going back to her office, Lindsay drove to the library. She circled the crowded parking lot twice before she found a space in the adjacent key lot.

Even if the trees weren't budding out, Lindsay would have known it was spring because most of the dogs accompanying the students were puppies. She stooped to pet an adolescent chocolate Lab tied to a bicycle rack waiting for his master. He licked her hand and wagged his tail.

"I hope they'll be back soon, sweetie," she said, rubbing his ears.

Some of the largest oak trees on campus lined the quadrangle in front of the library. Several students were stretched out on the grass in their shade. North Campus was the oldest part of campus, its age reflected in the white-columned Greek revival buildings. One could start on the north side of campus, abutting against downtown Athens, and, walking southward, view a chronology of architecture from 1785, when the University of Georgia was founded, to the present. Middle Campus incorporated the dark red brick buildings of the thirties and fifties and looked very somber. The walk would finish with a brand-new structure that many— unkindly, Lindsay thought—referred to as the "Purina Building" because of the conspicuous checkerboard pattern of its brickwork. Lindsay preferred the old part of campus.

She left the puppy straining at his leash and went into the library. It was crowded with students in an assortment of attire ranging from the black head-to-toe Goth look to ragged retro-hippie to casual yuppie. Lindsay had thought multicolored hair was on the wane, but as she walked up to the third floor, she passed a male and female with moussed and spiked lime green and mauve hair, respectively, sporting matching dog collars and nose rings. The young woman was explaining to her companion why aluminum sulfide can't be recrystallized from water.

The Hargrett Library was the home of the rare book and manuscript collection, the Georgia Room, and the university archives, as well as files of newspaper clippings that mentioned anything or anyone connected with the university. By the desk, a campus policeman was talking to an archivist.

"Perhaps you simply misplaced it," suggested the policeman.

Lindsay glanced at the look on the archivist's face, which stated more clearly than words that she was an archivist and therefore had not misplaced the item, that she never misplaced items, and, moreover, that it was her business to label and index items so that they could always be found. Lindsay smiled and walked past them to the filing cabinets. She quickly found the section she sought and looked under Athens, UGA, Foster, Shirley. She pulled out a file about half an inch thick and took it to a table.

Many of the clippings were about various exhibits and awards for Shirley Foster's work. One from the *Athens Observer* dated seven years ago was a Close-Up interview about an exhibit of her fabric designs at the university. There was the typical row of three black-and-white photographs the *Observer* took of the interviewee: Shirley smiling, head turned slightly to the right; Shirley grinning, showing white, even teeth; Shirley laughing—puckish, delighted, joyful. She had been an attractive woman: shoulder-length dark hair worn in a frizzy halo around a fair face, dark, deep-set eyes, dark eyebrows, and the large mouth of a singer.

Lindsay skimmed the article. Shirley told the interviewer that she hadn't wanted to become a designer in the beginning, that her original interests had been in history and archaeology. The interviewer had asked her why she hadn't pursued archaeology. "In this country," Shirley had responded, "archaeology is considered to be part of anthropology. I believe in the European tradition—where archaeology belongs in the history department. Archaeologists here tend not to understand the historical context of what they study but treat each site as a separate phenomenon." Lindsay raised her eyebrows and wondered if the sheriff should put the archaeologists of North America on the list of suspects. She continued reading.

How did you get from archaeology to textiles?

"I've always liked art and creating things. My grandmother taught me sewing and needlework. I don't know, really. I think reading about specimens of Greek cloth dating from the seventh century B.C. tickled my fancy. Fabric that old—it was interesting. I began to notice how many illustrations of weaving and spinning were on vases, tapestries, friezes. Look at faerie tales and myths—Penelope, for instance, weaving her tapestry and taking out the threads every night. And the story of Rumpelstiltskin. The story was about a girl who could spin so well, she could spin straw into gold. Sleeping Beauty pricked her finger on a spinning wheel's spindle. What that told me is that all through history, spinning and weaving were very important. Women spent all their spare time doing it. It was as economically important as agriculture. And no one was working on it, at least there were very few scholars."

So, you wanted to become one of the very few experts?

"I wanted to know more about it. We often think of our distant ancestors dressed in drab colors or in animal skins of one sort or another. But if you realize that they were dressed in very colorful cloths of indigo blues, vivid yellows, brilliant reds with names like dragon's blood— how could anyone not be fascinated by that? It was a more colorful world than our images have allowed us to see, a more colorful world than many historians have painted for us."

Tell us about your family. Were they important in your career choices?

"They were very important. Not in the specific choices, but both of my parents are well educated and love reading and the arts. My father has all the classics in his library and he encouraged me and my brother to read all of them. His favorite is Dickens. He named our house Bleak House. I think that is as great a gift as any parent can give their child."

Do you do the same for your children?

"Of course. . . ."

The article finished with a description of the fabric designs in the exhibit and with Shirley saying she would like to see a section of the museum devoted to cloth and the various instruments used through the ages to make it.

Lindsay replaced the clipping and looked for articles that mentioned Shirley's disappearance. There were many. The articles in the *Athens Banner Herald* and the *Atlanta Journal-Constitution* said that Shirley Foster had disappeared four years ago this past month. When she failed to show up at her parents' dinner party, they and her husband had called the police.

One of the last persons to see her was her secretary, Norma Henderson, who said she had waved good-bye to Dr. Foster as she went out the office door at 9:00 in the morning. Nothing seemed wrong. Dr. Foster said as she left that she was going first to Rabun County, then to a party in the evening. The police never discovered where in Rabun County she was going. Related newspaper stories over the next several weeks said that she had disappeared without a trace, and neither she nor her car had been found, nor had any of her credit cards turned up. There had been no suspects in her disappearance. The police suggested the possibility that she may have been abducted by a stranger somewhere in the mountains.

Lindsay made copies of the articles and left the library, then wondered to herself as she climbed into her Rover why she had bothered looking up anything on Shirley Foster. As soon as she finished with the bones, her part in the case would be over.

Lindsay drove home to meet Edgar Dante, John Booth's cousin. He looked enough like Booth to be his brother, except for the lighter shade of skin color, a thin moustache, and amazing green eyes. He brought with him a drilling machine, a truck loaded with pipe, another cousin, and two other helpers.

"Know where you want it?" he asked.

"I don't suppose there's any way you can tell where there's water?" she said.

Edgar grinned.

"Do you have a suggestion?" Lindsay looked at the land close to her house for a good place, which was hard, not knowing what a good place for a well looked like.

Edgar Dante also studied the terrain around her house, finally pointing to a spot. "I'd start there, if it was my well."

"Start?"

"I can't guarantee we'll hit water. I made that clear on the phone."

"Yes, you did."

"It's eight dollars a foot for the first hole. If it's a dry hole, the next one is six dollars a foot. I'm giving you a discount 'cause you know John."

"I appreciate it. How deep do you think the water will be?"

"Can't tell. Probably deeper than your other one. Is it drilled or bored?"

"Bored. It's thirty feet."

"If it's as little as thirty feet you're going to have yourself a real deal. But I wouldn't count on it. I dug a well for a guy about five miles from here." He pointed in the direction of her gate. "It was a hundred feet. That's not too bad, but it don't say nothing about your well. You never know what the rock formation is doing under the ground, which way it's going to go. I've got enough rods for a thousand feet." Lindsay winced as she multiplied. "We probably won't go that deep. Probably start another hole before we go that deep. I'll tell you if I think it's a dry hole. I won't go just running up the bill on you, even if you are a friend of John's."

Lindsay smiled weakly and watched as they connected the equipment and began to drill. At a little over a hundred feet they paused, inspected the bits of ground rock and dirt coming from the drilling, discussed among themselves, shook their heads, and continued drilling. At a hundred and fifty feet and no water, Lindsay began to get nervous. She bit her lower lip as she watched them work, glad now that she had accepted the consulting job from Will Patterson. She had just acquired the land next to hers, though it was mostly deep gullies and thick woods, because it was the source of the stream that ran through her property. The income from the Patterson job was to help restore her savings to good health. But now—

The sound of the drilling was so loud she didn't hear the truck drive up and was surprised to feel someone lay a hand on her shoulder.

"Well gone dry? Sorry, didn't mean to startle you."

"Leigh—no, I'm sorry, I forgot you were coming today. And yes. It went dry."

"Lot of people building houses in the area, lowering the water table," he said.

"I irrigated the back pasture from the old well, too. I'm sure with the dry weather and everything else, it just put too much drain on it. I think the noise may have Mandrake a little upset," she added.

Leigh Bradley was Lindsay's vet, here to give her horse, Mandrake, his annual physical and round of shots. Lindsay had been suspicious of Leigh when she first saw him. He wore cowboy boots and a western shirt, giving her the feeling that he might be the kind of guy who has the attitude that you have to show a horse who's boss in order to control it. In Lindsay's eyes, this attitude did not make for a good vet and could ruin a good horse. She'd seen her mother send several vets with such an attitude packing. Over half of them wore cowboy boots. It didn't help that he was good-looking, either. Men that good-looking are often spoiled. Leigh, however, had discredited all of Lindsay's prejudices. He knew how to deal with horses gently, and he was very good with Mandrake.

"This is Brooke Einer," he said, introducing a petite, brown-eyed blonde in black jeans and a pink blouse covered by a black denim jacket. "She's interning with us."

"Hi," Brooke said, holding out her hand. "Leigh tells me you have a beautiful horse."

"I think so," said Lindsay, shaking Brooke's hand. She started to lead them to the stable when Edgar Dante came over to her.

"We're down another hundred feet. We're going to break for lunch now." Lindsay saw the men bring out brown bags and Thermoses. "Okay if we eat here?"

"Of course," Lindsay told him. "Can you stop the drilling while you eat? My vet's here to examine my horse and the noise has him a little upset."

"Sure, we can do that," said Dante.

She led Leigh and Brooke to the stable where she had put up Mandrake while the drilling was going on. The stable was her father's portion of her birthday present. He had sent a check to help her build it. It was larger than her house, with three stalls on either side of a wide throughway and a loft on one end for hay. One stall was a tack room, another was a small bedroom in case she needed to stay with her horse some nights. The other three were for visitors. Occasionally, Susan or another friend brought a horse over and they rode together.

"He is beautiful," said Brooke, stroking his nose.

Mandrake pawed the floor of his stall and moved his head up and down. Lindsay went into the stall, talked to him in a low voice, stroking his black velvet neck gently. She clipped a lead to his halter and led him out.

"He does seem a little edgy," said Leigh, brushing the horse's nose with his hand and rubbing his neck before feeling his legs.

"He doesn't like being put up, either," said Lindsay.

Leigh deftly examined Mandrake, explaining to Brooke what he was doing and why.

"He's fit, as always," pronounced Leigh. "Brooke, if you'll get the vaccines, we'll finish up." Brooke went to the truck and brought back the shots for Mandrake, who stamped his hooves and gave a long whinny. "Don't like what's coming, do you, boy?"

"Should I get the twitch?" asked Brooke.

"No," said Leigh.

"My uncle's a vet, and he says that with an unruly horse you have to make it clear who's the boss, especially with stallions."

Lindsay looked at Brooke's feet. Running shoes.

"I'll tell you who's boss: Dr. Chamberlain here, and if she finds us twitching her horse there'll be hell to pay." Leigh measured the dosage into the syringe and gave Mandrake his shots. "There, that wasn't so bad," he said, rubbing the spot. "Mandrake never gets unruly. Do you, boy?" He patted his neck. "He's the best-trained horse I've ever seen. You want to show Brooke how he does on his imaginary longe?"

Lindsay led Mandrake outside to the paddock area and unhooked his lead. She held out her arm as though she were holding a longe line attached to Mandrake's halter and clicked her tongue. He began trotting in a circle around Lindsay as she turned so that she always faced him. "Canter," she said in a low voice. Mandrake sped up into a canter for a turn around Lindsay. "Change," she said, and he changed leads, from his right to his left, and cantered one more time around before she gave him the command to stop.

"That's amazing," said Brooke.

"Yep," Leigh said. "As you can see, Mandrake is not an unruly horse. With all due respect to your uncle, you never need to show a horse who's boss. It's all in knowing how to interact with them. Some people can, and some people can't."

Lindsay was surprised at the sharp edge to Leigh's voice. Apparently, he was fed up with Brooke and her uncle. Lindsay would be surprised if Brooke was offered a position at Leigh's clinic when she graduated.

They drove away, and Lindsay returned Mandrake to his stall just as the well drillers started up again. They were at 300 feet and still drilling. She stood and listened to them talk about such and such a well where they had to go 600 feet. She wanted to groan. At 320 feet, they struck another vein of granite, and gray rock dust bubbled up from the ground with mud from the water they used in the drilling process. At 350 feet, she paced. At 360, she stopped and watched, holding her breath as they put on another rod.

Chapter 3

AT 370 FEET water came gushing out of the ground like a geyser, wetting all of them. Lindsay let out her breath in a big sigh of relief and watched them take a bucket and stopwatch and measure the flow. Dante came over to Lindsay, grinning.

"Good news is you've got about thirty gallons a minute. That's more than the pump will handle, so water pressure should never be a problem."

"Don't tell me there's bad news," she said.

He held out a glass jar with rust-colored water. "You need to have it analyzed. It looks like you have an iron problem. It's common all through this part of the country. I can give you the number of a place that installs water filters."

Lindsay took the jar and stared at the water. "That deep, you'd think it would be pure," she said.

"It's good water. Just has some minerals that need to be filtered out. Right now, we'll put a sleeve down to the rock and drop the pump and wiring down the well—" He stopped and listened to one of his men who had yelled something to him. "Looks like the water level is up to forty feet," he said. "That's some pressure behind it. That's good. We'll drop the pump about 150 feet."

Somewhere, Lindsay thought, the water level for that aquifer is a mere forty feet under the surface. She wondered where that was.

Lindsay went inside and looked up the address of the place on campus where she could get her water analyzed. When Dante finished, he knocked on her door with the bill.

"You can pay it in two installments, if you want," he said.

Lindsay glanced over the bill: 370 feet of drilling, water pump, wiring, sleeve, and labor. She took a deep breath and wrote out a check for $2,100.

"The next installment due next month?" she asked, half expecting him to say no, tomorrow.

"Next month will be fine. I'd see about getting a filtering system before you run the water though your pipes, if I were you," Dante said.

Before going to campus Lindsay dropped off her water sample to be analyzed. Then she drove to South Campus where new, modern multicolored brick buildings were popping up like dandelions after a rain. She stopped at the Ramsey P.E. Center to shower and change her clothes.

When she arrived at Baldwin Hall, home of the Archaeology Department, Lindsay encountered Reed Cavanaugh and Kenneth Kerwin, two Archaeology faculty members in the faculty break room. She poured herself a cup of coffee. Reed was nursing his own cup, and Kerwin was reading the latest volume of the *Journal of Historical Archaeology*.

"Been reading about you in the paper," said Reed. "Looks like we're in for several more weeks of speculation about Shirley Foster." From his expression, Lindsay felt as though he would like for her to come sit down and tell him about the case. Reed was not a person who acted out of idle curiosity, and she realized that he had probably known Shirley Foster. In fact, probably several of the faculty had known her.

"I imagine there was a lot of publicity when she disappeared," said Lindsay.

"Oh, you can't imagine it. It made it scary for a lot of the girls on campus at that time, too."

"Did you know her?" asked Lindsay. She took a sip of coffee. As usual it was awful.

Reed nodded. "Nice lady. I liked her."

"She didn't have a very good opinion of archaeologists here in the U.S.," Lindsay said.

Reed laughed. "You must have been reading one of her interviews. I remember one in the *Observer*." He chuckled. "Shirley was just tweaking our noses. She was like that." He laughed again, shaking his gray head. "We never minded, though. She was a very playful girl."

"How about you, Kenneth? Did you know her?"

Kenneth Kerwin waited until he finished reading a paragraph before he looked over the top of the journal. "Not really. Academically, of course. She was interested in textiles, and she occasionally asked me questions about old mill sites in Georgia. She was a good scholar. A loss for the university." He went back to his reading.

"What can you tell us?" Reed asked Lindsay.

"Nothing, I'm afraid," she answered.

"Well, can you confirm what's in the newspaper?" he asked. "It said she had been burned in a curious manner. That wasn't the way she died, was it?" Reed looked as though he wanted Lindsay to tell him, "No, she really died peacefully in her bed."

"There was some burning. The sheriff believes it was an attempt to dispose of the body. It's an exaggeration to call it curious." The only "curious" elements were the intensity of the heat, the burn pattern, and the careful burial. Not a lot, but it nagged her just the same.

"What killed her?" asked Reed.

"Will you people please!" Kerwin said. "Reed, we did know the woman, for heaven's sake. It's bad enough that Lindsay spends her time doing this. Don't encourage her to bring in the grisly details to us." He got up from the sofa and left the room with his journal.

Lindsay and Reed watched Kerwin's retreating back. "Exactly what did you ever do to him?" Reed asked.

"Oh, I kind of gave him a hard time about the way he handled the media during the Ferguson business," said Lindsay.

Reed chuckled. Lindsay got up and poured her coffee in the sink. "Who made this stuff?"

"I did. Don't you like it?"

"It's awful." Lindsay started out the door.

"Don't forget the faculty meeting next week. You know what's up, don't you?"

Lindsay turned and leaned against the door frame. "No, what?"

"Administration wants to merge Anthropology and Archaeology."

"Why?" Lindsay asked.

"They say efficiency, but who knows? It's something political. This coffee is awful." He poured out his cup and left the break room with Lindsay.

As Lindsay was going past the departmental office, Edwina, one of the secretaries, called out to her.

"Yes?" Lindsay asked.

"You got a phone call first thing this morning. Some woman. Said it was important but wouldn't leave a name."

"Did she say what it was about?" asked Lindsay.

"No. Just that she would call back."

"Thank you, Edwina."

Lindsay walked down the series of hallways and stairways to her office in the basement. She sat down in her chair and turned on her computer. As it was booting up, she thought about the possibility of merging with Anthropology, a huge department with over twenty faculty members. Positions would be eliminated. That meant the dean probably had plans to downsize Archaeology. *Downsize,* what a word. Lindsay sighed. She was the third to last person hired and had no tenure. She could guess who would be the first to go—not the tenured faculty. She would have to watch her step and not get into any arguments with the dean's favorite, Kenneth Kerwin. She would have to keep a low profile these days. She couldn't afford to lose her job.

Toward the end of the day, Lindsay called to get the report on her water analysis.

"Yeah, hard water," the voice on the other end told her. "You have both iron algae and iron mineral. I imagine it must be dyeing all your whites a rusty color."

"Not yet," Lindsay said. "It's a new well."

"That'll be good then, you can get a filtration system before the stuff contaminates your pipes too much. I'll send the report to you."

Lindsay thanked him and called the number Edgar Dante had given her. They invited her to come by their office on her way home. The slender, brunette saleswoman at Crystal Clear Water, Inc. shook her head sympathetically when Lindsay told her what minerals she had in her new water supply. After giving Lindsay a sales pitch, the woman armed her with a load of brochures and a list of a few people in town who had the system that she could call for testimonials. That evening, Lindsay called several people and decided to have the system installed. She didn't have much of a choice. She was tired of lugging water home in plastic containers and showering at the Ramsey Center, and the water apparently wasn't going to clear up. Every time she tried the spigot on the well, the water ran an ugly brown-red color.

By the end of the week, Lindsay had a new twelve-foot-by-twelve-foot well house, a system of chemical, charcoal, and brine filtering tanks, a set of instructions on how to maintain them, and pure water. She also had an enormous bill that the company graciously financed, telling her the payment booklet would arrive in the mail shortly.

Now, she thought, sitting at her desk in her office, I'll

just have to figure out how to pay for all this. She was relieved when the phone rang and took her out of the depressing thoughts of her finances.

"Dr. Chamberlain, John Booth here. I've finished cleaning the bones. Anytime you want to come down, I'll be here."

"Thanks. I'll come this afternoon."

"Cousin Edgar take care of you okay?"

"Just fine. I've got an abundance of crystal-clear water."

The detritus left on bones is important in discovering cause of death, but Lindsay still preferred clean white bones to examine. The bones of the woman whose x-rays identified her as Shirley Pryor Foster, Ph.D., lay on the shiny metal table in the autopsy room and had, for the most part, a pristine glow like polished ivory. Booth, who was the only one assisting Lindsay that morning, had done a good job. Lindsay acknowledged her satisfaction with a nod as she examined the bones as if for the first time.

Shirley Foster, forty-year-old full professor in both the Art and History departments, was five feet, eight inches tall. She had taken ballet for several years and practiced diligently, as indicated by the large attachments for her calf, thigh, and hip muscles. She probably quit because she was plagued by pain from stress fractures in her feet. She had the beginnings of arthritis in her hands, but it was mild, perhaps even unnoticeable to her except in cold weather. The blow to her face resulting in the LeFort fractures was hard enough to have caused brain damage; however, her bones were thinner than normal and probably broke with a lesser force. She was completely ambidextrous, something Lindsay rarely saw. Even people who can use both hands well usually favor one over the other. Shirley Foster's pelvic girdle gave no indication that she had ever delivered a child.

Lindsay looked at the polished cross section of a tooth under a dissecting microscope, paying particular attention to the cementum, the bony layers surrounding the root of the tooth. She saw indications that Shirley Foster was undernourished for a time in her life. The lack of proper nutrition was also suggested by the slightly thinner cortex of her long bones. Lindsay thought about the capped teeth and wondered if Shirley had been bulimic as a teenager or young adult.

"This arrived today." John Booth showed her a large white envelope.

"What is it?" she asked. Booth opened it and took out a set of x-rays and a letter. Lindsay recognized the x-rays as Shirley Foster's teeth. She read over the letter that Booth held in front of her. "Ah, it's the dentist who capped her teeth. He is from New Jersey. I thought so. He thought she was bulimic as well. Attach these to the report."

Lindsay began a careful examination of each of Shirley Foster's bones, looking for any mark or nick that might indicate how she was killed. She found nothing.

"I'm finished. You can release her bones for burial if the coroner approves it," she told Booth. He nodded. "Unless something shows up in the tissue samples, we may not be able to tell how she died."

Lindsay finished her report in Eddie Peck's office before she went back to campus. She was relieved to be finished. Even though Shirley Foster disappeared before Lindsay came to work for the university, there was something haunting about examining the bones of a fellow faculty member.

Lindsay's usual parking space behind Baldwin Hall was taken by a shiny black Jeep loaded with wooden crates. All the other spaces in the small lot were full, so she had to park in the lot for the Psychology Building across the street. She took a copy of the *Red and Black,* the campus newspaper, from the rack on the way into the building. Across the front page the large black headline read: "Another Student Killed on Corner of Jackson and Baldwin Streets." It was the second student killed there in as many years. Students were so prone to step out into the street without looking, as if being on campus put them in a state of grace, immune to realities such as sudden death. And unfortunately, too many cars traveled too fast on both of those streets.

According to the article, Gloria Rankin, a twenty-seven-year-old Ph.D. student in the Classics Department with a master's in chemistry from the University of Chicago, was dead on arrival at Clarke General after being hit by the North/South Campus bus. She was a beautiful woman, straight nose, slender, oval face, and blonde hair—and so young. There was also a photograph of the scene, but Lindsay didn't look at it. She tucked the paper under her arm and shook her head as she walked to her office in the basement of Baldwin.

"I guess you heard about that girl," Sally said, nodding toward Lindsay's newspaper.

"Yes, I just read it. Did you know her?"

"No, but I know the driver of the bus, Luke Ferris. He's Liza's older brother."

"You're kidding," said Lindsay, "Liza's brother? Isn't he the guy who sometimes works for Frank and Kerwin sorting artifacts?"

"Yeah. He's terribly upset. There are no charges against him. It wasn't his fault, but he quit his job and Liza thinks he'll probably drop out of school this quarter."

"That's so sad. The parents—all of them—must be just grief-stricken."

"The Ferrises are beside themselves. And for it to have happened to Luke . . . he's a real sensitive guy. He's been treated for depression before. I guess this will really push him over the edge," Sally said.

Lindsay shook her head again. "It seems unfair that one simple mistake could require such a high price."

"I know. When I think of the number of times I've crossed streets on campus without looking—"

"Well, don't do it anymore." Lindsay's gaze rested on the tall, rectangular wooden crates stacked against the wall by her office. "What's that?"

"This really gorgeous guy's bringing them in."

Lindsay raised her eyebrows. "That must be his Jeep in my parking space. Who is he?"

"He didn't say. He just asked when you'd be back and started bringing them in," said Sally.

"These crates are old." Lindsay walked over to the closest one and brushed the faded stenciling with the tips of her fingers. "OOF-6/35, is that what it says?"

"Looks like it," said Sally. "What does it mean?"

"I don't know. The other crates don't seem to have any markings—" Lindsay began when a tall, lean man in his mid-thirties, dressed in tight-fitting jeans and a plaid shirt, came in carrying another of the mysterious wooden crates on his shoulder. He set it down gently beside the others and turned to Lindsay. He had short brown hair, blue eyes, and a day-old beard.

"Sinjin," said Lindsay, going to him, hesitating only a moment before she hugged him.

"Hello, baby sister," he said, kissing her cheek.

"Why didn't you tell me you were coming? Can you stay?" She searched his face and found no expression she could read.

"You didn't get a call from Dad?"

"Maybe it's on my voice mail. I've been away from my office." Sally edged closer to Lindsay and her brother. "Oh, this is Sally Flynn, my graduate assistant. Sally, this is Sinjin Chamberlain, my brother." Sally stuck out her hand, and Sinjin took it briefly, smiled, and nodded his head.

"So, what's in the crates?" asked Sally.

Sinjin turned to Lindsay. "Dad asked me to bring them

to you. They were found in one of Papaw's outbuildings. Apparently been there since the thirties."

"Wow," said Sally.

"You're kidding," said Lindsay. "No one knew they were there?"

"You remember that jungle of kudzu behind Papaw's workshop? There's a shed in the midst of it. No one has been in it in years, apparently forgot it was there. Great-aunt Maggie, in a fit of yard-work fever, found the building and the contents. Dad opened one of the crates, found some clay pots, and thought you ought to have them."

"So, you've been visiting Mom and Dad?" Lindsay felt a pang of disappointment that her father had probably sent him. She had hoped the visit was Sinjin's own idea.

"I was there a couple of days," he said.

"You can stay a few days here, can't you?"

"I don't know. Maybe overnight, if you have room."

"If she doesn't, I do," Sally volunteered. Sinjin looked at her briefly, eyebrows raised, and back at Lindsay. "Well, I have some things to do," said Sally. "I'll just slink back over to my corner and do them."

Lindsay laughed as Sally retreated to her space in the faunal lab. "I just finished my guest room. I'd love to have you stay."

"All right. I do have some business in Atlanta," he said, looking around at the archaeology lab.

"Let me show you the place." She grabbed his arm and pointed at the floor. "This building was once a gymnasium. You can still see the markings on the floor if you look hard enough." Sinjin looked briefly at the dust-covered wooden floor that had lost its shine ages ago, then followed Lindsay to a set of floor-to-ceiling oaken drawers covering two opposite walls of the lab. The brass pulls made them look like giant card catalogs in an old library.

"The artifacts we're currently working with are stored here." They were large flat drawers, three feet long, two feet wide, and four inches deep. Anything deeper would have been wasted space—artifacts could not be stacked on top of one another. Lindsay pulled out a drawer halfway. The bottom was entirely covered with large sherds—pieces of broken clay pottery.

White butcher paper covered all the tables in the lab. Two students sat at one of the tables gluing pieces of sherds into a whole pot. The glued pieces were held together by clothespins while the glue dried and were kept upright by being embedded in sand.

"These are broken pots from a house floor at the Jasper Creek site. That's the one—"

"Dad told me about your adventures at that site. How's your leg?"

"Fine. No permanent damage," she said, patting it as if to verify its soundness. The truth was, it still hurt some when she stood on it for a long time. "They're fitting the pieces of the pots back together. Each piece of sherd has been mapped to the exact spot it was found. After they finish piecing them together we'll be able to tell from the scatter pattern if the pots were resting on a shelf or on the floor prior to their breakage."

"Is that important to know?" he asked.

"Perhaps not by itself, but the little bits and pieces of information accumulate, and after a while we know quite a lot. If we find similar artifacts in a similar household arrangement in another site several hundred miles away, for example, we know that the two peoples were probably related in some manner."

Sinjin looked over the jigsaw puzzle of sherds lying on the white paper. "Do you have to find a special kind of person to do this?"

"Yeah," said one of the students who was gluing the pieces together. "A half-wit."

Lindsay smiled and led her brother to a room at the end of the laboratory. "This is our faunal reference collection." The room was furnished with rows of metal shelves containing hundreds of identical shoeboxes. Sally sat at a corner desk reading a stack of papers.

"Each box contains bones of some animal," said Lindsay. She pulled down a box and opened it, revealing the white paper-thin bones of a bird. "We try to get an adult male and female as well as several sub-adults of the same species. We use them to compare with animal bones recovered from a dig, to be sure of our identification."

"You must be right at home among all these bones," he said, looking at the many boxes. "Where do you get them?"

"Oh, some are from zoos when an animal dies. Many are roadkill." She replaced the box on the shelf.

Sinjin looked at Lindsay. "My sister collects roadkill?"

"Only if it's not been too flattened," Lindsay replied. Sinjin laughed out loud and Lindsay grinned at him. "Yeah, well, you got to do what you got to do."

"How do you . . ." Sinjin searched for the right word. "You know, extract the bones?"

"We skin the animal and put it in a garbage can with a collection of very efficient dermestid beetles. The bones are pretty clean after a few days. We clean them up further with chemicals."

"Nice work," he said as they left the room.

"It's easier than jumping into fires."

"I try to avoid jumping into fires."

Lindsay laughed. "I'm glad you're here. It's nice to see you looking so well," she said. She frowned suddenly. "Dad's all right, isn't he?"

"Perfectly healthy as far as I know."

"And you—you're okay, aren't you?"

"I see I should come more often. I'm fine. This is just a visit. How about I take you to dinner? Is there a good place to eat in this town?"

"Sure, but why don't I—"

Out of the corner of her eye Lindsay saw one of the students point her out to a well-dressed couple.

"Excuse me a moment," she said, and walked over to them. "Can I help you?"

The couple looked to be in their sixties. The woman had beautiful, silver coiffured hair. Her hand was tucked in the crook of the man's arm. The two of them, she in a blue silk dress and he in an expensive suit, stood out like peacocks in the dusty archaeology lab.

"I am Stewart Pryor and this is my wife, Evelyn. We would like to speak with you privately about our daughter, Shirley."

Oh, no, thought Lindsay. They want me to investigate their daughter's death.

Stewart Pryor took a manila envelope from his breast pocket. "You have to change your report" he said. "It's wrong."

"Report?"

"You did, did you not, examine our daughter's remains?"

"Yes, but—"

"Then we must talk to you." His jaw was firm and his mouth set in a way that indicated to Lindsay he intended that she would cooperate.

"You have an office near here?" asked his wife, looking around at the students and unconsciously brushing the skirt of her dress.

"This way, please." Lindsay led them to her office and seated them in front of her desk, then took her place behind it. Mr. Pryor laid the envelope between them. "I don't understand—"

"We will explain it to you," said Evelyn Pryor. "You say in here"—she leaned over and tapped the report with her finger—"that our daughter had no children. She did. A lovely daughter, Monica, and a precious son, Jeffery."

"I didn't say that she had no children. I said her bones show no indication of her having borne children."

"Monica and Jeffery are not adopted," said Stewart Pryor in a way that said the matter was closed.

"What is it you want me to do, exactly?" asked Lindsay.

"Shirley's mother and I want you to change the report. We don't want her children to ever see it," Mr. Pryor said.

"Autopsy reports rarely make it into the papers. In fact, I just finished it. How did you get it so soon?" Lindsay opened the envelope and examined the pages that were obviously photocopies of the originals.

"That's not your concern," said Pryor, sitting rigidly in his chair.

His wife dug in her purse and pulled out a snapshot that she handed to Lindsay. "What, then, do you make of this?"

Lindsay examined the picture and wrinkled her brow. The snapshot was of Tom and Shirley Foster. Tom had his arm around Shirley's shoulder. Both were smiling. Shirley was obviously very pregnant. The analysis of Shirley Foster's skeleton had been thorough. There had been absolutely no scars of parturition anywhere in her pelvic area. Her bones showed no evidence that she had borne even one child, much less two, yet here she was, very pregnant.

"What are you going to do about that?" Evelyn said.

"Mr. and Mrs. Pryor, this doesn't alter what I observed on her bones, and it was my observations that I reported. Understand, my analysis is only one part of a larger report on her."

They gave her a look that indicated they thought her to be stubborn beyond reason. Mrs. Pryor sighed and turned to her husband. "There's the other thing."

"You say here that we starved Shirley when she was a young girl, and that she might have had some mental disease. Shirley was a talented girl, a smart girl. She was a straight-A student. She graduated from high school when she was sixteen. She worked hard." His lips quivered as he spoke about his daughter. "Shirley never gave her mother and me a minute's trouble. She was a good girl."

"We didn't starve her," said Mrs. Pryor. "You make us sound like bad parents."

"I didn't say you starved her. I—"

"You as much as did," said Evelyn.

"I said there were signs that she did not receive the amount of nourishment she needed for proper bone growth. This could have been due to some condition that caused her not to absorb nutrients, or from not eating proper food, or any number of things. I said as much in my report. I also noted that all her teeth were capped. I simply stated that there is a possibility that she was bulimic."

"You are saying Shirley had some mental disorder," said her father.

"No, I—"

"There was nothing wrong with her, nothing. She worked hard, always did. There is nothing wrong with that."

"There is an attachment from her dentist with the original report. He put in her records that he capped her teeth because of substantive erosion of the enamel. He recorded that the erosion was consistent with the presence of stomach acid associated with frequent vomiting."

"She capped her teeth because she was thinking of becoming a ballerina," said her mother. "She was a wonderful dancer. You can't fault her wanting to look her best."

"I don't fault her. Mr. and Mrs. Pryor, you must know that I can't change my report because you ask. I have to report what I observed."

"You were wrong about Monica and Jeffery."

"I know this must be hard for you—"

"You don't know anything." Evelyn Pryor's words came

out in a hiss. She leaned toward Lindsay, her dark eyes glittering. "Our daughter was a perfect child. She always did what Stewart and I wanted and never disappointed us once." She relaxed back in her chair. "Our mistake was insisting she marry Tom Foster, and I will regret that until the day I die. We thought he was a good man. He owned a good business; he came from a family with roots here. His grandmother and my mother were at Winthrop together. We were wrong about Tom, and now she's dead." She took a lace-trimmed handkerchief from her purse and dabbed her eyes.

"We are grateful to you for finding her so that we can bury her, but you have to change that report. I don't want people talking about Shirley like she was crazy," Stewart Pryor said, taking his wife's hand.

"I'm sorry, I really am, but there's nothing more that I can do for you," said Lindsay.

"We'll see about that," said Pryor. They both stood, gave Lindsay a curt nod, and left.

Sally was entertaining Sinjin with tales from their digs when Lindsay came out of her office.

"That looked serious. They don't want you to be a detective, do they?" Sally asked.

"No, I think they are just working through their grief." She looked at Sinjin sitting on the corner of one of the mysterious crates waiting to be unpacked. "I don't suppose Dad gave you any of Papaw's papers to go with this cargo?"

"Nope."

Sally was grinning like she had news she was dying to tell. "I just figured out that OOF might be Ocmulgee Old Fields. And 6/35 might be June 1935. Your grandfather did work in Macon in the thirties, didn't he?"

"Yes, very clever, Sally," Lindsay said. "In the morning, we'll open the crates and see what's in them. How about getting some of the honors students to help unpack and catalog."

"Sure. Where are we going to put them?"

Lindsay looked around the lab. That was a good question. Space was at a premium, and there were several administrators on North Campus, home to a bastion of bureaucrats, who believed a university is no place to house "dirt and old garbage," as one of them put it.

"Clear a space in the storage room and put up those metal shelves stacked in the corner. We'll shelve them temporarily until we can catalog them. If the contents turn out to be from Ocmulgee, I'll contact them and maybe they'll have a place to store them. I hope there's some indication somewhere of what sites they're from."

"I'll get on it right away." Sally turned to Sinjin. "It was really nice meeting you. I hope you hang around a while." She gave him a dazzling smile and left to tend to the storage room.

"Nice kid," muttered Sinjin as Lindsay locked up her office.

"Yes, she is. Look, I've got some steaks in the freezer that I marinated in Jack Daniel's before I froze them. Why don't we have a cookout at my place? You'll love it out in the woods."

"Sounds good. I'd like that better than a restaurant. While I'm thinking of it, do you have a map of Atlanta? I've got some business there tomorrow."

"Sure." She wanted to ask him what it was; she wanted to ask him to stay longer. Instead, she walked out with him, climbed into his Jeep, and let him drive her to her Rover. As they pulled out of the drive, the police were taking measurements at the corner of Jackson and Baldwin.

Chapter 4

THE AROMA OF mesquite from the grilled steaks still filled the air as Lindsay and Sinjin sat on the porch steps of her log cabin, drinking cold bottles of beer and looking out over the pasture where Mandrake grazed. It was a warm night and the light was fading. An occasional lightning bug blinked its yellow light.

"You still dance?" he asked.

"Not as much. Both Derrick and I are too busy these days to practice. We haven't entered a contest"—Lindsay paused, wrinkling her brow—"in about four years, I suppose. I miss it."

"Weren't you dating him?"

"Yes."

"You still dating?"

"No."

"I kind of liked him the time we met at Mom and Dad's a few years ago," Sinjin said, taking a swig of his beer.

"He's a nice guy."

"Something happen? Ellen had the idea that the two of you were pretty serious for a while."

Lindsay thought for a second. She didn't remember ever talking to her mother about herself and Derrick. "We were, but we kind of broke it off. He broke it off. He doesn't like the detective work I do occasionally. He thinks I'm addicted to danger."

Sinjin looked over at her and swallowed a drink of beer. "Are you?"

"You say that as if you're asking me if I'm an alcoholic."

"I, of all people, know how addictive an adrenaline rush can be."

Lindsay closed her eyes, trying to imagine her brother jumping out of an airplane, parachuting into a forest fire. She couldn't. "Why do you do it?"

"What?" he asked. "Smokejumping?"

"Yes, when—" She didn't finish, but Sinjin did.

"You're asking why I'm a fireman when I could get a better job. A little snobbish, aren't we?"

"I didn't mean that."

"Well, you come by it honestly. Dad wonders the same thing."

"That's not fair. I meant when you could do something safer."

"Safer, like being an archaeologist?"

Lindsay reached over and gave him a gentle shove. "Like being a forester. That's what your degree's in."

"I am a forester. You never answered my question. Are you addicted to danger?"

"I just like solving puzzles. I don't like the danger."

"Are you sure?"

"Do you think I get a kick out of being kidnapped, shot, and thrown in a cave and left to die?"

Sinjin stopped, his bottle halfway to his mouth, and looked at her. "What?"

"I thought you knew."

"I knew about your getting shot in the leg. Dad and Ellen called when that happened. They told me you were fine, but I haven't heard about the other stuff."

Lindsay gave him a brief summary of her adventures, glossing over the dangerous parts. Sinjin listened open-mouthed.

"Are you sure Derrick isn't right?"

"Derrick used to help me solve crimes. I don't know why he's so uptight about me doing it now. Besides, none of that stuff that happened was my fault."

"No, but when you go after criminals, they are apt to retaliate. You know that."

"Are you about to lecture me?"

"Maybe. What about this thing you're involved in now, about those people who showed up today? You aren't investigating something for them, are you?"

"No. I was called to look for a body and I assisted with the autopsy. It's my job."

"I thought your job was to study ancient cultures."

"That, too. Look, Sinjin, why don't you stay for a while?"

"Would you like that?"

"Yeah, I would."

"We'll probably end up in an argument."

"Maybe not. I'd really like to get to know you better. Are you still with Kathy?"

"No. She left."

"I'm sorry."

"So am I. She's kind of like Derrick, I guess. The last fire before she left was a bad one, and she decided she couldn't take not knowing if I'd come home a crispy critter." He took another long drink of beer. "Do you think I could ride Mandrake some?"

There were only three people Lindsay would allow to ride her black Arabian stallion: Susan Gitten, who sometimes house-sat for her and trained horses of her own; her mother, Ellen Chamberlain, who raised and trained Mandrake; and her brother.

"Sure. The tack is in the stable."

Sinjin drained the last of his beer and set the bottle down on the porch. "That's the one thing I owe your mother. She taught me how to ride, and I've always enjoyed it. Those were the only times we got along."

Lindsay started to disagree with that but changed her mind and said nothing. She and Sinjin were getting along now and she liked it.

Darkness came rapidly now, and Lindsay could barely make out Mandrake in the pasture.

"I think there were more lightning bugs when I was a little girl," she said.

"Yeah," agreed Sinjin. "There don't seem to be as many these days."

In the morning Lindsay sent her brother off with a map of Atlanta. He looked tense, as if he'd had a sleepless night and was not looking forward to his destination. She wanted to ask him where he was going, but had he wanted her to know, he would have told her.

When Lindsay arrived at her office, the lights were on in the main lab and the door to the faunal lab was open. She could hear the chatter of students talking as they worked. Bethany was helping Luke Ferris glue pot sherds together. Lindsay had unlocked the door to her office and turned on the light when Liza Ferris tapped on the door frame.

"Yes, Liza?"

"Dr. Chamberlain. I hope you don't mind." She hesitated.

"Mind what?" Lindsay locked her purse in the bottom drawer of her desk and sat down.

"Well, my brother . . . you know, the accident. Well, he hasn't been back to his classes and, well, he's worked for Dr. Carter before, and he knows what to do."

"What is it you're asking, Liza?"

"He needed something to keep his mind occupied, and I didn't want him to stay alone in his apartment. He's taking the accident very hard and it wasn't his fault. Anyway, I thought since he already knows how to do the work, I'd have him do some sorting. You know how there is always so much to do. And it's the kind of work where you can talk to people and—" She let the rest hang in the air.

"Are you asking my permission or pardon?" asked Lindsay.

Liza smiled. "I guess both."

"Well, he's worked for Frank before. We can put him on as a temp. We do need to get the stuff sorted."

"Thanks, Dr. Chamberlain."

Liza left and Lindsay turned on her computer. She looked up at another tap on her door. It was Robin, one of Rachael Bienvenido's students.

"Hi, can I help you?" asked Lindsay.

"Amy didn't show up yesterday and I heard that she is in Atlanta today. We're supposed to be working on the South Carolina faunal remains. She's missed a lot and I've had to do them myself, and I'm way behind."

"Are these the ones from Bienvenido's colleague?"

"Yes, and there's a deadline. I don't think I can make it."

Lindsay sighed. "OK, will it help if I do some sorting this morning?"

"Well, yeah, but—would you?"

"Sure." Lindsay rose from her chair and went with Robin to a table near the faunal lab. Liza and her brother, Luke, were at a nearby table sorting bags of grid square fill. She had met him once when he was doing work for Frank, the department chairman. He had started out as a graduate student in archaeology a couple of years before Lindsay came to UGA. He had dropped out of school to work. Now he was back as a graduate student in accounting. He had been working as a campus bus driver but still came around the labs occasionally, picking up extra work with Frank and some of the other faculty.

Luke was fairer than his sister, with light brown hair to her dark brown. He had a pretty handsomeness to his looks that made him popular. His smile always held a flirtation. Lindsay suspected that he had gotten by as a kid on his looks—and still did. He was in his late twenties, a little old to be taken care of by his younger sister, she thought. But then, the accident was a tragic thing, and if the dark circles under his eyes were any indication, it had deeply affected him.

Lindsay glanced briefly at his work and saw that he did seem to know what he was doing. As he worked he was telling the others about the legend of the archaeology student who was discovered living in the building during the forties, showering in the bathrooms and sleeping in the narrow passageways that contained the pipes and wiring of the building. She had heard the stories but didn't believe them.

"That'd be fun to try," said Brandon. "Just to see if you could do it and not get caught."

"The showers have been taken out," said Liza. "I think someone would sniff you out."

"Well, heck," said Brandon, "there are lots of places on campus to get a shower. Just crawl out of the ductwork and jog over to the Ramsey P.E. Center."

Lindsay shook her head and turned to Robin. "Are these the ones?" Robin nodded. Lindsay counted the boxes stacked by the wall and labeled with the South Carolina site designation number. "There's quite a bit left."

"I know."

"Well, let's get to it." She pulled several boxes marked with the same feature number and set them on the table. Robin had already placed empty boxes for identified bones near the worktable. Lindsay pulled up a chair, opened a box of bones, and began sorting them into various smaller boxes: *O. virginianus, V. fulva, S. carolinensis, S. floridanus, M. gallopavo, M. carinatum, T. carolina, C. canadensis*—deer, fox, squirrel, rabbit, turkey, sucker, turtle, beaver.

"You're fast, Dr. Chamberlain," said Robin, watching Lindsay work.

"That's why I get paid the big bucks." Lindsay smiled at her and put the bones of a frog in a box.

"There's another thing," said Robin, handing several pieces of paper to Lindsay. They were sheets reporting bone count and MNI—minimum number of individuals.

Lindsay examined each sheet. "The MNI looks too high. Is that your concern?"

"Yes," Robin said.

For some reason unknown to Lindsay, the concept of minimum number of individuals was one of the hardest for her beginning students. Determining the MNI is more than counting the bones, she told them. A left and a right deer femur the same size together indicate at least one deer. They may also represent two different individuals, but you can't know for sure. One, you know for sure. You know two left femurs means two individuals. Amy knew how to calculate the correct number, or Lindsay wouldn't have let her work in the faunal lab. She was either careless, or simply put something down in order to hurry through her work.

"I don't want to get Amy in trouble," Robin said, "but, well—"

"You're not. If she's in trouble, she did it to herself. We can't have the faunal lab producing bad data." Lindsay took one of the data sheets and figured MNI for a feature. Amy's count was way too high. "What about her identification of the bones?" asked Lindsay.

Robin shrugged.

Lindsay's chair scraped across the floor as she got up. "These are the identified bones?" She pointed to the shelf space behind the table. Robin nodded. Lindsay pulled several boxes down to check them. She could not help but hear the students talking at the other tables.

"I'm sorry about what happened, Luke. I know it must be hard. How are you doing?" asked Bethany.

"Yeah," agreed Brandon, "that was tough luck."

He nodded. "It's hard. I wrote a letter to her parents. I don't know if that was a help to them or not. I hope so."

"I'm sure it was," Liza said.

"The worst part," said Luke, "is the dreams. Three out of the last five nights I've had the same damn dream."

"I'm good with dreams," Robin said. "If you feel like it, tell it to me."

Lindsay was beginning to rethink the idea of allowing Luke to work in the lab, but she couldn't very well monitor what the students talked about. Perhaps she was the only one who was squeamish. She'd been too close to death the last few days and didn't want to hear about it here.

"I'm driving the bus, and I . . . and it happens. I jump out and suddenly I'm Hercules dressed in this red cape. I don't know why Hercules and not Superman, but that's who I turn into in the dream." He looked sheepish telling the story. "I have this cape, white tunic, and a gold headband on. I get out of the bus and she is there under the wheel."

Lindsay took a deep breath.

"Oh, how awful for you," said Bethany.

"It was. I mean, it didn't really happen that way. She was actually, uh, knocked several feet from the bus. But in the dream there she is, and I'm trying to lift the bus off her and I can't, even though I'm Hercules. It's the same each time. I wake up in a cold sweat."

"That's an easy one," said Robin. "You feel guilty because you couldn't save her and in your dream you try. You even transform yourself into a superhero to try."

"That makes sense," said Brandon.

Lindsay had to admit to herself that it did. It must be a terrible thing to have killed someone, if you have any conscience at all, even if the death was an accident. Lindsay wondered if the killer of Shirley Foster was experiencing feelings of guilt. She wondered what his—or her—dreams were like.

"It looks like Amy sorted the bones correctly," said Lindsay, returning the bones to the shelf. "That's a relief. Just the calculations are wrong."

"What's the deal with Amy, anyway?" Liza asked. "She's missed a few of Dr. Cavanaugh's classes, too, and he hasn't been happy. You know how he is—he expects you to come to class."

"She's met this guy," said Robin. "She's crazy about him and he lives in Atlanta. She's been going up there a lot. He comes from this old Atlanta family."

"That's a hard society to crack," Liza said. "Those old families are an exclusive bunch in Atlanta. Savannah, too. I guess every city has them."

"All families are old," Lindsay said, without looking up from her work, "and basically the same age."

"What do you mean?" asked Brandon. "My family sure isn't one of those old guards."

"You just don't know your ancestors, and they haven't lived in the same place for generations. That's the difference. All people alive today are the product of an unbroken line from the beginning of humankind. That seems incredible to think about, but it's true," Lindsay said. She was glad to be off the topic of Luke's dreams.

"Yeah," said Liza, as if she had never thought of it that way. "That's so obvious."

"You're right about so-called old families, though," Lindsay said. "They do maintain their boundaries in society."

"I'd just be glad to know anything about my family," Bethany said. "My parents adopted me. I was left on a church doorstep and there aren't any records of where I came from."

"There's one thing," Lindsay said. "You may not know

your near relatives, but you know that your distant ancestors were Celtic."

Bethany looked at her wide-eyed.

"How's that?" Brandon asked.

"Because the genes for red hair are only carried by the Celts. That's one of the ways their spread throughout Europe is traced. If you have red hair, you have some Celtic blood." Lindsay was surprised by the look on Bethany's face. It was as if she had given her a great gift. "You know, you can take a course in Celtic history in the History Department. Brenna Tremayne is very good. Why don't you take it one quarter?"

"Yes, I will. Thank you, Dr. Chamberlain, thank you."

"Dr. Chamberlain?" Lindsay looked up to see a teenage girl walking toward her. "My name is Monica Foster. May I speak with you?"

Lindsay took a moment to respond. "Yes. We'll go to my office. Robin, when Sally comes in, tell her the problem with the backlog and see if she has time to help. I'll do some more when I can. And when you see Amy, tell her I want to see her."

Monica Foster's damp blonde hair curled in a multitude of tiny ringlets around her face. She smelled faintly of chlorine. She must have come from an early morning swim, thought Lindsay. Shirley Foster's daughter was a petite, athletic-looking girl, not nearly as tall as either of her parents.

"My office is in here." She showed Monica in and motioned her toward a chair. "I'm very sorry about your mother."

"I'm glad you found her. Not knowing what happened— that was hard."

"What can I do for you?"

"I know my grandparents came to see you yesterday."

"Yes."

"Mother never told them that I was adopted."

Lindsay opened her mouth, then shut it.

"She told me, of course, but she just didn't want Gran and Grampa to know that she and Daddy couldn't have any children. I don't know why, really. It was silly. It was Daddy, anyway. He had the mumps or something."

"I see." Though she didn't completely.

"I guess you're wondering why I'm telling you this?"

"It had crossed my mind." Lindsay smiled at her.

"I was able to sneak a look at some of the report. Dad, Gran, and Grampa don't know it. They don't want me to know the details. I was twelve when she disappeared and they often think that's still how old I am." She stopped and took a breath. "You were right about so many things. Mother told me she quit ballet because her feet hurt. And the bulimia thing, I knew about that, too. Mother told me because she wanted me to learn from her mistakes. She told me what she did when she was in ballet, trying to keep her weight down and being hungry all the time and afraid of growing taller. Anyway, you knew all of that."

"What is it you want?" asked Lindsay as gently as she could.

"I want you to find out who killed my mother. Everyone's saying it was Daddy, but I know it wasn't. He's not a murderer. He wouldn't have done it. I want you to find out who did. I know my grandparents think it was him, but I know it wasn't. He loved Mother."

"I'm not a detective."

"You've solved crimes. I've read about them."

Lindsay winced. "This is an open case handled by Dover County. Specifically, it's Sheriff Irene Varnadore's case."

Monica frowned. "Irene's all right. At least she isn't going to hang it on Daddy, unless someone makes her."

"I really can't do anything while the authorities are investigating. Besides, I've already spent my expertise by examining the remains. That's about all I can do."

"You won't help me?"

"I have no authority."

Monica looked at Lindsay's bookshelves, as if searching for an argument among the books and journals. "I don't know what to do," she said finally.

"They won't arrest your father unless they find a lot of evidence pointing toward him," Lindsay said.

"You don't understand. It's what people think that's important. I don't want them to think Daddy did it. And if he's the only suspect, then the police won't look for anyone else."

"Who do you think did it?"

Monica's face brightened, as though the asking of the question meant Lindsay would reconsider, then her shoulders sagged. "I don't have any idea. I've thought about it a lot—when she disappeared and now. I've listed all her friends. I've tried to think about who didn't like her, but everybody liked Mother."

Lindsay felt the temptation, like prickly sensations in her brain. Then the image of Derrick, looking disapprovingly, intruded into her mind. Derrick's over, she thought.

"You'll consider, then?" Monica's voice brought Lindsay out of her reverie.

"Do you know Will Patterson?"

Monica slumped farther in her chair. "He thinks Daddy did it."

"But you know him. He's been working on your mother's case for a long time. It was he who brought me in. Whatever he thinks of your father, I believe he wants to find out who killed your mother. Besides, it's my understanding he and your dad used to be friends."

"A long time ago. Mother and Will were still pretty good friends when she died. They were engaged once, you know."

"No, I didn't."

"Yeah. Gran and Grampa didn't want Mother to marry him. They had Daddy picked out for her."

"How did Will feel about that?"

"You don't think Will did it—after all that time? Surely not." Monica shook her head. "That was in high school. Both of them got over it."

"What about Irene Varnadore?" asked Lindsay.

"She didn't like Mother. You know how it is. Mother was the prom queen, got a Ph.D. and Daddy. Irene was jealous, but I can't imagine her murdering Mother." Monica shook her head. "Everyone who knew Mother—her friends and family—they all loved her. A stranger did this. Maybe if the police looked for, you know, similar murders, they would see that some serial killer did it."

"Is that what you believe?" Lindsay asked, and Monica nodded. "Was it a coincidence that the stranger buried the body on your father's family land?"

Monica was taken aback for a moment. "The killer could've stalked her. He could have known about Daddy's land."

"What about the other relatives? Your father's people?"

"Now there's a thought. Georgina didn't like Daddy either—they're cousins. Georgina's a secretary here at UGA. Daddy's brother is mad at Daddy, because of the land. And there's another cousin. All of them are fighting over Daddy's property. They could have done something to Mother to get back at him."

Lindsay was unable to simply say no to Monica. "I'll tell you what. I'll ask someone if they've searched the records for similar patterns, and I'll talk with Will Patterson. That's all I can do right now."

"Thank you, Dr. Chamberlain. Maybe something will come of that." Monica stood up and held out her hand. Lindsay shook it and ushered her out the door.

Sally had arrived and had commandeered Brandon. They were busy looking over her grandfather's crates for stencils and other markings, copying them down.

Lindsay turned her attention to the crates. It seemed impossible that her grandfather would forget about having stored five crates of artifacts. She tried to remember the times when he was in his workshop. It wasn't often. He always said he wanted to retire and be a cabinetmaker, but he never did. His love of archaeology was too deep. She tried to remember the building behind the workshop. All she remembered was the kudzu.

"This is the crate opened by your father," said Sally. "He re-nailed it. Do you want to start with it?"

"Yes. What we'll do is unpack and record everything. Brandon, get a camera from the main office and photograph each artifact. We can do a more thorough cataloging later."

"I'll use mine. It's an old-fashioned 35 millimeter and takes great pictures," said Brandon, fishing in his backpack.

They moved the crate close to a table and Sally pried it open. Sitting amid shredded paper and old newspaper packing material was a large, cord-marked ceramic jar with a globular body and two ceramic strap handles on a tapered neck.

"This is really nice," said Sally.

"What kind is it?" asked Brandon

"I don't know," Sally said, looking at Lindsay.

"It looks like a Fort Ancient jar."

"Fort Ancient?" asked Brandon.

"Late prehistoric culture in Kentucky," said Lindsay.

"Kentucky?" Sally asked. "I thought these were from Georgia."

"This one isn't," said Lindsay. "The only reason that we thought it might be from Georgia was that the stenciling on one of the crates seemed to indicate it."

Brandon snapped a picture of it and Sally wrote a description on an item list.

"If you find any notes or papers, be sure to handle them with care. By this time I'm sure they will be brittle and fragile. Put the newspapers in a box carefully and let Greg take care of them when he comes in," Lindsay told them.

They found two more ceramic pots and a cache of triangular projectile points. The next crate contained two chipped stone maces, a pair of yellow pine figurines of a seated man and woman, five engraved conch shell gorgets, and three tetrapod bottles—all Mississippian and all, Lindsay believed, from Kentucky.

"Where are the newspapers from?" she asked Sally.

Sally carefully took one of the old packing papers from the box and looked at the masthead. "One says: *Macon Telegraph,* June 18, 1935." She picked up another one. "This one's from the *Kentucky Herald,* August 5, 1934."

"Let's get the others unpacked and recorded," said Lindsay uneasily.

The next crate had similar Mississippian artifacts. The fourth contained hundreds of smaller items: copper bracelets, clay platform pipes, ceremonial knives, chipped stone hoes, stone celts, engraved stone tablets, mica and copper crescent headdresses, numerous ground stone gorgets, and a large, beautiful shiny mica cutout of a hand with an eye etched in the center.

"Wow," said Brandon. "Nice. I'm doing my honors paper on Mississippian eye motifs. I'd like to use a photograph of this." Sally held it for him and he took several pictures, having Sally turn it one way and another.

"Don't use up all the film on this one piece," said Lindsay.

Brandon grinned and patted his backpack. "I've got plenty of film."

"What's your paper about, exactly?" asked Sally.

"Some articles say that the hand-eye motif may symbolize the holding of a crystal in the hand to foretell the future, the way some southeastern Indians did. I'm hypothesizing that the crystal was a kind of primitive remote sensing, like finding where game is located." Brandon eyed the mica as though wondering if he had taken enough photographs. "Anyway, I'm comparing the onset, frequency, and disappearance of the motifs in the archaeological record with weather patterns of that time. I know that's the hard part, and I don't know if I can find that data, but I think it's a neat idea."

"It is a neat idea," said Sally. "I'd like to see what you come up with."

"You might check with Ronan in Geography and Hoffstedder in Botany," said Lindsay.

"Great. Thanks, Dr. Chamberlain."

"What's this?" Sally held up what looked like a paddle with animal teeth at one end.

"It's a cut animal jaw. It's thought that it was inserted into the mouth of a skull, something to do with burial practice," said Lindsay absently. "All these are Adena artifacts, also, I think, from Kentucky."

"These are really valuable, aren't they?" said Brandon, "and they're in such good condition."

"Yes, they are," said Lindsay. She noted that neither Brandon nor Sally asked why the artifacts had been stored by her grandfather all those years ago.

It was getting late in the day. Brandon kept checking his watch and Lindsay was tired. She decided to wait until tomorrow to open the last crate. She locked the storage room and sent the students home.

"Is your brother going to stay a few days with you?" asked Sally as she helped Lindsay clean up.

"I don't know. Maybe."

"I'll put this box of old newspapers in my workspace," said Sally.

Lindsay nodded in agreement.

"He's a great-looking guy," Sally said.

"I've always thought so."

"I don't suppose he's talked about me?"

Lindsay smiled. "Well, he did say you're a nice kid."

"*Kid*? He said I'm a nice *kid*?" She stopped and turned to Lindsay, her arms around the box full of old newspapers.

"Well, he is thirty-six," said Lindsay.

"That's not old," Sally answered.

"No, but how old are you?"

"Twenty-one—and a half. I'm not all that much younger than you."

"He thinks I'm a kid, too."

"How long do you think he'll stay?"

"I hope it's a while. I don't know when he has to get back to his job."

Sally put the box on the shelf next to her lab space. "What does he do?" she shouted across the room.

Lindsay didn't answer until Sally returned. "He's a smokejumper."

"A smokejumper? What's that?" Sally threaded her arms through her backpack and strapped her bicycle helmet on her head.

"He helps put out large forest fires, in remote locations. The firefighters parachute in with their equipment. It saves a lot of time."

"Wow. It sounds dangerous."

"It is."

"Who does he work for? I mean, fires happen all over."

"The U.S. Forest Service."

"Interesting guy."

"I'll tell him you said so. You can go on home, Sally. Thanks a lot for your help."

"Sure. See you tomorrow. By the way, some guy came by to see you. He didn't leave a name. Said he'd be back."

"Do you know who it was?"

Sally shook her head. Her bike was parked just inside the door against the wall. Lindsay held the door open for her as she walked it outside and closed the door behind her.

The lab was quiet. Everyone had gone home. Lindsay went back to her office and sat down at her desk. She stared at the photograph of her grandfather standing in front of the platform mound at Macon. Large tears filled her eyes and spilled down her cheeks.

Chapter 5

LINDSAY DID NOT hear the lab door open. Sinjin's sudden appearance made her jump.

"I didn't mean to startle you," Sinjin said. His clean-shaven face from that morning now had the beginnings of a shadow on his jaw. He had removed his tie and his white shirt was open at the neck, sleeves rolled up. He looked tired. Sinjin drew up a chair and sat down across from her. He could see she had been crying. "You all right? Did you hear from Derrick or something?"

Lindsay shook her head. "The crates . . ."

"Was everything broken? I tried to be careful."

"No, everything was in great shape." Lindsay sniffed, took a Kleenex from her drawer, wiped her eyes, and blew her nose.

"What about them? You aren't getting sentimental about Papaw are you?" He said it as if he couldn't imagine it. "I know you and he . . ."

Lindsay shook her head. "The artifacts are in excellent, mint condition. Nothing broken or damaged. They're from at least three cultures: Fort Ancient, Mississippian, and Adena."

"Fort Ancient? Isn't that Kentucky?"

Lindsay nodded.

"I still don't understand what the problem is."

"The artifacts are from different sites and different times. There are no sacks of pot sherds, or broken arrowheads, nothing that is not well-preserved and whole."

"What does that mean?"

Lindsay shrugged. "It looks like looters' stash. In one crate alone I counted about $25,000 worth of artifacts on today's market. I don't know what price they would have fetched in the thirties."

Sinjin whistled. "You mean I was hauling something that valuable—that's what, five crates? That's potentially $125,000 worth of stuff. Where is it now?"

"I locked it in the storage room."

"Why didn't you lock the door to the basement? Anyone could have walked in."

"I forgot."

"Jesus, Lindsay."

"You don't understand," she said, tears threatening to spill over again. "What were they doing hidden away in Papaw's shed? What was he doing with them? And what were they doing in crates labeled Ocmulgee Old Fields?"

"Are you afraid he was involved in black-marketing artifacts?"

Lindsay shook her head vigorously. "He couldn't have been."

"But you think he might have been."

Lindsay bowed her head and looked at her hands resting on her grandfather's desk, absently tracing her fingers on the scratches made by countless artifacts that had been examined on its surface. "I don't know," she said.

"What are you going to do?"

"They will have to go back to where they belong. I just don't know where that is. I just don't want people to think, I mean . . ." Lindsay couldn't finish.

"I see you're upset. Let me drive you home and I'll bring you back tomorrow. I stopped by this Chinese place and got us dinner. You can leave your Rover here can't you?"

Lindsay nodded.

• • •

They ate dinner at Lindsay's small oak dining table, which sat by a large window with a view into the woods. Lindsay had opened the window to let in the sounds—the cries of raptors and songs of passerines, the tapping of woodpeckers, the rustling and chattering of squirrels, the wind in the trees. Occasionally Lindsay had heard the distant yipping of coyotes and wanted Sinjin to hear them, too. But he worked in deeper woods than hers and had probably heard many more animals than her tiny patch of wilderness had to offer.

As she ate, Lindsay wanted to talk about anything but the artifacts. Sinjin didn't seem to want to talk about his business in Atlanta, so they talked about the movies they liked. Sinjin liked science fiction and hated musicals, Lindsay liked musicals and comedies, but not science fiction. They both liked mysteries. It turned out that *Double Indemnity* was a favorite for both of them.

"Maybe we can check it out before you leave," said Lindsay.

"Maybe so." He looked out the window. "There's still some light left. How about I take Mandrake out for a while?"

"Sure. He hasn't been ridden this week. He'll enjoy it."

Lindsay watched them race across the pasture, then slow and take a trail into the woods. Sinjin's presence filled a deep yearning for a relationship with him that she had had for a long time, but he seemed distracted, and she didn't know how to ask him about anything personal.

Her thoughts drifted to Derrick, who was finishing his doctorate in archaeology at the University of Kentucky. She wondered if she should call and talk to him about the artifacts. There was a time when she could talk to him about anything; there was a time even before they started dating that he was her best friend. Now she hesitated even to call him about something that concerned both their fields.

This is silly, Lindsay thought. She went up to her room and picked up the phone. A copy of the *Athens Banner Herald* that she had meant to read was lying on the floor. She picked it up and noticed a long article about Shirley Foster in it as she listened to Derrick's phone ring. She was about to hang up when he answered.

"Derrick?" she said. There was a moment's pause. She could hear music in the background. "If this is a bad time, I can call back." She tried to sound professional, as if this were an archaeologist-to-archaeologist call. Which it was, she told herself.

"Lindsay. How are you? You sound upset. Is everything all right?"

Oh, no, she thought. She meant to sound so matter-of-fact. "No, well, yes, something has come up and I need to talk to someone about it, but if you're busy . . ."

"No. That's all right. What do you need?"

She began pouring out the story quickly because she didn't want Derrick to think she was calling about something personal—something between them.

"Wow," he said when she was finished. "I know what you must be thinking, but don't jump to any conclusions about your grandfather. You don't know what the story is."

"It looks so suspicious," she said.

"Well, yeah, but I'm sure there's a reasonable explanation for why thousands of dollars worth of artifacts were concealed under a mountain of kudzu on your family's property."

Lindsay felt herself relax. Derrick was sounding like the old Derrick she knew.

"I was thinking of delivering them to the University of Kentucky so the Office of State Archaeology could determine their disposition."

"I'd hold off on that for a little bit. Remember who's in charge these days: Harold van Deevers."

"Not him?"

"Yep, the guy you humiliated at the last North American Archaeology Conference."

"Well . . . he had a decimal in the wrong place. If I hadn't pointed it out, someone would have."

"Yes, but it was you, and it completely destroyed his thesis."

"It wasn't a very good one anyway."

"No, but he doesn't like you at the moment, and being the guy he is, he'd like to have the opportunity to put a pox on you and your house."

"But Papaw was an important archaeologist in Kentucky."

"Yes, he was, and that and a quarter won't even get you a cup of coffee anymore."

"What should I do?"

"Let me have a look at them. Can you store them?"

"Yes."

"I can't get away for a while, but as soon as I can, I'll come and have a look, and we can decide something. In the meantime, just forget about them. They've been lost for sixty years; they can wait a little longer."

"Thank you, Derrick."

"Anytime, you know that."

Lindsay heard his door open in the background and a female voice announce her presence. "It sounds like you have company. I'd better let you go."

"I'll be in touch. Don't worry about the artifacts, or your grandfather."

She replaced the phone in its cradle and sighed. That wasn't what she wanted him to say. She wanted him to tell her that he didn't have to go, that it was only some woman selling magazines, and he could talk all night if that was what she wanted. She didn't get to tell him that her brother was visiting. She didn't get to tell him anything personal.

Lindsay picked up the newspaper and began to read the article about Shirley Foster. Before she disappeared five years ago, Shirley had been at the university for fifteen years and was a tenured professor. She had won awards for her designs and taught courses in the history of textiles and fabric design. She had just published a book called *Women's Work: Weaving, the Oldest Profession.* She was internationally known and a world traveler. Shirley Foster also belonged to the Athens Council of the Arts and was an expert on fine wines. She was survived by her husband, Tom Foster, CEO of Glass Edifices; daughter Monica, 18; son Jeffery, 10; parents Evelyn and Stewart Pryor; and a brother, Chris Pryor.

Lindsay suddenly remembered that Eddie had found an IUD during the examination. Yet Tom Foster was supposed to be infertile. Had Shirley Foster been seeing someone? Who? Lindsay wondered. She was brought out of her thoughts by the sound of her front door opening and closing.

She hurried downstairs. "How was the ride?" she asked as she walked into the entranceway and came face-to-face with Tom Foster.

"I knocked," he said.

"I didn't hear it."

"I did knock. I don't go around breaking into people's houses. I was about to call for you."

"Why didn't you call on the phone first?"

"I tried on the car phone on the way over. Your line was busy." He waved a dismissing hand. "That's not what I came to talk about."

"Why did you come?"

"I need to talk to you about Shirl."

"I was just going out on the porch to watch my brother ride," Lindsay said, gesturing toward the door. Foster grumbled impatiently but followed her out to the porch. She scanned the pasture and woods for Sinjin but didn't see him.

"I know this is irregular."

"Yes, it is."

"It's about this . . . investigation. I don't like what you and Will are trying to do."

"I'm not trying to do anything. My involvement in the investigation is over."

"I know Stewart and Evelyn came to see you." He didn't mention Monica's visit, and neither did Lindsay. "What did they want?"

"That is really not your concern."

"Not my concern! Dammit, can't you see what they're trying to do?"

"Why don't you tell me?"

"They want to get their hands on Shirl's money. Her grandmother left her a bundle. They would like to get custody of Monica and Jeffery, too, but that'll stop when they find out they're adopted."

"They showed me a picture. . . ."

Tom laughed out loud. "Shirl got one of those things they use in the movies, you know, to make actresses look pregnant."

"Why?" asked Lindsay.

Tom shrugged. "You've got to understand Shirl and her family. For all her accomplishments, and there were many, she was terrified of disappointing her parents." Tom shook his head. "When we were in school, all her mother had to say was, 'We know you won't disappoint us, dear,' and it would send Shirl into a panic. I didn't understand it, never did, still don't. Chris's the same way."

"I still don't understand why she was pretending she was pregnant."

"She didn't want them to know the kids were adopted. She was afraid they'd reject them. They had some rather unkind things to say about a niece who was adopted. I think Shirl enjoyed putting them on, too."

"But how did she pull it off? Surely she didn't wear that thing every day, and she'd need several."

"We were out of the country in the months leading up to both adoptions. Shirl spent a lot of time in Europe at various universities, and I traveled a lot for business. That's the way we'd do it. When I'd have to take a trip to several countries, Shirl'd make plans to do research. Every few weeks we'd meet in Paris or someplace." He sighed. "Those were good times. Before she started running around with Will."

"What?"

Tom Foster grinned. "You didn't know that, did you?"

"No." She paused.

Foster stood there still grinning as though he had slipped something over on her, and it annoyed her.

"But didn't her mother or anyone ask her questions about her pregnancies?" Lindsay asked—to make him stop smiling as much as out of curiosity.

"Humph. Her mother'd never talk to her about anything like that. And as for friends, the close ones know. The others, well, Shirl'd handle it. She was good at that." He was silent a moment. He kicked an acorn from Lindsay's porch and crushed another one under his foot. "I loved Shirl, but she had her faults. I won't drag them out in the open on account of Jeffery and Monica, but she was far from perfect."

"I still don't understand what you want from me, Mr. Foster."

"I don't want you and Will Patterson trying to pin this thing on me. People are talking and it's bad for business. I've already lost two big orders."

"Didn't Will Patterson and you used to be friends?"

"In high school. We were kids then. Kids are stupid sometimes."

"What happened?"

"We both fell in love with Shirl. That was all."

"And you won."

"With the help of her parents. I admit that, but she loved me. We had good times."

"And bad?" asked Lindsay.

"The only bad times were brought on by Will Patterson. Stupid drunk. Look at him—private detective, my ass. He makes his living peeping through keyholes and taking pictures of people cheating on their spouses. He and Shirl never did break it off completely. He'd come off a drunk, Shirl'd feel sorry for him, and they'd go at it."

"I still don't understand why you think I have some role in this."

"Will hired you. He said you were working on the case and you had a good track record."

Lindsay raised her eyebrows, wondering why Will had said such a thing or if Tom had misunderstood. "He hired me to find where Shirley was buried." Lindsay sensed that Tom Foster simply had some free-floating fear that she and Patterson were plotting against him but he didn't know how. As if Patterson by himself was weak, but teaming with Lindsay made him stronger or more credible.

"Did you ask yourself how Will knew where she was buried? I didn't even think she was dead. He didn't get any anonymous call."

"Why were you so sure she wasn't dead?"

"Because the missing hundred thousand dollars never turned up."

Chapter 6

"**A** HUNDRED THOUSAND dollars?" Lindsay said, pronouncing each word to make sure she had heard correctly.

"Yeah, didn't you know about that?"

"No. There was no reason I should."

"When she disappeared, so did a hundred thousand dollars from her account. I figured it was some scheme she and Will were up to."

"What kind of scheme did you have in mind?"

Tom shrugged. "I just thought they were planning to run off together. When he didn't leave, I thought maybe she wanted to start a new life somewhere. It's been done."

"What about her children?"

"As I said, it's been done."

"The hundred thousand dollars, was that her entire fortune?"

"No, but I figured she left the rest for the kids, you know, to ease her conscience for leaving them."

"You thought she just walked away from her life—having two children, with a terminal degree in her field and tenure? A hundred thousand dollars is a lot of money, but it strikes me that someone from her social and income levels, having left her credentials behind, would need more to start a new life. Did you look for her?"

Tom Foster's face flushed red and his voice rose a level. "See, there you go. I knew you would start laying the foundation for blaming me. Yes, I looked for her, but not hard. I figured if she wanted to go, more power to her. At least she left the kids." And part of her money, thought Lindsay. "I just came out here to tell you to tell Will Patterson to leave me alone."

"Who do you think killed her?"

"Will might have. Maybe they were planning to leave together and she changed her mind. Maybe he did it on one of his drunken binges. I don't know. Could've been anybody did it. As I said, Shirl wasn't as blameless as everyone thought."

"How do you mean?"

"Just what I said. She liked to have her fun."

"Didn't that make you angry?"

Foster snapped back, "Now there you go again. It won't work." He pointed a finger at Lindsay's face.

"Put your finger down. I think it's time you go," said Lindsay, thinking that perhaps she had asked one question too many.

"Not till I've had my say," he said. "I want you to deliver a message to Will for me."

"You will have to tell him yourself. We aren't working together."

"That's not what I hear. You tell him—"

"I'm not telling him anything. I'm no longer involved in this case."

"You sure ask a lot of questions for someone who's not involved. Why did Shirl's parents come to see you if you aren't involved?"

"I think you should go now."

"Not until—"

"You heard my sister. I think you ought to stand down." Sinjin's voice was calm, almost friendly. He walked up on the porch. A faint aroma of hot leather and horse wafted through the air.

"I wasn't intending to harm her," said Tom Foster.

"I know. Nevertheless, when she asks you to leave her property, you must."

"I don't want any trouble, here or anywhere. That's all I want to say." He turned and walked to his Mercedes and drove away.

"I must say, baby sister, you're really good—the way you asked him all those questions and got him to answer. I'm particularly impressed by the way all the suspects are coming to you. You do have a talent."

Lindsay rolled her eyes. "How was the ride?"

"Great. Mandrake's a fine horse. Do you get to ride much?"

"Every chance I get, which is usually a couple times a week."

They walked into the house together and Sinjin started for the guest room, stopped, and turned toward Lindsay.

"Seriously," he said. "I eavesdropped for a while. For someone who is not investigating this case, you sure ask questions like you are."

Lindsay exhaled. "I suppose so. But people keep coming to me."

"Do you think that perhaps Derrick may be a little bit right?" he said.

"No."

"Whatever you say."

"How about dessert and coffee?" Lindsay asked.

"Sounds good. Let me shower."

Lindsay had chocolate cake and hot coffee waiting in the living room when Sinjin returned from the bathroom, smelling like shampoo and soap. He wore faded blue jeans and no shoes. His white T-shirt had large wet patches where he had not completely dried off. He tried to train his damp hair by running his fingers through it.

"You look refreshed," Lindsay said, handing him a slice

of cake as he sat down in one of the leather chairs by the empty fireplace.

"The ride on Mandrake and the shower worked the kinks out. This is a nice place you have here. I like it better than that apartment you lived in last time I visited."

That was six years ago, and she had lived in another apartment and a rented house since then, but she didn't tell him. She simply said, "I like it a lot."

"So, what you been up to, besides finding out Papaw might've been a pothunter?"

The words stung Lindsay. "He wasn't a pothunter."

"I imagine there's a few Indians who would disagree with you." He took a bite of cake. "This is pretty good. You make it?"

"No. It's from a neighbor. I suppose you think I'm a pothunter, too," Lindsay said, handing him a cup of coffee.

Sinjin eyed her over the cup as he drank. "Sorry, I suppose I shouldn't have said that."

She sat down in the matching chair opposite Sinjin and put her coffee cup to her lips and blew gently to cool the hot drink. "I called Derrick to ask him about the artifacts," she said.

"And?"

"He said to hold off on doing anything with them right now. Said he'll come down when he can and take a look and we will decide something."

"Decide something?" Sinjin said between bites of cake.

"Derrick is of the opinion that I should keep a low profile right now. The guy I would have to deal with in Kentucky is an archaeologist I kind of embarrassed at an archaeology conference." Lindsay poked at her cake with her fork.

"What did you do?"

"I only pointed out a mistake in his life's work. I mean, part of what we do at those meetings is point out one another's mistakes." Lindsay's effort at humor failed. Sinjin didn't look amused.

"Is this whole thing with the artifacts really a big deal? I mean, besides being embarrassing?"

Lindsay shrugged. "Not really. I can just say they were lost. They were. There may be some talk about what Papaw was doing with them, but—I just didn't want that. Doesn't it matter to you?"

"No."

"Why?" Lindsay asked.

"We weren't that close," said Sinjin, looking into his coffee.

"Yes, you were."

"No, we weren't. You were close to him, but I wasn't. I liked fishing and playing around in the woods better than I liked going with him, digging in the dirt, hunting for arrowheads. He had no use for me."

"That's not true."

"Lindsay, you weren't there. You don't know."

"Is that why you don't visit very often?" she said.

"How often do you visit me?" Sinjin set down his empty plate and cradled his coffee in his hands.

He had a point. She sipped her coffee. It burned her mouth. "We're both gone a lot," she said.

"Yeah."

"How did you and the folks get along?"

"Pretty good." Sinjin leaned back. "Dad's getting too old to argue with me, I suppose. He's kind of mellowed out."

They were silent for a while, drinking their coffee, looking into the empty fireplace. Her house seemed suddenly very quiet.

"I suppose I just never learned to be close to you guys. You, Ellen, and Dad were always the family. I was an outsider."

"You never were," she said.

"How would you know? You were just a baby."

"It didn't look that way. You—"

"It didn't look that way! Through the eyes of a little kid

who everybody—never mind. My mother wasn't supposed to die. She was having her tonsils out, for Christ's sake. I'd had mine out and I was fine." He stopped talking and Lindsay couldn't think of anything to say to fill the gap of silence. Sinjin stared into his coffee cup. "I was seven when she died. No one would tell me anything. Then Dad married again, and it was as if my mother never existed. Ellen wasn't my mother. I'm sure she probably tried, but I wanted my mother. Then you were born and everybody adored you—including me, by the way. I don't know, it's like once you get into the habit of not getting along, you just don't know how to."

"Why were you always mad at me?"

"Because you were an insufferable little twit." He looked up from his cup and grinned. "Besides, I wasn't always mad at you."

"Insufferable twit? I wasn't! How?"

"Every time Dad and I had an argument about what direction my life should be taking, you were right there telling me what I should be doing and how I shouldn't upset Dad. My baby sister, lecturing me."

"Did I really?"

"Yes. You were such a proper little kid. The best thing you ever did was to run away with that Harley fellow and go down into that cave."

Lindsay smiled at the memory. "It's wasn't easy being the perfect daughter."

"No, I don't suppose it was. We're both grown up now and we can act like adults."

"I'm glad you're here. I hope you no longer find me insufferable."

"You're not too bad."

Lindsay set her empty cup down on the hearth. "Sally's been putting in a lot of overtime work in the lab, and I'm taking her out to dinner tomorrow night. Would you like to come along? I'm not matchmaking; I just thought you'd like to come."

"Sure, why not?"

"I have to warn you. Sally's getting a crush on you."

Sinjin raised his eyebrows. "She's what, sixteen?"

"No, she's twenty-one."

"Still too young." He shook his head. "College students are looking younger and younger these days. I must be getting old." Sinjin rose from his seat and gathered up his plate and coffee cup. "I think I'll go to my room and read a while before going to bed. See you in the morning."

"I'll take these." Lindsay took his dishes from him and stacked them with her own.

Before he went upstairs, Sinjin went to the front door, checking to be sure it was locked. It looked automatic, like something he always did before going to bed.

"Sinjin."

He turned. "What?"

"Can't you tell me what's going on with you?"

He said nothing.

"I want us to be closer. I want to be your friend as well as your sister."

He stared past Lindsay for a long moment, lost in thought. When he spoke, the look of pain on his face made Lindsay hold her breath. "Kathy left me for someone else. She's pregnant . . . says it's his. She said I should know it's not mine, because I was never around. But I have to be sure. I've had lawyers working on forcing a paternity test after the baby is born. Kathy and her . . . this guy . . . live in Atlanta. I came to talk to lawyers here. I wanted her to do it voluntarily. Anyway, that's it. Common little problem, I know, but . . . well, there it is."

"Oh, Sinjin, I'm sorry." Lindsay walked over to him. She wanted to hug him, but she didn't. She just stood there holding the empty dishes. "Please stay as long as you need."

"Thanks."

The next morning Lindsay did not look forward to opening the last crate. She had lain awake half the night trying to think of different reasons her grandfather might have stored the artifacts in a shed and forgotten about them—but these were not forgettable artifacts. The other half of the night, she stayed awake worrying about Sinjin. The look on his face was so full of hurt.

Sinjin drove her to the campus because she had left her Land Rover there. Her Rover—she looked at it as Sinjin pulled in beside it. Now, with everything else, the monthly payments were going to be a big drain. She rubbed her forehead. Something else she would have to deal with.

"You all right?" Sinjin asked.

"Fine. Why don't you come in and have a look at the artifacts?" He followed her into the lab and to the back storeroom. "I'll inventory them and decide how to handle them later," she said, as she showed him the shelves filled with the orphaned artifacts.

"I think you're worrying about this too much. It probably has some simple explanation," Sinjin said.

"You're probably right," agreed Lindsay, locking the door behind her and walking down the hallway to the lab.

"Where you taking me to dinner?" asked Sally. She was standing over the last crate with a crowbar.

"Where would you like to go?" asked Lindsay.

"How about Rafferty's?" Sally turned to Sinjin. "You can come with us."

"Thank you, I'll do that," he said.

Sally grinned, took the crowbar, and with one swift motion pried the lid up on the crate. As the top came loose, the front of the crate fell open. A skeleton tumbled out onto the floor. The skull rolling across the hardwood sounded like a bowling ball. It stopped at Sinjin's feet.

But it was not the rolling skull that caught Lindsay's eye. It was the fact that the skeleton was wearing a shirt and tie.

Chapter 7

SINJIN BENT DOWN and picked up the skull. Sally stood with her mouth open. Lindsay searched for something to say. None of them noticed the door opening onto the stairs leading to the Archaeology Department.

"Lindsay?" Lindsay looked up to see Dr. Frank Carter, head of the Archaeology Department. With him was Associate Dean Ellis Einer, one of the administrators on North Campus who viewed archaeology the way some view rotting fish—with a wrinkled nose and a wave of the hand and wondering what value it could possibly have.

"My God!" Einer said. "Isn't it enough that you store those things here . . . I thought you were supposed to repatriate them, or whatever you call it, and why in the world is it dressed that way?"

"Lindsay?" repeated Frank, staring at the remains.

"We have to call the police," she said in the most authoritative voice she could muster.

"The police?" said Einer. "Whatever for?"

"Aboriginal remains," said Frank, clearing his throat, "are not found in modern clothing."

Einer looked puzzled for a moment. "My God. Oh, my God. You mean . . . that this . . . this thing is a body?" He pointed to it as though he were afraid they would mistake what he referred to.

"Yes," replied Lindsay.

"Well, where did it come from?"

"I'll call campus police," said Frank, excusing himself and walking into Lindsay's office.

"It just arrived," said Lindsay, hoping he wouldn't ask any more questions.

"Then it isn't ours?" said Dr. Einer.

"No," said Lindsay.

"Good. Then, while we are waiting for the police, perhaps we can have a little talk." Lindsay raised her eyebrows. "Is there somewhere, ah, private?" he said.

Frank was getting off the phone with the police as Lindsay and Einer entered her office.

"They'll be right over," Frank said, and left the two of them alone.

Lindsay took a seat behind her desk and motioned for Dr. Einer to sit down. He glanced briefly at the chair seat before sitting. Einer was not a slim man, but the expensive cut of his navy blue suit camouflaged the spread of his upper body quite well. The sharp crease in his pants, however, made his legs look even thinner by comparison. His silver-gray tie went well with his hair. Lindsay thought his wife must have picked it out for him.

"Dr. Chamberlain," he said in a low voice, "a delicate matter has come to my attention." Lindsay bit her lip to keep from smiling. "You know how important donors to the university are." Lindsay nodded. "Mr. Stewart Pryor, who I must confess is one of my oldest friends, has asked me to look into a situation you are involved in that concerns his daughter. I told him, of course, that there is nothing official that I can do, but perhaps I could take a little unofficial look into the matter."

Lindsay wanted to tell him that this was none of his concern, but unfortunately, she might need his goodwill very soon, so she chose her words carefully.

"Quite understandably, they are suffering an enormous

amount of grief and didn't realize that they were asking me to falsify a legal document."

"There is some question of a mistake—"

"No."

"Stewart was quite certain—"

"The deceased was his daughter. He's concerned that the observations I made will reflect badly on her. But I assure you, there is nothing in my report that would do that. And I only reported what I observed."

"Well, of course, there's nothing I can tell you to do—"

"No, there isn't. It's a tragic situation. I wish there were something we both could do to ease it for them, but there isn't." Ellis Einer wrinkled his brow. Lindsay could see him thinking of another way to attack the situation. She tried to cut him off. "I was very thorough in my examination of the remains. I verified the problem they are worried about with an outside source. I am certain of my observations. The parents are choosing to put an unfavorable interpretation on the observations that I made, but their conclusions are unwarranted."

"I see. Dr. Chamberlain, I'm not quite sure what it is you do here. Why were you examining Dr. Shirley Foster's remains in the first place?"

Lindsay opened her mouth, but hesitated for a long moment before she spoke. "I discovered the remains and assisted in the autopsy," she said.

"And why was that? You're an archaeologist, aren't you?"

"Yes, and I'm also a forensic anthropologist."

"Oh, I see. I didn't realize we had one of those. Well, thank you for your time, Dr. Chamberlain." Lindsay nodded and Dr. Einer rose and started to leave. "You and Dr. Carter can take care of the police?" He gestured at the door.

"Yes."

"Good."

He left her office and she could hear him talking to Frank about the Archaeology Department's request for more lab space. Their voices faded away as they walked through the lab. What an impression, she thought. Just when we need something from him. Lindsay laid her forehead down on her hands.

"Look at it this way," said Sinjin from the doorway, "it can't get much worse."

Lindsay looked up at him. "Don't say that."

She rose wearily from her chair and went back into the lab to look at the skeleton. The crate that had been its sarcophagus was the same style as the others but was the only one that was labeled. It had dark stains on the inside, and except for some dirt it was empty of anything but the skeleton. There were a couple of knotholes in its wooden side panels.

Lindsay took a piece of typing paper from one of the tables. Frank was still talking to Einer, but Sinjin and Sally were watching her. She took the paper and slid it under the dirt.

"What?" Sally asked.

"Don't ask," Lindsay said. She took the page of dirt and carefully folded it and put it in her desk. Sinjin looked at her questioningly. "I know," she said, "but the police will probably send it back to Kentucky and out of my reach." Sinjin said nothing.

The campus police came. So did a reporter from the campus newspaper, the *Red and Black*. She began snapping pictures immediately.

"So, this may be someone your grandfather knew?" the officer asked.

"I have no way of knowing that," Lindsay answered.

"But the crates were on his property?"

"The crates have been there covered over with kudzu for over sixty years," said Sinjin. "We don't know exactly when they were put there or that our grandfather even knew they were there."

Lindsay could hear the continuous clicking of the camera and wondered if maybe the reporter would run out of film.

"When did kudzu come into the United States?" the reporter asked, as if she had just thought of an important clue. "Wasn't it in the fifties? That would mean the shed wasn't actually covered until . . ."

They all turned to look at her and she snapped a picture. It was Sally who answered. "*Pueraria lobata*—that's kudzu—was introduced into the United States in 1876," she said, giving her a winning smile. The reporter looked disappointed.

After the police came and resealed the skeleton in the crate and took it away, and the reporter had taken all the pictures she wanted and asked all the questions she could think of, they all finally left and Lindsay went back into her office. She opened her desk drawer and put the dirt she had collected from the crate into two vials and replaced them in her desk.

Although the nametag said Bruno, the server bearing frozen margaritas for Lindsay and Sally and a beer for Sinjin was a tall, young blonde woman. She turned to Sinjin, gave him a sparkling smile, pen poised over her order pad.

"Steak medium rare, salad with hot bacon-honey-mustard dressing, and baked potato with everything."

Sinjin looked at Lindsay. "Little sister?"

"That sounds good to me."

"Sally?" asked Sinjin.

"Ditto."

The waitress took up the menus. "Easy. It won't take long." She gave Sinjin another dazzling smile and left.

"Well," said Sally, "that skeleton—wasn't that bizarre?"

Lindsay almost choked on her drink.

"You have a talent for understatement," Sinjin said.

"What will happen to it?" Sally asked.

"The county medical examiner will have to confirm that the remains are those of a modern, not ancient, individual." Lindsay cleared her throat. "Authorities in Kentucky will be notified, and I imagine the remains will be shipped back to McCleary County where they originated. I don't imagine they'll be a high priority, since they were stored for . . ."

"That's another thing." Sally tapped her straw against her glass. "How do you know the bones were on you all's land that long? I mean, couldn't someone—say, ten years ago—have sneaked those crates in there?"

"I don't know." Lindsay sipped her drink and closed her eyes, thinking about Frank's and Ellis Einer's expressions. "It's someone else's problem now."

"So you won't get to examine the bones?" Sally asked.

Bruno brought the salads, and Lindsay took a few moments to push the red cabbage to the edge of her plate before she answered. "No. Since the bones came from my family's property, it wouldn't be proper for me to examine them."

"Who do you think will?" Sinjin asked.

Lindsay shrugged. "There are several good people they can get."

"The police didn't ask as many questions as I thought they would," Sally said.

"The reporter made up for it." Lindsay stared out across the dining area to a far corner.

"What?" asked Sally, turning in her seat, following Lindsay's gaze. "Isn't that those people from yesterday?"

"The Pryors." Lindsay bent her head over her salad.

"I hope they don't come over and ask you to change the report," Sally said. "I can't believe they sent an associate dean to pressure you."

"I think they were simply dealing with their grief. Some people do it in strange ways. I doubt I'll hear from them again." She grinned at Sinjin. "Tell Sally about your job."

"Yes," agreed Sally. "Lindsay said you jump into fires."

Sinjin made a face at Lindsay. "That appears to be her impression. . . . Uh-oh," he said. "The young guy from the Pryors' table got up, and it looks like he's making a beeline for us."

Lindsay took a bite of salad as Chris Pryor approached, hoping he wouldn't expect her to talk with her mouth full of lettuce.

"I'm very sorry to disturb you, Dr. Chamberlain. My parents insisted."

"We're trying to have a peaceful meal," said Sinjin.

"I know, I'm sorry. I'll leave before your main course arrives. I was wondering if I could make an appointment to speak with you?" He took a seat in the empty chair across from Sally, between Lindsay and Sinjin.

"Have a seat," said Sinjin.

"I have nothing more to do with the case," Lindsay said. "And as for changing the report . . ."

Chris waved a hand. "Forget the report. I'm sure Tom Foster will spill the beans about the adoptions to my parents sooner or later. My parents love my sister. They will never accept anything bad about her. They'll end up blaming Tom for everything bad, and they will never believe the bulimia. This is not about the report." The waitress came with her tray, hesitating at the new arrival, and Chris stood up.

"He was just leaving," Sinjin told her.

"My parents heard that you're a good detective. They want you to work with Will Patterson."

Lindsay shook her head. "This is an active case. I really can't get involved."

"But you do work on murder investigations. Could I at least come talk with you?"

"It won't do you any good."

"I can at least tell my parents I tried." He pressed his lips into a tight line.

"Very well," Lindsay agreed. "Can you be at my office by 7:30 in the morning?"

"Seven-thirty?" He took a deep breath. "Yes, thank you very much."

"You're a pushover, Lindsay," Sinjin said, watching Chris Pryor walk back to his table.

Lindsay was up early, but Sinjin was already gone. More business in Atlanta, she assumed. She wished she had gotten to know Kathy better. Maybe if I had been closer to him—she shook her head. It didn't do to speculate. Her thoughts turned to Chris Pryor.

She had just arrived at her office parking lot when Chris pulled in beside her.

"You'll get a ticket," she said as she got out of her Rover.

"It won't matter," he said, following her into the base-ment lab and to her office, where he continued their conver-sation. "As I said last night, my parents want me to persuade you to try to find out who killed Shirley."

"Will Patterson is the detective. I only identify bones."

"They've heard people talk about you. I think they're sorry they made a bad impression on you the other day, but they wouldn't admit that for anything."

"I don't harbor any ill will, but I couldn't investigate this case anyway, while it's active."

"I understand that. Mainly, I had to come here because Mom and Dad asked me to. Sometimes they won't be denied." He gave Lindsay a charming crooked smile.

"Why did Shirley go to such great lengths to make them believe she was pregnant?"

"It was her compromise. She pretending to be the perfect daughter, then doing what she wanted. It was a game, really."

"But you knew."

He nodded. "We were close. She was my big sister. I

don't suppose you allow smoking in here?" He put a hand inside his jacket.

"No."

"I thought not." He pulled out his hand. "I believe all the buildings on campus are smoke-free zones, aren't they? I don't smoke much, just occasionally. Shirley smoked occasionally, too. We kept it from our parents." He shook his head. "Adults we may be, but we hid our smoking from them. They would have disapproved—even though Dad smokes a pipe." He leaned forward, his elbows on his knees, as though he were about to confide something to Lindsay. "They'll keep after you and after you until they get their way." He smiled a tight, humorless smile and straightened up. "They aren't really mean people. They won't try to get you fired or anything if you don't do what they want, but they will ask their friends at the university to talk to you. You know, apply a little pressure from above—and they'll keep doing it until you give in."

"Have they tried working with the sheriff of Dover County? She's handling the case," said Lindsay.

Chris shook his head. "Irene Varnadore wants to make sure that anyone but Tom Foster takes the blame. My parents want to make sure that he is blamed."

"Do you think Tom killed her?"

"I don't like to think so—he's Jeffery and Monica's dad and he got me started in my business—but I do. Their marriage was never that good, and Tom was a jealous man. I think he was tired and wanted out."

"Divorce is easier."

"Not with the prenuptial agreement Dad had drawn up when Tom and Shirley married."

"I thought your parents liked Tom Foster in the beginning."

"They did, but that doesn't make any difference where money is concerned."

"Was your sister wealthy?"

"Yes, she was. My grandmother left her a sizable fortune."

"And you?"

"She left me some in a trust that periodically dribbles out some spending money. Mom and Dad thought it best that way. I won't starve, and I will always be comfortable."

"Do you work?"

Chris smiled, then grinned. "Point well taken. As a matter of fact, I do. I have a shop on Clayton Street. Glass Imagerie. It's a takeoff on . . ."

"I get the allusion."

"Shirl thought it was clever."

"Glass Imagerie is an art gallery for glass sculpture, isn't it?" said Lindsay.

"Yes, mostly glass. I have some nice things. I hold classes, too. I also manage some local artists and occasionally locate paintings and sculpture for buyers. I found the friezes for the new bank downtown. They're from an old Greek revival building torn down in New York. Garish building, the kind Ayn Rand hated in *The Fountainhead*. The friezes look good on this building here, though."

"I've seen some of your glasswork in the window. They're quite lovely."

"I do okay, even without my trust fund."

"You think your brother-in-law killed your sister. Are there any other suspects?"

"I thought you weren't interested."

Lindsay smiled. "I'm curious."

"Everyone liked Shirl. I don't know of anyone who hated her enough to kill her. I can't think of anyone besides Tom Foster with a motive."

"Do you remember the last time you saw her?"

Chris's eyes were suddenly shiny with a film of tears.

"Yes. It was the day before she disappeared. We were going over the plans for Dad's sixtieth birthday party. It was going to be the next week. Nothing too big, just a few people at the botanical gardens. Shirl was good at organizing things."

"What about the missing hundred thousand dollars?"

Chris sat bolt upright in his chair.

"What?"

"You didn't know about it?"

"No."

"That's what is missing from her account. With that much money in her possession, even a stranger could have killed her for it," Lindsay pointed out.

"Yes. I see. You're right. But so would her husband. What was she doing with that much money, I wonder?"

"You have no idea?" Chris shook his head. "Do your parents know about the missing money?"

"No. They certainly would have said something. Come talk to them, please."

"What good would it do?"

"Perhaps none. Perhaps you could at least consult with Will Patterson. You know, give him some good ideas. Or you can tell them to their face why you can't take the case."

Lindsay relented. "All right. I'll have to check my calendar."

"Fine." Chris drew a map to the Pryors' home. "Thanks. Call me when you can come and I'll meet you out there."

Chris had left by 8:15. Lindsay had no idea why she had agreed to go to the Pryors' home, except that she was curious—about the burning pattern on the bones, about the missing money, about Shirley Foster herself, about a lot of things. Lindsay doubted it was a stranger who killed her—she was buried on her husband's family's property. A stranger would have just dumped her body or put it in a shallow grave. A stranger might not care whether the body was found or not. Whoever killed Shirley Foster didn't want her body found— at least, not right away. Who had dug the deep grave in the woods and placed her so carefully in it? And who, Lindsay wondered, called in the anonymous tip to Will Patterson about the body being buried on the Foster farm?

Lindsay was jerked out of her thoughts by the sound of the phone. From the long ring, she knew it was from somewhere on campus.

"Lindsay, Frank here. The police are sending someone over to get the rest of the artifacts. Can you pack them up?"

"Sure. What are they going to do with them?"

"Harold van Deevers from the University of Kentucky wants them sent to his office. The authorities have agreed to allow him to receive them."

Lindsay made a face. "All right. When will they be coming to pick them up?"

"In a couple of hours."

"Very well." She hung up the phone. "I imagine Harold van Deevers is getting a great charge out of this," she said aloud as she retrieved the key from her drawer.

The dark storage room had the characteristic dusty smell of old artifacts. The shelves were filled with boxes containing bags of dirt taken from grid squares inside the structures of the Jasper Creek site, all waiting to be sorted or to undergo chemical flotation. All the small things that had accumulated on the floor of the house structures—bone, sherds, daub, rock, charcoal—would be classified, labeled, and stored for later analysis. Now, they sat waiting for students to get to them. Sometimes it took years. Lindsay coughed and turned on the light. She didn't even notice all the boxes from the Jasper Creek site sitting neatly on the shelves, because the new shelves at the far end were more conspicuous. They were completely empty.

Chapter 8

LINDSAY STOOD STARING at the empty shelves, willing the artifacts to reappear. Maybe someone had just moved them, she thought. To where? She locked the storage room and walked back through the darkened lab. It was quiet. She turned on the lights, which brightened the space but did nothing to dispel her uneasy feeling. The huge sets of artifact drawers, silent keepers of the treasures, loomed tall over the worktables. Portions of pottery stood in their sandboxes, looking like ancient ruins in miniature, surrounded by hundreds of sherds to be fitted into place. Boxes of half-sorted animal bones waited on another table for students to come and identify, weigh, and measure them—a process that would eventually determine the MNI from the site and provide a good estimate of the amount of meat protein the inhabitants consumed. Someone had brought several site reports and stacked them next to the boxes of bones. Lindsay absently ran her thumb over the edges, flipping through the pages as she looked around the room for anything out of place.

The next table contained boxes and boxes of black chert debris in the process of being measured and categorized—a tedious time-consuming task. The resulting data would reveal which stages of flint toolmaking occurred where the debris was found. These broken bits of rock, bone, and pots yielded far more information of much greater value to archaeologists than the artifacts that were missing, but on the collector's market they were worth less than nothing. To looters, they were objects to be thrown aside, forever separating them from their location—and destroying their value to the body of historical knowledge. Lindsay closed her eyes. Papaw wasn't a looter, she thought. He couldn't have been.

She opened her eyes and looked under all the tables, thinking that maybe someone had, for some unknown reason, packed the artifacts away and stored them there. Nothing. She unlocked the faunal lab. Nothing but the metal shelves and shoeboxes. She looked in Sally's lab space. The box of old wrapping material was shoved under Sally's desk. She took it to her office and locked it in the closet, not that anyone would want to steal brittle old newsprint.

"Damn," she said as she dialed Sally's number. "Sally, do you know if anyone moved the Kentucky artifacts to another location?"

"No. Why?" There was a long pause. "Jeez, are they gone?"

"I'm afraid so," said Lindsay.

"Oh, no. Who?"

"I have no idea. Maybe someone just moved them. I'll give Frank a call." Lindsay hung up the phone and dialed Frank's office phone.

"Frank, did you ask someone to move the Kentucky artifacts?" she asked.

"No. Why? They aren't missing, are they?"

"They aren't on the shelves."

There was a long pause that was beginning to become uncomfortably familiar.

"Have you talked to any of the students?"

"I called Sally. She doesn't know anything."

"Damn."

"Yeah."

"Who do you think?" he said. "I hope not one of the students."

"No. I can't believe it was any of them. We'd better call the police. They'll be able to tell if the door was forced or anything."

The same campus policemen who had come the previous day answered the call regarding the missing artifacts. Fortunately, the reporter wasn't with them this time. They took the theft seriously, but not with the same concern they did when the computers in the Political Science Department were stolen—until Frank gave an estimate of their value to collectors.

One of the policemen whistled. "Did the student workers know their value?"

"Not the exact value," said Lindsay. "They knew the artifacts had value to collectors, but they work with artifacts all the time."

Lindsay made a list of who was present when the artifacts were unpacked and gave it to the police. "I know all of these students," she said. She saw the skeptical look in their eyes, the look that said people are capable of doing all sorts of things you would never think they would do. "I do know them," she reiterated. "None are thieves."

"But they may have seen someone," said one of the policemen.

"Yes, they may have seen someone," she agreed. "We took pictures of each artifact. Brandon should have them. I'll ask when he returns."

"Could you and Dr. Carter make a list of the missing items, including the value of each, and provide a picture?" they asked.

"Sure," answered Frank and Lindsay together.

The police examined the door and found nothing that suggested forced entry. "We'll send someone over to check for prints, but don't get your hopes up about that." They put up crime-scene tape, blocking the door to the storage room.

As the students came in and took up their work in the lab, Lindsay asked them about the artifacts. Did they know if they had been moved? Had they seen anyone they didn't know hanging around?

"The police are interviewing everyone who works here," she said. "Please try to remember anyone at all who may have been down here."

"Maybe it was the person who killed the fellow in the crate," one of them suggested.

"He may have died over sixty years ago," said Lindsay.

"Maybe we should tell the police to check the retirement homes," said another.

"Seriously," said Bobbie, a graduate student who had just come in and set down her backpack. "What if the missing artifacts were in some family's folklore? You know, like stories of great-grandfathers tossing the family silver down a well. Only, in this case, it was a big hidden cache of artifacts, and when they surfaced, some family member came to claim them." Lindsay looked at Bobbie for a moment, pondering her suggestion. Bobbie's interests lay in family lore—that was her mindset, and it was an intriguing idea, if a little far-fetched. "Why don't you call your family," Bobbie continued, "and see if they told anyone about the find?"

"I will. That's a good idea. Very creative. Thanks, all of you." Lindsay felt a pang of guilt as she looked at the earnest faces of her students—that they should come under this cloud of her family's making. Where, she wondered for the thousandth time, had her grandfather gotten the artifacts? "I'm really sorry, guys, for all this . . ."—she threw up her hands—". . . this mess."

"That's all right, Dr. Chamberlain. It's kind of interesting," a student said.

"Yeah," said another. "You're always involved in interesting things."

Great, thought Lindsay, she had developed a reputation for the sensational. She went back to her office and sat down at her desk to think. The artifacts had been stolen; no one had moved them. She hated to admit it. The phone signaled the distinctive two-ring pattern of an off-campus call.

"Lindsay Chamberlain," she said into the receiver as Brandon entered her office and handed her an envelope.

"Lindsay, this is Harold van Deevers. How are you?"

She made a face into the receiver as she took the envelope from Brandon's hand. "The pictures," he mouthed to her, then he waved and went out the door.

"Harold. I'm fine. And you?"

"That's not what I hear. I just got off the phone with Frank Carter."

Then why are you calling me? she thought.

"I'm very upset about the disappearance of the artifacts," he continued.

"We all are," she said.

"I don't understand how it could have happened."

"The police are trying to ascertain that right now." Lindsay emptied the contents of the envelope onto the desk.

"In fact, I don't understand what your grandfather was doing with them."

"If you talked to Frank, then you know that this whole situation is mysterious." Lindsay picked up the pictures one by one and looked at them.

"I was hoping you could shed some light on the matter," he said.

Stop dancing around and come to the point, Lindsay thought as she looked at a picture of a Manion Phase clay pot. "If I had any light to shed, I would have certainly shed it to Frank and the police. I fear I'm in the dark about the whole thing."

"It would help if you adopted a more cooperative attitude," he said.

"Attitude will not get the artifacts back. I'm taking all the steps I know to try and recover them." It's behavior, not attitude, you should be looking at, Lindsay thought. And that's just what's wrong with your papers—not enough emphasis on the behavioral meaning of your data. "Exactly why have you called me?" she asked.

"I'm not pleased with the way any of this has been handled." His voice showed a little more hostility, and Lindsay wondered if she should have been more contrite. "You should have notified me immediately after you discovered the artifacts. Your behavior has not been professional in this matter."

"Harold, the collection of artifacts caught me completely by surprise. The labeling on one of the crates indicated that they were from Georgia. I identified them as being from Kentucky by what I thought were Fort Ancient pottery and assemblages. As you know, pottery is not my forte."

"Do you have any idea what they were doing among your grandfather's possessions?"

"Not a clue." Strange he didn't mention the skeletal remains, thought Lindsay. Frank must not have told him about that. "Frank and I will make a list of the items. I'll fax you the information as soon as we finish."

"I would appreciate it. Good talking to you, Lindsay."

"And you, Harold." They hung up and Lindsay frowned at the door. He only called to needle her about the artifacts, she knew, but was he right about how she had handled them? Was she more concerned with protecting the image of her grandfather than doing what was right with the artifacts? What was right? Where did they belong? She began looking at the pictures and making a list. She would let Frank deal with the appraisal.

She heard a tentative knock on the door and looked up to see Bethany, her long red hair tied up in a ponytail, standing in the doorway.

"I have come to do some sorting, Dr. Chamberlain. Could I have the key to the storage room?"

"You can't go in there until the police finish."

Bethany's eyes widened. "There hasn't been another body discovered, has there?"

Lindsay smiled. "No, but some artifacts are missing."

"Somebody stole bags of dirt?"

"No. The day before yesterday I stored some other artifacts in the storage room and they're missing. You haven't seen anybody hanging around have you?"

Bethany shook her head. "Do you have anything for me to do? I kind of need to get some hours in."

"I don't have anything. I think Dr. Kerwin needs some copying done."

"Not Dr. Kerwin," Bethany groaned. "He wants all his staples at exactly a forty-five-degree angle. I can never do them to suit him."

"I don't suppose you'd like to help Greg with the faunal specimens?" Lindsay suggested. Bethany wrinkled her nose.

"Ask Dr. Bienvenido if she needs anything."

Sally arrived just as Bethany left. "Have you found the artifacts?"

"No. I've looked everywhere."

Sally sat down. "Who do you think did it?"

Lindsay shook her head. "I have no idea. The police are going to dust for fingerprints, but I have a feeling they won't find anything."

"This is very strange. Who do the artifacts belong to? You?"

Lindsay shook her head. "Not to me. I suppose my father could lay claim to them, if he were inclined, but he wouldn't. Right now, I imagine the Office of State Archaeology in Kentucky—if the artifacts are from Kentucky. We don't know that for sure."

"Maybe the police will come up with something."

Lindsay patted her on the shoulder. "You're an optimist, Sally. I hope you're right."

"Thanks for dinner last night. I really enjoyed it. I'm glad your brother came."

"He and I enjoyed it, too."

"I don't suppose he said anything about me."

"I think he did ask how old you are again," Lindsay answered.

"Boy, is he hung up on age." She rose and sauntered out the door. "I guess I'll go see if Andy's finished with the sandbox. I brought my plastic bucket today."

"Sally," Lindsay called.

"Yes?" she said, turning and leaning into the doorway.

"Would you take this list and these pictures to Frank for me?" Lindsay rose and handed an envelope to her. "I'm going to the medical examiner's office and see if they'll let me look at the bones of our mystery guest. But don't tell anyone unless they ask."

"You want me to go with you?"

"No. I'm probably not supposed to have access to them, and I certainly don't want to be accused of contributing to the delinquency of a minor."

"Cute." Sally took the envelope.

"Eddie, can I look at the bones?" asked Lindsay.

"You can, but may you? That's the question." He grinned at her from behind the desk in his small office.

"May I?"

"I don't see why not." He rose from his desk and walked with Lindsay to the morgue. "What's the story on these? They were in your grandfather's trunk or something?"

"Not exactly. They were in a wooden crate stored in one

of my grandfather's outbuildings that's been covered with kudzu ever since anyone can remember."

"Fascinating—all that time." He shook his head.

"Do you know who's going to examine them?" Lindsay asked.

"I believe we're supposed to ship them back to Kentucky. But no one said you couldn't look at them first."

Eddie took the box of bones to the autopsy room and helped Lindsay unpack them and lay them out on the table. John Booth appeared out of nowhere and assisted them.

"Have you looked at them?" asked Lindsay.

"We collected some insect casings and packed the clothing separately. That's about all."

"A guy," said Lindsay, looking at the pelvis.

"Well, then, we don't have a cross-dresser," said Eddie.

Lindsay smiled at him. She examined the surface of the pubic symphysis. "Wouldn't you say early twenties?" she asked, running a thumb across the ridges and furrows of the bone.

"Works for me," said Eddie.

Lindsay took a quick look at his teeth. "Lots of cavities, few trips to the dentist." She examined a femur and the sternal end of a couple of ribs. "We'll say between twenty-two and twenty-five."

"I like these quick and dirty methods," said Eddie. "Saves time."

"When you don't have to write the report, it's fast and easy," she said. "He was left-handed." Lindsay pointed out the beveling on the margin of the left glenoid cavity.

"Look between the fifth and sixth ribs," said John, pointing to his right side. He grinned at Lindsay, showing a row of white teeth. She raised her eyebrows and picked up the ribs in question.

"The sixth rib has a cut," said Lindsay.

"From the front," said John.

"Yes," she said, feeling the rough edge of the nick in back of the rib. "How did you know?"

"Went through the shirt, stained it." John flashed his white teeth again.

"Well, that was easy," said Eddie. "He was stabbed. With a knife?"

"Looks like it," Lindsay answered, examining the v-shaped nick. "Give me a small sliver of paper," she said.

John tore an edge from a piece of paper he took out of the trash can. Lindsay put the edge in the nick. "Look at the direction it's oriented," she said.

"Downward and toward the center of the body," Eddie commented.

Lindsay looked over the other ribs. "Here's a nick on the anterior surface of the right tenth. It looks like the killer held the knife in his left hand and stabbed the guy in his right side. Is that what it looks like to you?"

Eddie nodded. "Killer was taller, too, by several inches." He took a ruler and walked over to Lydell, an anatomy skeleton standing in the corner, and pulled him away from the wall. He dragged a stool next to Lydell and stepped up onto the stool. "Let's see," he said.

Lindsay watched him as he held the ruler at the proper angle while bending his knees and moving up and down until he found a height that would have been natural for someone wielding a knife. "What would you say that is?"

"'Bout five or six inches taller, I'd say," said John.

"I agree," said Lindsay.

"Couldn't the fellow be sitting down and the killer come up behind him and stab him over the shoulder?" John asked. "'Course, I guess he'd have to hold the knife upside down to make those cuts in the top of the rib, wouldn't he?"

"I had a case once," Eddie said, "fellow stabbed from behind, over the shoulder. Cut the bottom of the rib."

"I don't believe the angle would be as steep," said Lindsay.

John Booth rubbed his fingers over the nicks. "Amazing what you can tell from tiny cuts in the bone."

"Yep, keeps Miss Lindsay here in business," Eddie said, and as John held the ribs, he measured the distance from the sixth rib to the inside of the tenth. "I'd say it had to be a knife about nine inches long."

"Anything else from the clothes?" Eddie asked John.

"Bloodstains. Shirt and pants," John responded. "The guy bled."

"The crate?" Lindsay asked. "It was stained as I remember. Blood?"

"Maybe. Body fluid certainly," said Eddie. He shrugged. "They can test it in Kentucky."

"So, he may have been dead when he was put in the crate," Lindsay commented. "How long might it have taken him to die?"

"Let's see. It hit the lung, the liver, probably a vessel. I imagine he bled to death. It'd be quick, probably just a few minutes."

"The way he was bent, he had to be put in the crate either before the onset of rigor or after rigor resolved," commented Lindsay.

"True. If they put him in the crate after rigor, they might have had to wait as long as thirty hours."

"Anything else from the clothes?" asked Lindsay. "I don't suppose there was a driver's license?"

"Nothing at all in his pockets," John said. "Judging from his clothes, I reckon he was about five foot four and weighed about 130 pounds."

Lindsay took the bone board and measured the left femur. "Four hundred and forty-one millimeters," she said.

Eddie searched around in one of the cabinets. "Here we go," he said, lifting out a thick book. "What's the race?"

Lindsay examined the skull again. "White," she said.

"Five feet, five inches," said Eddie. "Pretty good, John."

"There's a healed break in the right femur," said Lindsay. "And in the right tibia."

"It's hard to break a femur," said Eddie.

"Right tibia didn't heal well. One leg was shorter than the other. Was he wearing corrective shoes?" Lindsay asked John.

"No," said John, "but his shoes were scuffed pretty bad and the heel of the right shoe was wore down on the inside."

"You should be a detective, John," said Eddie.

John showed Lindsay the shoes inside the plastic bag. She dug in the pocket of her jeans for her hand lens and examined the sides and bottoms of the soles through the plastic.

"Can you tell where the dirt's from?" asked Eddie.

Lindsay gave him a sideways glance. "Sure," she said, and he grinned at her.

"They ought to be able to do something with that up there in Kentucky," said Eddie.

"You come from Kentucky, don't you, Dr. Chamberlain?" asked John Booth.

"Yes, I do."

"I thought so. Where 'bouts? I have some people up there."

"Stearns."

"Pennyroyal," said Booth. "Mine are up in the Bluegrass."

"Actually, Eastern Mountains, but it's up against Pennyroyal," said Lindsay.

"I know what Bluegrass is, but what's Pennyroyal?" Eddie asked.

"Geographic regions," Lindsay said, "like Piedmont or Coastal Plains here in Georgia."

"Where'd you go to school?" asked Eddie.

"UT."

"Tennessee, Kentucky. You're a little mountain girl, aren't you?"

"Pretty much. Look at this," she said, turning the humerus over in her hand. "Femur's the same."

"Those groves down the bone?" asked Eddie.

"Yes, the poor fellow had to do some very hard, back-breaking labor in his short life." She quickly looked at the vertebrae. "He had back problems, too. His vertebrae are a little too worn for his age."

"Poor guy," said Eddie. "What do you think?"

Lindsay shook her head. "I don't have a clue."

"You think they can find out who he is?" asked Booth.

"Not without some miracle," said Lindsay. "You'd better pack him back up and ship him off. Thanks for letting me take a look."

"Sure. You think your grandfather had something to do with this guy?"

"He was stored behind his workshop. I just don't know, and . . ."

Eddie's cell phone rang. He searched his pockets for it, finally locating it in the front pocket of his lab coat. "Yes?" Pause. "Lindsay, it's for you. Sally."

Lindsay took the phone. "Yes?"

"Lindsay, you need to come back. The police took your brother to the police station."

"Sinjin? Why?"

"Just come back."

Chapter 9

SALLY WAS STANDING outside waiting when Lindsay pulled up behind Baldwin. As soon as the Rover stopped, Sally jumped in the passenger side.

"What's this about?" asked Lindsay.

"Some student said they saw Sinjin's black Jeep parked out back last night."

"His Jeep, or one like it?" Lindsay drove out onto Jackson Street.

"They said his, but every other Jeep on campus is a lot like his."

"That can't be all," said Lindsay.

Sally looked down at her hands clasped tightly in her lap. "They found some stuff in his Jeep."

Lindsay was silent a moment. "What stuff?" she asked.

"One of those tripod jars and a few points."

"I see." Lindsay remembered his being surprised at the artifacts' value, then banished the thought from her mind.

"He didn't do it," Sally said.

"No, he didn't," Lindsay said, turning on Lumpkin. "How did you find out about it?"

"He came by your office looking for you just as the police showed up. It was really bad timing. Frank was there, too."

Neither said anything as Lindsay drove the rest of the way to the Public Safety Building. Sinjin was coming out the door when Lindsay drove up. He looked angry.

She stopped the Rover, got out, and smiled at him, hoping it looked natural and not forced. "Hi, need a ride?"

"Yeah."

Sally climbed into the back seat, leaving the passenger seat for Sinjin.

"What was that about?" asked Lindsay.

"They think I took the artifacts."

"That's ridiculous. If you wanted to make off with them, you could have done it anywhere between here and Kentucky."

"Yes, if I had known their value."

Lindsay wanted to ask him if he had any idea how the artifacts got in his Jeep, but she didn't know how to not make it sound like an accusation.

"My Jeep is parked behind your building," he said. "If you'll take me there, I'll meet you at your house—if you can go home."

"Sure. You told them where you were when your Jeep was supposed to be parked outside Baldwin? Didn't they check it out?" said Lindsay.

Sinjin was silent for a long time. "I went to see Kathy."

"Didn't she tell them?"

"No. She denied it."

Sally made a surprised sound from the back seat. Lindsay pressed her lips together in a tight thin line. "Why?" she asked.

"She didn't want Sid to know."

"Sid?"

"Her new—whatever," he said.

"Did you explain the importance?" asked Sally, leaning forward to the front seat.

"I didn't talk to her. The police did."

"What now?" asked Lindsay.

"They have a problem with who actually owns the artifacts. Since they have been with our family for over sixty years, they don't quite know what to do."

"Did they tell you not to leave town?" asked Sally. Sinjin turned and looked at her. Sally scooted back in the seat. "I'm sorry," she said. "I know this is none of my business."

Sinjin gave her a crooked smile. "Thanks for bringing the cavalry." He turned around and stared out the front window.

Lindsay took Sally back to Baldwin. Sinjin got his Jeep and they drove back to her cabin in the woods.

"You had any lunch?" she asked, heading for the kitchen.

"No. I'm not very hungry." He poured himself a glass of cold water from the refrigerator and drank it down.

"I'll make some sandwiches. You can eat one if you want."

"I didn't take the artifacts," he said.

"I didn't think you did," Lindsay said. She took a loaf of bread in plastic wrap from the bread box. "This is great bread. I bought myself a bread machine for my birthday."

"You thought it," he said, pouring another glass of water.

"No, I didn't." Lindsay opened the refrigerator and took several plastic containers and various jars out and put them on the chopping block where she began preparing lunch.

"Then why didn't you ask how the artifacts got in my Jeep?"

Lindsay stopped spreading mayonnaise on the bread, put down the knife, and looked at him. "Because I was afraid you would think I thought you did it, if I asked." She paused. "How did they get there?"

"I don't know."

"Why did Kathy lie?"

"I told you, she was afraid of hurting her relationship with Sid."

"That's not a good reason when your freedom could depend on her answer."

"She's pregnant. She feels vulnerable."

"What's the story on you two?" Lindsay asked. "Why did you go see her?"

"She didn't have anything to do with this," he said.

"She might, if she wanted to . . ."

"Keep her out of this. Kathy wouldn't do this to me. How could she, anyway?"

Lindsay picked up the knife and began making the sandwiches again. "Well, I envy her. I wish Derrick loved me that much."

"Maybe he does, but he can't bear to stand around and watch you get hurt."

"Sure."

"Have you talked to him?"

"Just business. What did the police say?"

"What I told you. They searched my Jeep and found those few artifacts. Some student reported having seen my Jeep parked there last night."

"You mean, one like it."

"No, he gave them my tag number."

"What? And the police didn't think that was strange?" Lindsay handed him a sandwich on a plate. "Roast chicken."

"Thanks. The guy was suspicious of a car being there at night and took down the number, they said."

"Come on, this is a university community. We do research. Every building on campus has people working late every night. I've worked overnight many times and no one has ever reported my vehicle. Besides, the Baldwin parking lot is hidden around back of the building. You can't really see it from anywhere but the cemetery, and you don't walk through it to get to anywhere—unless you're going to Baldwin or to the cemetery." She finished making her sandwich and got a Diet Dr. Pepper from the refrigerator, and they both sat down at the kitchen table.

"I don't think they'll press charges, because of the uncertainty over the ownership of the artifacts. That reporter was there. The one from the *Black and Blue* or whatever. The one who took all the pictures of the skeleton."

"I'm sorry this happened to you," Lindsay said.

"*I'm* sorry. I know this must be an embarrassment for you," Sinjin said. "It doesn't matter about me."

"Do you really think that?"

"No. I care what you think, what Dad and Ellen think. Hell, I even care what Sally thinks. I hate this."

"So do I, and I'm going to get to the bottom of it. The artifacts will surface somewhere. Eat your sandwich." Lindsay took a bite of hers. "I went to examine the skeleton today."

"They let you?"

"Sure, no problem. The medical examiner knows me. They were about to pack him up to send him to Kentucky."

"What did you find out?"

"The guy was in his mid-twenties. He walked with a limp from a bad accident that broke his right leg in a couple of places. He worked very hard all his life. The only other place I've seen muscle attachments like that is in the remains of African-American slaves."

"So . . . ?" Sinjin asked, eating his sandwich.

"I don't know." She hesitated. "Pennyroyal, Bluegrass, Western Coal Fields," she said.

"Now you've lost me."

"During the examination, we were talking about the geographic regions of Kentucky, and it just reminded me. Someone who worked in a coal mine all his life, starting as a kid, could have that kind of bone remodeling. It's also a place he could have broken his leg that badly." Lindsay smiled and finished her sandwich.

"You like this, don't you?" Sinjin said. "Maybe not when it's so personal, but you like to solve the mysteries."

"Yes, I do."

"You're good at it."

"Thanks."

"I'm good at managing fires and the people who fight them. And I enjoy it. Did you know that last year there were 49,000 fires in U.S. forests, and people like me kept all but 300 from becoming major fires?"

Lindsay raised her eyebrows. "Wow."

"Yes, wow. I like my job."

"I'm sorry if I've been less than supportive."

"That's all right. I just wanted you to know."

"Tell me about you and Kathy. I'm not investigating her. I just want to know about your life."

"Not a lot to tell. Funny, I was going to ask her to marry me when I came back from the last fire. Guess I waited one fire too many. When I got home she was gone. She left me a note. Told me the whole thing about Sid."

"I'm sorry."

"Yeah, me too. After a fire, all the smokejumpers and hotshots go home to their families, and I always envied them. That's why I came to visit you and Dad. I wanted to patch things up and have a family again."

"You've always had a family. Things weren't that bad, were they?"

"I've always felt that you and Dad looked down on me. Like I had all this potential and couldn't live up to it. I never liked being looked down on by my baby sister."

"That's not true. I never—"

"Isn't it?"

"I suppose I was a little snobbish. I thought you ought to work at a university, like everyone else in the family. I'm sorry. But I never looked down on you. I just thought you were stubborn and didn't want to do what Dad wanted you to do."

Sinjin laughed. "Didn't want to do what Dad wanted. Do you hear yourself? It never occurred to you that I just wanted to do what I wanted?"

"I suppose not."

"How about you? Are you doing what you want?"

"Yes, I am. I love archaeology and I love the forensic work. I get to do both here."

"Will all this scandal hurt your job situation?"

"No, it shouldn't."

"Do you have tenure?"

"No."

"Then it could, couldn't it?"

"I don't think so."

"I'll tell you what. I have a lot of time off coming. I'll stick around a while and help with this mess."

"I'd love having you here. I'll get Susan to bring one of her horses over and we can go riding together some."

"I'd like that."

"You and Sally have a little in common," Lindsay said.

"What's that?"

"Her boyfriend e-mailed her a Dear Jane letter."

"*E-mailed?* That's worse than a note taped to the bedpost. Poor kid."

"Yeah, and the girl he left her for is such a jerk."

"Sally's a cute girl."

"Yes, she is. Smart, too."

"Are you matchmaking?"

"Not really. I just thought you'd like to learn more about the people I hang out with here in the Archaeology Department."

"You know, the guy in the crate didn't have to be from Kentucky," said Sinjin. "He could be from anywhere. If the crates originated in Georgia, he was probably from here."

"That's true," Lindsay agreed.

"Maybe he was one of the WPA or CCC—or whatever they were called—working the digs at Macon with Papaw."

"You don't think Papaw . . . did this, do you?" asked Lindsay.

"No, I can't imagine it," admitted Sinjin.

"I'd like to go see the Pryors this evening. Would you go with me?"

"Keeping me under supervision, huh?"

"No. I . . ."

"Just kidding, baby sister. Sure, I'll go. The Shirley Foster murder, huh? Never a dull moment around here."

On their way to the Pryors', Lindsay's mind kept returning to Kathy's failure to support Sinjin's alibi. "What did Kathy want?" Lindsay asked.

"Don't bring her into this," said Sinjin. "She doesn't know anything about the artifacts."

"She's involved some way. She had you come to Atlanta, then lied to the police about it."

"It was your university police. She probably thought it was some rinky-dink thing of no importance."

"Campus police have the same authority as city police. The fact is, they have complete jurisdiction over crimes that happen on campus. It's not a small thing, lying to them."

"Drop it."

"No."

"Dammit, Lindsay!"

"When do the police think the artifacts were taken?" she asked.

"Sometime early this morning. Supposedly, my Jeep was parked behind Baldwin around four in the morning."

"When did you leave for Atlanta?" Silence. "She asked you to come early, didn't she? Did she give you some excuse—that Sid worked an early shift?"

"Sid's a lawyer. He doesn't work shifts. Do you think everything concerned with me is blue collar?"

"Dammit, Sinjin, that's not fair."

"Neither are your questions."

"I'm trying to help."

"Well, you're not."

Lindsay was working up a sizable suspicion of Kathy, but she dropped the subject. Instead, she told Sinjin about her interview with Chris Pryor.

"Sounds like a spoiled brat to me," he said.

"I think it must have been hard growing up in that family."

"Why? Just because his parents had high expectations?" Sinjin shook his head. "It may have been hard, but there are worse things."

"Yeah, but it's not like we'd have to fool *our* parents about something as important as adopting children."

"The Foster woman didn't, either. She could have just told them, and they'd have to deal with it. It's just the way Shirley and Chris chose to live their lives. Once you become an adult you don't have to act like a kid anymore."

"Maybe. But it's hard when expectations are so high you sometimes feel you can never meet them," said Lindsay.

"Are we talking about Shirley here?"

"I don't know."

Lindsay drove the rest of the way in silence. Sinjin didn't say anything either. She reached Church Street and turned off onto a paved driveway. Behind a stand of water oaks, a large white house came into view. The center portion of the house was vernacular architecture, of a standard design, probably not built by a known architect schooled in formal architectural styles but by anonymous builders using traditional materials and traditional forms. The house had been added to over the years, and the chimneys that were formerly outside were now inside. A large front porch ran the length of the house.

"Nice house," Sinjin said, standing on the porch.

"It may be on the historical register," Lindsay said. "Seems like I've seen it somewhere. I think perhaps it once was a girls school."

this was Stewart Pryor's chair. Lindsay sat on the couch. Chris brought a chair from the library table.

"I'm glad you came," he said to Lindsay.

"I'm not sure why I did."

Lindsay glanced at her brother looking at the photographs on the mantel. Probably curious about what Shirley Foster looked like. Along with a portrait of Shirley, there was one of Chris and one containing several people at what looked to be a cookout. Lindsay rose and walked over to the mantel to look at the picture. "When was this taken?" she asked.

"About four or five years ago at one of Shirley's departmental parties at, I believe, Dr. Pierce's house," Chris said.

Among the people in the photograph was Chris, holding hands with a very pretty blonde, and Shirley was making faces at the camera. Standing beside Shirley was Kenneth Kerwin from the Archaeology Department. He was looking adoringly at Shirley.

"See something?" asked Chris.

"Nice picture," she said as she sat back down.

Stewart Pryor came into the room, wearing slacks and a plaid burgundy and gray smoking jacket. The plaid was not bold but was of a very fine weave. Lindsay didn't think anyone but her father wore a smoking jacket anymore. She introduced Sinjin to Pryor. Sinjin shook his hand and sat down on the couch next to Lindsay.

"I appreciate your coming." Pryor took a pipe from the stand and filled it with tobacco from a pouch in his pocket, tamping it down in the bowl with his finger.

"That's a lovely smoking jacket," Lindsay said.

"It is, isn't it? Shirley made it. She wove the fabric herself. She made several for me—different ones for special occasions." He patted his pocket and, finding it empty, walked to the mantel, took several matches from a crystal jar, and slipped them in his pocket. He used one to light his pipe, and the aroma of cherry filled the air. "She made me a beautiful Christmas jacket. Dyed it herself to get a special color of red. She took it to display at the museum, and some damn fool lost it—took it, most likely. Everyone wanted Shirley's work." He sat down in the chair that Lindsay had decided must be his.

Sinjin, Chris, and Stewart Pryor stood again as Evelyn came in with a tray of coffee in white china cups and set it on a small glass-topped table in front of the couch. It had been a while since Lindsay had seen that done, men standing when a lady entered.

"It is very nice of you to come," she said to Lindsay— "and to meet you," she said to Sinjin. "Do you work at the university as well?"

"No, I'm visiting Lindsay for a while," replied Sinjin.

"How very nice. How do you like your coffee?" Lindsay and Sinjin both asked for it black. "And what do you do?"

"I'm a firefighter. I put out forest fires," he replied.

"Oh, how interesting," she said. Stewart muttered an agreement.

It was not overt, but Lindsay saw the subtle look of condescension in their polite smiles, and it shocked her. Was this how she and her father appeared to Sinjin? Surely not. It was not the way she felt, was it? She suddenly felt very much ashamed of herself. Lindsay wanted to jump up and shout at them, tell them that she had no intention of listening unless they could act better. But the whole episode was so imperceptible, she doubted they would know what she was talking about.

"Chris told me that you want me to consult with Will Patterson," Lindsay said, a little too abruptly.

"Yes," Stewart said. "We've heard from several sources that you are particularly good at solving . . ." He hesitated momentarily. "Good at solving crimes in which a length of time has passed. As much as sixty years, I've heard."

"I'm not a detective and I'm sure Chris told you that I . . ."

"I want my daughter's murderer found. I am willing to pay a great deal of money."

"It's not a matter of money."

He held up a hand. "I know, the active case thing. Will is working on the case. He assures me that there is no problem."

"Perhaps not for him."

"I can assure you, not for you, either."

"Mr. Pryor, I'm not sure what you think I can bring to the case. It seems to me that Will Patterson is doing a good job. He, essentially, found where your daughter was buried." Lindsay saw a look of pain cross Evelyn Pryor's face and deeply regretted coming. She didn't know why she did or why she kept flirting with this case. But it wasn't her idea, she reminded herself. People kept coming to her.

"You found her. You found Shirley," said Stewart.

"Yes, but it was his idea to bring in an archaeologist."

"Will is fine with more recent crimes. This one—" He paused and inhaled smoke from his pipe. His teeth gently clicked on the stem. "This one needs something else. I believe that Shirley's husband killed her. As long as Irene Varnadore is the only official investigating, Tom Foster will never be a suspect."

"Do you have any specific reason to suspect her husband?" asked Lindsay.

"Money. Tom had control over it as long as she was missing. Now that she's been found and her will is to be probated, all that will change. We advised Shirley on her will, of course. Tom had his own money. He didn't need Shirley's. The money stayed in the family. A trust for the children and, I'm sure, something for Chris—that was up to her, I told her. The rest to her mother and me. I'm sure that sounds selfish to you, but it wasn't. Money must be cared for if it's to grow. I've made a lot of money in petroleum products, even when everyone else was losing their

shirts. I know how to handle money. I know how to keep
track of it. I had Shirley structure her will in such a way as
to make sure her children had a sound fortune in the event
that Shirley's death preceded ours." He stopped and
inhaled on his pipe again. "That's not supposed to
happen—children passing away before their parents. But
there it is." He seemed weak suddenly.

"Tom Foster could use her money as long as she was
missing. Is that it?"

Stewart nodded. "When we were planning her will, I
never thought about the possibility of her disappearing.
That's my fault. If I had thought of it, she might still be alive."

"My expertise has already been used in her behalf. I
really don't believe I can . . ." Lindsay left the sentence
hanging when the phone rang. Evelyn rose to answer it, and
Lindsay sipped her coffee to avoid saying anything.

Evelyn Pryor returned almost immediately, her face
white. "That was Sheriff Varnadore," she said. "They've
made an arrest in the case."

Chris and his father stood. Stewart took the pipe out of
his mouth. "Who?"

"Some young man named Luke Ferris. I don't know who
he is."

Chapter 10

LINDSAY HAD COMPLETELY forgotten about the faculty meeting until Sally reminded her, and she rushed upstairs to the conference room. The eight other faculty members that made up the Archaeology Department were seated around the table. Frank was at the head, holding a sheaf of papers in his hand. Copies of the *Athens Banner Herald* and the *Red and Black* were making their way around the table.

"Well, if it isn't Nancy Drew. Nice of you to join us," said Reed Cavanaugh. Reed looked like Albert Einstein gone native. He wore his long, steel gray hair tied back, but numerous strands had escaped and stood electrified around his head. As usual, his shirt was torn. Lindsay suspected he tore a rend in all of them to keep up his image. He grinned, baring a neat row of teeth as Lindsay rolled her eyes at him and sat down beside him.

Across from her was the newest faculty member, Trey Marcus, an underwater archaeologist. He had a neat stack of papers and glossy photographs in front of him. He twirled his pen in his fingers as he listened to Frank. Frank had hoped that hiring him would swell the ranks of the undergraduates. Marcus had been in the department only one quarter, but his class was already promising to be one of the most popular. Had Lindsay not known he was an archaeologist, she would have thought him a marine, with his compact build and short black hair. He was serious and single-minded about his work, which took him to some interesting places around the world.

"The question has come up again of combining departments with Anthropology," said Frank. "We were just about to discuss the pros and cons."

"Just a minute," said Kenneth Kerwin. "We may not have a department to combine, if this kind of thing keeps up." He tapped his finger on the front-page picture of the previous day's *Red and Black,* which showed Lindsay, Sinjin, Frank, and Sally standing around a wooden crate. The headless skeleton lay in a heap on the floor, its skull sitting on a table.

"I doubt that our department will be dissolved because of a few newspaper articles," Frank said.

"My God," said Reed, "we wouldn't be a bona fide archaeology department if we didn't have a scandal going on."

"Make fun if you want," Kenneth said, "but I assure you, they are not laughing on North Campus."

"That's right," said Rachael Bienvenido, an ecological archaeologist and expert in the archaeology of South America. "Let us all know that you have political connections."

"Aren't we getting a little far afield of the problem?" said Caspar Sandes, whose favorite place to dig was, unfortunately, in Iraq. For him, archaeology meant Old World archaeology. "That's Lindsay's problem, not ours. Ours is this proposal Frank has in his hand. What kind of space are we going to save by combining with Anthropology—a suite where a department head resides? What they want to do is to start eliminating faculty and research space. You all know what North Campus thinks of Archaeology. It doesn't matter if there is a scandal going on or not. And don't think for a minute, Dr. Kerwin, that your little *Gone-With-the-Wind* archaeology won't be considered for the ax. Frankly, they don't give a damn."

"I resent that characterization!" Kenneth shouted. "We know very little about the post-Civil War rise of the textile industry. . . ."

"Miss Scarlett, Miss Scarlett, I don't know nothing about birthing no babies!" The high-pitched squeal came from Reed.

"Jesus, Reed," said Rachael, "you sound like a pig."

Frank put his hands to his face.

"And you? What do you have to offer?" Kenneth shouted, pointing to Reed. "Archaeology of American Indians is obsolete. They won't let you dig up anything anymore. There is nothing left to do in the United States except historical archaeology."

"I think that is a bit of an exaggeration," muttered Frank. "Does everyone object, then?"

"I certainly do," said Kenneth. Everyone raised a hand.

"I'll write a formal response to the proposal and tell the dean that the faculty vote was unanimous against joining departments with Anthropology."

"Wait, wait!" shouted Kenneth. "That isn't what I voted for; I objected to Caspar's characterization of my work."

"Caspar's opinion wasn't on the table," Frank said. Lindsay thought she detected a bit of a smirk.

"We need to take another vote. I want to change mine. I think there would be many advantages to combining departments. We are, after all, anthropologists as well as archaeologists."

"That has nothing to do with it, Kenneth. It's about space and budget," said Caspar. "Pay attention. You voted."

"I was railroaded."

Frank sighed. "OK, now we need to talk about the budget and space. Because of all the new construction going on all over campus, some space in older buildings has come open, and we have a good chance of getting some. Not everyone on North Campus hates us."

As the discussion began, Lindsay perused the newspaper articles, ignoring the arguments and protestations.
The first article, the one with the picture of the skeleton laid
out on the floor, was not bad. It presented the event as a
mystery and was almost humorous. But the article the next
day had a picture of Sinjin with the campus police and
named him as a possible suspect. It talked about the artifacts and raised the question of what they were doing
hidden away in the storage shed belonging to Lindsay's
grandfather. It quoted "sources" who said the campus
police were investigating the possibility that Sinjin, who
was on campus but not affiliated with the university, might
be implicated in some family business of black-marketing
artifacts. The article mentioned Lindsay, an archaeologist
following in her grandfather's footsteps, who recently
examined the bones of slain faculty member Shirley Foster.
Lindsay felt sick. It looked as though the reputation of her
grandfather was the least of her worries. She was brought
out of her thoughts by the sound of her name.

"I'm not sure I understand how Lindsay rates the dispro-
portionate number of student workers," said Rachael.

"And lab space," added Kenneth.

"I don't have either," Lindsay defended herself. "Two
undergraduate student workers and two graduate assistants
are paid out of the faunal lab budget. I have no students
assigned specifically to me. If they seem like my students,
it's because I'm in charge of the faunal lab. I would like to
remind all of you that the faunal lab not only pays for itself
but operates in the black."

"I trust your ability to profit from archaeology," Kenneth remarked.

"What?" said Lindsay, rising from her seat, leaning forward on the table and glaring at Kenneth. "Would you care
to clarify that statement?"

"Kenneth," said Rachael. "That's too far, even for you."

Kenneth muttered something under his breath. Lindsay realized that she was standing and sat down. She could feel the heat in her face.

"The lab space," said Lindsay, "is there for everyone to use. The students who work in the lab are working on materials from Jasper Creek, 9dv7, Whitley Folsom, Maya Lake, and Miller Creek, which, Kenneth, is your project. The students use the faunal lab to identify the animal bones, they all use the chemical flotation equipment, and they all use the space. And the reason the faunal lab budget is in the black is that during this past year we processed animal remains for seven universities around the country. This has not only given our students valuable experience but also enhanced the reputation of the department."

"But you give all the students their assignments," said Rachael. "Not just the ones paid out of your budget. That's why some of us think they are your students."

"Only because they come to me when they have no assignments, and that's because my office is down there. I'd be glad to switch offices with any of you and let them come to you for their assignments."

"Why don't you send them to the main office?" suggested Frank.

"I will," Lindsay said. "The ones who are not paid out of the faunal lab budget."

"Why are the contracts late?" asked Per Solveig.

"What contracts?" asked Frank.

"The ones for nontenured faculty—Lindsay, Stevie, Trey, and I haven't gotten the letter renewing our contracts. What's the holdup?"

"I don't know. I'll find out," said Frank.

"You know we need that information. If we aren't being renewed, we need time to look for positions elsewhere."

"I'll look into it," Frank repeated. "I'll find out what the problem is."

Everyone was quiet for a moment and Trey cleared his throat. "I have a colleague who will be visiting next week. She is working on the LaBelle and has quite an interesting presentation that I think students and faculty would enjoy. I know Kenneth is scheduled to speak at the next Archaeology Club meeting, but I thought perhaps he would delay his talk a week and allow Clerisse to speak."

"I've already prepared—" began Kerwin.

Frank interrupted him. "That would be fine. We'll announce it in the campus newspaper. There may be other university students who would like to hear it. Anything else?"

"I don't have my computer yet," paleontologist Per Solveig complained.

"Right now, we don't have a budget for new computers," said Frank.

"That's only because you don't like them," said Per.

"No, that's not it at all. We have to buy lots of equipment. Right now, we are trying to build up the palynology lab."

"Stevie's getting a new computer?" Per asked.

"The lab gets that computer and other equipment to analyze the pollen data," Frank said.

Stevie Saturnin, whose speciality was pollen analysis from archaeological sites, said nothing. Her wispy blonde hair hung in her face like a shield. She rarely said anything during faculty meetings, but rather sat back in her chair looking uncomfortable. Stevie preferred the quiet solitude of working with a microscope to human interaction, and at the moment, Lindsay couldn't blame her.

"I need a computer," said Per.

"What for?" asked Reed. "I get along fine with my Apple IIe."

"What? What?" Trey Marcus sat up straight in his chair. "You are using an Apple IIe?" He looked amazed. "You can't get any data on a five-and-a-quarter-inch floppy!"

Reed grinned. "That sounds like a brassiere size."

Trey turned red. Stevie slipped farther down in her seat.

"Reed, for heaven's sake," exclaimed Rachael.

"What?" he asked, looking around the table innocently. "You going to accuse me of creating a hostile work environment, Rachael?"

"I'm going to show you a hostile work environment," she said, leaning toward him, glowering.

"And what about you, Chamberlain," Trey said. "You use an outdated computer?"

"No, I have a 486," Lindsay said.

Trey groaned, carelessly tossed his pen into the air, and looked away, shaking his head. "Look," he said as he rose from his chair, placing his hands on the table and leaning forward.

"I believe he's serious about this," said Reed.

"Do you guys know what century you're in? You can't do your work without modern computers."

Reed tapped his forefinger to his temple. "Good work comes from the brain, not some mindless computer, and I do my work just fine, thank you."

"You think you do, but there are analyses that you can't . . ." He paused. "I'll tell you what, Reed. Give me some of your data and a couple of hours, and I'll show you what you can do."

"OK, you're on," said Reed, grinning.

"And if I can convince Reed, you all get new computers. Agreed?"

"Agreed," said Reed.

"Now wait a minute," said Frank.

"I agree," Per said. "Let's vote."

It carried, and Frank looked at Lindsay as if she had betrayed him. She smiled back at him. Frank shook his head. "I think we've covered enough in this meeting, and I have work to do." He picked up his papers and left the room.

Lindsay rose with the others. She glared at the papers

lying on the conference table, wanting to scoop them up and shred them to bits. She wanted to go out to the newspaper racks, take all the newspapers, and burn them. Instead, she left the room and walked to Frank's office.

"You know, I think new computers would be a good thing," she said, leaning against Frank's doorjamb. Frank sat at his desk, frowning and shuffling through papers.

Bobbie came in and put a folder on his desk. "Is this what you're looking for?" she asked.

"Yes, that's it. Thanks, Bobbie." He looked up at Lindsay as Bobbie left the office. "If we can afford them," he said.

"What's wrong with you? It's not the faculty meeting."

"No, it's not that. The dean wants Kerwin to be head of the department. The dean has his own ideas about Archaeology's place in the mission of the university."

"You're getting a lot of pressure?"

"And this thing with the missing artifacts isn't helping."

"I'm sorry. They came out of the blue. I'm sure Dad thought he was doing a good thing by sending them to me."

"I know. It's not your fault. Do you think your brother took them?"

Lindsay walked into Frank's office and sat down. "No, he didn't."

"I'm not accusing. But if, on top of everything else, we get Mina Jones picketing us again about Native American artifacts, that may be all that Administration needs to take over."

"Take over?"

Frank shrugged. "Put Kerwin in charge, force a merger with Anthropology. That would destroy us. You know what Anthro thinks of most of us."

"Is it that bad?"

"Could be. North Campus is just waiting for the right moment. It depends on a lot of things. There are some who want to bring in Francisco Lewis as head. I heard they've been talking to him. Administration would go for that. Lewis is controversial, but they seem to like celebrity faculty."

"Lewis would want to come here?"

"Seems so. But you know how gossip is."

Lindsay stood up to go.

"Look, Lindsay, you don't have tenure. You have to be careful. I can only protect you so far. My position as head is not all that strong." He paused. "And if they do manage to bring in Lewis . . ."

"The faculty would never go for it," said Lindsay.

"If we are merged with Anthropology, we'll be outnumbered. Anthropology likes Francisco Lewis. It would be a majority vote."

"Oh, I hadn't thought of that," Lindsay said.

Frank shook his head. "It's easy to get paranoid. That may not be Administration's thoughts at all. If it is, be advised, Lewis likes to bring in his own people, and right now he has a liking for a bright young physical anthropologist named Gerri Chapman."

Lindsay sat down again. "Frank, I haven't done anything. Why, all of a sudden, am I in trouble?"

"It's all politics and who your friends and enemies are. You know that. I'm not sure you understand that you have an envied position here—with the archaeology, the zooarchaeology, and the forensics."

"You mean, because I do the work of three people, there are people out there who want my job?"

"Yes, and the forensic archaeologists outnumber the available job positions," Frank reminded her.

"Gerri Chapman isn't a forensic specialist," said Lindsay.

"Politicians don't care about competence."

"Ellis Einer doesn't even know what I do."

"Others do."

"I can only do my job. I don't know politics," Lindsay said.

"Be careful how you do your job. These forays into detective work don't help you." He hesitated. "I got a call from an associate dean early this morning. They are concerned that you allowed a possible murderer to work with the students."

"What? What are you talking about?"

"Luke Ferris. You had him working in the lab last week."

"And you had him a few weeks before that, and Kerwin a few weeks before that. Am I supposed to be clairvoyant? Or held to a higher standard than the rest of you?"

"I know and I agree."

"Just how did they know about Luke Ferris working in the lab?"

"I imagine one of the students just happened to mention it to Kerwin, and he jumped on the phone and complained to his buddies. You know how he is. If the dean knew that Kenneth had his eye on the dean's job eventually, he'd not be so cozy with him."

"This is really stupid." Lindsay rose and moved toward the door. "I'm sorry about the computer vote."

"That's all right. Trey has to convince Reed, and you know how stubborn he is."

Lindsay went back to the conference room and retrieved a copy of the newspaper with a clear picture of the skull. She took it to the copier and made several enlargements. She went back to her office with them and sat down. Her gaze drifted to the picture of her grandfather standing in front of the mound at Macon, leaning on his shovel. She felt a strong desire to turn his picture to the wall. She put her hands on her temples and closed her eyes. Maybe Sinjin would like to have lunch. She phoned her house—no answer. Just as she replaced the receiver, the telephone rang and Lindsay picked it up. "Yes?"

"Dr. Chamberlain?" asked a male voice on the other end.

"Yes."

"This is Gerald Ramirez of the *Atlanta Journal-Constitution.*"

Lindsay closed her eyes and rubbed them with her fingertips. "What can I do for you?" she asked.

"We would like your comments on the missing artifacts that your grandfather had stored away on his property."

"I don't know anything about them," said Lindsay, wishing she had some clever words that would send the media somewhere else.

"The police seem to think your brother took them," the reporter said.

"That would be silly, since he drove them down from Kentucky," said Lindsay.

"The police believe that he didn't know their value at that time," persisted the reporter.

"Does that make sense to you? He grew up around artifacts," Lindsay answered.

"One report suggested that your family may have been involved in the black-marketing of artifacts."

"If that were true, no one would be questioning whether or not my brother knew their value before he got here. And, furthermore, it would be much easier to deal with them where they were found than to haul them down here across two states and cause all this trouble."

"Did you know the value of the artifacts?"

"Yes."

"Do you know the identity of the person whose body was found in one of the crates?"

"No. I don't have a clue."

"Have you asked any member of your family about the skeleton?"

"Not yet. I'm sure the Kentucky authorities will ask them. The shed where the crates were found had been covered in kudzu since the thirties. None of us knew it was there."

"Why didn't you report the artifacts to the Kentucky authorities as soon as you found them?"

"I wasn't completely sure they were from Kentucky. That had to be established."

"But you thought they were?"

"Yes, from the ceramics. Ceramics are not my speciality. I would have verified their origin before I sent them anywhere. Markings on one of the crates indicated they probably were from Georgia."

"Has the Archaeology Department had any other artifacts stolen?" asked the reporter.

"No," she said, then realized that she didn't know. "Not to my knowledge." That was a good question. It hadn't occurred to her to look. Most of the really valuable artifacts that used to be housed in Baldwin were now stored in the basement of Nancy Hart Hall.

"Thank you, Dr. Chamberlain, for answering my questions," said the reporter.

"Sure." She hung up the phone, but her hand stayed on the receiver, as though a deep thought paralyzed her. Frank wanted her to keep a low profile, but people were asking questions, and staying still wouldn't make her any less of a target than being on the move. She opened her desk drawer, took out the two vials of dirt samples from the crate, and wrote "Chamberlain" on the glass with a black Sharpie. She put the vials in the pocket of her jeans. As she opened her door to leave, Sally and Liza Ferris were standing in the doorway. Sally had her hand raised, poised to knock. Liza was sobbing.

Chapter 11

"DR. CHAMBERLAIN," LIZA said, "you've got to help Luke. He didn't kill Shirley Foster, I know he didn't."

Lindsay sat back down at her desk and gestured for them to come in. Sally closed the door behind her. "Liza, I'm not sure what I can do." Liza's eyes were red and swollen; her nose looked red and irritated.

"He didn't do it." She looked Lindsay in the eye. "You know what it's like to have a brother falsely accused." It almost sounded like an accusation. Liza was pulling out all the stops to help her brother. Lindsay supposed that she would, too.

"Why did they arrest him?" asked Lindsay.

Liza held her hands in her lap and stared a moment at the shredded tissue she held there. "They found a key of some sort and traced it back to him, and when they talked to him, he sort of admitted he had been the last one to see Shirley Foster alive." She looked up at Lindsay. "Oh, I don't know all the details. He won't talk to us, and the sheriff won't tell us anything."

"Does he have a lawyer?"

"Yes, but he needs someone to find out who really did it. He didn't do it, I know he didn't." Tears rolled down her cheeks. "This is killing us. All of us."

"Where is he now?" asked Lindsay.

Liza's face lifted. "You'll help, then?"

"As I said, I'm not sure what I can do, but perhaps he'll talk to me," said Lindsay.

"He's at home. Not his apartment, but with Mom and Dad. They had to mortgage the house to get him out."

"I'll start by talking to him, and see."

"Oh, thanks, Dr. Chamberlain. I know you can clear him."

Lindsay was not so sure. Nor was she sure she should even get involved, but Liza looked so desperate. And Lindsay's obstinate streak was telling her to do the opposite of what everybody else was telling her. Lindsay stood. "I'll give you a call later, and we can set up an appointment to meet with Luke. Right now I have to run a few errands."

There were two palynology labs at the Riverbend research facility, one operated by the Geology Department and the other by Archaeology. Some in the administration found two palynology labs redundant, but not Lindsay. The geology lab examined sedimentary core samples for clues to the age of rock and its oil potential. The clues they looked for were in the form of fossil pollen and spores, requiring the use of acids to dissolve the rock, leaving the pollen to be examined under a microscope.

The archaeology lab used the same method—a series of acid baths to reduce soil samples to pollen, but their interests lay along a human time scale, not a geologic one, a difference of thousands of years versus millions. Archaeologists could reconstruct the prehistoric diet, learn what plants were in cultivation, and identify prehistoric food crops and food storage pits.

Different time scales, different functions, and different acid solutions—reason enough for two separate labs. The geology lab used as much as a 70 percent concentration of hydrofluoric acid, the archaeology lab 5 percent, which was dangerous enough. Hydrofluoric acid was an acid Lindsay respected. A burn over just 10 percent of the body meant death. Even washed off the skin, fluoride ions ate away flesh and bone. Inhaled, fluorine gas mixes with moisture in the lungs, turning into hydrofluoric acid and destroying the lungs. Odd to think that anything mixed with water could become lethal.

Lindsay parked her Rover at the Riverbend labs and went straight to Stevie Saturnin's palynology lab, a fifteen-by-twenty-foot room equipped with a fume hood, a centrifuge, an emergency shower, several sinks, and a desk. One wall was lined with cabinets filled with chemicals to do the work of finding pollen in a dirt sample: potassium hydroxide to dissolve humic acids, acetolysis to dissolve cellulose, hydrochloric acid to dissolve carbonates, nitric acid to dissolve pyrite, and, of course, hydrofluoric acid to dissolve silicates. In the end, the dirt would be gone and the polymer sheath of the pollen grains, vulnerable only to oxidation, would be left.

Stevie was sitting at a desk and Mason, her technician, was about to turn on the fume hood and don his rubber gloves when Lindsay walked in.

"Hi," said Stevie. "Some faculty meeting."

"I hope we don't have many more of those," Lindsay replied.

"What can I do for you?" Stevie asked, smiling at her. One on one, Stevie was more personable.

Lindsay reached into the pocket of her jeans and brought out one of the vials. "I was wondering if you would process this for me?"

Mason walked over to look at the vial. His hair had been cut since Lindsay last saw him. His close-cropped hair revealed plainly the silver ring in his earlobe.

"Not much dirt," he muttered. "I can process it with the batch I'm doing now. I can have it ready by tomorrow. Will that be all right?"

"That would be great," Lindsay said.

"I'll do a pollen count tomorrow then," said Stevie.

"Thanks," Lindsay told them.

"No problem," said Stevie.

Lindsay noted that neither Stevie nor Mason had asked her where the sample came from or why she wanted it processed. Mason simply smiled and took the vial to the fume hood. I must really be getting a reputation, thought Lindsay. She walked down the hall to the geology lab and peeped in to see if there was anyone she knew. Jaleel was there talking to the technician, his feet on his desk.

"Well, Lindsay, been reading about you," Jaleel said, his white teeth showing broad against his black face.

"Me, too," she said, hoping he'd drop the subject.

"Looks pretty bad, but I've been telling folks you'll come out on top."

The technician, a husky blond fellow Lindsay didn't know, looked uncomfortable.

"Thanks for your vote of confidence," she said.

"I saved the newspaper picture of all you guys standing over that skeleton looking surprised. Got it on my door. That's the damnedest thing," he said, "Opening up that crate and having a body fall out. I tell you, you people in Archaeology are always into something."

"We have a reputation to keep up," Lindsay said. "It's hard and time consuming, but it's our job."

Jaleel tilted his head back and laughed. "What brings you here?"

Lindsay pulled out the other vial. "Can you tell me where this dirt came from?"

"Does a bear do it in the woods?" He laughed. He took the sample from her hand. "Not a lot here, but I may be able to. What is it? Or should I ask?" he said, grinning.

"I'm just trying to come out on top," she said, and he laughed again.

"I'll look at it when I get back to the department and give you a call."

"Thanks."

"Anything I can do to help," he said, winking at Lindsay.

Sally and Bobbie were waiting in her office. Both had big grins on their faces.

"We are so clever," said Sally, her brown eyes sparkling. "You aren't going to believe it."

Lindsay sat down at her desk. "Surprise me, please."

Sally took a drawing from a folder and pushed it toward Lindsay. "You remember I told you that some guy came to see you the day we unpacked the crates of artifacts?"

Lindsay thought for a moment. "Sort of."

"Well, you know that cute police sketch artist we met in Eddie Peck's office that time?"

"Yes," said Lindsay.

"Well, Bobbie and I took him to lunch, and I talked him into doing a sketch of the guy. I couldn't remember very much at first, but the more I talked to him, the more I remembered."

Lindsay looked down at the picture and up at Sally. "I don't recognize him."

Bobbie held up a hand and grinned. "There's more. Sally showed me the picture, and I thought I recognized it." She put a poster on Lindsay's desk. "I'm auditing a course at the law school—and boy, that was hard to get permission to do—anyway, this was one of the speakers a few weeks ago. It was still on the bulletin board. I've been seeing it every day as I leave class."

Lindsay looked down at the flyer. The pictures did look very similar, from the coat and tie to the professionally styled haircut. Sidney Barrie, UGA Law School alum and member of the firm Easton, Easton, and Shackleforth, was to speak on "Ethics and Corporate Law."

"It's worth a try," Sally said. "The police could talk to him."

Something was nagging at Lindsay as she examined each of the pictures.

"Lindsay?"

She looked up at Sally and Bobbie. "I'm sorry, what did you say?"

"We could give his name and this sketch to the police."

"Sidney, Sid—lawyer," said Lindsay out loud. "Not yet. Would you allow me to keep this?"

"Sure, but . . ."

"You two really are clever. This may be just what I need to get the artifacts back." Bobbie and Sally beamed.

"They're showing *The Rocky Horror Picture Show* at the Tate Center late this evening," Sally said. "A bunch of us are dressing up and going. Want to come? You can bring Sinjin."

"I'll pass, I think." Lindsay grinned at them. "But thanks for asking. Be sure to take pictures of yourselves."

When they had gone, she took out the Atlanta phone directory and looked up the name Kathy Falkner. There wasn't one. Then Lindsay remembered that Kathy may have recently moved. She dialed information, and there was a listing for a Kathleen Falkner. Lindsay knew she had the right number when the woman answered the phone. She had met Kathy once when she and her parents visited Sinjin, and she recognized her husky voice.

"Kathy, this is Lindsay Chamberlain."

Kathy said nothing.

"Sinjin's sister."

"Yes, I remember you. What do you want?"

"I'm leaving Athens, on the way to Atlanta. I want you to meet me at the coffee shop at Lenox Square in two hours. Do you know where that is?"

"Yes, but why should I do that?"

"Because you lied to the police about Sinjin and, conse-quently, caused a lot of trouble."

"I . . ."

"Don't bother to lie to me. I'm not really in the mood. Meet me. You can ask Sidney Barrie to come if you want."

"What do you want?" she asked.

"To talk to you," Lindsay responded.

"You can do that now," Kathy said.

"No. I'm leaving now. Be there." Lindsay hung up the phone.

Kathy Falkner was a startlingly beautiful woman with black hair, crystal blue eyes, and flawless skin. It was easy to see why men fell in love with her. It was not so easy to under-stand why they stayed in love with her. Lindsay eyed her as she positioned herself in the booth. Kathy didn't look preg-nant, but she did look slightly rounder than when they had met before. Sidney Barrie, looking like an ad in *GQ,* slid in beside her. He watched Kathy adoringly whenever she spoke.

"This is real uncomfortable." Kathy shifted her position as she sipped a milkshake through a straw. She wore a pink silk shirt over white slacks. A necklace with a single dia-mond twinkled at her throat. Lindsay also noticed a sizable diamond on her finger.

Sid directed his attention to Lindsay and the adoring look in his eyes changed quickly. "Was this necessary?"

Lindsay thought Kathy was trying to play for sympathy. She wanted to tell her not to bother, that although Sinjin loved her, and Sid obviously did, she, Lindsay, did not. But the thought that Kathy might be carrying her niece or nephew made Lindsay hold her tongue. Instead, she asked her calmly, "Why did you insist on seeing Sinjin at such an early hour of the morning?"

"Didn't he tell you?" Kathy asked.

"No. He's still very loyal to you." Lindsay hoped that would give her a twinge of guilt. "But for whatever reason you wanted to see him, why so early in the morning?"

"Sid and I are getting married. I had fittings all day and I needed to see Sinjin, all right? I know that sounds selfish, but . . ." She shrugged.

It did, but Lindsay didn't say so. "Why did you lie to the police?"

"I didn't think it was a big deal. It was the campus police that called, for heaven's sake. How serious could it be?"

"It was very serious. You caused problems not only for Sinjin but for me as well."

"Look, I'm sorry. I'll call them back and tell them I made a mistake."

"No, you won't." Sid laid a hand on Kathy's arm as if she were about to reach for a phone. "Whatever trouble you and your brother have gotten yourselves into, it doesn't have anything to do with us. If you want to know why Kathy wanted to see your brother, it was to get him to leave her alone and drop this silly blood-test idea. It's not his baby. He agreed to drop it. Now, if you persist in harassing us, I'll have to take action against you, and it won't be fun."

"Let me tell you what I think," said Lindsay, staring him straight in the eyes. "You came to visit me, probably with the same story, hoping I could influence him, or to have me deliver a little threat to him like the one you just made to me." Lindsay saw his eyes flicker and Kathy look over at him, and knew she had made a hit. "It was on a day when we were unpacking artifacts. You overheard us discussing them and, for whatever reason, decided to steal them."

"Now, just a minute," said Sid, leaning forward.

Lindsay raised a hand to stave off any comment. "After all, $125,000 is a lot of money, and you aren't a partner yet."

Sid opened his mouth, but nothing came out.

"A hundred and twenty-five thousand dollars?" Kathy whispered.

"You asked Kathy to call Sinjin and get him away from home, to make sure he had no alibi. You stole the artifacts, then called the police and reported seeing Sinjin's Jeep parked behind Baldwin."

Sid gave a nervous laugh. "There's no proof I was ever there."

Lindsay whipped out a copy of the sketch and the flyer. "My graduate assistant saw you. She had the police sketch artist do this. She'll pick you out of a lineup." A little melodramatic, thought Lindsay, but it had an effect.

"I wasn't there," he said.

"My assistant says you were. With her sun-bleached hair and Hershey chocolate eyes, some tend to think her a little southern valley girl. But I assure you, she's a good witness."

"In court, this would be thrown out," began Sid.

Lindsay leaned forward. "You don't understand, do you? That doesn't matter. I'm here to tell you from recent personal experience that all that has to happen for your reputation to be damaged is for an article to appear in the paper. 'Sidney Barrie, of the law firm Easton, Easton, and Shackleforth, was questioned about the disappearance of valuable artifacts. He denied, etc., etc.' You know the rest. What would Easton, Easton, and Shackleforth think of that?"

"OK, Kathy can call . . ."

Lindsay shook her head. "I'm not here to blackmail you. Kathy can make the call or not, according to her conscience. I want the artifacts back. You can ship them to me in care of the Archaeology Department."

"Look. OK, I came to see you, just to talk to you about your brother. That's all. You weren't there, and I left. I don't know anything about the artifacts. I didn't take them."

"How can I believe that, when Kathy here comes up

with the improbable explanation that she had fittings all day and could only see Sinjin early in the morning? Then she deliberately lies to the police."

"I did have fittings, and I didn't know it was anything serious. I didn't think it would matter."

"It mattered a great deal to a lot of people, and unless I get the artifacts back, it's going to matter to you. You can give them to me or to the police."

Lindsay gave the waitress money for her salad and drink, grabbed up the copies of the sketch and flyer, and walked out to her Rover. Sid followed her, Kathy close behind.

"Look. You have this all wrong," he said. "We can't give them back, because we never took them."

"You've got until tomorrow to either return the artifacts or show me you didn't do it. And that's going to be hard, since you've lied once and are stopping Kathy from telling the truth." Lindsay got into her Rover and left them standing in the parking lot. Now she would have to go home and tell Sinjin what she had done. That was going to be hard.

Lindsay looked at her watch when she pulled into the Baldwin parking lot. It was only three o'clock. She remembered what the reporter had asked about other missing artifacts and needed to take a look. Instead of going to her office, she walked across campus to Nancy Hart Hall.

Nancy Hart, named for a Revolutionary War heroine from Georgia, was a small, old Greek revival–style building, constructed in the 1930s of red brick and nestled between two other buildings. Lindsay walked between the two white columns and opened the large double doors. The floor of the entranceway was made from polished local gneiss. The walls were an indescribable blend of light beige, green, and yellow, and hadn't been painted in years. Large, thick chips of old paint were peeling off the walls and collecting on the floor. The first floor still had a few offices, mainly retired faculty for whom office space couldn't be located anyplace else on campus. The top floor was empty.

Lindsay took the stairway to the basement. She inserted her key in the padlock that secured the heavy, dirty white wooden door to the artifact room. She had to shake the key in the lock before the shackle would release, then push hard on the old door to get it to open. The room was dark and dusty-smelling, but thankfully, Lindsay didn't smell any moisture. She hated that the artifacts were stored here. They desperately needed more lab space so students could study them.

She flipped on the light switch. The artifacts, many collected as far back as the thirties, were in boxes on the same type of metal shelves as were used in Baldwin. Against one wall was an old desk that students used when analyzing the items. She walked between the aisles and opened a box. She had been here many times helping her students do research using the artifacts in storage, and she knew what was there and where everything was supposed to be. Right away, in the first box, she found that several bird effigy pipes were missing. She went to another box that should have contained a complicated stamped Swift Creek bowl. It was gone. She went to box after box. Not all were empty; in fact, many boxes had only one or two artifacts missing. It was clear, however, that someone had been systematically stealing them. Lindsay tried to think when she was there last. It wasn't that long ago. Last quarter? Nothing was missing then. Frank would have to be told. Another scandal. He would hate it. She hated it. Lindsay dusted off her hands and walked toward the door. Before she put a hand on the knob, she heard the sound of a click. She hesitated a moment, then turned the knob and pushed the door. It was locked.

Chapter 12

LINDSAY HEARD QUIET footsteps walking away. "There's someone in here," she yelled, banging on the door with her hand and trying to get their attention. The sound of footfalls continued up the stairs.

This isn't an accident, she thought. Who? Someone guarding the artifacts for themselves. Who? Lindsay dropped her hands to her sides and listened to the silence of the room. She was in no immediate danger. She could eventually attract someone's attention by banging on the door. Then again, there was nothing down here but Archaeology storage, and she hadn't told anyone where she was going. Fear rose from her belly and stung her throat. This is silly, she thought. She wouldn't be locked in here until she died, not in the middle of a campus of thirty thousand people. To her knowledge, it had never happened.

There were no windows, but there were lights. It could be worse, it could be dark. But, despite her determination to stay calm, she felt a growing sense of being trapped underground. OK, this isn't that bad, she told herself as she concentrated on breathing slowly, keeping panic at bay. Lindsay looked at the ceiling covered with peeling plaster. On the other side of that ceiling was the bottom of the first floor. That gave her an idea. Perhaps someone was in an office. Maybe the broom closet held something she could use to bang on the ceiling. She opened the closet door and turned on the light. An old mop was standing in the corner, along with a bucket filled with cleaning supplies, none of which looked like they had been touched during the past decade. As she put a hand on the mop, she noticed a small door behind the bucket. The crawl space for the building's wiring and plumbing. Would that lead to the outside? It would perhaps at least lead to another room where the door might not be locked. She moved the bucket and pulled on the door handle. It wouldn't budge. There was a small keyhole below the knob. She examined the walls for a key hanging on a nail but found none. She looked in the drawers of the old desk. There were pens, pencils, paper clips, Sharpies, White Out, paper, all in disarray, but nothing that looked like a key.

It was an old door with an old lock, and old, cheap locks can sometimes be opened with any key that will fit in the keyhole. On her key chain, the key to her tack room looked to be about the right size. She tried it in the keyhole, but it wouldn't turn. She rattled it in the lock, turned it again, and heard a click. She pulled the door open, revealing a gaping black hole. Lindsay stared at the darkness a moment, reluctant to move. "This isn't that bad," she told herself out loud.

Lindsay had a small flashlight on her key ring. Vowing, after her experience of being lost in the cave, never to be without light again, she had bought several flashlights of all shapes and sizes and had placed them in her Rover, in her office, at home, and on all her key rings. The switch on the tiny flashlight was the type that had to be held down for the light to stay on. She shone it into the darkness. In the few feet illuminated ahead of her, she could see the mass of ancient cables bracketed to the wall of the crawl space, covered with dust and cobwebs. Lindsay tried to orient herself in the building. Which direction led to the outside? The entire crawl space couldn't be that long. This was not like a cave, she said to herself. Backtracking wouldn't be that big of a deal.

Lindsay was struck with a sudden thought. What if whoever locked her in meant to come back, perhaps with some-one else to do her harm? Stupid, she thought. Why would they do that? It would only bring more attention to what they were doing. It would raise the stakes for them tremendously. She shook the thought. She was just scared. However, as a precaution, she turned out the lights in the main room and in the closet. Maybe if they came back, and she wasn't here, it would all look like a mistake, like they were being paranoid. She took several deep breaths and crawled into the space and closed the little door tight behind her. "Oh, God," she said softly to herself. "Calm down. This isn't that bad. I'm not trapped. I can go back out the door anytime and turn on the lights." The sound of her own voice gave her courage, and she began crawling down the tiny conduit.

Lindsay felt something drop into her hair and frantically brushed it away. Don't think about what's in here, she admon-ished herself. She crawled along the tiny space, shining the small light on the wall. She thought she heard small creatures scampering, but decided it was best to ignore them. Snakes, she thought. She had forgotten about snakes. She was about to shine her light farther ahead when the beam hit another door like the one she had entered. There was no keyhole on her side of the door, but when she tried the knob, it opened. She emerged into a darkened closet similar to the first one, but this one was completely empty. She listened. Silence. Carefully, she tried the knob to the closet door. It wouldn't turn. It was locked. She pushed hard on the door. It wouldn't budge. She was afraid to make noise. She closed her eyes, trying to think how many rooms were on this side of the building. The Archaeology storeroom was the first. This room was the second. There should be one more.

Lindsay climbed back into the crawl space, more easily this time, and continued, ignoring the things that might be crawling on her. After twenty feet or so, she came to another door like the first two. She pushed, willing it to be unlocked.

It was, and she found herself in another closet. She switched on the light. The closet was stacked with dusty boxes labeled Fredrickson Foundation Archival Files, with dates ranging from 1972 to 1982. She had no idea what the Fredrickson Foundation was, but that was not surprising, the university had hundreds of foundations. She tried the closet door. It was unlocked. Her small light showed the next room to be empty. The only furniture was a desk against one wall, listing to one side from a broken leg. This room had two doors and, unless Lindsay was mistaken, one led to the outside. She walked across the room to the opposite door. It opened onto a patio surrounded by shrubs. She stepped outside, breathing the fresh air into her lungs for several moments before she closed and locked the door behind her.

Lindsay ran her fingers through her hair to get rid of unwanted creatures. She dusted off her jeans and shirt and walked around to the sidewalk in back of Nancy Hart Hall. Classes were changing and students came pouring out of the buildings. She started across campus. Looking over her shoulder, she saw a couple of campus police enter Nancy Hart.

"Dr. Chamberlain."

Lindsay jumped and turned.

"Sorry, I didn't mean to frighten you."

"Hello, Brandon," she said. "What are you doing this far away from Archaeology?"

"I have a French class. Heard anything about the missing artifacts?" Lindsay was momentarily confused as to which missing artifacts he was talking about. She shook her head. "At least we have a good record of them," he said.

"Yes, we have that, thanks to your pictures."

"Do you think there's much chance they will be found?"

"I hope so," said Lindsay.

"Well, see you later. I've got to get to class." He was off. Lindsay stood for a moment watching his retreating back.

She saw the police come out of the Nancy Hart Hall, talking into phones or radios. She walked back to her Rover.

Lindsay didn't tell Frank of her discovery. Instead, he told her about the call that the police received about someone in the storage room of Nancy Hart. They went there and found it locked, got in with the help of the building custodian, found nothing amiss, and called him.

"I think it would be a good idea," Frank said, "for us to go to Nancy Hart and check the storage."

"I agree," she said.

For the second time, Lindsay discovered the missing artifacts. As she helped Frank check the boxes, she had no doubt that whoever locked her in meant for her to be found there. With more artifacts missing, and her connection to the missing Kentucky artifacts, it would look damned suspicious.

"This is not good," said Frank. "I hate to think about the bad press we're going to get over this. Your brother doesn't know about this storage, does he, Lindsay?"

"No!" she said. "No. How could you even think that? Sinjin's not a thief, and there's no way he could know about these artifacts."

"You might have told him—"

"I see. Then you don't trust me, either? Is that what you mean?"

"That's not what I said—or even meant. I don't know what I meant. Forget it. Do you remember the last time you were here?"

Sure do, Lindsay thought to herself. "When I was helping Brandon and Liza with a project last quarter, nothing was missing, certainly not the effigy pipes. That was what Brandon was working on. What did the caller say to the police?"

"Just that he came over to visit one of the offices in the building, heard noises, peeped in the door, and saw what looked like someone stealing. He called the police," said Frank.

"Who was the caller?"

"He told the police he didn't want to get involved any further, that he'd done his duty."

"Where did the call come from?"

"Good heavens, Lindsay, the police didn't tell me that. If you insist on being a detective, find these artifacts."

"I'll take that as an order," she said.

"No, forget I said anything. Let the police handle it."

They went back to the Archaeology Department. Frank called the police and told them what he and Lindsay had found. Lindsay started down to her office, wondering why she hadn't told Frank about what happened. She was afraid to, that's why. Not of Frank, but he would have to tell the police, and they would have to be suspicious, and whoever locked her in Nancy Hart wanted that.

She was lost in thought when a hand grabbed her arm and pulled her into an office.

"Sit down, Lindsay, and listen to this." Lindsay stared at Reed Cavanaugh and Trey Marcus. It was Reed who had pulled her into the office. Both were grinning like they'd been up to something clever.

"Reed, you nearly gave me a heart attack. What is it?" asked Lindsay, catching her breath.

"Lindsay, you wouldn't believe what Trey here has been showing me. I had no idea—the mapping capabilities alone, not to mention global positioning—"

"Global positioning?" said Lindsay. "I take it Trey has convinced you?"

"Indeed, he has. The only problem is the budget at the moment. Now, here is what we have come up with. The palynology lab and the faunal lab are in the black. We thought that you and Stevie could make a good-faith donation to the cause, and the department would, of course, put up the rest."

"I don't need a new computer," said Lindsay. "That should save—"

Trey shook his head. "I have a cute little black laptop picked out for you."

Lindsay shrugged, giving up. "I'll look at the books and see what I can do. Have you asked Stevie?"

"Not yet," said Trey.

Lindsay rose. "Well, good luck, guys."

She smiled all the way back to her office. She could imagine what Frank would say when he discovered that Trey had won Reed over to the cult of technology.

Sinjin brought home dinner again. This time it was souvlaki, rice, Greek salad, and baklava for dessert. "This is good," said Lindsay, taking a sip of wine. "You're going to have to visit more often. I never eat this well by myself. Where did you find Greek food?"

"There's a little restaurant up the road from you that serves, among other things, Greek food," Sinjin said, taking a bite. "I called Dad today."

Lindsay winced. "Mom and Dad. I completely forgot. I imagine this made the Kentucky papers, too."

"Yeah, it did."

"What did he say?"

"He's feeling pretty guilty for sending you the stuff."

"He didn't believe that—"

"—that I took them. No, I don't think he did. But, he is confused about the whole thing."

"Aren't we all."

"I asked him to send any of Papaw's papers that he has. He said you have most of them. I found them in your study. I hope you don't mind. I've been going through them."

"No, I don't mind at all."

"He'd prefer we not talk to the great-aunts about it. But

if anybody knows anything, it should be them. Maybe I'll talk to Maggie later."

"You've been busy," said Lindsay.

"I thought I'd help you solve this. Now, speaking of guilt, I haven't seen you look so guilty since you took all my model planes to the gully and threw them over the edge trying to get them to fly."

Lindsay gave a hint of a smile. "I'm sorry about that."

"I'd outgrown them anyway," he said, smiling.

"Sinjin," Lindsay said as she wrapped her hand around her glass, "I spoke with Kathy today."

Sinjin was good at angry looks. Lindsay cringed. "What did you talk about?" His voice was quiet.

"The artifacts and why she lied about your visit early Thursday morning."

"Why, Lindsay?" He threw his napkin on the table. "This is my business. It has nothing to do with you. Damn it, I told you to leave her out of it."

"It has a lot to do with me. Her lie affected me as much as it did you."

"How?"

"I take it you haven't seen the papers."

"No."

"Unfortunately, I didn't bring any home for you to read, but they implicate me. You can let Kathy ruin your reputation, but I can't allow her to ruin mine. This is how I make my living." Lindsay took out the sketch and the flyer. "I had a visitor the day we unpacked the artifacts. I was gone when he came, but Sally saw him. She got a police sketch artist we know to draw this." Lindsay pointed to the picture. "Another graduate student, Bobbie Lacayo, recognized him from this poster."

Lindsay watched Sinjin's face. The anger at her wasn't completely gone, but it had softened. He stared at the pictures. "They look like the same person."

"Yes, they do."

"What did Kathy say?"

"That because it was the campus police asking, she didn't take the situation seriously."

"That's possible," Sinjin said. He still believed in Kathy. Lindsay envied her. Derrick must have seen the papers, and he hadn't even called, even as a friend.

"Have you told the police?" Sinjin asked.

"No."

"Are you going to?"

"No."

Sinjin looked from the photograph of Sid to Lindsay. "Why? He may have taken the artifacts."

"He may have," agreed Lindsay.

"Then why?"

"I'm not going to push this issue for two reasons. One is, I think there's a good chance that the sequence of events was just a coincidence. Another is, I think Kathy is carrying your son or daughter, and if that's true, I don't want there to be anything between our family and theirs to cause a grudge that will interfere with this child being a part of our family."

Sinjin said nothing for a long moment. "Kathy wanted me to drop the paternity issue. She convinced me that it couldn't be mine, and I didn't want to cause her any more stress, so I agreed."

"A blood test isn't stressful. It's pretty easy. It's only stressful if you are afraid of the outcome," Lindsay said. "Here is what I think. Sidney Barrie obviously adores Kathy. He wants to marry her. He doesn't even care if she is pregnant with another man's child. However, he doesn't want the other man in her life at all. So, he and Kathy agree to convince you that the baby is not yours, and because you still love Kathy and believe her, you won't push it." Lindsay paused a moment to allow what she said to sink in.

Sinjin said nothing for several moments. "Do you mind

if I take Mandrake out for a ride?" he said at last.

"No, go ahead," she said. A good ride made her think more clearly, too.

Lindsay cleared the table, loaded the dishwasher, and went to her bedroom. She had a light table in the corner beside her desk. Its glass top was slanted, like a drafting table, and lit from underneath. On the glass top she placed the enlargement she had made of the newspaper picture of the skull. The light from beneath the glass gave the skull an eerie glow. Placing a white piece of paper over the picture, she began to draw, using the skull as a substructure for the face.

She had seen enough pictures of archaeology workers in the thirties to know what hairstyle to draw. When she finished she lifted the drawing from the table and looked at the face of the man whose skeleton had fallen out of the crate. The face looked back at her with sad eyes. The sad countenance was unconscious on her part, she supposed, but a man who had worked hard all his life at backbreaking labor, had severe injuries that always ached, and was poor probably had a sad face. This was the face she would look for among the photographs taken at her grandfather's digs.

She switched off the light on the table and placed another sheet of paper on the glass and began to draw. This time, the picture was of the man standing in the clothes he wore at the time of his death, standing with one leg shorter than the other.

He was wearing a tie, she thought. The archaeologists wore ties, but not the workers. Workers usually wore overalls and work pants. Church? Was he killed on a Sunday? He had gotten all dressed up to go someplace to die. It was probably supposed to be someplace special. How sad. She shook her head.

Warming to her subject, she drew one more picture. This time, in addition to the man standing, she drew another figure, taller, left-handed, his back to her, stabbing his victim through the ribs with a long knife. It was then, as she examined her work, that she realized that her grandfather was five-foot-eleven and left-handed. She grabbed the picture, started to wad it up, and stopped. A lot of men were that height and left-handed. In 1992 all three men who ran for president were left handed. "Papaw didn't do this," she said to the face of the man.

Lindsay looked at the clock. It was past twelve and she hadn't heard Sinjin come in. She went downstairs and opened the front door and found him sitting on the porch.

"Are you all right?" she asked, sitting down beside him.

He nodded. "Do you believe what you told me? Did she say anything that would make you believe that the baby is mine?"

"Yes, I believe it, and no, she didn't say anything. I can't explain it. It was just seeing them, seeing the way he looked at her, talking to him. I just knew what he would be like. I may be wrong, but I don't think I am."

"Does she love him?"

"I think she feels safe with him."

"And she didn't feel safe with me?"

"Why didn't you marry her sooner and start a family?" asked Lindsay.

"The job I do is dangerous. I know that. I was going to quit sometime and raise a family, but I'd never put a child in danger of losing a parent. I know what that's like."

"You answered your own question then." Lindsay saw car lights through the trees, coming down the long drive. "Who do you suppose that is?" They watched as the car came closer. "I believe it's Sally. I wonder what she's doing here at this time of night."

Chapter 13

SALLY STOPPED THE car in front of Lindsay's cabin and got out. She looked a fright, with bright purple Egyptian eyeshadow and her hair standing wild around her head. She was wearing a short maid's uniform.

Lindsay and Sinjin stared at her for a moment.

Sally answered their stare. "I'm Magenta."

"Sally, are you all right?" Lindsay asked. "Is that makeup or a scrape on your face?"

Sally put a hand to her face. "It's a scrape. Look, I'm sorry to come out here so late, but I need to talk to you. Something happened."

Lindsay took Sally's hand and led her inside. Sinjin followed.

Sally sat on Lindsay's couch and fingered the buttons on her torn skirt. "I must look awful."

In the light, Lindsay could see the torn hose and smudges on Sally's clothes. "You look frightened. What happened?"

Sinjin brought Sally a glass of ice water and sat down at the other end of the couch, his brows knitted together in a puzzled frown.

Sally's hand shook slightly as she took a sip from the glass. "Several of us went to see *The Rocky Horror Picture Show*. I left early."

"Why?" asked Lindsay.

"It's silly, I guess. Brian and Gerri Chapman were there. I think they're in town for Brian's mother's birthday. Anyway, they weren't dressed up, and I was, and I don't know, it just wasn't fun anymore, so I left."

"That must have been hard," Lindsay said.

Sally shrugged. "I'll get over it. Anyway, I started off toward Baldwin where I'd left my car. I thought someone was following me. I wasn't sure at first, but I felt really spooked. He was dressed like Frank N. Furter. This sounds so stupid."

"I don't understand," Sinjin said. "He was dressed as a hot dog?"

"No," said Lindsay, "like Dr. Frank N. Furter, a character from the movie."

Sally took a deep breath. Lindsay moved to the couch and put an arm around her shoulders. "I wasn't very smart," Sally continued. "I tried to lose him by going between buildings. No one was around, and before I knew it, he grabbed me and threw me to the ground. I thought . . . I thought . . ." She took her sleeve and wiped the tears that were spilling onto her cheeks. "Some people came around the building, and I called for help. I thought maybe he'd get scared and run off, but they just yelled 'elbow sex,' laughed, and went on."

"They yelled what?" Sinjin asked.

"It's something from the movie," Lindsay said. "They didn't realize she was being attacked, apparently." She turned her attention back to Sally. "Can you tell us what happened?"

"All he did was whisper in my ear in this stage voice. Then he left, and I lay there for a while. I guess I was crying, I don't know how long. I finally got up and went to the police. I just came from there. They were very nice. I talked to a Detective Kaufman. He sent someone to look for him right away, but there were so many Frank N. Furters."

"What did he whisper to you?" asked Lindsay.

"It was a warning. He said to tell Dr. Chamberlain if she doesn't stop trying to be a detective, it'll be worse next time."

"Oh, God, Sally." This is my fault, thought Lindsay. "Did he say anything else?"

Sally shook her head.

"Why don't you stay the night with us?" Lindsay said.

"Would you mind? I'd rather not drive back tonight. I'll sleep on the couch."

"You take the guest room," said Sinjin. "I'll take the couch."

"I don't want to put you—" began Sally.

"That way I can guard the door," Sinjin said.

"Thanks. I was really scared. I'll bet I aged ten years at least." She smiled through her tears, and Sinjin laughed out loud. It took Lindsay a second to get it.

"I suppose you did," said Sinjin.

Sally followed Lindsay to her room and sat on the bed while Lindsay searched for a nightgown.

"Would you like to shower?" asked Lindsay.

"That would be great. I came straight here from the police station. I thought you ought to know. What do you make of it?"

"I don't know. It may have something to do with the artifacts. Sally, I'm so sorry."

"It's not your fault. Please, if I thought you would blame yourself, I wouldn't have come out here."

Lindsay pulled out a nightshirt, eyeing Sally's small frame. "This is short on me, so maybe it won't be too long on you. Here's a robe to go with it. They'll be a little big on you, I'm afraid."

"That's okay, I appreciate it and your letting me stay here."

"That's the least I can do, and I'm glad you came here. Are you hurt? Did you see a doctor?"

Sally shook her head. "I'm all right. Just some scrapes. Scared mostly."

"It's over now. You'll be safe with us. There's some stuff in the medicine cabinet to put on your cuts."

"What's Kathy like?" Sally asked.

"I've always thought she was a little self-absorbed, but—" Lindsay shrugged.

"What does she look like?"

"Like Elizabeth Taylor in her *Butterfield 8* days." Sally groaned and Lindsay smiled at her. "Take all the time you need. We'll be downstairs."

Sinjin watched Lindsay come down the stairs. "How is she?"

Lindsay sat down heavily on one of the sofas. "She's fine. I feel responsible. It's one thing when what I do affects only me—"

"This isn't your fault."

"It may be. Someone locked me in the basement of Nancy Hart Hall. Apparently, when locking me in the storage room didn't work, whoever it was escalated his attack."

"What? Why didn't you tell me?"

"I was getting around to it."

"Well, tell me about it now."

Lindsay told him about the artifacts missing from Nancy Hart, how someone had locked her in, and how she had escaped through the utility duct. "I didn't tell the police. I'm ashamed to say it, but I was afraid. I felt like they would believe I really was there to steal artifacts. But I'll have to tell them now. I can't have my students threatened."

"How did he know Sally was your student?" asked Sinjin.

Lindsay hesitated. "What? I don't know. That's a good question. A stranger wouldn't know that, would he?"

"Unless he'd been casing the place. Sally's picture was in the paper, wasn't it?"

"Yes, but I'm not sure anyone who only knew her from a

newspaper picture would have recognized her dressed up like that."

"Perhaps not. It looks to me like someone you know."

Lindsay said nothing, wondering what to do. The shower running upstairs and the ticking of the living room clock sounded loud in her ears. Not knowing what to do scared her. "That was nice of you to give up your bed," she said.

"It's nothing."

"I'm sorry I interfered in your business. I felt I had no choice."

"Why didn't you come to me with all this?"

"You would have tried to stop me. You would have been angry," she said.

"You didn't trust me. If I thought Sid was stealing—involving Kathy—"

Lindsay bit her lower lip. She wanted to shout at him. Tell him what she thought of his idealized view of Kathy. But what would she say if someone had accused Derrick? She would defend him beyond all reason, but then, Derrick was trustworthy. Kathy was not.

Silence settled between them again for several moments. "Look," said Sinjin. "The thing you said about the baby, about not following through on Sid—" He stopped. "That was decent of you."

"You're more important," she muttered without looking at him. "I'll get you some sheets for the couch."

Lindsay sat up and looked at her clock—2:00 A.M. She wondered what had awakened her, then she heard the stereo. The pleading strains of Lorraine Ellison singing "Stay with Me" drifted up the stairs. She put on a robe and walked down to the living room. Only the desk light was on, barely illuminating the room. Sinjin was on the couch with his feet propped up on the coffee table. Sally was curled up in a chair. They were listening to blues, drinking beer, and watching the lights on the stereo.

"You all can't sleep?" Lindsay asked.

Sinjin took another sip and set his bottle on the coffee table. "Did we wake you? I've been teaching Sally how to enjoy wallowing in a broken heart."

"Sitting in the dark, drinking beer, and listening to soul music?" said Lindsay.

"That's it," said Sinjin.

"You should have gotten me up. I need to learn that, too," she told him.

"Go get yourself a beer out of the fridge and join us," he said. Lindsay got a bottle and settled herself in the other chair. "Now, you can't talk about it. You have to listen."

"I can't complain that Derrick hasn't even called to see how I was doing, even as a friend?"

Sinjin sat up. "Oh, Lindsay, he did call. This afternoon. I'm sorry."

"He did? What did he say?"

"He wanted to know how you were and if there was anything he could do."

"And what did you say?"

"I said things were kind of hard for you and he might call back and talk to you. He said he will tomorrow."

"Give me your beer," Sally demanded.

Lindsay smiled and settled back and listened to the music.

Lindsay had specifically asked to see the detective who had talked to Sally and was directed to Detective Davis Kaufman. She knew many of the campus police but had never met him before. From the uncluttered look of his office and desk, she guessed he hadn't been at his job on campus long. Most campus police were young. Captain Grant, head of campus security, liked young people for the job because of their endless energy. This detective, however, was older, perhaps in his late thirties. He had steel-gray hair, matching eyes, and looked as though he wouldn't have any trouble keeping up with the younger officers.

"At first I thought it was an accident," said Lindsay, carefully choosing her words. "I thought someone had locked the door as they left the building, not knowing I was inside. I didn't know how long I would be stuck down there, so I found a way out. I feel now that the attack on my assistant might have something to do with the missing artifacts, and thought I'd better report what happened to me. It may not have been an accident."

"You think someone is trying to stop you from investigating the artifact theft? Why would they do that?" he asked. She imagined he got many a confession with his steely, unblinking gaze.

"I only think that because of the message delivered to Sally."

"And are you investigating?"

"The artifacts stolen from Baldwin were in my family's possession until my father discovered them and sent them to me. I naturally am making every effort to get them back."

"They're yours?"

"No. The question of rightful ownership is uncertain. They probably belong in Kentucky, and if so, will eventually be repatriated to their Native American tribal affiliation."

"You think someone is impressed with your detective skills enough to believe that you are likely to discover who stole the artifacts, and whoever that is wants you stopped?"

Lindsay didn't know if he was trying to make her defensive on purpose or there was some reason he resented her, but she definitely felt his hostility. "I know, it doesn't sound plausible, but there it is."

"You have no idea who locked you in the building?"

"No."

"How did you know to escape through the utility conduits?" he asked.

"I didn't really. I knew they were probably there. I wanted to get out. The episode may mean nothing. I just thought I should tell you, in view of what happened to Sally Flynn."

"All right. Do you have any other information that you have forgotten to tell us?"

Lindsay met his gaze with hers and declined to be either defensive or hostile. "I'm sure you have already thought of it, but the person who attacked Sally knew she worked for me. It's definitely not a secret, but a stranger wouldn't know it." Lindsay saw a slight waver in his eyes. He hadn't thought of it and it was rather obvious. She rose and held out her hand. "Thank you for seeing me."

He rose and took it. His grip was firm but not rudely hard. "Let us know if you think of anything else." Lindsay felt relieved that he asked her no more questions. She got to the door when he spoke again. "Dr. Chamberlain. Did you discover the artifacts were missing when you were down in the basement the first time?"

That was the question she had been dreading. It would lead to all sorts of questions as to why she hadn't reported it immediately. To tell them that she was afraid of being blamed, her real thought at the time, now sounded silly—and guilty. She turned around and faced him, and looked him in the eyes.

"I suspected it. That's why I went down there to begin with. None of the boxes, however, were completely empty, and we do research with them all the time. It was not out of the realm of possibility that someone had checked them out or had repacked some of the artifacts to make them more convenient to study. Frank Carter, the department head, and I confirmed that they were missing."

"You know, don't you, that the person who locked you

in reported that a theft was in progress?"

"I have heard that, but it doesn't make sense, does it?" said Lindsay. She realized that he indeed suspected her of being the thief.

"How is that?" he asked.

"What would they see in the short time and narrow view they had? The door was mostly closed while I was there. The faculty who have offices in the building know me. It is not an uncommon occurrence that I work with the artifacts. Neither is it uncommon that I take sample artifacts to show my archaeology classes. What would this mysterious Good Samaritan see that would make them suspect I was stealing these artifacts and not working with them? No one has ever reported it before when I or any of the students have carried artifacts out of the building. Isn't it odd that they would do so now and throw suspicion on me, then not a day later, one of my students is attacked and given that cryptic message? But I'm sure you've already thought of all that."

"Good day, Dr. Chamberlain."

"Good day." Lindsay left his office and started out of the building. Another of the campus police stopped her. Now what, she thought.

"Dr. Chamberlain," said the young man. "Just tying up some loose ends. Can you tell me why Gloria Rankin, the student who was hit by the bus, was coming to see you?"

Chapter 14

"GLORIA RANKIN WANTED to see me?"

"That's what she said when she left Park Hall, just before being struck and killed," said the officer.

"I have no idea," Lindsay said. "I didn't know her. Wasn't she in the Classics Department?"

The officer nodded.

"They do archaeology also. It may have been an archaeology question."

"If you think of something, let us know."

"I will. I'll ask the secretary if Miss Rankin called." Lindsay left the Public Safety Building, relieved to get away. She was actually starting to feel guilty.

Gloria Rankin did call, Lindsay realized, but didn't leave her name. Edwina had said a woman called. Maybe the caller left a message that Edwina hadn't given her.

Lindsay stopped at the Golden Pantry in Five Points and bought a bottle of Tums before driving back to Baldwin. She chewed a couple before starting the Rover. Now she had to tell Frank that she had already known that the artifacts were missing before she looked at the boxes with him. What a tangled web, she thought.

"That's the silliest thing I've ever heard," said Frank. "You really think I would blame you for the theft of the artifacts?"

"No, but I thought you would be obliged to tell the police, and they would blame me. I think that's what the person had in mind when they locked me in and called the police."

Frank was silent a moment. "It does look that way, doesn't it?"

"Who do you think is behind it?" she asked.

"I don't know, and I don't like it. How's Sally?"

"She's doing fine. I told her not to come in today, but I think she probably will anyway."

"Kerwin will make something of this," Frank said.

"I know." She rose to go. "Let me know if you hear anything."

Edwina was sitting at the front desk, working at her computer. She stopped as Lindsay approached and looked at her with a face that said, I have to be polite to you, but I wouldn't if it were my choice. It was an expression that Lindsay had received many times from Edwina. Kerwin had been gossiping again.

"Edwina, last Thursday, I think it was, you said a young woman called. She said it was important but didn't leave a name. Did she say anything else?"

"We get many calls here. Once I deliver a message, I put it out of my mind."

"It's important. I wish you would try."

Edwina put on the expression of one trying to remember, but Lindsay strongly suspected she was acting. Lindsay's gaze rested on Edwina's monitor screen. She was updating Kerwin's résumé. Lindsay noticed one of his publications: Kerwin, K. (1995). "Rayburn Mill site: Post Civil War Industry." *Journal of Historical Archaeology* 4:17-29. It reminded her of something. She shook her head. There were too many puzzle pieces floating around in there.

"I just can't remember," Edwina said.

Lindsay was startled to hear Edwina's voice and, for a second, forgot she had asked her a question. "Thank you for trying, Edwina. I appreciate it."

Edwina returned to her typing and Lindsay started for her office. She stopped when she heard her name and turned to see Dr. Stevie Saturnin catching up with her in the hallway.

"It's from a cornfield," Stevie said softly, her blonde hair hanging in her face.

"The dirt sample is from a cornfield?" Lindsay repeated. Stevie nodded. "Thanks. I hope it wasn't too much trouble."

"None at all," Stevie said and went on her way down the hall, sorting through her mail.

A cornfield, thought Lindsay. One of the last places the fellow who ended up in an artifact crate stood was a cornfield. A nice, hard fact. Lindsay liked hard facts. She wasn't sure what she could do with it, but it made her feel good to have it.

Liza Ferris was waiting in front of Lindsay's office when she came down the stairs and turned the corner. "I talked Luke into speaking with you, Dr. Chamberlain. Could you come today?" Liza asked.

Lindsay looked at her watch. "Would two hours from now be all right?"

Liza nodded and handed Lindsay a folded piece of paper. "I wrote down the directions for you. It's not far from here."

Lindsay took the paper. "I'll see you in a couple of hours." She looked at her watch again. She was having lunch with her brother at twelve. Perhaps he would like to do some detective work first.

She walked back up to the departmental library to look for the volume of *Historical Archaeology* containing Kerwin's article, the one she had seen Edwina typing on his résumé. She ran her finger down the row of neatly shelved journals. The volume was not there. She looked among other volumes, on the tables, under the tables—it was not there. Kerwin would probably have it, but she wasn't going to ask him just yet—not until she had read it to see if it would jog her memory. Whatever it was that it reminded her of may not have to do with anything. She returned to her office and just caught her ringing phone before it rolled over to her voice mail.

"Lindsay. Derrick here." Lindsay's stomach churned. "Sinjin said you've had it kind of rough the past few days."

"I'll weather through it. What have the papers been like up there?"

"Oh, you know how papers can be."

"My poor parents."

"Funny about the skeleton. It could only happen to you."

"At least he's too old for people to blame that one on me."

"Is it that bad?"

"There are artifacts missing from Nancy Hart."

"Then it's not just the artifacts that were stored with your family. There's something bigger going on. They aren't blaming that on you, are they?"

"They're trying."

"You're kidding. Are you investigating it?"

"Derrick, let's not—"

"I'm not. I'm just wondering if you found out anything."

He's not going to like this, thought Lindsay, then realized it probably wouldn't matter to him anymore. They weren't together. She told him about the incident in Nancy Hart and about the attack on Sally. There was a long moment of silence before Derrick said anything.

"Lindsay, my God, I didn't realize it was that bad. When Sinjin said you were having a hard time, I had no idea—"

"Sinjin didn't know about all of that when he talked to you. Before that, it was mainly political stuff, fallout from the newspaper articles. Did you know that Francisco Lewis wants to come here?"

"What? He's alienated half of the U.S., and now he wants to go for the other half?"

"Unbelievable, I know. I wonder how this fits into Kerwin's plans to become department head. I don't understand any of it. I thought Kerwin was the dean's favorite. Anyway, speaking of Kerwin, I'm looking for an article by him. You take *Historical Archaeology,* don't you?"

"Yes."

Lindsay gave him the volume and page numbers. "Could you fax it to me?"

"I can do that right now. It should be there in a couple of minutes."

"Thank you, Derrick."

"Do you—" he began.

"What?"

"Nothing. Later, maybe. Take care. I'll fax the article."

When she replaced the receiver in its cradle, she realized she was gripping it so tightly her fingers were hurting. She jumped when the phone rang under her hand.

"Lindsay Chamberlain," she said.

"This is Sidney Barrie. Kathy called the campus police and explained to them that she thought their call was a prank until she read the paper. She told them that your brother was with her."

"Thank you. Thank Kathy for us."

"Ms. Chamberlain. We, I can't give the artifacts back, because I didn't take them. If you report—"

"Something else has come up that may take this in another direction. If you didn't take the artifacts—and I'm prepared to believe you didn't—I have no desire to have the newspapers find out about your visit. I know what it's like to have suspicion unfairly focused on me, and I wouldn't wish it on anyone." Lindsay thought she heard a sigh of relief.

"I appreciate that. This isn't going to hang over our heads, is it?"

"No."

"Then good day to you. I'm glad this is finished."

Lindsay breathed her own sigh of relief and rose to go to the main office to get the fax. Her phone rang again.

"Chamberlain," she said, and when she heard it was Jaleel from the geology lab, she realized she was hoping it was Derrick calling her back. Get over it, she admonished herself. "Jaleel, hi, were you able to find out anything about the soil sample?"

"Keep in mind the sample was small, but the profile looks like Piedmont and Coastal Plain," he said.

"So, it's where the two regions meet?" asked Lindsay.

"I'd say so, right around the Macon area. Does that help?"

"Yes. Yes, it does. Thanks."

"No problem. Tell me about it sometime," he said.

"I will. Thanks again."

She hung up the phone. A cornfield near Macon—possibly the last place the fellow in the crate had stood. But who was he? Sinjin said Dad was sending the rest of Papaw's papers. There should be tons of old photographs of the excavations from that time. If she looked through them, perhaps she could find a picture of him—if the portrait she drew looked anything like him, and if he was actually at the digs with her grandfather.

It was almost time for Sinjin to be arriving. She hurried up to the main office to get the fax from Derrick. Nothing was on the machine. She looked in her mailbox. Nothing. Kate, the office manager, walked through, putting a large envelope in one of the mailboxes.

"Kate, do you know if I had a fax come in?" Lindsay asked.

"I think I heard one come in a few minutes ago. It's not there?"

"No. Do you know who was in the office?"

She stopped and thought for a moment. "Edwina was just here. She went out to lunch. Dr. Marcus and Dr. Kerwin, and I think Liza and Brandon were up here. Maybe one of them got it and is going to bring it down to you. I'll ask around."

"Thanks, Kate."

Kenneth Kerwin's office was across the hall from the main office. Lindsay glanced in as she walked by. Kerwin sat at his desk, surrounded on three sides by floor-to-ceiling shelves jammed with books, journals, and papers. He never used the overhead light, relying instead on a green banker's lamp on his desk. He raised his head from his work and fixed his gaze on Lindsay. He looked like a wizard in a cave, and he looked frightened of her. She left him sitting there and went downstairs.

As she turned the corner into her office, she found Gerri Chapman sitting in her chair.

"Trying it on for size?" Lindsay said. Gerri looked up and jumped.

"You startled me. I was just looking for something to write on."

"There's a pad of paper by your left hand."

"Oh. If it had been a snake it would have bitten me." Gerri took a piece of paper and started writing. "You've been getting a lot of press lately," she said.

"Yes, I have." Lindsay still stood in the doorway, wondering when it would occur to Gerri to get up.

"Bad luck, huh?" said Gerri, smiling.

"Strange luck, at any rate."

"Lindsay, how are you!"

Lindsay turned and greeted blond, suntanned Brian and gave him a hug. "I'm fine, Brian. You look good. Been out in the sun, I see."

Gerri relinquished Lindsay's chair and came out to join

them. "We saw Sally last night. She didn't look too good," she said.

"Does anyone look good after being mugged?" asked Lindsay, watching Brian.

"What? Mugged?" he said. "Sally was mugged?"

"Yes, I thought you knew, from what Gerri said."

"No," said Gerri, "I just meant she didn't look like she felt well. I saw her leave."

"When she left the Tate Center, she was attacked behind the Psychology Building. She wasn't hurt, but she was very frightened."

"I didn't know about it," said Brian. "You sure she's all right?"

"Yes. She spent the night at my place."

"Did they catch who did it?" Brian asked.

"No."

The door swung open and Sally came in with her bicycle. The red scrape across her cheek looked tender and inflamed. She stopped when she saw Brian and Gerri. "Hi, Brian. How've you been?"

"I'm fine. Lindsay said that you—"

Sinjin came in, and Sally seemed glad for the interruption as Lindsay introduced him to Gerri and Brian.

"Ready for lunch?" he said to Lindsay.

"Sure. I've got an errand to run first. I hope you don't mind."

Lindsay got her purse from her office, closed and locked her door, and started to leave. Sinjin walked over to Sally and kissed her lips.

"We're still on for tonight, right?" he asked.

Sally stuttered, "Well, uh, yeah."

"Good, I'll pick you up at seven."

As they went out the door, Lindsay saw Brian staring at Sally and Gerri staring at Brian. Sally was staring after Sinjin, looking surprised—and smiling.

• • •

"That was nice," said Lindsay as she climbed into Sinjin's Jeep.

"Well, I thought it might be nice to take Sally out to dinner, maybe a movie. It'd also give ol' Brian something to think about."

"Well, it was sweet."

"That's me, a sweet guy. Where do you want to go for lunch?"

"Do you mind going with me to interview Luke Ferris first?" asked Lindsay.

"You're kidding, aren't you?"

"No. Liza asked me to come by."

"Jesus, Lindsay. Are you sure Derrick isn't right? Why are you doing this?"

"Liza's a student. She needs help."

"Come on, that's not an answer," Sinjin said.

"I don't know. I suppose it's because I'm not supposed to. I guess all those years of growing up doing as I was told have taken their toll."

"That's not an answer, either."

"I don't have an answer, other than that I feel like if I could just answer all the unanswered questions, my life would straighten out. Here are the directions. Turn right up here on Lumpkin." Lindsay saw a large package on the back seat from Stearns, Kentucky. "Is that Papaw's papers?"

"Yes. I thought I'd go through them. Maybe find out where those crates came from."

"I'd like to have a look at the photographs. Did I show you the portrait I drew of the skeleton?"

"No. What? From the skull? You think you can recognize this guy?"

"Maybe. I'd like to try. I did find out that the dirt in his crate and from his shoes was from a cornfield in the Macon area.

Though I don't know what good knowing that will do me."

"That's impressive. How did you determine that?"

Lindsay told him about the soil analysis she had the palynology and geology labs do for her. "He may have been killed on a Sunday or on some special occasion or maybe at a meeting he thought was important."

"OK, Sherlock. How did you arrive at that?"

"He wore a shirt and tie."

"So did Papaw."

"Workers didn't, and this fellow was a worker. It showed in his bones and his teeth. The shirt and tie were for a special occasion."

"Better tell me which way to turn."

"Oh, sorry. Turn left at the stop sign. Derrick called," she said.

"And?"

"And nothing. He called. Funny, though. I asked him to fax me an article written by Kenneth Kerwin. He did, I'm sure, but someone took the fax before I got to the machine. I think it was Kerwin. The article is missing from the departmental library, too."

"What's the article about?"

"I don't know. I saw the title in his résumé and it reminded me of something, but I can't put my finger on what. Kerwin is hiding something. He knew Shirley Foster well. He said he didn't, but I think he had a thing for her. That's the way it looked in that picture on the Pryors' mantel."

"You don't miss a thing, do you?"

"I missed telling you where to turn back there. Can you turn around in that driveway?" Lindsay read the rest of the directions aloud as he turned around. "It's not far."

Liza met them at the door. Liza's mother and sister were older versions of her—dark hair, dark eyes, pretty. Her father looked like a former football player: muscle gone to bulge, light brown hair, and blue eyes like his son.

"Thank you for coming," Mrs. Ferris said. "Liza said you can help us. I know Luke didn't do this thing he's accused of. We just don't understand it."

"I'll talk with your son," said Lindsay. "But please don't get your hopes up that I can work any miracles."

"At least he'll talk to you," Mr. Ferris said. "He won't say a damned thing to us. He's sitting out there now, alone in the gazebo."

Lindsay and Sinjin walked down a path bordered by purple creeping phlox to a small screened-in redwood gazebo with gingerbread trim. Luke was sitting alone inside. He looked like a kid. Lindsay tapped on the screen door.

"Dr. Chamberlain, thanks for coming," he said, rising to open the door.

"This is my brother, Sinjin. I hope you don't mind him being with me."

Luke shook his head. "I just can't talk to my parents yet."

They sat on the bench built around the inside of the gazebo. A small table in the center held a towel, a pack of cigarettes, matches, and a glass ashtray. "This is nice," Lindsay said.

"Dad and I built this last summer. They had one a long time ago that burned down." Then, after a moment's hesitation, he looked down at his feet and said, "My parents had to mortgage the house to get me out of jail. I didn't kill her. I swear I didn't."

"Why did the sheriff come to you?"

"In a minute," he said, nodding toward the house from where his mother was coming, carrying a tray with a pitcher of tea and a plate of cookies. Sinjin opened the screen door for her.

"Just some refreshment," she said, and Lindsay thanked her.

Sinjin put the tray on the table and got glasses of tea for himself and Lindsay as Mrs. Ferris walked back toward the house.

"I used to work in the Chemistry Department doing custodial work. I had a sub-master key that I forgot to turn in. It must have been in my jacket pocket and fell out the night Shirley Foster died. The sheriff traced it to Chemistry and they had a list of people who hadn't turned in their keys. I don't know why they never called me about it. Anyway, they found out that I had also worked for Shirley Foster. Bingo. They came to my apartment. What could I say? I told them I found her body, but I didn't kill her. They didn't believe me."

"Did you see anyone else that night?" Lindsay asked, leaning forward.

Luke shook his head. "When I got there she was . . . she was lying on the bank. She was dead. Burned. That's all I know."

Chapter 15

"**I** KNOW YOU don't believe me," Luke said. "I don't blame you. The sheriff doesn't believe me either."

"You just found her lying there? Could you tell how long she might have been there?"

Luke shook his head, still staring at the floor. "Not long. She was still . . . uh . . . there was still smoke."

"Why were you out there?" asked Lindsay.

Luke pursed his lips. "I don't know. She asked me to come."

"She gave you no indication why?"

Luke shook his head. "She said she had a surprise and that she would correct her mistake."

"You don't know what she meant?"

"I challenged the grade she gave me on a paper. I figured it was that."

"You didn't think it odd that she wanted to meet you way out there in the woods to change a grade?" asked Lindsay.

"Well, sort of, but I just thought it was, well, you know—"

"You thought she would change your grade in exchange for some sexual favor?" asked Sinjin.

"It seemed that way," answered Luke. Luke had quit looking at the floor, and he now fixed his eyes on the scalloped molding in the gazebo. Lindsay wasn't sure if that meant he was not telling the truth, or if he was embarrassed.

"Had she ever given you any indication before of those kinds of intentions?" asked Lindsay.

"No. Not really. I mean, she was friendly, but she was that way with everybody. I never took it personally before."

"How did she ask it? I mean did she just say meet me at the lake at midnight?"

"She didn't actually say it in person. She left a note for me."

"Do you have the note?"

He shook his head.

"What did you do after you found her?" Lindsay asked.

He put his hands to his face. They were shaking. He seemed to have tears in his eyes. "What could I do? She was dead. I just left."

"Why didn't you call the police?" asked Lindsay.

"I was afraid. I didn't want to be involved. She was past any help."

"But what about her family? Didn't you think they'd want to know what happened to her?"

"I thought they would find her. It was her property. Her car was there. We had departmental picnics there. It wasn't like it was in the middle of nowhere."

"Do you mind if I have one of those cigarettes?" asked Sinjin.

"What? No. Go ahead. They're my sister's. She comes out here to smoke sometimes."

Sinjin took a cigarette from the pack and a match from the box. He flicked the match with his thumbnail and it ignited with a hiss. Sinjin lit the cigarette and put the flaming match in the ashtray. Lindsay was surprised. She didn't know Sinjin smoked. Luke watched the ashtray as the match turned to a thin piece of charcoal and burned out.

"But when they didn't find her—" began Lindsay.

"What? Oh." Luke looked at her and shrugged. "I didn't understand it."

"You didn't go back and look?" she asked.

"No! No, I couldn't. God, no, I couldn't. I just thought— I don't know what I thought. I just wanted to forget it."

"Is that why you quit school?" Lindsay asked. Luke nodded.

Sinjin put out the cigarette. "Not my brand," he muttered.

"Did you make the anonymous call to Will Patterson?" asked Lindsay.

Luke shook his head. "I don't know who he is."

"What do you think?" Lindsay asked as Sinjin drove out of the Ferrises' drive and onto the street.

"He's lying," said Sinjin.

"Why do you think so?" she asked.

Sinjin shrugged. "He's not a good liar. He couldn't look at either one of us. Surely you saw that. Where do you want to eat?"

"There's a place in Five Points where we can get a sandwich, or there's a little Mexican place down the street, if you prefer. I wonder why he didn't just report it?" asked Lindsay.

"How about Mexican? He was afraid they would blame him, because he's a firebug. Probably set things on fire as a kid. May still do it occasionally."

"How do you know that?" Lindsay asked.

"The gazebo burned down. There's no electricity in it," said Sinjin.

"Couldn't it have been struck by lightning?" she asked.

"Could have. But lightning more often hits the tallest object. It would've probably hit one of the pines. I didn't see any evidence of it. I think he set it on fire."

"That's kind of a jump. Going from a burned gazebo to him setting things on fire."

"He likes fire. Did you see his eyes when I lit the match?" Sinjin asked.

"Is that why you lit the cigarette? I didn't think you smoked."

"I don't, and yes, that's why. I wanted to see his face. I've seen that look before. He's fascinated by fire."

Lindsay groaned. "I feel bad for Liza and her family."

Sinjin pulled in the parking lot of the restaurant. They ordered their food and took it to one of the outside tables.

"A strange thing happened today as I was leaving the police station," Lindsay said. "A policeman asked me if I knew why Gloria Rankin was coming to see me. She was the student hit and killed by the bus that Luke Ferris was driving."

"That is odd," said Sinjin. "A coincidence?"

"I don't know," Lindsay answered.

"Did you know her?"

"No, I didn't."

"Do you think her death was an accident?"

"The police think it was," she said.

"Yeah, but the police think you and I are the Bonnie and Clyde of the archaeology world. I have another angle on the artifacts," Sinjin said over his beef burrito. "But it isn't good, either."

"What's that?" asked Lindsay.

"I talked to Dad again. Steven and Anne are pitching a fit about Dad sending the artifacts to you in the first place."

"Maggie's Steven and Anne?" asked Lindsay. "Dad's cousins?"

"Yes. The ones who are always putting a price tag on everything. They seem to think the artifacts are part of the family inheritance, and because they were found behind the house their mother lives in, they want their share of them."

"They could only profit from the artifacts if they were sold to collectors," Lindsay said, trying to take a bite of taco without spilling the filling out the end.

"That wouldn't bother them. Dad reminded them that he owns the house and property where Maggie lives. He thinks that shut them up, but I don't know."

"They're what, Dad's age? I can't imagine them driving

down here, breaking into the storage room, and stealing the artifacts. I don't think they even know where I work," Lindsay said.

"Their kids might have come—with enough incentive," said Sinjin. "I agree, it's a long shot. But—" He shrugged. "I just thought I'd throw it out."

"Poor Dad."

"He wanted to come down and help," Sinjin said.

"You told him everything is all right, didn't you?" said Lindsay.

"Yeah. I told him I'd stick around until it's solved."

"When do you have to be back to work, or on duty, or whatever?" Lindsay asked.

"I've got another two weeks, provided there are no major forest fires. And there probably won't be. Fall is the big season for fires—after the summer has dried everything out."

"I'm glad you're staying. I hope you're not too bored."

"That's one thing about you, baby sister, life around you isn't boring."

Lindsay went to the library to look for Kerwin's article. The bound volume containing the *Historical Archaeology* journals from 1994 and 1995 was not in its place, nor was it on any of the library tables, the sorting shelf, or in the copy room. Journals didn't leave the library for more than one night, and then only in the hands of faculty members who had broad library privileges. Unless it had been stolen, it had to be in the library. She asked a staff member if it was checked out.

"Journals aren't usually checked out," the student worker told her.

"I can't find it anywhere. Could a faculty member have it?"

"It's not in the computer, but it could have been done by hand. It's probably in a carrel. I'll put a search on it."

Lindsay left the library and walked to her office, wondering who on campus might subscribe to the journal. Probably not the classical archaeologists. She'd ask Derrick to fax the article to her again. This time, she'd stand over the fax machine until it came in. But Derrick didn't answer when she called him, and she hung up without leaving a message. She sighed and walked out into the lab. Robin was working with the bones.

"Amy hasn't come by my office," Lindsay said.

"She quit," said Robin, punching numbers into her calculator. "Getting married."

Lindsay sat down and helped Robin sort through the animal bones. She went through several boxes almost automatically. All the mysteries in her life at the moment were swimming around in her head, frantically trying to arrange themselves into some order she could understand. She couldn't even decide which event went with which mystery. After a while she stood up. She needed to talk with Eddie Peck.

"I hope I've helped some," she said to Robin. "I have something I must do now."

"Yeah, thanks, Dr. Chamberlain. You've helped a lot. Dr. Bienvenido got a time extension on the analysis."

"Would you like me to find another student to help you?"

"Brandon said he would like to. Is that all right?" Robin asked.

"Sure. Have him go to Kate or Edwina and get the paperwork filled out so I can pay him."

Lindsay went into her office, closed the door, and called the medical examiner, Eddie Peck, who always seemed to know the details about the cases of the people he autopsied.

"Yo, Lindsay," he said, "been reading about you."

"You and everyone else in the Southeast," she said.

"Not that bad, is it?"

"Mostly embarrassing," she said.

"What can I do for you?"

"Maybe nothing. I have a question that's none of my business to ask."

"Okay, shoot," he said.

"I found out that the student Gloria Rankin was on her way to see me when she was hit by the bus. She was enrolled in the Classics Department, so she may have simply wanted to see me about some archaeology question. But that strikes me as odd, since it was Luke Ferris's bus that hit her, and Luke's the brother of one of my students—and he's been arrested for the murder of Shirley Foster. I don't know what any of this has to do with anything. But I wanted to ask you if there was anything unusual or suspicious about Gloria Rankin's accident that you could tell me."

"Whew, let me see. All that's interesting—and could mean nothing, as you say. There weren't many witnesses. It happened during classes and it was raining, not hard, but enough that not many people were outside. One guy observed the accident from the parking lot next to the Psychology Building, and a couple saw it from across the street as they were coming out of Baldwin. All said the driver couldn't have prevented hitting her. The guy in the parking lot said she almost jumped in front of the bus. The couple at Baldwin didn't see her until she was knocked down in the street. Just before that, they said she was standing on the curb. The bus was virtually empty, and no passengers saw anything."

"That seems pretty straightforward." Lindsay was disappointed, but she didn't know why.

"There's one other thing," Eddie said. "She had a bruise on her back that was a bit of a puzzle. She had massive bruising on her torso, as you can imagine, from the impact of the bus, but that was mostly on her side. And she had some scrapes and bruising resulting from her contact with the surface of the street, of course. But this troublesome bruise was small and round, about a centimeter in diameter, off to itself in the lower lumbar region. I thought she might have landed on a rock or something. That's not much, but I did wonder about it."

"What happened after she was hit?" asked Lindsay.

"Ferris stopped the bus and ran to her. So did the witnesses. She was alive but pretty bad off. They all did what they could. The female witness had a cell phone in her purse. She called the ambulance. They got Miss Rankin to the hospital within the golden hour, but she had too many internal injuries."

"That's so sad."

"Yes, it is. I get a lot of sad cases."

"I don't see how you do it. I appreciate the information."

"It wasn't much. Most of it was in the papers. You hang in there. I've found that most everything blows over."

"Thanks. I hope so."

Lindsay left her office and walked across the street to where the accident had happened. There were marks on the street in dark paint: an *X* about ten feet from the corner on Jackson Street where, Lindsay presumed, Gloria had been hit, a line where the bus had stopped,and another *X* where she had lain in the street.

Running parallel to the sidewalk was a wall that held back the embankment and tapered to ground level. The highest point of the wall was waist high. The embankment was landscaped with shrubs and trees. Lindsay climbed onto the wall and looked among the shrubs. She didn't know what she was looking for, but it occurred to her that it was a place to hide. She saw nothing, no disturbance in the ground, no broken flora. This is silly, she thought. Not everything's sinister. Accidents do happen—in fact, had happened before at this very spot. She was about to leave when she looked up and saw it. She wasn't sure it was what she was looking for, but it was an anomaly nonetheless. An umbrella hung from a branch in one of the trees. Lindsay took it down without touching any metal or plastic parts. The name etched into the handle read *Rankin*.

"Perhaps an unnecessary precaution," Lindsay told the policeman as he examined the baggies she had placed over the handle and tip of the umbrella. "But it was strange to find it hanging in the tree."

"It's best to be careful," he said. "Why were you looking there in the first place?"

Lindsay shrugged. "I've been overly suspicious of everything lately. When you said she came to see me, well—"

"So you looked in the trees?" he said.

"It occurred to me that she may have been pushed. If that were true, the person who pushed her might have been hiding among the shrubs. It's pretty thick there, and the wall could provide cover. I just happened to look up and see it."

The policeman smiled as though he thought that was funny. "Thank you for bringing this by and being careful with it, but if you suspected something, you really should have let us handle it."

"You're right, of course, but I assumed the police had already examined the area, and I just needed to satisfy my curiosity."

Lindsay had turned to leave when she heard her name. She recognized the voice and wished she could pretend that she hadn't heard. She turned back and faced Detective Kaufman.

"Yes? What can I do for you?" she asked.

"I'll walk you to your car," he said.

Lindsay's Rover was parked just outside the door, so they didn't go far. She stood by her door and waited.

"We got a call from your brother's alibi. Seems she thought we were joking when we called her the other day. Changed her story."

"Shouldn't you be talking to my brother, to tell him?"

"I believe he was called," he said.

"I'm glad to hear it. It's a terrible thing to be accused of something you didn't do," Lindsay said.

"I tried to get a search warrant for your place," he said. Lindsay raised her eyebrows. "Seems you have friends in high places. I couldn't get one."

"Detective Kaufman, I assure you, I'm not well connected. If you couldn't get a warrant, it's because you didn't have grounds for one." They stared at each other for a moment. Lindsay felt that if she broke her gaze, she'd lose, but what exactly, she didn't know. "I can't figure out why you are focusing on me. There's nothing to connect me with the thefts," she said at last.

"I usually find that where there's smoke, there's fire, and I smell a lot of smoke."

"No, Detective Kaufman. Sometimes there's only a smoke-making machine. That's one of the problems when your metaphors are clichés, you get caught in thinking patterns that blind you to alternative solutions."

He didn't speak for a moment but seemed to study her face. Probably fancied that he could look at a person and tell if they were lying, she thought. "Give me an alternative solution," he said.

"I'd like to, but I don't have one. I've gone over and over who knew about the artifacts—" She stopped, realizing that she had done the same thing. She had overlooked one other person, simply because he didn't fall within her definition of suspects. Associate Dean Ellis Einer could have known about the artifacts, couldn't he? He was there when the skeleton fell from the crate. Frank may have told him.

"You thought of something?" He looked at her through narrowed eyes.

"Yes, but there's nothing linking him but circumstances."

"Tell me who you suspect," he said.

Lindsay shook her head. "No. I won't put anyone else in the position I'm in until I have more to go on."

"Don't go off investigating on your own," he said.

"Does this mean you are willing to entertain the notion that I may not be guilty?"

"I might entertain the notion. That doesn't mean you aren't my prime suspect."

Lindsay thought that sounded rather melodramatic. She opened the door to her Rover. "Fine, just as long as you're still looking elsewhere." She got in, closed the door, and started the engine. Kaufman turned and walked back into the Public Safety Building. Lindsay wondered what had set him so doggedly on her trail.

"No, Lindsay. No. Forget that. We have enough trouble without you trying to accuse an associate dean of theft."

"Look, Frank, we have talked with everyone who was here when the artifacts were unpacked. I didn't think of him, because he was here the following day. But he knew about them, didn't he?"

"I didn't talk to him about the artifacts. We talked about extra space for the department. That's all, so drop it. You know what he thinks about storing artifacts in university space. You think I'd casually tell him we got a shipment of unprovenanced artifacts and are storing them here? Unless you told him, he didn't know."

"It's a thought."

"Forget it. Concentrate on where we're going to find the money for new computers."

"So, Reed and Trey have talked to you?"

"Yes, and I can't believe that Trey convinced him. They said that you and Stevie are willing to donate money from your budgets."

"Yes," said Lindsay. "I really think it might be a good idea to chip in. You know, create a little social cohesion in the department."

"Maybe. I don't like attracting attention by spending a

lot of money right now."

"Do you get the *Journal of Historical Archaeology*?" Lindsay asked.

"No, but it's in the departmental library."

"The issue I'm looking for is missing."

"I'm sure Kenneth subscribes to it," Frank said.

Lindsay thought it wise not to tell Frank about any suspicion she might have of Kerwin, especially in view of the suspicions she had just raised about Einer. Frank admonished her once more as she went out the door not to involve Einer. Lindsay said nothing, and she could see by the look on Frank's face that he was uneasy.

Lindsay passed Kenneth Kerwin's door. It was cracked open, but he wasn't there. She looked up and down the hallway and into the main office. No one was in sight. She slipped into his office and stood there for a moment. The uneasy feeling of standing with her back to the door made her move aside, almost behind the door. She scanned his desk and his shelves and saw what she was looking for. There were two identical volumes of the missing journal side by side. She took one copy from the shelf and moved the books closer together to cover the gap just as she heard Kerwin's voice in the main office.

Lindsay held her breath. She could hear her heartbeat in her ears. She stood still for a moment, then eased herself farther behind the door and listened. She could hear him talking to Frank. He was still angry over the vote. It sounded as though Frank was trying to leave the main office, so that meant Kerwin would be facing the door. He would see her if she left. Damn. She looked briefly over his office. There was no closet in which to secret herself, no window to climb out—not that either of those options would work anyway. She stood motionless, barely breathing. Abruptly, their arguing stopped, and Kerwin came marching into his office. Lindsay's heart stopped. She clutched the journal behind her back. Just as suddenly, he marched out again, and Lindsay could hear him following Frank down the hall and, presumably, into the men's room. Lindsay wasted no time. She slipped out the door and almost ran down to her office by the back way.

She closed the door and sat down at her desk, breathing hard, not from exertion but fright. What in the world was I thinking? she asked herself. That has got to be the most appalling bit of behavior I've carried out in a long time— secretly going into a fellow faculty member's office and absconding with a piece of personal property. The fact that one of the copies probably belonged to the department was a minor technicality.

She opened the journal to Kerwin's article. It was not long, a simple analysis of the importance of the Rayburn Mill site to the creation of several present-day communities. There was a map showing the location of the site and nearby communities within a ten-mile radius. An accompanying aerial photograph showed the remnants of the ancient connecting roadbeds. It was interesting—Kerwin was not a sloppy researcher.

The site was on a river. The old roads led to each community like the spokes of a wheel. The former relationships of the communities to one another and to the old textile mill were lost to current memory. The old roads grown over and new ones leading elsewhere indicated shifted patterns of economic focus. There was a footnote citing Shirley Foster as the source of information on the way textiles produced at the mill were used and of their importance to European textile manufacturing. The citation was referenced as a personal communication. There was nothing odd or unusual about that. Researchers often cite information received in conversations and correspondence with colleagues. Kerwin never denied knowing or even working with Shirley Foster on a professional basis.

What, Lindsay wondered, did Kerwin not want her to see?

The only reason she was suspicious of him was because of the photograph in which he seemed to be looking adoringly at Shirley. That could be nothing, or it could be that he simply thought her to be a beautiful woman, which she was. The fact that he seemed to be hiding the journal could have been an unfortunate coincidence. And what did it matter anyway? She had more pressing concerns—like her exhausted finances. She opened her drawer to look for the bottle of Tums she had bought that morning.

Lindsay put the journal and the Tums in her briefcase and saw her checkbook lying inside. She took it out and thumbed through the checks. She knew buying the parcel of land would make things tight for a while, especially in view of the work she was doing to renovate her cabin. But owning the source of the stream was a good investment.

She had left a cushion in her savings account for emergencies, but she hadn't expected the $10,000 emergency that her well going dry had presented. Now there was the other half of the bill for the well, the monthly payments for the filtration system and the payments for her original parcel of land, not to mention Mandrake's upkeep. And there were the payments for the Rover. At the time she bought it, she could well afford an expensive automobile, but now—she reached for the phone and called the Ford dealer a few miles from where she lived.

"Well, hey, Miss Chamberlain. You going to let me talk you into trading that old Land Rover for a new Explorer?"

"Yes."

"What?"

Lindsay smiled. He clearly was making a joke and didn't expect that. "It will have to be a used Explorer. I want to lower my monthly payments substantially."

"Tell me what you want, and I'll get on the computer right away."

Lindsay gave him a list of things she would like to have but emphasized the importance of keeping the cost down.

"No problem," he said. "You have a color you particularly like?"

"Oh, if a green one comes along, like the Rover, I'd like that. But right now, I'd accept one with just the primer."

He laughed. "I'll give you a call in a couple of days."

Lindsay hung up the phone. She felt better. She gathered up her purse and briefcase and walked outside to her Rover. She would go home and go through her grandfather's papers and visit with her brother.

Lindsay pulled onto the road and started to turn down the highway toward her home but instead turned in the opposite direction. There were still a few hours of light left, and she decided to visit the Rayburn site.

It wasn't far, just across the line into Dover County. She'd been there before. The excavation of the site had been finished for several years, but the manager's house hadn't been located. Some of the students working on the site had come up with an idea of where it might be. Lindsay had helped them dig a few test trenches, but in the end they had failed to find anything.

Lindsay turned off onto the dirt road that led to the Rayburn Mill site. The road was still in use by the occupants of the one house off it, a large gray structure under a grove of trees. Past the house, the road became overgrown, badly eroded, and rugged. She drove the Rover as far as she could, got out, and walked the rest of the way.

Not much was left of the site. The rock foundation of the factory itself was overgrown. The filled-in squares of the once excavated row houses boasted a thick carpet of tall weeds waving in the breeze—all that was left of the dwellings where several generations of factory workers had lived. Lindsay remembered the student who analyzed the animal bones collected from the rear of the house sites.

The workers' diet had included chicken, rabbit, deer, and squirrel—indicating a significant hunting component in their personal economics. There had probably been gardens, too, but Lindsay didn't recall if any had been described in the research report.

The whole site was surrounded by woods. A river flowed by the place where the factory once stood. There were no boats on it now, but during the time of the mill's operation, the river was the route for taking the mill's wares to the coast for shipment to markets around the world. Across the river, thick woods now grew. The site that, according to Kerwin's article, had once been a bustling focus of commerce was now a peaceful place in the process of being reclaimed by nature.

Lindsay didn't know what she hoped to accomplish by coming here—find some clue to Kerwin's behavior? What? Did she *need* to find a clue to Kerwin's behavior? She shrugged and walked around the place, visualizing what it was like when it was alive. She could make out one of the old roadbeds through the woods. There was something about old roadbeds that seemed to last forever: the faint dip in the ground, the slightly shorter trees, the bare remnants of the road's sides—like a ghostly avenue superimposed over the woods. She smiled and stepped back onto a place where there was no ground. She fell into darkness.

Chapter 16

LINDSAY LANDED ON her feet, jarring her entire frame, and collapsed to the ground. For a moment the breath was knocked out of her and she gasped involuntarily, trying to get her lungs working again. In the next moment a wave of pain went up through her bones. When the pain left and she caught her breath, she stood up on shaky legs and looked around her. She was surrounded by dirt walls.

"Oh, damn, not again," she cried and looked up through a round hole at sky and tree canopies. "The well. Damn, I forgot about the well." Why, she thought, hadn't they filled it in? "Damn."

She stood on the dry well bottom of soft earth and forest litter and tested her legs. She felt her arms. She seemed to be all right. She had landed on her feet, and her skeleton had absorbed the shock of the fall. Had she landed on her side, she might have been seriously injured.

How to fall correctly was one of the things her mother taught her. "You will fall off your horse sooner or later," she had told her. "Try to land on your feet. If you are going over headfirst, you need to break your fall with your hands, so don't have your reins wrapped around them."

Once, on the rare occasion of her mother teaching a riding class, she was giving the same instruction to a little boy. The boy's father overheard her and came marching over. "Don't teach him to fall!" he had shouted at her. "That's teaching him to fail!" Her mother looked at the man for several moments, raking her gaze over him from head to foot before she spoke. "That's the stupidest philosophy I've ever heard. Falling isn't a failure. It's obeying the laws of gravity when you get thrown off balance. Are you going to explain your school of thought to the horse?"

Her mother, however, had given her no instructions on getting out of a well. "I don't suppose anybody's up there?" Lindsay shouted. Her question was met with silence.

The old well was less than twenty feet deep. If the dirt walls weren't too soft, she could climb out. Lindsay felt the sides with her fingertips. The walls felt like sandpaper-hard earth. It probably wouldn't cave in on her, but it might be hard to get hand- and footholds. About four feet from the top, she saw a root growing from the wall. That could be good. She fished in her pockets and only came up with a quarter. She had left her keys in the Rover, and her pocketknife was in her purse.

"I'm going to have to start wearing a tool belt everywhere," she said aloud. Damn, she hadn't told a soul where she was going.

She took the quarter and began scraping a toehold. The earth was hard, not impossible, but it would be slow going. She dug toeholds up the side of the wall as far as she could reach, aiming for the root.

Lindsay thrust a toe into one of the holes she had scraped out and began to climb, alternately using the gouges for fingers and toes. This isn't that hard, she thought. I'm becoming really good at escaping from holes in the ground. As she climbed, she scraped out more handholds. Her arms and hands were becoming exhausted.

The earth was softer nearer the top, and the digging

went faster—so did the climbing. She was almost to the root when one of the holds crumbled under her weight, pulling her off balance. She grabbed for the root as she started to fall, holding on to it like a rope, dangling from the side of the well. She hung there for a moment before the root started pulling out of the wall like a thread unraveling from a sweater. Suddenly, she was back at the bottom of the well, holding a long piece of root in her hand. The action had loosened the soil, and now there was a deep gash down the side of the well.

Lindsay examined the loose dirt, wondering if there was a danger of the well caving in. She felt her heart pound as fear took hold of it. The light overhead was growing dim as the sun began its descent. It wouldn't be long before she had no light. Already, it was growing darker in the well. She toyed for a moment with the idea of throwing the end of the root up and seeing if she could snag something, an idea immediately abandoned as stupid.

It was not until Lindsay determined that the gash had made her original path too unstable and she should just start again that she realized she no longer had her quarter—not a great tool, but the only one she had. Lindsay was determined she was not going to spend the night in the well, even if she had to use her fingernails to claw her way to the top.

The quarter wasn't visible and Lindsay searched the ground, feeling through the leaves and pine straw with her hands. Her fingers stung as bits of stems pricked them as she hunted. Something hard scraped her flesh, and she drew back her hand. Blood oozed from a thin scrape across the tips of her fingers. She dug through the leaves for the offending object. It was a railroad spike. She grinned, forgetting about her scraped fingers in the joy of finding such a useful tool.

Lindsay went back to work again, digging toeholds with the spike. The work went faster. She climbed, dug more holds, and occasionally stuck the spike in the side of the well and pulled herself up. She was almost to the top when a hand appeared in front of her face.

"Can I help you?"

Lindsay was startled for a moment and stared at the hand. It was a woman's hand. She followed it up and looked into the face of Sheriff Irene Varnadore. Lindsay gratefully took her hand, and the sheriff pulled as Lindsay levered herself up and out of the well.

"Thanks," she said, leaning over, breathing heavily.

The sheriff shrugged. "You were almost out. How did you get in?"

"Stupidity and carelessness," said Lindsay, brushing the caked dirt from her clothes as best she could.

Irene Varnadore didn't look like a sheriff, dressed as she was in plum slacks and pink blouse. Law enforcement duds were remarkably defeminizing.

"Are you hurt?" Irene asked.

"I don't think so. Just dirty, exhausted, and humiliated."

Irene looked at her cut hand. "You need to wash that," she said, adding almost hesitantly, "I just made a pot of beef stew. Would you like to come to my place and clean up and have dinner?"

"That sounds good. Yes, I would." Then it came to her to wonder about her good fortune. "How did you come to be here?"

"I live in that house a mile back. You must have passed it. I saw a vehicle drive by. There's nothing down here but this old place. At first I thought it was just kids looking for a place to park, then there was something about the Rover that seemed familiar. I thought I'd check it out."

"I'm grateful you did."

Irene shrugged again. "I really didn't do anything."

"It's a comfort to know that somebody noticed me passing by."

Lindsay climbed into her Rover and followed the sheriff

to her house, a modern-looking modular design with gray siding and a steep, slanted roof with dormer windows on the upper floor.

Inside, the look was southwestern, with geometric motif rugs on pine floors, wood and leather sofa and chairs, cactus, and driftwood accessories. The house was uncluttered and clean. Lindsay left her shoes at the door.

"There's a bathroom down that hall and to the right. Towels and washcloths are in the wicker cabinet."

Lindsay followed her directions into an old-fashioned bath with a pedestaled lavatory, claw-footed tub, and a brass towel stand. She chose a matching rose-colored towel and washcloth from the cabinet and washed her face and arms, dusted off her clothes, and cleaned her cut fingers. She fished in her purse for a brush and ran it through her tangled hair. She found a sponge in the cabinet and cleaned the bathroom of the dirt she had brought in. She thought she should call Sinjin and tell him she would be late but remembered he was out with Sally.

Lindsay followed the sounds and found Irene setting a tureen of beef stew on the dining table set with silver, china bowls, and iced tea. This room looked older than the rest of the house. The wood in the flooring was a larger cut than in the other floors and was fitted with wooden pegs. The brick in the fireplace was old, with a newer walnut mantel holding an assortment of photographs.

"Go ahead and sit down," said Irene. "I'll just get the cornbread." She left and returned shortly with round steaming bread on a plate.

"Were you expecting company?" asked Lindsay, suddenly feeling like she was taking someone's seat.

"Jesse—he's a highway patrolman I see—we had a date to eat and watch a couple of movies. Nothing much. There's a pileup halfway between here and Atlanta, and he had to go. I heard about it on the scanner," she added.

"It was nice of you to ask me in." Lindsay spread the napkin in her lap. They ate the first few bites in silence. The beef was tender, and the vegetables were cut in large chunks. "This is so good," said Lindsay.

"It's my grandmother's recipe. The bread, too," Irene told her.

"This looks like an old part of the house—"

"It is," said Irene. "My grandparents bought it in the thirties. It was old then. They built onto it. Didn't follow the original design, though."

"I wonder if this was the mill manager's house," Lindsay mused. "Was this part of the old textile mill?"

"I don't know. Could be, I guess."

"Archaeologists tried to find the manager's house and couldn't. It'd be interesting if it was here all along, just changed with the times."

"I heard Luke Ferris asked you for help." Irene didn't seem displeased, just curious.

"Yes, but I'm not sure there's anything I can do," Lindsay said.

"Did he tell you his story? You don't need to answer, I can tell by the look on your face he did." Irene shook her head.

Lindsay tried to look noncommittal and thought she probably failed. "It's just that I know his sister, and him, too, a little. I just can't imagine it."

"People do funny things. His story's weak all the way around. Whatever I thought of Shirl, I don't believe for a minute she planned a rendezvous with him."

"It seems unlikely, but things like that do happen," said Lindsay.

"Maybe. But Shirl's great love was Will Patterson. She might cheat on her husband but not on him."

"You all used to be friends, didn't you?"

Irene nodded. "Sort of. When we were in high school I felt honored that she chose me as her friend. But I was just a sidekick. Shirl was the main attraction. At the time I thought some of her starshine would rub off on me. It didn't. I'll bet you were popular in school."

"Not especially," responded Lindsay.

"What, you weren't a cheerleader, prom queen?"

Lindsay shook her head. "Not even close. I didn't even have a date for the junior prom. Most of my extracurricular activities centered around horses. My mother raises and trains Arabians. I did a lot of horse show stuff. That and tagging after my grandfather on digs."

"I went to the proms, but Shirl always got me the dates. I think I resented her for that."

"Weren't you relieved to graduate and find out the world isn't like high school?"

"In a way. But when you keep the same circle of friends, it's hard to break the typecasting. I even dated Will myself for a while, after Shirl started seeing Tom. Didn't work out."

"Why didn't Shirley just marry Will in the first place?" Lindsay asked.

"She should have. Her parents had her life laid out for her on a blueprint, and she just went along. I guess I did feel sorry for her some—and for Chris, too. Their parents treated him like the original screwup. His father was furious over his opening that little shop instead of going to work for him. I think Stewart Pryor has dynastic delusions or something."

Irene took another bite of cornbread and a sip of tea. "Getting into law enforcement was the best thing that ever happened to me. That and Granny leaving me this house and property. Mom and Dad tried to get me to give it to my brother and his wife. They told me that, since he had a family, this'd be a great place for their grandchildren to grow up. They had it all figured out. Buster would pay me something every month. Like I'd ever see a penny. Earleen actually came over to measure the windows for drapes."

"They must've been surprised when you refused," said Lindsay.

Irene grinned. "You'd have thought I was the most selfish bitch alive." She stopped smiling. "I wasn't going to be second best anymore. Like you said, life's not high school. I told Mom and Dad that I wanted a family, and if Buster and Earleen couldn't house their family, they should stop having kids. I said that in front of Earleen, too." Irene smiled again. She was attractive when she smiled. Lindsay thought the coroner was right, that perhaps she just wasn't at her best around Tom Foster. "You dating anybody?" she asked Lindsay abruptly.

Lindsay shook her head. "Not now. He didn't like my detective work. But I miss him," she added.

"This guy I'm seeing is nice. I kind of hope something comes of it. I'd still like to have a family. I saw where that actress Adrienne Barbeau had twins at fifty. That kind of gives me hope."

"I imagine it was very hard on her."

"I suppose so. You ever want kids?"

"Yeah, I do. Right now, I'd even settle for a niece or nephew."

"You have brothers and sisters, then?" asked Irene.

"I have a brother. He's visiting me now. He's a nice guy."

"What's he do?"

"He's a smokejumper," Lindsay said with pride.

"Really? I got a cousin who's a hotshot. Name's Zeke Varnadore. Ask your brother if he knows him. It's a pretty tight community of people, I understand."

"I'll ask him. I hate to admit it, but I don't know a lot about what he does. What's a hotshot?"

"Ground crew who fight the fires. Similar to smokejumpers, but they don't get to the fire by parachute." Irene seemed pleased to tell her. "What's your brother's name?"

"Sinjin Chamberlain."

"Sinjin? I don't think I've ever heard that before."

"Short for St. John," Lindsay told her.

"St. John. I like that. It's better than Buster." They both laughed.

Lindsay finished her stew and the last of her cornbread. "This was great. I thought I was going to be in that well all night."

"What were you doing at the old mill?"

Lindsay shrugged. "It was a fellow faculty member's dig. I read his report, and something about it bothered me. I came out to see if I could figure out what." If Irene thought that was an odd explanation, she didn't say so. Lindsay wouldn't have blamed her if she had. It was an odd explanation.

The phone rang and Irene got up to answer it. She came back and sat down. "That was one of my deputies. I've had them dragging the lake for Shirl's car, and they just found it. Would you like to go with me and have a look?"

The lakeside site was lit with large spotlights that shone off a low fog hovering over the water. As Lindsay and Irene approached through the woods, the car was emerging from the fog, pulled by a large tow truck with a winch. The first thought Lindsay had when she saw the car was what a shame someone had pushed it into the lake. It was a dark blue Jaguar and had water pouring out of every crack and opening. A deputy started to open the door.

"Wait," Irene told him. She peered in the window. Lindsay followed her.

There wasn't anything on either the front or back seat. The keys were in the ignition. It looked like the gearshift was in neutral.

Irene carefully opened the driver's side door and took the keys. "Let's have a look in the trunk," she said.

The trunk was full of water, but it was leaking out quickly. Other than what might have been a soggy, flat cardboard gift box, the trunk was empty.

"What do you think happened to the money?" asked Lindsay as Irene drove her back to her Rover.

"Right now, I'm assuming Luke Ferris squirreled it away somewhere. We haven't found any hidden assets. But that doesn't mean he hasn't spent it or maybe has it hidden, trying to figure out how to launder it."

"How does one go about laundering money, anyway?" asked Lindsay.

"Put it through some legitimate business, falsify receipts. It's best if you have a cash business. I knew a guy who stole fifty thousand from his employer. He took up painting with watercolors and went to craft fairs, selling his pictures. His cousin ratted on him. He said the paintings were so bad, no one could possibly be buying them."

They both laughed.

"Luke Ferris has no way to launder any money," Lindsay said.

"Granted, he may not know how. But that doesn't mean he doesn't have it stashed away somewhere. He could be afraid to spend it."

"What was Shirley doing with all that money anyway?" asked Lindsay.

"Who knows? Something she didn't want Tom or her father to find out, that's for sure."

Irene pulled up beside Lindsay's Rover and stopped. Lindsay put a hand on the door, ready to get out.

"I'd get a tetanus shot if I were you," said Irene.

"I keep up-to-date," said Lindsay. "You run into all kinds of things on digs."

"I imagine so. Look, I've read about your troubles in the papers."

"Yeah. I'm trying to figure out some way to clear my name. There's this campus policeman who's sure I'm guilty."

"Kaufman. I know him. He's a friend of the guy I date." For a moment, as Lindsay looked at Irene, she wondered if Sheriff Varnadore had set him onto her, then dismissed the idea. "The reason he thinks you're guilty is someone at the university has been putting a bug in his ear. Says they've been trying to get something on you for a long time and can't."

Lindsay opened her mouth, shocked. "Why?"

"I don't know. I told him you have a good reputation among law enforcement people."

"Did he tell you who said that about me?"

Irene shook her head. "Look, I think you're all right. I'll try to find out who it is, if you want."

"I would be grateful. Thank you."

"You tell me anything you dig up on Shirl's murderer. I think it's the Ferris kid, but I'm not looking to hang him just to close out a case."

"I will, but I've been trying to avoid getting involved. People just keep coming to me. Thanks so much for your hospitality," said Lindsay. "I was in need."

"My pleasure," Irene said.

Someone at the university, thought Lindsay on the drive home. Who? Student, faculty, staff, administrator? Probably not a student; she couldn't imagine Kaufman giving a student that much credibility, but you never know. She turned into her driveway. Through the trees she saw a light on. Sinjin was home. She smiled to herself. Even with everything going on, it was nice to have him visit.

Sinjin stood in the middle of Lindsay's kitchen with his mouth open. "Am I going to have to hire a keeper for you? First the basement, and now you tell me you've fallen down a well. Let me see those hands." He shook his head at her broken fingernails. "I'm really getting to see Derrick's point of view."

Lindsay tried to ignore his ribbing. She didn't want a lecture, either. She took back her hands. "Did you and Sally have a good time?"

"As a matter of fact, we did. What were you doing wandering around out in the middle of nowhere, at a site that's already finished?"

"I don't know. Something bothered me about Kerwin's site."

"Exactly what bothered you? You didn't like his methodology?"

Lindsay ignored his sarcasm. "No. I can't put my finger on it. I have this vague feeling it has something to do with Shirley Foster, but I can't imagine what."

Sinjin grabbed the colas he had poured for the two of them and guided Lindsay to the living room. "Didn't you say she was some textile expert? That was a textile mill—"

"And she gave him a personal communication—" Lindsay stopped still.

"What?" asked Sinjin, putting down her drink.

Lindsay fished in her briefcase and pulled out the journal, flipping to the references in Kerwin's article. "That's it. Personal communication from Shirley Foster, November 14, 1994. That was the day she disappeared. She went out with him to the Rayburn Mill site. That's what she told her secretary—that she was going to Rayburn. Shirley's secretary misunderstood and thought she meant Rabun County in north Georgia. The little weasel never told anyone that he was the last person to see her alive. That's why he was trying to keep me from seeing the article."

"Do you think he killed Shirley there and moved the body?" asked Sinjin.

Lindsay sat down. Put like that, it seemed unlikely. She had no love for Kenneth Kerwin, but she couldn't imagine him killing anyone or having the stomach to try and dispose of a body in such a grizzly way.

"You in there?" asked Sinjin, waving his hand in front of her face.

"I was just thinking. None of this makes sense."

"You work that out while you were down in the well?"

Lindsay grinned. "What did you and Sally do?"

"She took me to downtown Athens. They were having a jazz concert in the street. We went to a sidewalk cafe and listened while we ate. Then we went to the Civic Center and took in *Cats*. I'd never seen it; not bad. After that we had tea at Sally's." He smiled, showing a row of straight white teeth. "I had a good time. I'd forgotten what dates are like. We even ran across Brian and what's-her-name. I think he was a little jealous."

"Sally must have had a great time," Lindsay said.

"I'd like to think she did. She's a nice kid."

"She's not a kid."

"I know." He grinned. "Did you know she has a Mickey Mouse teakettle? One of Mickey's round ears forms the handle." He made a circle with his hands. "You, know, I'd forgotten you can actually spend time with a woman and not argue."

"Sally's always a breath of fresh air." Lindsay stood up and stretched. "I'm exhausted. Climbing out of an abandoned well is hard work. I think I'll go to bed. I'm sorry I'm such a bad host; I had hoped when you came to visit me, you'd enjoy yourself."

"Actually, it hasn't been half bad. Before you go upstairs, I've got some pictures for you to look at, if you feel like it. I've been going over Papaw's papers and looking at the picture you drew—you're pretty good, by the way. I came up with some photographs."

Sinjin laid out a book with pages marked with Post-It notes, along with several photographs in a folder. Lindsay looked at each one. Most were fuzzy and looked like they could all have been the face she had drawn. Many were pictures of the archaeology crew working or posing for the photographer. Lindsay's grandfather was in several of them. One picture was of the main archaeologists with workers resting in the background. She paid particular attention to the clothes and shoes. All wore work clothes. One had his legs crossed. With her hand lens she examined the shoes. They all had on more or less the same type of shoes, but what she was looking for was an indication of a wear pattern on the soles similar to the wear pattern belonging to the skeleton. Unfortunately, the pictures weren't clear enough to see any details.

She looked through the pictures again. This pass, she noticed a man standing, leaning on a shovel. His whole frame was skewed, causing his left hip and shoulder to be higher than his right. She took her lens and examined the face.

"This one," she said to Sinjin. "Look how his skeleton is asymmetrical."

Sinjin took the picture and looked. He turned it over. "It has the names of the archaeologists but just says 'and diggers' for the others." He handed it back to Lindsay and she set it aside and looked again through the other pictures, looking for the same face. A picture that showed several workers seated in a row showed the same man. Lindsay turned the picture over. Names were listed on the back, with the heading L-R. She read the third name.

"Hank Roy Creasey. Is that what it says?"

"Looks like it," said Sinjin. "Do you think there's any chance of finding out anything about him?"

"First, I need to establish that this is the picture of the man in the crate."

"How you going to do that?"

"Actually, that won't be hard. I can do that tomorrow."

She picked up the folder and flipped through the photographs Sinjin hadn't marked.

"Maggie sent most of those," said Sinjin. "I called a few days ago and asked her. I didn't tell her what they were for."

"How was she? Did she say anything about what's going on with the artifacts and the skeleton?"

"She had seen the story in the newspaper," Sinjin said. "She was worried at first. I told her it was really nothing—that it was just such an odd story that the newspapers picked it up. I told her the skeleton might have been from an Indian burial and was just wrapped in old clothes. I didn't think lying to her would hurt, and it might save her some grief."

Lindsay agreed. "Did you talk to Elizabeth and Lenore?"

"Oh, yes." He smiled. "I couldn't get off the phone without talking to them. They're fine. They asked about you."

"I just hate this," Lindsay said.

"Yeah, so do I."

There were several photographs of her grandfather when he was young—some with various family members, some with her father, one of him with a young couple with their arms intertwined. He was grinning broadly in all of them. Many of the photos Maggie had sent were more recent, and a few were of Lindsay and her grandfather. She smiled as she went through them.

"You were a cute little thing," said Sinjin. "I like the one where you're holding the string of fish."

Lindsay remembered the trip. Her grandfather hadn't liked fishing particularly, and it was a rare trip with him, her father, and Sinjin. She was about five and Sinjin fourteen. They all were grinning.

"I didn't catch all those fish myself, did I?"

"Not all of them. We gave them to you to hold."

She looked at her grandfather's face. He looked amused, not like someone who years previously had committed murder. It seemed to Lindsay that if a man like her grandfather had done such a thing, it would show on his face like a scar.

"This looks like Maggie's husband." Lindsay showed him an Ocmulgee picture with her grandfather and his brother-in-law Billy, standing in front of a mound.

"I think Papaw gave Billy a job when the mines closed after a cave-in or something like that."

Lindsay looked at the next picture. It was of Sinjin when he was about seven, her father, and a very beautiful woman. Her father was laughing and had an arm around the woman's shoulder. They all looked happy. Lindsay realized that the woman was Sinjin's mother. It was odd to see her father behaving so lovingly toward someone who was not her mother. This picture must have been taken about a year before she died. Odd how events happen. If Sinjin's mother hadn't died, Lindsay would never have been born. It was a strange thing to think about.

"This is a nice picture," said Lindsay. "Do you remember it?"

"A little."

Sinjin was looking at Lindsay rather intensely. She wondered if he was wondering what she was thinking. She went to the next picture in the stack. This one was of her graduation party. She had just received a combined Bachelor of Arts and Bachelor of Science degree and her father and mother were giving her a party at her grandfather's house. It was a few months before he died. He was ill at the time and was sitting in a lawn chair, wrapped in a blanket, even though it was June. All her great-aunts were there, Maggie, Elizabeth, and Lenore. So was Sinjin. Her mother was cutting a cake. She remembered that it was a happy day. Her grandfather had been proud of her. She started to put the picture down but was struck by the look of pain on her grandfather's face. Funny, she remembered that he was feeling really good that day. Then she noticed it. He was staring out at the kudzu patch. Lindsay looked up at her brother. He had seen it, too, and was waiting for her to notice it.

"What do you think?" she said, her voice so soft it was almost to herself.

"I think he knew what was out there, and toward the end of his life, it preyed on his mind."

Chapter 17

LINDSAY STOPPED AT a photo shop on the way to her office and ordered two enlargements of the picture of Sinjin with their father and his mother, one copy for Sinjin and one for herself. She wanted to do something for him, something that showed him how much she liked his being here, something that showed him she understood him a little better. She also wanted to remind herself that Sinjin and her father had a family before she and her mother arrived, and that his family was important, too.

Lindsay was not looking forward to going to her office today. She planned to confront Kerwin. After pulling into her parking space, she sat for a moment, gathering her strength, rehearsing in her mind what she was going to say to him. When she did get out and head to her office, she found Rachael Bienvenido standing outside her door, pacing.

"Can I help you?" Lindsay asked, unlocking her door.

"Yes. It's about Dr. Cardell's analysis," said Rachael, following her into the office. She sat down in a chair, raking a hand through her short hair.

Lindsay seated herself behind her desk. "That's the faunal analysis Robin is working on?"

"Yes, she tells me they are going to be late. That's not so much of a problem, but she also tells me that Amy made errors in the calculations."

"She did, but I've been correcting them. I've also

checked her bone identifications, and I'm helping Robin finish up."

Rachael seemed to relax. "I'm glad about that. Aura Cardell is a friend as well as a colleague, and I feel responsible."

"I always check up on the work the faunal lab does. The students who work there know to come to me if there are any problems."

"That's what I wanted to hear. I'm talking to Aura this afternoon, and I wanted to be able to give her a good report."

"You can do that. I'm sorry about the problem with Amy."

Rachael shrugged. "Girls these days. They fall in love too easily and give up their dreams. Who can figure them?"

"Rachael, did you know Shirley Foster?"

Rachael leaned forward in her chair. "Lindsay, take my advice. Get off this—what did Reed call you, Nancy Drew? Drop this Nancy Drew thing. You're a good researcher. When you say you're identifying animal bones, I don't worry. I know it will be correct. This other stuff is doing you no good at all. Forget it." She rose and left Lindsay's office.

Lindsay sighed. Perhaps she should. But instead of taking Rachael's advice, she took out the photograph with Hank Roy Creasey and trotted up to Trey's office.

"Chamberlain, come in. What can I do for you?" asked Trey, pulling up a chair beside his desk for her. "You making out OK these days?"

"As well as can be expected. How's the computer acquisition coming?"

"Frank wants to wait. Something's going on. I don't know what."

"Too bad. I was kind of looking forward to a new computer. Anyway, I have a computer question."

"Shoot."

Lindsay laid the photograph of the skull from the newspaper and the one of Hank Roy Creasey down on the table. "They have special software in the medical examiner's office, but I thought there might be a way you could do what I need faster. I would like to superimpose these two images, the skull and the face. They have to both be the same size image—"

"Hmm. Yeah, I can do a quick job with a paint program."

Lindsay watched as he scanned each photograph into his computer at 1000 dpi and brought up the images into a paint program, placing the two images on the same screen. She tried to follow the menus as he moved the mouse with the ease of an expert and selected from the apparently hundreds of things the program could do. First, he measured them, then resampled them, making them equivalent in size. Next, he drew a marquee around each one and selected "transparent" from a pull-down menu. Finally, he overlaid one image on top of the other. The entire procedure took perhaps ten minutes from the initial scan to the printout. Lindsay was impressed.

The composite that came out of Trey's printer was an eerie face of bone and flesh, a face with eyes inside bony sockets. The bones of the skeleton's nose and cheeks fit perfectly over the nose and cheeks of Hank Roy Creasey. The orbits were directly over the eyes, the teeth matched perfectly, as did the chin, jawline, and forehead.

"Looks good to me," said Trey. "So, this is the infamous stowaway in the crate?"

Lindsay nodded. "Yes, it's him. His name is Hank Roy Creasey. Other than that, I have no idea who he is."

"But now you have a name. That's pretty good."

Lindsay agreed—that was pretty good. "Thanks for doing this," she said. "That's amazing—and using an ordinary paint program."

"That's kind of a new use for it. Say, Chamberlain," Trey said, as Lindsay rose to leave. "You know my friend who is coming down to talk about the LaBelle?"

Lindsay nodded.

"Well, she and her husband like to dance, and I was wondering if, uh, well, do you dance?"

Lindsay grinned broadly. "Yeah, I dance."

"Did I say something funny?"

Lindsay shook her head. "No. Are you asking me to go dancing?"

"Trying to."

"I love to dance. If I'm not in jail, I'd like to go."

"Things aren't that bad, are they?" asked Trey.

"Depends on who you talk to. If you ask one of the detectives on campus, it's only a matter of time."

"It sounds absurd. What are you doing about it?"

"I'm looking for the machine that's pouring out all the smoke. One's bound to turn up. Thanks again for your help. Let me know about the dancing plans."

Lindsay put the photos in her office before she went to see Kerwin. She was not looking forward to it, but it was one element in the puzzle that had to be cleared up before she could make any sense out of the rest of it. Maybe after that she could leave it alone.

Kerwin was sitting at his desk writing on a pad of yellow paper. He didn't use a computer or typewriter but wrote his articles longhand and had Edwina type them. Lindsay walked in and closed the door behind her.

"Please don't stand on ceremony, come in and sit down," said Kerwin.

"You were the last person to see Shirley Foster alive. You let the police bust their butts looking for any sign of her in Rabun County, a good seventy miles from here. You knew she meant the Rayburn site when she told her secretary where she was going."

Kerwin blanched and looked over to his bookshelf.

"Why did you hide that article? Did you kill her?" Lindsay asked.

"No, damn you, no. What are you trying to do to me?"

"There's proof you saw her on that last day. It's in the article you've been trying like the dickens to keep from me. You said you didn't know her—"

Kerwin interrupted her. "I did not. I said I didn't know her well. I knew her professionally—"

"Exactly. You knew her only professionally, yet there is a picture of the two of you at a departmental barbeque that says otherwise. What did you do—ask her to go out in the middle of nowhere, make a pass, and when she turned you down, you got furious and killed her?"

"No, you've got it all wrong. I . . . I . . . She wasn't inter-ested in me, yes, but, I . . ." Kerwin looked at his desk and up at Lindsay. "God, I only tried to kiss her. That was all." He sat, the two of them looking at each other. "What are you going to do?"

Lindsay picked up the phone. "You are going to tell your story to Sheriff Irene Varnadore."

"No, I can't." He pulled the phone out of her reach.

"It will sound better coming from you than from me." She leaned across the desk and took the phone away from him and dialed Irene's office number.

"Sheriff Varnadore," said Lindsay, "Kenneth Kerwin, one of our faculty, has some information about Shirley Foster's last day and wants to tell you about it." She handed him the phone. Lindsay could hear the sheriff saying "Hello? Hello?" as Kerwin stared at the phone. Lindsay guided it to his ear.

"Sheriff," he squeaked. "Ah, Sheriff, I just realized something. When Shirley Foster told her secretary where she was going, she meant the Rayburn Mill site and not Rabun County. She, uh, wanted to see the excavation. I showed it to her, we talked, and I left." He paused a moment. "She seemed fine. Happy, even." Pause. "No, no one was there. We were basically finished with the excava-tion. The crew was gone. I left in my car. She was in her

car, and I had assumed she left, too. It was several days later
I heard on the news that she was missing, and I simply never
made the connection." He paused again and smiled up at
Lindsay. "However, Luke Ferris was a member of my field
crew, and I believe he worked for Dr. Foster as well. He
could have followed us." Lindsay narrowed her eyes at him.

"I just wanted to tell you. I didn't know quite what to do,
and Dr. Chamberlain told me that you are the person to talk
to." He paused, listening. "Certainly, I'll hold." He placed
his hand over the mouthpiece. Kerwin was good at the
smug expression. "Well, Dr. Chamberlain, does that meet
with your keen ethical sensibilities?"

"Luke was one of your students. He worked with you.
Have you no loyalty to him?"

"Not if he's a murderer. And if he's not, the truth won't
hurt."

"What about that little truth that you made a pass at her
and she rejected you? Why didn't you tell the sheriff that?"

"It will be your word against mine, and right now you
don't have much credibility." He gave a jerk of his head as
if to add, "so there."

"It will be my word against yours, but people will know
it's true. You aren't a man who hides his feelings well—
like the smug little twist of your mouth that you have now.
They will remember those little social gatherings and professional meetings, how you acted, and the little looks you
gave her. They will know it's true and they will always
wonder if maybe you did it after all."

Kerwin frowned. "You're bluffing."

"What's to bluff?"

"I really doubt you'll be here much longer anyway, Dr.
Chamberlain. I think you'll find your number's up."

"Are you the one whispering in Kaufman's ear?" Lindsay asked.

"Who's Kaufman?" From the look on his face, she was

tempted to believe he really didn't know, but Kerwin was just mean enough to do something like that.

"Kenneth, I allowed you to talk to the sheriff as a courtesy, because you are a fellow faculty member. I could have gone to the sheriff, and she could be the one in here asking you these questions and wondering why you let the police waste all their time and taxpayer money looking in the wrong county. Are you such a mean-spirited bastard you can't see that?"

"I can't see you did me any favor."

"I'm sure you don't." He took his hand from the mouthpiece and listened, frowning. "But I've told you all I know." Pause. "I'm not sure when I'll have the time." Pause. "Yes, I'll make the time." Pause. "This afternoon, yes."

Lindsay smiled and turned and walked out of his office. She could almost feel him staring at her back and wishing his gaze was arrows. She walked to her office, hoping she hadn't gotten Luke into any deeper trouble. But on the other hand, he might be guilty. She wasn't sure that he wasn't. She sat at her desk wondering what to do next when the phone rang.

"Lindsay, it's Derrick. How're you doing?"

"I'm doing fine." She decided not to tell him about falling down the well.

"Lindsay, I've heard a rumor."

It was unlike Derrick to be cryptic or hesitant to speak. The acid in her stomach churned up a notch. "Oh?"

"Actually, it's from a reliable source. It's a done deal."

"What?"

"The dean is making a division out of Anthropology and Archaeology. A separate, but not separate, kind of arrangement. They're bringing in Francisco Lewis to be division head. He plans to bring in some of his own people. Among them, Gerri Chapman."

Lindsay pressed her lips together, as if that would stop the stinging in her eyes. She liked her job—the students, the faunal lab, the forensics. Unconsciously, she pulled open a drawer and fingered the file with all the information she was collecting to apply for tenure. She knew what she had to do to get promotions at the university. She wrote the papers and got them published in the right journals. But this was so out of her control.

"Lindsay?"

"That must have been what Kerwin meant."

"What's that?" asked Derrick.

"Oh, he hinted that I wouldn't be here much longer. Of course, I should have realized something was up when I came in and found Gerri trying out my chair."

"She wasn't—"

"'Fraid so. Derrick, thanks for being the one to tell me."

"Would you like me to come down?"

"Would you?" She leaned forward, holding the receiver tight in her hands.

"If you want."

"Don't you have the film crew coming to start the documentary about the Cold River site?"

"They can start it without me."

Lindsay smiled into the phone. "I would like it very much, but it would also give me a great deal of pleasure to watch you tell about your site on public television."

"Then you come visit me when you can," he said.

"You have a job for me?"

"Yes."

"I'd like that. When I know something about my future, I'll come for a visit."

"How's the problem with the artifacts?" asked Derrick. Lindsay told him everything she knew. She also told him about the conversation she just had with Kerwin. "You think Kerwin is trying to set the police on you?" he asked.

"I thought so. I wouldn't put it past him, but he didn't seem to know what I was talking about when I mentioned the detective's name. I don't know who it is. Derrick, would you do me a favor?"

"Sure."

"I found out that the skeleton in Papaw's crate was a man named Hank Roy C-r-e-a-s-e-y. I'm going to look in the old Macon and Atlanta papers here for his name. I was wondering if you would look in the Kentucky newspaper archives?"

"You're kidding, you found out who it was? Lindsay, you're amazing."

"Sinjin helped a lot."

"Sure, I'll look it up for you. I'll give you a call when I find out something."

"Thanks, Derrick, for everything."

"Sure, baby, take care."

"I will." She started to hang up when she heard him call her name. "Yes?"

"I miss you," he said.

"I miss you too." Lindsay felt tears sting her eyes.

"Do you think we could talk sometime?" he asked.

"I think we could do that."

"Good. I'll free up some time and call you and we'll make some plans."

"That would be good." Lindsay set the phone back on the cradle and stared at it. Derrick was always there when she needed him.

In the basement of the library Lindsay sat down in front of the microfilm reader, looking through 1935 and 1936 editions of the *Macon Telegraph* and the *Atlanta Journal.* She narrowed her search to the years 1935 and 1936 because those were the years on the newspapers wrapping the artifacts and the date stenciled on the crates themselves. Newspapers weren't indexed. She hadn't known that. Her academic research took her exclusively to professional journals and not to newspaper archives. She found out when she asked the librarian in charge of the newspapers where the indexes were. The woman looked at her without speaking, her lips almost, but not quite, turning up in a smile. Lindsay realized immediately what an enormous task it would be to index daily newspapers from their first issue until the present, and most libraries all over the country were understaffed. So, Lindsay was there straining her eyes looking in the microfilm reader for the name Hank Roy Creasey, Hank Creasey, H. R. Creasey, and every spelling she could think of anybody Creasey. She found nothing. It was time to give it up and go home. Maybe Derrick would find a reference in Kentucky, though Creasey could have been from anywhere.

On her way out of the lobby, Lindsay noticed the archivist of the Hargrett Library getting on an elevator. Lindsay stopped in her tracks, turned abruptly, and followed the woman up to her office.

"Mrs. Andrews?" Lindsay said.

"Yes?" The woman looked at her, smiling, ready to answer her questions.

"I was in here a few days ago looking for some clippings, and I overheard you talking to a campus policeman. We in the Archaeology Department have had some of our artifacts stolen and, well, I was wondering if—"

"If we are suffering from the same thing? The answer is yes. Some of our rarest books and maps are missing. The policeman suggested that perhaps I misplaced them."

"Right now, they think I might have, er, misplaced artifacts."

Mrs. Andrews shook her head. "I don't know how they expect to find anything. I read about the artifacts missing from the Archaeology Department and actually called the policeman in charge of our theft. I don't know if he looked for a connection."

"Do you know if any other antiquities are missing on campus?"

The librarian motioned Lindsay into a chair. She sat down at her desk. "I called the museum. They're looking at their inventory again. They haven't found anything missing recently, but you know, about a year ago they had some thefts. I also talked to the Classics Department. They have several things missing. I told the policeman about all of those cases."

"What did he say?"

She stretched out her arms on her desk and linked her fingers. "He thanked me."

"I have another question, and I would like you to forget it after I ask you." Mrs. Andrews raised her eyebrows. Lindsay took a piece of paper and wrote two names on it. "Have either of these men visited the Hargrett Library in the last few months?"

She put on her glasses, which hung from a chain around her neck, and looked at the paper.

"The second name has come on more than one occasion in the past several months to look at the rare books. Don't tell me you suspect him?"

"I have only the thinnest evidence on which to suspect him. That's why I wish you would forget I said anything."

"I like my job here. I won't say a word. But it would be a bad thing if he were involved."

"Yes, it would." Mrs. Andrews didn't ask what she intended to do. Lindsay wouldn't have known what to tell her if she had.

Lindsay was strangely relieved that Kenneth Kerwin hadn't visited the rare book room. As much as she disliked him, she didn't want anyone in Archaeology to be associated with stealing antiquities. On the other hand, it was probably only a coincidence that Ellis Einer had visited the rare book collection from which items were missing and was also present on the day after the artifacts were unpacked in the archaeology lab. As she told Mrs. Andrews, it was the thinnest thread that connected him. But it nagged at her. He was also someone a man like Detective Kaufman would listen to.

Lindsay's phone was ringing when she opened her office door. It was Irene Varnadore.

"I thought you'd like to know, we found a witness who was there on the evening Shirley Foster died," she said.

"Really, someone saw what happened?"

"Yes. I thought you would like to hear her story."

Chapter 18

"**T**HE FOG SETTLED itself above the water like a low ceiling, and the moon shined on it, making it blue gray and everything else bright shades of black and gray. It was raining earlier and the water still dripped off the trees. There weren't no wind, and the water on the lake was still, like a black mirror, a good night for fishing."

Mrs. Lila Poole looked to be in her late sixties, with a head of white hair and a lean, wrinkled face. She sat in the sheriff's office drinking a cup of hot coffee, wearing a pink-checkered house dress. Mrs. Poole moved like a much younger woman. She had sat down in the chair the sheriff brought for her with an ease that showed she still had strength in her legs.

"You were there fishing?" asked Irene.

"Who's she?" Lila pointed a wrinkled finger at Lindsay.

"Dr. Chamberlain. She found Shirley Foster for us. I'd like her to hear your story if you don't mind."

"You want me to tell it again? I told it to your deputy."

"I want you to take your time and tell me everything you remember."

"You going to record it?"

"Yes. Then I'll have it typed up and you can sign it."

"Fair enough. You asked me if I was fishing. What else would I be doing out there in the dead of night? Yes, I was fishing. That missy what thinks she owns the land—"

"Tom Foster's cousin, Georgina Sothesby?"

"Yes, her. She calls it poaching. Poaching! Who does she think she is? By my thinking, if they can't figure out who owns it, it don't belong to nobody." She nodded with a jerk of her head. "Like I said, I was fishing. Done caught me a whole stringer full when Mrs. Foster came. I was about to go, but I didn't want to get caught, so I just stayed in my place."

"Your place?" asked Irene.

"My favorite fishing spot down by the lake. Now, we're going to be here all night if you keep interrupting me."

Irene smiled. "Sorry. Go ahead."

"She came, Mrs. Foster, parked her car in the road, and walked down to the lake. She don't mind me fishing. She knows I gotta eat. But I stayed where I was, just the same. People out by themselves don't want to be bothered. She just stood there looking at the lake. Sometimes pacing back and forth, with it getting darker and darker. It wasn't long before another car come up and parked behind her. This feller got out. He left his headlights on, and they was like a spotlight.

"He come walking down to the lake. She turned and saw him and started walking toward him. Once, she held out her arms and said something. I didn't hear what it was. Then her arms dropped to her sides." Lila Poole started shaking her head back and forth. "I will remember what happened next for the rest of my life, and as God is my witness, it's the truth.

"That poor woman burst into flames right before my eyes. There weren't nobody around her. The feller who drove up was still a ways off. There weren't nobody there but the three of us, and she just caught fire. I thought at first it was God what done it, but I knew Mrs. Foster, and she weren't no worse than others in this world, and a lot better than most. It had to be the devil's work. It was like a piece of hell got a'holt of her.

"She screamed. Oh, how she screamed." Mrs. Poole put her hands to her ears. "I didn't know what to do, I sat there in the bushes with my mouth open, scared to move, afraid that fire and brimstone would start coming out all over. The feller came running, yelling for her to 'drop the rolls, drop the rolls.' I don't know why he was worrying about some bread burning when she herself was burning like she was. She weren't carrying nothing, she didn't have no bread. She run and jumped in the water." Mrs. Poole raised her hand as if taking an oath. "And I swear to you this is the truth, she burned brighter in the water. She was close to where I was, and I looked at her glowing in the water, and I knew it was a demon that got her. I put my hand over my mouth. I was afraid I'd attract whatever it was that had a'holt of her.

"The feller got him a stick and fished her out of the water. It was hard, but he done it and he started beating her with his coat, trying to put out the fire. I thought he was a brave feller. He kept yelling, 'Oh, God! Oh, God! Oh, God!' over and over. But God wasn't having none of it that night."

Irene looked over at Lindsay. Each raised their eyebrows at the other.

"I knowed you wouldn't believe me. I don't blame you. I wouldn't if someone told it to me and I didn't see it with my own eyes. But it's the truth."

"Why didn't you come forward when Shirley Foster was missing?" asked the sheriff.

"What? And tell that story, and me being there where I ain't supposed to be? Besides, she was gone. They should have found her, but she was gone. I didn't know what took her and didn't want none of it."

"Why did you come forward now?" asked Irene.

"She was found. That poor boy got hisself arrested and, unless he's the devil, he didn't do it. Couldn't have."

"What do you make of it?" asked Irene after the deputy left to take Lila Poole home.

"I don't know. I've never heard anything like it," said Lindsay. "What are you going to do?"

Irene shook her head. "I don't know. I don't believe it, but she does. I know Lila Poole. She's eccentric, but she's never been known to be a liar and never been in any trouble. The only complaint about her has been from Georgina Sothesby about her poaching. And frankly, nobody cared but Georgina." Irene took out a cigarette and searched her desk drawer for matches. "Maybe Ferris threw something at her. Maybe Ferris's folks talked Lila into telling that story, but I can't imagine Lila going for that. I'll talk to the district attorney. You got a match?"

"No, I'm sorry."

Irene looked around in the drawers of the other desks in the office, finally finding a book of matches. She lit her cigarette and took several drags. She shook her head. "That's a strange story."

Lindsay didn't return to the department but stopped by the library, the photo shop, a frame shop, and the grocery store before she went home.

"I'll make us dinner," she said as she came in the door, carrying sacks of groceries. "I hope you don't mind steaks and salad again."

Sinjin took the sacks from her. "Sounds good. I'll fire up your grill."

Lindsay busied herself with making dinner, washing the baking potatoes and salad fixings, cutting the vegetables, all the while forcing Derrick's news about the department reorganization to the back of her mind. She mentally categorized recent events, matching clues with their respective mysteries. When she got to Sally's attack, she realized she didn't really know where to put it. She had assumed it had to do with the missing artifacts, but it might just as easily have had to do with the murder of Shirley Foster. It was very inconsiderate, she thought, of the attacker not to mention which investigation she was to abandon.

"Think that salad's tossed enough?" asked Sinjin.

"What? Oh, I was just thinking."

"Want to tell me about it?"

"I was just—I'm going to lose my job, and I love my home out here in the woods so much," she blurted, as tears ran down her cheeks.

"What? Because of the artifacts? Lindsay, I'm sorry. Is it because of the artifact mess?" He reached out and pulled her to him, stroking her hair.

Lindsay cried into his shirt, then pulled away, wiping her eyes with a paper towel. "It's not the artifacts. It's a political reorganization thing," she said.

Lindsay took the salad to the table, tossed the potatoes in the microwave, put the steaks on the grill, and sat down with Sinjin before she told him about Derrick's call.

"Is he sure?" asked Sinjin. "It might be just a rumor."

"Derrick's pretty connected. He was sure that Lewis is coming."

"It doesn't necessarily mean you'll lose your job. I mean, they can't just fire you for no reason, can they?"

"They can just not renew my contract for next year. I don't have tenure, and none of us nontenured faculty have gotten our contract renewal letters."

"I tell you, the next time I visit you and Dad asks me to bring anything, I'll make sure I toss it in the river on the way out of town."

"You mean you were coming to visit me anyway?"

"Yeah, why?"

"I thought Dad had asked you to bring the crates and that's why you came. I guess you had to go to Atlanta, though."

"No. I was mainly handling that by phone. I wanted to come see you."

"I'm glad," was all Lindsay managed to say, but she felt grateful to know that.

"Look, Lindsay. Things aren't over till they're over. Don't give up."

"I won't. I'll see what my options are." Lindsay went out to the deck to turn the steaks.

"Some detective named Kaufman called to talk to me," said Sinjin when she returned. "He's not the same one I talked to at the station. Apparently, he's taken over the case."

"I've met him. That's another thing, someone from the university sicced him on me. I don't know why, or who, or what it has to do with. I think the sheriff of Dover County is trying to find out who's behind it. I'm sorry you're in this with me. What did Kaufman ask you?"

"About the artifacts found in my Jeep. I told him the same thing that I told the others. Perhaps a little sharper."

Lindsay smiled. "I'm afraid I was a little sharp with him, too. At least he knows it runs in the family." Lindsay put down her fork. "Let me tell you what I heard today." Lindsay repeated Lila Poole's tale almost word for word. "It was spooky."

"You don't believe it?" asked Sinjin.

"What do you think?"

"She's just superstitious. A more rational person would have seen something different."

"No," said Lindsay, shaking her head. "She wasn't superstitious. Just the opposite. She expects things to make sense. When she saw something that had no natural explanation she could think of, the only alternative was to go to the supernatural."

"Lindsay, people don't catch fire. The human body's not

prone to spontaneous combustion like oily rags." He took one of the candles on the table and passed a hand through the flame several times. Lindsay winced. "See"—he held out his hand to her—"not even red. I would have to hold it over a flame for quite a while for my skin to actually catch fire. People just don't burn that easily."

"Some people have," she said. "I've read—"

"Lindsay, in every reported case of so-called spontaneous combustion, there is a logical explanation."

"But I saw a picture of a woman burned in a chair. The chair was ashes, but nothing around the chair was burned," Lindsay persisted.

"So? Look, Lindsay, a stuffed chair can smolder for hours, reduce the chair to ashes, and hardly flame up. Someone probably dropped a cigarette in the cushions, the chair smoldered, and caught her clothes on fire."

Lindsay took the steaks off the grill and retrieved the baked potatoes from the microwave. She dressed her potato with butter and the steak with ketchup and took a few bites before she spoke again. "The body is made up of, what, 60 percent water? What if the water broke down, through some mechanism, into hydrogen and oxygen, which somehow helped cause a reaction between static electricity and hydrogen in the body? Couldn't the body catch fire then?"

Sinjin was about to cut a piece of steak; instead, he put down his fork and stared at her for a long moment. "What do you do up in your room all evening, watch *X-Files* videos?"

"It's not possible?"

"No. Where did you get such an idea?"

"I went to the library and looked up a couple of articles on spontaneous human combustion."

"I'm surprised they carry the *National Enquirer*."

Lindsay made a face. "What about Mrs. Poole's story?"

"Luke or someone could have threatened her, or she's mistaken in what she saw. Seeing a person burn to death is a very traumatic experience. I can tell you that. It's not surprising that it left a disturbing impression. Besides, if she had burst into flames through some kind of spontaneous combustion, wouldn't the inside of her ribs show signs of burning? Did you find that?"

Lindsay had to admit that all signs of burning were on the outside of the ribs. But she wasn't willing to dismiss Mrs. Poole's testimony. "What about the burning underwater part? Doesn't napalm, for instance, burn underwater?"

"Yes, many things burn underwater. I'll give you that. The kid could have thrown something like napalm at her. Maybe the woman didn't see him do that. It was getting dark, remember."

"She said the car lights were on."

"That still wouldn't necessarily give enough light to see everything going on. There would be strong shadows and unlighted areas."

"Where do you get napalm? Is it something someone could make?" Lindsay asked.

"Yes, it's very easy. I could make it probably from the things you have around here."

Lindsay grimaced. "Could someone like Luke make it? Don't you have to be some kind of expert?"

"No, you just need the recipe and enough sense not to burn yourself up."

"But why would someone like Luke do that? That's such a mean way to kill someone. Luke doesn't strike me as someone who would do anything that mean to another person."

"Lindsay, a lot of antisocial people appear to be nice guys. Didn't the medical examiner take tissue and fabric samples?" Sinjin asked. "A chemical like napalm would show up, wouldn't it?"

"I'll give him a call and see if the results are in."

"Do that. You'll find out there was some outside ignition source that caught her clothes on fire."

"The fire was very hot. It's hard to burn bone, but three of her distal phalanxes were missing, and others were burned white. That's a very hot fire."

"Do you mind if we quit talking about burned bodies while I'm eating red meat?" Sinjin asked.

Lindsay grinned at him. "Sorry."

"That guy, Hank Roy Whatsit. His photo a match with the skull?" asked Sinjin after a few moments of silent chewing.

"Yes, he was. I meant to tell you. I asked Derrick to look for him in the newspaper archives in Kentucky. I looked him up in the local papers but didn't find anything."

"We're making more progress than I figured," Sinjin said, taking his last bite of steak. "We know who the poor beggar was. If we can locate his next of kin, at least we can tell them that he died standing in a cornfield wearing his Sunday best." He put down his fork and knife. "I'll do the dishes. Sally said she's coming over after dinner and bringing a movie, *Double Indemnity*. You don't mind, do you?"

"I'd like that." Lindsay helped Sinjin clear the table. "You and Sally seem to be getting along."

"Like you said, we have a lot in common. She's a lot of fun. I'd forgotten about fun. Kathy and I hadn't been getting along for quite a while. I hadn't noticed, because it got to seem natural."

Lindsay left Sinjin to finish up in the kitchen while she straightened the living room. She was taking the silver-framed photograph of Sinjin with his father and mother out of the bag when he walked into the living room.

"I got this for you," she said.

Sinjin gingerly took the photograph from her hands, sat down in a chair and looked at it, touching it with his fingertips as if he could feel his mother's face through the glass.

"I made an enlargement for me, too. I hope you don't mind," she said.

"Mind? No, I don't mind," he said. He looked up at her

and smiled. "Thanks, baby sister. This is . . . this is really nice."

"It just seemed . . . ," she began and stopped. "I think I hear Sally's car driving up." Lindsay went to the door.

"Hi," Sally greeted, a video in one hand and a large tin of three different flavors of popcorn in the other. "Sinjin told you I was coming, didn't he? I hope that's okay."

"Come in. I need a diversion."

Lindsay had Sinjin bring the television from her room. "I didn't realize it would be this much trouble," Sally said. "I'm sorry."

"It's no trouble. I have hookups down here. I had two TVs, but one burned out."

Sinjin connected the TV to the VCR and sat on the couch. Sally sat cross-legged beside him. Lindsay sat in her favorite chair, curled up with her feet under her. They watched Barbara Stanwyck talk Fred MacMurray into killing her husband—how easy it was for her. Lindsay wondered if there were women with that kind of power in real life. She couldn't imagine it. She also wondered if people in the forties really talked that way—tossing clever lines back and forth so casually and with such deadly accuracy. Fred MacMurray lit matches with his thumbnail, the way Sinjin did. Lindsay smiled and scooped up a handful of popcorn.

"That is such a good movie," Sally said. "I don't know why they don't make them like that anymore."

"What about *Body Heat*?" said Sinjin. "Corruptible nice guy and simmering broad."

"*Body Heat*?" said Sally. "No."

"Yeah, that was almost as good," said Lindsay. "And *Chinatown,* and *LA Confidential.*"

"Okay, they can make movies like they used to when they try," conceded Sally. "I'd never noticed it before, but did you see how much the young Fred MacMurray looked like Pierce Brosnan?

Lindsay rose and stretched. "It's those dark Irish good

looks. Very nice. I'm going to turn in and leave you two to discuss film noir. We'll have to do it again. It's been the most relaxing time I've had in a long while."

"I need to get home. Thanks for having me out," Sally said.

"I'll walk you to your car." Sinjin gathered up her popcorn tin and walked with her out the door, just as Lindsay's phone rang.

"Lindsay, this is Irene Varnadore. I hope I didn't wake you."

"No, not at all."

"I'm sorry to call so late, but I just got back from a date with that friend I told you about. Davis Kaufman and his wife went with us. Davis told me a little about who put the bug in his ear, and for what it's worth, I told him that I thought he had you pegged wrong."

"Thanks. I really appreciate that. Who is it?"

"Some bigwig in the administration. All Davis would say was that it was an associate dean."

"Lindsay, you have nothing whatsoever to link Dr. Einer with the thefts. This isn't like you," Frank said, scowling at her from behind his desk. "Do you know how many associate deans there are on campus?"

The next morning Lindsay had marched into Frank's office first thing. She stood in front of his desk now, looking down at him. "It's slim, I know, but there's a connection. And why would whoever it was tell Detective Kaufman that he had suspected me of stealing antiquities for a long time?"

"It was probably a miscommunication. Lindsay, I don't need this, and you don't either."

"I have nothing to lose. I believe my fate is sealed," she retorted.

He was silent for a long moment. "So, you've heard."

"Yes. Why didn't I hear it from you?"

"I haven't known long. It's something Francisco's been working on. And look, I don't know where you'll fit in."

"You won't need two osteologists, and Dr. or Ms. Whatever-her-status-is, Chapman's been sizing up my chair. I know I won't fit in."

"Well, I don't know that, and it won't happen without a fight from me. I hope you don't intend to just give up."

"No, I won't give up."

"Good. Now drop this thing about Einer. You won't get anywhere with it. Frankly, there's more circumstantial evidence that connects you than him."

"I won't publicly accuse him, if that's what you mean. He's inoculated himself pretty well where that's concerned. Kaufman wouldn't believe me, now that Einer has gotten to him. He'd just think I was trying to get even or something."

"If Kaufman talks to me—and he will if he's any kind of decent detective at all—I'll tell him he's wrong."

"Thanks."

"Leave the Einer thing alone, but don't lose heart over the other thing."

"I won't."

As Lindsay came down the stairs and rounded the corner, she almost ran into Brian, standing in her doorway. He looked guilty.

"Hello, Brian. How are things?"

"Lindsay, can I talk to you?"

"Sure. Come in. Take a seat. How's your thesis coming?"

Brian sat down uneasily in the chair in front of her desk. "Good. I'm tracing the chert source for the lithic material at the Cold River site. I'm evaluating different methods to get a chemical analysis of the material." Brian stopped talking. Lindsay said nothing, then they both tried to talk at the same time.

"Go ahead," Lindsay said.

"Look, Lindsay, I don't want you to think I have anything to do with what Gerri's been up to. I didn't know until last night what she's been planning."

"I don't think that, Brian."

He relaxed a little. "I broke up with her. I can't believe she's been going after your job. She's pretty cold about it. Told me it's not personal. Good jobs in osteology aren't that easy to come by, she said. Said she isn't doing anything different from what everybody does, using their contacts to get a job. But it really stinks."

"Don't concern yourself about it," Lindsay said. "I don't blame you for anything Gerri may be involved in."

Brian still looked miserable. "I told Gerri a lot of stuff. Not anything bad. I don't know anything bad. Just how you like to solve crimes, and the stuff Derrick told me about the missing artifacts. I'm afraid she may have used things to her advantage, you know, in talking Lewis into giving her the job here. Derrick is really pissed at me."

"It's all right," said Lindsay. "Don't beat yourself up for trusting someone. Like you said, there aren't any bad things to know. If they sounded bad to Lewis, then it's because Gerri made them sound bad. It's not your fault."

"Thanks, Lindsay. I would hate for you to think I was in on this. I guess Sally's pretty steamed?"

"I don't know that she knows. We haven't talked about it."

"She dating your brother?"

"They've gone out a couple of times, I believe. Are you going back to Kentucky?"

"Yeah, today. I'm trying to catch Sally. Does she come in today?"

"Usually, but I've given her some time off. That attack at *The Rocky Horror Picture Show* really scared her."

"It must have. I hope she didn't leave the show early because of me and Gerri." Lindsay didn't say anything. Brian sighed and rose from his chair. "I'll see if I can catch her at her apartment before I leave." He offered his hand and Lindsay took it.

"Don't worry about me, Brian. I'm all right." Lindsay felt sorry for him as he walked out her door. She bet he was sorry he had dumped Sally.

Her phone rang. "Dr. Chamberlain, this is Detective Kaufman. Would you come down to the Public Safety Building, please?"

"You have some news about the artifacts?" asked Lindsay.

"I'll tell you when you get here."

Chapter 19

LINDSAY WAS SHOWN to a chair in Kaufman's office by the receptionist. After five minutes of waiting and no Kaufman, Lindsay decided that it was just some tactic of his, and she wasn't going to play. She got up and was walking out the door when he entered, stepped behind his desk, and sat down. Lindsay turned but remained standing.

"Please sit down," he said. Lindsay sat on the edge of the chair. She thought she probably looked as if she were ready to bolt at any minute. It was the way she felt. "I just have a couple of questions." The two of them looked up as Frank walked into the room. He sat in the empty chair near Lindsay, looked at her and shrugged.

"You were saying?" Lindsay asked Kaufman.

"We found some of the artifacts."

"You did?" Lindsay and Frank said together.

"Where?" asked Lindsay.

"They were still in the basement of Nancy Hart. In a closet in boxes marked Fredrickson Foundation Archival Files." Lindsay opened her mouth and raised her eyebrows. She had passed them when she was finding her way out of the basement. "We found your fingerprints in the near vicinity."

Lindsay was tempted to roll her eyes. Her fingerprints weren't on file; he must have gotten them when she was here the other day. Maybe on a coffee mug? She almost laughed. "I saw the boxes when I was in the closet. If you remember, I escaped from the basement through the closet and out the back door."

"Yes. I remember that's what you said. We also found this in the box with the artifacts. Do you recognize it?" He held up a silver letter opener.

"I have one like it. My aunt gave it to me. Mine is engraved with my name. If that one is engraved, I assume it's mine."

"It is."

"Then it must be mine."

"Do you know how it got in the box?"

"No, but I imagine someone put it there so you could haul me down here to ask me about it."

Frank winced. "You said *some* of the artifacts. Not all of them?"

"No. There was just one box," Kaufman answered as he picked up a box from behind his desk and set it on top. Lindsay and Frank peered inside at two small pots and a couple of clay effigy pipes.

"Not much," said Frank.

"We figure the rest were moved," said Kaufman.

"There was a whole stack of boxes," said Lindsay.

"And you don't know how your letter opener got in the box?" Kaufman asked again.

"She said she didn't," answered Frank.

"Detective Kaufman," said Lindsay, "to what use would I have put a silver letter opener while absconding with boxes of artifacts? The only thing you can do with it is open letters. It doesn't make a good knife, and I carry a Swiss Army knife in my purse. The letter opener is only there because it has my name on it."

"When did you last see it?"

"I don't know. It's usually on my desk, and I don't always lock my office. Anyone in Baldwin, or the university for that matter, could have gotten it. There's been a parade of people—students, faculty, police, reporters, and even Ellis Einer, an associate dean—through my office in the past few days."

Lindsay watched him closely. He twitched slightly at the mention of Einer. She thought she had scored a hit. It occurred to her, watching him thinking up another question to ask her, that he might be in on it with Einer. It would be easy for a campus policeman to park behind Baldwin and take the artifacts. No one would notice anything amiss about a police car in the lot at night. Perhaps there had been no anonymous call, or perhaps he made it. Lindsay was on the verge of asking him just that when Frank spoke.

"Detective Kaufman, can't you see she's right? And look at these artifacts. All are chipped or broken. They picked the ones with the least value to leave behind to salt with incriminating evidence. Just how did you know to look in the closet in the first place? Another one of these ubiquitous anonymous calls?"

"As a matter of fact, when we discovered that there was this virtual back door to the artifact room, I thought it would be a better way than going through the front door to steal the artifacts without being seen. And it occurred to me that they could also be stored there, too. It didn't look like anyone ever cleans or uses the place."

"That was very good thinking," said Frank. "Apply some of that to Lindsay. I know her; I've known her for a long time. I don't know why someone is trying to throw suspicion on her, but they could have just as easily thrown it on me or any of the faculty or students who use the artifact room. This line of investigation is a dead end, and I would very much like to get the artifacts back. Have you looked on the collector's market at all for them to show up?"

"Yes, I have, and they haven't, but that doesn't mean there wasn't a private sale. I'm focusing on Dr. Chamberlain because she's a common denominator."

"Not in the antiquities missing from the library or from

the Classics Department," said Lindsay.

Kaufman looked at her in surprise. "What?"

"The librarian informed campus police that valuable maps and books are missing from the rare book room. You mean the information didn't reach you?" Lindsay went on before he could answer. "Talk to Linda Andrews. She's the archivist at the Hargrett Library where the rare books are kept."

"And you say some things are missing from the Classics Department?" asked Kaufman, removing the box from his desk. Lindsay told him of her conversation with Linda Andrews. "So, you were in the rare book room?" asked Kaufman.

"After," said Lindsay, underlining the word with the tone of her voice, "the items were stolen, and I've never been to Park Hall. Also, I believe there were some things stolen from the museum a year or so ago."

"We know about that," Kaufman said.

"Now, if that's all, I'm leaving. When you finish with my letter opener, I'd like to have it back."

She and Frank stood up and left the building. "Nice going," said Frank. "When I first met you, you were shy."

"Yeah, well, it's all the stuff that's happened, I guess. I'm feeling backed into a corner for the flimsiest of reasons. No one could really expect to do anything but throw the weakest of suspicions on me with the evidence they've come up with. What would I be doing carrying around an engraved silver letter opener? By the way, why did you come?" she asked.

"Kaufman called. Maybe he's focusing on me next."

"No, he just wanted to interview me in your presence. I think it was just a tactic to maybe make me nervous."

Frank laughed. "Little did he know, you have nerves of steel."

"Steel wool, maybe."

• • •

Frank drove back to Baldwin, but Lindsay decided to visit Park Hall. With my luck, she thought, I'll run into Kaufman. She parked behind the building and went in, looking for the Classics Department office.

The receptionist was a woman in her late fifties, slim, dressed in an light blue Oxford shirt and navy skirt. She wore black cat-eye glasses on a dark chain draped around her neck. The plaque on the desk identified her as Mrs. Annette Hargrove.

"I'm Dr. Chamberlain from the Archaeology Department. We've had some of our antiquities stolen, and I was wondering if you have any missing from the Classics Department."

The woman began nodding her head and motioned for Lindsay to sit down. "I told them they were missing. They think Dr. Lennox checked some of them out. She's out of the country now, and she certainly wouldn't take any with her."

"They?" asked Lindsay.

The woman waved a hand at the offices. "The faculty. They are very good classicists, but, well, they just don't think anybody would steal anything."

Lindsay smiled. "I discovered it through a librarian."

"Linda Andrews." She nodded. "She called and asked the same questions."

"Has anyone else called or come by to ask about them?"

"No, they haven't."

"I've been talking to a Detective Kaufman. He'll probably talk with you."

"Good. I've made a list of the missing items."

"He'll like that. I don't suppose anyone from the administration has been here lately."

Mrs. Hargrove shook her head. "Like I said, no one besides you and Mrs. Andrews has been interested."

"How about just visiting?" said Lindsay carefully. "I know that one of the associate deans has been interested in security in our department. . . ."

"No, not that I'm aware of."

"Thank you for talking to me. Maybe now that the campus police are aware of the problem, they can find the missing items."

"I certainly hope so," said Mrs. Hargrove.

Lindsay wanted to ask more questions, like where had the artifacts been stored, when was the last time she had seen them, but she knew the receptionist would probably tell Kaufman she had been here. He would ask Mrs. Hargrove what questions Lindsay had asked, and she didn't want to make any more trouble for herself. Instead, she changed the subject.

"I have another question. This is rather sensitive." Mrs. Hargrove took off her glasses and leaned forward. "One of the campus police told me that Gloria Rankin was coming to see me when she was struck by the bus. I didn't know her nor why she was coming. Do you have any idea?"

"Poor, poor Gloria. She was a nice girl, a nice girl." Mrs. Hargrove shook her head slowly back and forth. "I don't know, but she wouldn't have told me anyway. Her office mate, Theodora Ricarda, may know. She's down the hall in 210."

"Thank you."

Lindsay walked down the hallway of white marble, looking at the numbers on the wooden doors. She passed a glass case of statuary replicas of Hercules: Hercules throwing a discus, Hercules tearing off his tunic, Hercules leaning against a tree, Hercules fighting the Hydra. Among the statues were several journal articles and books about Herculean mythology written by faculty members. She looked to see if any of the articles were by anyone she knew. One was by Gloria Rankin, a review of *Trachiniae* by Sophocles.

Lindsay knocked on the door to room 210, and a husky female voice told her to come in.

"Theodora Ricarda?" A plump woman of about twenty-five with black hair, dark lashes, and beautiful blue eyes sat at a desk situated perpendicular to the door. Another similar desk faced hers. Bookcases teeming with volumes lined the walls. "My name is Dr. Lindsay Chamberlain. I'm from the Archaeology Department in Baldwin." The woman raised her eyebrows in what looked, to Lindsay, like disdain. "I was informed that Gloria Rankin was coming to see me the day she died, and I was wondering if she might have told you why."

"I don't feel comfortable talking about Gloria to a stranger." She looked back at the article she had been reading.

"I can understand that. The police asked me about it. I'm sure they will come and ask you. They are tying up loose ends." Lindsay turned to go.

"I don't know why. We didn't talk much."

I'll bet, thought Lindsay. "Was she working on anything to do with archaeology?"

"Not likely. She was interested in Greek and Roman mythology. That's her master's thesis on the shelf." Theodora pointed to the bookcase behind Lindsay.

Lindsay picked up a thin black volume. The gold lettering stamped into the cover read: *Medea: The Source of Her Sorcery,* by Gloria Louise Rankin. Catchy title, thought Lindsay. The book was dated 1993.

"What was her dissertation topic?"

"Nothing to do with Indians."

Lindsay smiled. "We study a lot of things. For instance, I'm an expert in bones. We have experts in lithics, underwater archaeology, pollen analysis—we also have Old World archaeologists."

Theodora shrugged. "She was doing something with glazes and fifth-century Greek vases, I think."

"What are your interests?" asked Lindsay.

Theodora brightened. "Ancient Greek poetry and linguistics. I love translating from ancient Greek."

"I think ancient Greek poetry is very beautiful." Lindsay hoped she wouldn't be struck down by lightning for lying. She actually had no idea what ancient Greek poetry was like.

"It is, isn't it? The form is like nothing else, and the imagery gives you such insights into the ancient Greek psyche."

Lindsay wondered if that were a pun and decided it wasn't. "You've been very kind to let me take up your time. If you think of anything, here's my card." She laid her University of Georgia business card on the vacant desk. "Thanks again." Lindsay was out the door before Theodora could ask her who her favorite Greek poet was.

The visit to the Classics Department had yielded nothing useful, Lindsay realized, and she had probably compromised her already shaky position by simply being there. Depressed, she drove back to Baldwin.

She sat at her desk and put her hands to her temples, trying to ease the tension from her muscles. Too many mysteries. She had the strangest feeling she was missing something important. She could almost feel the clues swimming around in her brain, waiting for the one piece that would make all of them make sense.

The phone rang, and Lindsay let it ring a couple of times before she picked it up. She was starting to dread answering the telephone.

"Miss Chamberlain? Jake Gilroy here. Think I have you an Explorer. Can you come by and look at it?"

"Yes, after work today, or maybe tomorrow?"

"Sure. It's a '95 program car. I think you'll like it and the price, too. We can probably give you a real good deal on your Rover."

"Thanks, Jake. I appreciate it."

Lindsay put down the phone with a sense of relief. If she could at least lower her car payments to make up for the property payment, that would be a big help, especially since

she was about to lose her job. Her job. It made her sick. Just
don't think about it, she told herself, you've got enough to
occupy your mind. Her gaze rested on the box of old newspapers that was still sitting in the corner of her office. She
had completely forgotten about them. She carefully took a
brittle page and flattened it on her desk. It was a *Macon Telegraph* from 1935. There was nothing in it but bad economic
news, advertisements, and an article about Babe Ruth quitting
the Boston Braves. Boston Braves? Interesting, she thought.

She picked up another paper. It was much the same. The
third was from Kentucky, dated two years earlier than the
rest. She scanned the yellowed and stained pages for anything related to archaeology or Hank Roy Creasey. She
read the obituaries. The fourth entry caught her eye. A
Henry Ray Creasey had died in a mine explosion. His body
had not been recovered. The obituary gave no other information, not even the next of kin.

Lindsay carefully examined the rest of the paper. On
the back page was part of an article about the mine explosion. It had killed several men: Henry Ray Creasey, Homer
Timmons, Lonnie Cross, and Ruddy Stillman. Lindsay
turned back and looked again at the obituaries. None of the
men except for Creasey were there. Henry Ray, Hank
Roy—Lindsay bet they were the same person. The last
paragraph in the article said that a plaque had been placed
at the mine to mark their grave. Lindsay looked over the
list of names again. Lonnie Cross, she thought. That name
sounded familiar.

Lindsay took a stack of index cards and began labeling
them with headings on the upper left corner for the three
main mysteries: Artifact Theft, Shirley Foster, Creasey. She
mentally crossed off Gloria Rankin. There was probably no
way of knowing why Gloria had been coming to see her.
But what was her umbrella doing in the tree? That was
easy: When she was hit, it was knocked into the street and

someone came by later, picked it up, and hung it in the tree. Why? Who knows why students do what they do? Not a good answer. They didn't want it. A guy found it and it was a girl's umbrella. He didn't want people to stumble over it, so he hung it in the tree. Okay, he walked into the bushes and hung it in the tree instead of just laying it on the wall. Lindsay picked up the telephone and called Eddie Peck, the medical examiner.

"Eddie," she said when he answered the phone, "that bruise on Gloria Rankin's back. Could it have been made by the tip of an umbrella?"

"Well, yes. Why?" Lindsay told him about the stray umbrella belonging to Gloria. "Hmm, interesting. Are you thinking that someone hid in the bushes and pushed her in front of the bus?"

"I don't know."

"A bold move," said Eddie. "But she was on the sidewalk. Wouldn't she be too far away?"

"Not in that particular place," said Lindsay. "The wall is low and there's a profusion of bushes and trees. It would be risky, but someone could have stepped forward out of the shelter of the trees, pushed her in the back with the point of the umbrella, and stepped back into the cover of the shrubbery. Didn't someone say it looked like she just jumped out in front of the bus?"

"Do you have any idea why someone would do that?" asked Eddie.

"I have no idea. It's just something nagging me. Like, why was she coming to see me?"

"I'll discuss the umbrella with the detective in charge," he said.

"Have you gotten any reports back on the tissue and clothing samples from Shirley Foster yet?"

"Yeah. One, and it's kind of strange. Arsenic."

"Arsenic? Was she poisoned?" asked Lindsay.

"I don't think so. It doesn't seem to be that much," Eddie said. "She could be one of those people who eat it. You know how strange you university people are."

"Yeah, I do. Have you heard about the woman who witnessed Shirley Foster's death?"

"I didn't know there was a witness. Tell me about it," Eddie said, and Lindsay told him the entire story. He whistled into the phone. "I take it back. It's not just you university people who are crazy. It's everybody."

"You don't think her story is true?" asked Lindsay.

"That Foster just burst into flames? No. People don't do that."

"That's what my brother says."

"Smart guy."

"What about napalm, or some substance like it?"

"It would account for part of what the witness saw. Another thing, if she was standing when she was burned, it would account for the burns being on her back as well as her front."

"Yes, it would, wouldn't it?" said Lindsay.

"There are several ways to make napalm," he said. "I'll have the lab check the samples for residue. That still looks bad for Luke Ferris."

"I know, but the witness was sure she didn't see him throw anything."

Lindsay hung up the phone and went back to her index cards. She made a set for Gloria Rankin. On the upper right side of the cards, she put subheadings: forensic evidence, interviews, rumors. She began filling out all the cards, listing everything she knew about each case, every mention anyone made about any of the cases. She then organized them according to their headings and subheadings. There was really quite a lot of information, but there also was quite a lot of information missing. And there were those things in her brain just out of reach of her conscious mind. Those annoyed her the most.

Lindsay shuffled through the cards. The only person she hadn't talked to about Shirley Foster was Will Patterson, and he probably knew her best. Lindsay put the index cards in her purse and looked up his address in the phone book.

Will Patterson had an office downtown in one of those buildings with a very narrow entrance and flight of stairs that led to the upper floors. If she were doing a film noir, Lindsay couldn't have picked a better place for a detective to have an office. He even had a glass window in his door with his name printed in black paint. Lindsay wondered if she ought to go home and change into a dress with shoulder pads and a hat with a small net veil and a single slender feather. She knocked on the door. It opened almost immediately. P.I. Patterson smiled and motioned her into the room.

Will Patterson had probably been a heartstopper when he was in his twenties, and even though the years had taken their toll—creases around his eyes, mouth, and forehead, graying of his hair, a slight roll around his waist—he was still an attractive man. He moved with ease. Lindsay thought she had seen him jogging on campus. He had a scar that creased his forehead and disappeared into his hairline. She wondered if he had been shot. If he had, it had certainly been a close call.

"Dr. Chamberlain. I was just thinking about you." Will stood back to let her enter. "I was wondering when you would get around to visiting me."

His office wasn't a disappointment. Unpolished hardwood floors, an old desk with a green blotter, cluttered with file folders, a spindle skewering several receipts and a letter, and a brass ashtray. One old oak filing cabinet stood in the corner beside a closed door. Along the wall past the door sat a beautiful antique cabinet with a washbowl. A moustache comb and scissors sat behind the basin. Will didn't have a moustache and Lindsay found herself wondering what he would look like with one. Against one wall was a green fake-leather sofa. The bookcase next to it was filled with various reference books.

On top of the bookcase was a violin under glass, which caused Lindsay to raise her eyebrows. Will was full of surprises. He did not look like a man who played the violin. On the wall hung a finely woven tapestry of Sherlock Holmes at Richenbach Falls. The falls, gray in all the drawings she had ever seen before, were a brilliant combination of blues and greens. Lindsay had no doubt that Shirley Foster had woven it.

Will sat behind his desk and Lindsay sat down in a red leather chair. She paused a moment before speaking. She had the strangest feeling, an odd familiarity. She looked at Will. He smiled at her. She looked around the room and then back at him. He was still smiling.

"Do you read mysteries?" she asked.

His smile turned into a grin, then a laugh. "No. Shirl did this. She had the most wicked sense of humor." His eyes took on a moist brightness. "How many detectives do you see?"

Lindsay looked around the room again. "Sam Spade, Hercule Poirot, Sherlock Holmes, Phillip Marlow." She rubbed the arms of the red leather chair. "Nero Wolfe, Lew Archer." Her eyes fell on the spindle with the single letter. ". . . and August Dupin."

"I believe that's most of them," he said.

Lindsay shook her head and smiled. "It gives an odd sensation, like the ghosts of past detectives hanging about your office."

"I think that was the effect she was after."

"What did you mean when you said you wondered when I'd come to see you?"

"I've been waiting for you to interview me," he said, leaning back in his chair.

"You're the detective," said Lindsay. "I've been trying to

avoid looking into this case. People just keep coming to me."

"I know," he said. Lindsay was silent. She stared at Will Patterson. The window behind him looked out onto Broad Street, and the light coming through the thin blinds was split into long horizontal shafts. It was hard to see the details of his face with the light behind him. Lindsay wanted to shade her eyes so she could look into his, but instead, she rose, went to the blinds, and turned the wand until the light was deflected away.

"Shirl would have liked you," he said. "I think you would have liked her, too."

"You've been sending everyone to see me, haven't you?" said Lindsay.

"Everyone I could. I had to manipulate Tom a little. Told him we were working together and you would find him out."

"You thought he might be a killer, and you sent him to me?"

"I thought he would come to your office. I didn't know he would drive out to your house."

"Still—" Lindsay let it drop. "Why? You're a detective."

His eyes sparkled under a sheen of moisture. "I'm too close. I don't like Tom. But I want Shirl's killer found, even if it isn't Tom. I know a lot of law enforcement people. They tell me you're good at connecting things. What do you call it—remote association? You're supposed to be good at old crimes. I knew you wouldn't do it if I asked you, so I arranged it so you couldn't help but investigate her death."

What a manipulator, she thought. "Do you think Luke Ferris is Shirley's murderer?"

"Do you?" he asked.

"I don't know. I have a hard time believing it. Have you heard his story?"

"Yes. The kid's lying. Shirl wouldn't have lured him out there for favors. He must be guilty."

"Exactly how do you know his story?" asked Lindsay. "I didn't think you and the sheriff were that close."

"I grew up around here and know just about all the deputies. They talk to me."

"Irene thinks Luke's lying, too. She said Shirl might cheat on her husband but not on you."

"She's right. Shirl wouldn't."

"When was the last time you saw her?"

Will wasn't offended by the question. In fact, he seemed to welcome it. "I have an apartment through that door. Few people know about it. Shirl and I stayed there sometimes. She stayed with me the night before she disappeared. Her children were visiting Tom's parents," he added, as though he wanted Lindsay to understand that Shirley was a good mother.

"What was her state of mind?"

"Happy. The happiest I'd ever seen her. She went to work early. I had a case I was working on and had to be in Atlanta by nine-thirty that morning. I was back by three that afternoon." He shook his head. "She'd left a note on my door. Wanted me to pick up some copies for her at Kinko's on the corner and take them to her office."

"Did she often ask you to run errands for her?"

Lindsay saw him bristle slightly, shifting in his chair. He didn't like any criticism of Shirley. "No. But the copying place was almost downstairs, and her office was just down the street. I suppose her student help wasn't available that day. You know how students are. It was no problem."

"Did you pick up the copies?"

"Of course. I gave them to her secretary. Shirl wasn't there."

"You know that means that Luke wasn't lying," said Lindsay.

"What?" He sat upright in his chair. "How do you figure that?" He glared at her now, daring her to tarnish Shirl's memory.

"The note she put on your door was not something she would ask of you. It was meant for Luke, her student worker. He obviously got your note, which, according to Luke, said something like, 'Meet me at Foster's pond at seven. I have a surprise and I intend to correct a mistake.' Luke thought it meant she was going to change his grade, but that didn't really make sense, even to him. The only thing he could figure was that she wanted a date. The note makes a lot of sense, if it was meant for you. She was going to give you $100,000 for something—I don't know what—and she was going to tell you she was leaving Tom to marry you."

Will was silent for a long moment, staring in Lindsay's direction but through her. Finally, he spoke. "I knew I was right to have you investigate this. There are two options, as I see it. Could be that when Luke showed up by mistake and he tried something, she resisted, and he killed her. Or Tom got wind of what she was planning, and he killed her."

"Luke wouldn't have come prepared with napalm, or whatever was used on her," said Lindsay.

"Napalm?"

"I can't think of anything else that would burn underwater, assuming the witness is correct."

Will nodded. "Lila Poole. I hardly credited her story, but you're right. It would have to have been premeditated. That takes us back to Tom," he added almost absently.

"There's another thing, though. My brother, Sinjin, thinks that Luke may have some kind of fascination with fire."

Will sat very still. "That adds a whole other dimension to it." His voice was almost a whisper.

"Maybe, but I don't have nearly enough information to narrow it to Luke, Tom, or some stranger. Do you know if she ate arsenic?" asked Lindsay.

Will wrinkled his brow. "Ate arsenic? No. Why the heck would she do that?"

"Do you think someone might have tried to poison her?"

"What are you saying?" he asked.

"The medical examiner found arsenic in the samples taken from her remains."

"Okay," he said, leaning forward in his chair. "How's this? Tom was trying to kill her slowly, made it look like she was just getting sick, but that was too slow and he made another plan."

Lindsay shook her head. "No one, including you, had any indication she was sick, and arsenic poisoning has definite symptoms."

He sat back. "You're right. But that's very strange. What do you make of it?"

"As I said, I don't have enough information yet."

"You will continue investigating?" he asked.

"I suppose so."

A thin, satisfied smile spread across Will's face. His dark eyes became like dull pools, absorbing all light. As Lindsay looked into their depths, it was as though she glimpsed his soul within, and it frightened her. It came into her mind suddenly and surely that Will Patterson was going to kill Shirley Foster's murderer once he knew who it was, and she was leading him to Luke Ferris. She sat back in her chair as if his gaze pinned her to it, realizing she was holding her breath. If he noticed her sudden unease, he in no way indicated it.

"That's good. I'm glad you are." He relaxed. Everything seemed normal again, and Lindsay wondered if she had only imagined the look in his eyes.

"Why would she give you a hundred thousand dollars?" she asked.

"I had a chance to buy a detective agency in Atlanta. It was a good agency, several operatives, lots of equipment. She offered to loan me the money. I kept refusing. She must have been going to tell me to buy the agency and that she'd marry me." He closed his eyes. "If we can find the money, we'll find who killed her."

"Not necessarily. We may only find who took the money. It may not be the person who killed her," said Lindsay. "Did you investigate any of Tom Foster's family? Could the problem with the Foster land inheritance have anything to do with what happened to her?"

Will shook his head. "I rode that horse pretty hard, but no theory I came up with made sense. They all actually liked Shirley. She thought the land should go to Tom's relatives, since she and Tom had so much money."

"What about people she worked with?" Lindsay asked.

"Another dead end. They liked her. I couldn't find a motive for anyone. Maybe a little professional jealousy here and there, scholarly disagreements, but nothing that anyone would kill for. I checked into their backgrounds. Everything normal. At least what passes for normal on a university campus." He grinned. "Money was the only motive I could find and that led to Tom."

"Tell me about Shirley Foster," Lindsay said.

Chapter 20

"**S**HIRL WAS SMART and funny." Will paused, looking inward. "And a lot of things. How does that song by Billy Joel go? 'She's always a woman to me.' That was Shirl. The song describes her to a T."

"Is that how everyone saw her?" asked Lindsay.

"I don't know. Most people liked her. I know most men did. Not that she was a flirt," he added quickly. "She was just . . . a man's woman."

Lindsay wondered exactly what that meant. "What was the thing with her parents?"

"I suppose her parents meant well, but they were very controlling. Who doesn't want to control their children? Their respect meant a lot to Shirley, but she was not a woman who liked being dominated, even by her parents, so she lied to them, often. Not to be mean but to maintain her privacy."

"Were they really that bad?"

"They're hardest on Chris. They always wanted him to go into the family business, but Chris didn't want to. Chris's father likes to apply what he calls 'economic pressure' on him periodically—you know, threatening to buy out the loan on Chris's gallery, for example. Not that it's much of a business, just local art."

"Local art can be expensive," commented Lindsay.

"If you say so."

"The gallery seems to be doing well. It's been there quite a while, and he's had a number of showings."

"I think Tom Foster has bailed him out a couple of times—and Shirley, occasionally."

"Is that why the Pryors don't like Tom Foster?"

"Part of it. Tom started Chris in business. Got him interested in working with glass. Chris is a talented artist, and it turned out that glass is his medium. Tom gave him space in one of his old factories. The Pryors felt that Tom was interfering in their business. Tom told them that Chris was an adult and to buzz off, only his language was probably a lot more colorful."

"Were you angry when they insisted that Shirley marry Tom?"

"What do you think? Of course I was, but . . ." He shrugged. "I probably wouldn't have made much of a husband. My old man drank and so did I. I guess that's what they didn't like about me. I didn't have good breeding—but I haven't had a drink in six years."

Lindsay was silent a moment. "When Shirley had the auto accident that caused the LeFort fracture, you were involved, weren't you?"

Will looked stunned for a moment. "You're quick. Nobody knew that but me and Shirley."

"Her accident was six years ago, and you stopped drinking six years ago. What happened?"

"I didn't leave her there, needing help and taking the blame, if that's what you're thinking," he said, frowning at Lindsay. "I was driving her little Mercedes convertible. I was drunk, but like a lot of drunks, I was good at hiding it. We were driving out near Cherokee Corner. I guess I lost control. I don't remember. We weren't wearing seat belts and both of us were thrown out of the car. I rolled down the embankment into some bushes. They found the car turned over and Shirley on the side of the road, thought she was the only one in the car, and took her to the hospital. When I came to a few hours later, I didn't know what had happened. The car had been towed away, and there was no sign that an accident ever happened. I didn't know how I got in the bushes, but that wasn't an unfamiliar experience for me. Anyway, I hitched a ride back to town to my office and spent the rest of the night in the apartment."

"You didn't remember what happened at all?"

"Not then. When I heard about Shirley the next day, I started remembering us being together, but I still didn't remember what happened. Shirley didn't either. She didn't even remember us being together. Later, I studied the accident report—you know, direction the car was headed, tire marks, which sides we must have been thrown from. I figured out I must have been driving. I told Shirley. She was still in the hospital all bandaged up from them having to . . ." He stopped for a moment, unable to finish. "I sat on the side of her bed and cried. Told her what happened. She got all agitated and I figured she hated me."

He shook his head, and Lindsay thought he would cry again at the memory. "She couldn't talk, but she could write. She told me not to tell anyone, broke the pencil writing exclamation points. I kept my mouth shut, but when she was better I talked to her about it again. She said that it was something between the two of us and it was nobody else's business."

Will Patterson looked straight into Lindsay's eyes. "She was terrified her parents would do something to me if the truth came out, and she made me promise never to tell, and that's the only reason I didn't."

The tension slowly eased from his face. "I started AA after that and haven't had a drink since. Not even when she disappeared . . . not even now."

"Why do you think Tom Foster may have killed her?"

"The usual—inheritance and life insurance—that was my thought in the beginning when she disappeared. But if he was going to collect, her body would have to be found, and it wasn't. After a while, I thought maybe some stranger kidnapped her. I tried everything I knew to find her. It wasn't until the Pryors hired me that I discovered that if she died, he got very little in her will, but if she disappeared, he got the use of all her money. It made sense to me that he killed her. I knew the two of them had argued a lot."

"Was there really an anonymous telephone call?"

Will stared hard at her for several seconds. "No," he said.

"It was just a wild guess, then, that her body was buried on the old Foster farm?"

"During my search for her, the only clue I uncovered was from a trucker on Highway 78 who saw her Jaguar go by. You get to the Foster farm by taking 78. Yeah, I know, that was slim, but I had nothing else, absolutely nothing. And if he buried her anywhere, it would probably be out there, and I thought a good archaeologist could find her. I was right."

"Were you surprised she was there?" Lindsay didn't know why she asked that question, perhaps to gauge the depth of Will's belief that Tom Foster killed his wife.

"Surprised? Yes. I realized that, until I saw the dome of skull uncovered, I had hoped that she was still alive and, for some reason of her own, had left all of us."

"I'm sorry."

"My hypothesis was born out. She was there on Tom Foster's land. Isn't that what you scientists use as proof of a theory—its predictability? It looks like Tom Foster's guilty."

Lindsay shook her head. "Wrong theories can still predict. The theory that the earth was the center of the universe allowed the prediction of planetary movement for a very long time. Just her body being on Tom's family farm doesn't tell us who killed Shirley Foster."

Lindsay left Will Patterson's office after agreeing to continue her investigation into Shirley Foster's death. She gave her consent for two reasons. One was the uneasy feeling she had about Will's intentions toward the person he might ultimately believe to be Shirley's murderer. She felt a responsibility toward Luke, Tom, and even Will himself to try to get to the bottom of Shirley's death before Will did something they would all regret. The second reason was that she felt as though the solution was close, hanging out there like the objects of the fictional detectives in Will's office, waiting for that one bit of information that would make everything fall into place.

Luke's family was having supper when Lindsay arrived, and everyone but Luke was glad to see her. She could see that he didn't want to talk to her, but she virtually marched him out to the gazebo and sat him down. She sat across from him and leaned forward, close, almost eye to eye.

"Luke, I want the truth. What happened that night at the lake with Shirley Foster?"

"I told you the truth," he said.

Lindsay was shaking her head even before he got the words out. "No, you didn't. I know you didn't, and the sheriff knows you didn't tell her the truth, either. Now, tell me."

"You won't believe me," he said almost in a whisper, turning his eyes from Lindsay's steady gaze.

"I don't believe you now, so you have nothing to lose."

Luke sat there a moment. As before, he looked in every direction but Lindsay's. "I did get a note from her, asking me to come to the lake."

"I know you did."

He looked at her, surprised. "You do?"

"Yes."

"How?"

"Tell me the truth, Luke. Now."

He took a deep breath, and the story began to flow out of him like a flood that had been dammed up inside him. "I drove out there. It was getting dark, but there was still some light. My car lights were on, and I could see into the woods. Shirley was standing looking at the lake. She turned and walked toward me. She smiled and held out her arms. Then she stopped and looked surprised, and I think she said my name. I got to within fifteen feet of her, I guess. I started to say something when she . . . she just . . ."

Luke rose from his seat and strode over to lean against the post of the gazebo. He had his head down and was rubbing his eyes.

"Tell me what happened," said Lindsay.

"She just burst into flames." He snapped his fingers. "Just like that, she was suddenly on fire and screaming. I didn't believe what I was seeing. I didn't know what to do. She started running toward the lake. The only thing I could think was what the firemen said when they visited my class as a kid. I screamed at her, 'drop and roll, drop and roll.' I know that sounds stupid."

"No. That's what she should have done," Lindsay said, gently.

Luke looked at her. "You believe me?"

"Finish your story."

"She jumped into the lake and—I swear to you that this is the truth—she burned faster. The water was boiling and bubbling with it. God, I didn't know what to do. I thought maybe there was a gasoline slick by the bank, you know, from a motorboat or something. I found a tree limb and tried to fish her out. I finally got the fork of the limb around her neck and pulled her onto the bank. I was afraid to touch her. She was still on fire. I took off my jacket and shirt and began beating her. Finally, the fire went out."

"What did you do then?"

"Pretty much what I told you before. I just left. There wasn't anything I could have done. She couldn't have been alive." Luke sat down across from Lindsay and met her eyes. "I swear I didn't kill her. I don't know what killed her."

"Did you see anyone else there?"

Luke shook his head and lowered it. "There wasn't anyone else there."

"There was. The sheriff found a witness."

He jerked his head up. "She did? Then they must have seen the same thing. Who was it?"

"Someone fishing. That's the same story they told."

"Then the sheriff will have to let me go!"

"The sheriff thinks you may have thrown something on Foster to set her on fire."

"No. No, I didn't. I swear."

"Did you see anything that might have been thrown on her?"

Luke's shoulders slumped. "She just caught on fire." He paused and looked up at Lindsay. "You believe me, don't you?"

"I want to. Didn't you used to set things on fire?" she said quietly.

"How . . . ?" he whispered. "No . . . I . . . when I was a kid. A few times. It was just a stage I went through."

Lindsay raised her eyebrows. "A stage?"

"I used to burn things in the yard. I never hurt anybody. Who told you? Liza?"

"No. What kinds of things?"

"Old papers, clothes, some toys. Nothing really valuable. I was a kid. I liked to watch the flames."

"How about the gazebo?" asked Lindsay.

"I . . . How did you know? Who told you? My family are the only ones who knew."

"Never mind that. What about it?"

"I was fifteen. I'd been smoking pot and I was mad at my

folks and, I don't know, I just wanted to see something big burn. But I don't do that anymore. I started going to a therapist—hey, he didn't tell you, did he? He's not supposed to."

"No, my brother suggested it."

"Your brother? I don't even know him."

"He's a firefighter. It's one of those things firefighters notice," said Lindsay, with a wave of her hand. "The point is: Do you see what the sheriff could make of it?"

Luke put his hands to his face. "God, yes. But I didn't kill her. What I told you is the truth. There's a witness. Surely, that means something."

"Yes, I think it will mean a whole lot, but we'll have to find out what made her burst into flames."

"I've heard some people just do that. I read up on it after . . . after that night. Something about body chemistry?"

"My brother says that doesn't happen."

"Well, is he the last word on fire or something?"

Lindsay smiled. "No, but he has a point. Think back. Can you remember anything about what happened right before she burst into flames?"

"I've thought about it—replayed the scene over and over. She walked toward me. Held out her hands to me— and they were empty. She wasn't carrying anything. When she got close, she dropped her hands and called my name. Then it happened."

"You didn't see the witness, you may not have seen someone else there. You didn't see anything, any object hurled at her? Think."

Luke shook his head back and forth. "I saw her clearly, and there was nothing but what I told you. Nobody threw anything at her."

"Thanks for telling me the truth," said Lindsay.

"I only lied before because it's such a fantastic story, I didn't think anybody would believe me. What did you mean before, when you said you knew about the note?"

"An old friend of hers got a note asking him to pick up some copies from Kinko's. She wrote two notes, one for you and one for her friend, and I believe she accidentally switched the notes."

"So, it's looking better for me?"

"I don't know. I think a little better."

Lindsay drove back to campus. The lot behind Baldwin was almost full, and she had to park in one of the spaces next to the cemetery. As she got out of her vehicle, she saw someone sitting on a bench on the far side of the graves. It looked like Shirley Foster's mother, Evelyn Pryor. Lindsay walked through the gate of the old, rusted iron fence and among the moss-covered brick sepulchers and gray granite tombstones to where she was sitting.

"Mrs. Pryor?" said Lindsay. "I thought that was you." There were dark circles under the older woman's eyes. She looked small, sitting there on the wrought-iron bench, holding a thin blue sweater around her to shield her from the cool breeze.

Evelyn looked up, puzzled for a moment. "This is—was —one of Shirley's favorite places to just sit and think."

"That's right, her office was in the Visual Arts Building." Lindsay glanced at the building that sat on the other side of the cemetery from Baldwin.

"I thought it was strange, at first, to sit in a cemetery, but it is nice and quiet," Evelyn said.

Lindsay took a seat on a nearby gneiss ledge over a grave. "I imagine the people buried here are accustomed to visitors." She rubbed the faded inscription with her fingertips. "I've always felt comfortable here."

Evelyn smiled. "I sometimes go to places Shirley liked. It helps." They both were silent for a while. If Evelyn minded Lindsay being there, she didn't indicate it. "Do you think this Luke Ferris did it?" she asked after a while.

"No, I don't. But I may be wrong. It just doesn't feel right," Lindsay said.

"Who does feel right?"

"I don't know."

"We should have allowed her to marry Will Patterson. I think she would have been happy with him. Shirley had to work hard at being happy." Mrs. Pryor fell silent and shivered. "Tom told us the children were adopted," she said unexpectedly. Her eyes glistened with tears. "I don't know why Shirley was afraid to tell us. I look back and try to think if we were too hard on her. I told Tom I love them anyway, and I hope he won't keep them away from us. This is so hard. Do you think Tom could have killed Shirley? Stewart is convinced he did. I can't bear the thought of it."

"As far as I know, the only thing implicating Tom is that she was buried on his property. I understand that Tom had control over her money while she was missing but would lose it after she was pronounced dead?"

Evelyn nodded. "In the event of her death, her money was to be left in trust to her children. Her father and I are the trustees. She left a sum to Chris but not to Will. That surprised me. Of course, her father didn't want her to leave her money to Will, but she didn't always do what her father wanted, and I know she still felt something for Will."

"Why didn't she leave any to Tom?" asked Lindsay.

"He didn't need it. We wanted to make sure the children would get it," she said.

Lindsay considered telling her about the switched notes and that she suspected that the missing $100,000 was meant for Will Patterson, but she decided against it.

"Stewart is not having an easy time," said Evelyn. "He and Shirley quarreled before she disappeared, and it eats at him."

"What did they quarrel about?"

"It was my fault. Chris needed money to keep his art gallery going. His father and I hadn't wanted him to go into business for himself. Art is good as a hobby or if he was going to be a professor like Shirley, but it's not a good career. We wanted him to work at the family business. But his shop seemed to mean so much to him. I gave in and loaned him the money. It wasn't much money. That little business didn't take much, and he did seem happy doing what he was doing. When Stewart found out that Chris had gotten a loan, he hit the roof. To protect me, Shirley told Stewart that it was she who had loaned Chris the money. She never liked it when Stewart and I quarreled. They argued. Shirley told him Chris would be better off if Stewart would let him find his own path." Evelyn sighed. "It wasn't a bad argument. We are not a family who yell at one another. But Stewart hates it that that was the last conversation he had with her."

"I know that must be hard. You seem like a close family."

Evelyn smiled. "We are."

"I'm sure your husband had many more good conversations with Shirley."

"Oh, they would talk for hours in front of the fire in the winter or out on the deck in the summer. Yes, there were many, many good conversations between them. I told Stewart that, but," she wiped away a tear, "we loved her so, and her absence is so . . . so relentless."

"I'll try to find out who did this," said Lindsay.

"I hope you will. I don't want to blame it on this boy if he didn't do it, but if he did, I don't want him to get away with it."

"I'll find out the truth." She rose and left Mrs. Pryor sitting alone in the cemetery.

Lindsay sat at her desk wondering how she would discover the truth about what happened to Shirley Foster. She reached for the phone and dialed Sheriff Varnadore.

"You work late," Lindsay said when Irene answered.

"So do you," she responded. "Probably why we are both still single."

"Possibly," Lindsay said, then told Irene her theory about the switched notes.

"Interesting," the sheriff said. "I think you're probably right. That may mean Ferris was frustrated when Shirl rebuffed him."

"Maybe, but it also means he was telling the truth about the note."

"True," she said.

"Surely, the evidence against Luke is weak now that there is a witness."

"The D.A. thinks otherwise, and he's the one who has to put it before a jury," said Irene.

"Was there anything in the car?"

"Not really, just what you saw in the trunk, and the regular kind of stuff in the glove box."

"Thanks for sharing," said Lindsay.

"If you find out anything else, let me know."

Lindsay hung up the phone. She liked Irene Varnadore, but that didn't stop her from wondering if maybe she had killed Shirley. Irene had a cousin who was a hotshot. She could find out about how to set fires. She didn't seem capable of murder, but she lived in Shirley's shadow for a long time, and Shirley was many things that Irene was not. Still, Lindsay thought, death by fire? Whoever killed Shirley Foster hated her, or they liked to watch people burn. She shivered. Why else would anyone kill in such a gruesome manner? But whoever buried Shirley seemed to care for her. They placed her in the ground carefully, with her hands on her body, as if placing her in a casket. Two people, then? One who killed her and one who found and buried her? Could Lila Poole have buried her? Why would she?

Lindsay couldn't shake the dark feeling she'd gotten from Will. Would he get to thinking about how Shirley died and go out and kill someone, possibly the wrong person? Perhaps Will killed her and wanted Lindsay to discover it. She rejected that idea as quickly as she had thought of it. Far too melodramatic. What would have happened if the notes hadn't gotten switched? Would Will have been the one to see her burst into flames? Would he have handled the situation better and extinguished the flames before they killed her? Lindsay had a vision of Will taking Shirley into his arms and holding on to her as the two of them went up in flames, eternally commingled. Lindsay shook her head: what an absurd thought.

But who killed Shirley? Lindsay had no idea. Maybe it was Luke Ferris, but he was arrested only because he was there. Lila Poole was there. Could she have been involved in Shirley's death? That was a thought. Both Luke and Mrs. Poole had the same story. The sheriff thought Luke threw something at Shirley. Perhaps Mrs. Poole did.

She's an elderly woman. What would she be doing lobbing flames at Shirley Foster? Perhaps someone else was there. A relative of Mrs. Poole? Luke didn't see Mrs. Poole, so perhaps he didn't see the other person, either.

What would be Mrs. Poole's motive?

Something to do with the land?

What?

Blank.

Mrs. Poole seemed sincere. So did everyone else. Maybe there was a third person that neither Luke nor Mrs. Poole saw.

First, find out how it was done, Lindsay thought. Maybe the *how* will lead to the *who*. Maybe she was going about it all wrong. Maybe she should look at the question from the opposite end. If she were going to cause someone to burst into flames, how would she go about doing it? Lindsay was jarred from her thoughts by a gentle tap on her door, and when she looked up she saw Trey standing in the doorway.

"Come in," she said. Trey closed the door behind him and sat down.

"I hope I'm not disturbing anything," he said. "You looked deep in thought."

"They were thoughts I don't mind being brought out of," she said.

"I understand that feeling. Frank changed the Archaeology Club meeting. Clerisse won't be giving her talk about the LaBelle. Seems we get to hear Francisco Lewis instead."

Lindsay frowned. "Do you know him?" she asked.

Trey shook his head. "Just by reputation, and that's kind of a mixed bag. Actually, I don't think he's that bad. Just likes to be a star. Good at getting himself in the media. Some of the faculty think he might be good for the department."

Lindsay looked doubtful. "I don't know him either. As for being good for the department, I don't know. Sometimes good media makes bad science."

Trey shrugged. "I suppose all of us nontenured faculty will have to stick together," he said.

"What do Per and Stevie think?" asked Lindsay.

"They're worried. Me, too. It isn't good that none of us have gotten our renewal letter."

"Georgia has a coastline. It's logical to have an underwater archaeologist. You should be safe. I think, however, that I'm going to be redundant."

"I've heard some rumors," admitted Trey, "but that's all they are."

"Maybe, but I can hear the vultures flapping their wings. All these problems I'm having aren't helping."

"Reed thinks you'll land on your feet," said Trey.

Lindsay smiled and thought about the well. "Maybe, but where will I land on my feet?"

"Would you still like to go dancing?"

"Maybe just dinner," Lindsay said. "I'm not in much of a dancing mood these days."

"By the way, I've heard about your dancing. I hear you're pretty fantastic."

"A friend and I used to enter contests now and then."

"I'm kind of your basic dancer," said Trey.

"I can do that, too."

"How's the hunt for the lost artifacts coming?" he asked.

"Not well. I have a few very weak suspects. Right now, I'm the best suspect the campus police have."

"This must be hard on you," said Trey.

"I'll figure something out."

When Trey left, their date was up in the air, like every other aspect of Lindsay's life at the moment. She could tell that Trey was as worried as she that their contract renewals for the next year had not come down from the dean's office. She knew that Trey had just bought a house and a boat he was outfitting for archaeological use. Although Lindsay understood politics very well, it still amazed her that it was never enough just to do your job well in order to keep it. To her, it seemed that should be the only requirement.

All the students had gone home for the day. Sally hadn't been in. She and Sinjin had gone to Macon together to search for information about Hank Roy Creasey and hadn't yet returned. Lindsay closed up her office and the lab, climbed into her Rover, and headed home. She turned on the radio to WUGA, the campus public radio station, and listened to Bach, trying to keep thoughts of death and missing artifacts out of her head for a while.

As she passed the Ford dealership, she noticed it was still open, and she drove up to the door, meeting Jake on his way out.

"Hey, great. You caught me just in time. Here it is over here." He led Lindsay to a forest green Explorer with tan leather seats and a moon roof. "Nice, huh?"

"It's beautiful," said Lindsay.

Jake put down his briefcase and dug inside for some

papers. "I worked up some numbers to show you." He handed her a piece of paper. "This includes the Rover as a trade-in and a $500 down payment. What do you think?"

The payments were far lower than what she had now. She was tempted to hug him. Even though this and the second payment on the well drilling would finish off her savings, her monthly bills would be a lot less. "This looks good."

"Great. Why don't you take it home, drive it around a little, and we'll sign the papers tomorrow." He handed her the keys.

Lindsay took them, unloaded her Rover, and drove the Explorer home. She collected her mail at the box near her gate, laid it on the seat, and drove the long, winding drive to her cabin.

She sat down at the kitchen table to relax, enjoy a glass of Cherry Coke over ice, and go through her mail. Buried among the sales catalogs and junk mail was the payment booklet for the loan to finance her new water filtration system. The system had better last a long time, she told herself, looking at the crystal-clear cubes of ice glittering like diamonds. She saved the best for last—a large envelope from Derrick. Inside were a letter and copies of several newspaper articles. She looked at his handwriting and thought about him. His letter said he couldn't find a reference for Hank Roy Creasey, but he did find three articles mentioning a Henry Ray Creasey, which he thought was close enough to warrant a look.

One of the articles was a police blotter with a short mention of a seventeen-year-old Henry Ray Creasey arrested for stealing a car and wrecking it. The second article was an obituary like the one Lindsay had already seen, but this one had a photograph. It wasn't a good photograph, and it lost a lot in the copying, but the man in the photo looked remarkably like the Hank Roy Creasey in the picture from her grandfather's files. The third article was about the explosion in the mine. It was from a different newspaper than the article Lindsay had found in the crate. It said that Creasey, after being severely injured, was carried to safety by a man named Malcolm Dodd. Creasey was not expected to live. The article went on to say that it was believed the mine was blown up intentionally and, apparently, prematurely. It was believed that the perpetrator himself was caught in the explosion. The suspected saboteur was a man named Lonnie Cross.

There was a fourth article, dated two years prior to the mining accident. It was about the looting of important archaeological sites and mentioned several collections that had been stolen. It said nothing about any suspects or if any of the artifacts had been found, nor did it mention what kind of artifacts had been stolen. During one of the robberies, an archaeology student working late at the lab where the artifacts were stored had been hit over the head with a heavy object and had died several days later from her injuries. Her name was Rebecca Warfield.

There weren't many female archaeologists back then, thought Lindsay. She must have been an interesting person. Probably had fought hard to get into a field dominated by men and died before really getting to practice her profession—died at the hands of looters.

Lindsay rubbed her eyes with the heels of her hands and sighed. There was too much death in her life right now. She changed clothes and went out to the stable to Mandrake. Caring for him gave her a sense of peace: moving the brush across his coat, talking to him, having him nod his head up and down as if he understood everything she said to him. When she was riding, nothing existed except her and her horse. She took the bridle from its peg in her tack room. It was dusk, but there was still a little while left before dark. She put the bit in Mandrake's mouth and the bridle over his head. She didn't saddle him but led him away from the stable and out of his pasture before she grabbed a handful of mane and jumped on his back.

Ellen Chamberlain's method of teaching Lindsay to ride was to teach her to ride bareback first. Lindsay had been able to gallop bareback down a trail, jumping over logs and small streams, before she ever rode with a saddle.

She rode Mandrake at a walk to the back pasture where a large expanse of grassy ground stretched before them. He was alert and spirited, his ears listening for her command. She urged him forward with a gentle squeeze of her legs and he took off across the pasture. She felt his strong muscles, and for all she knew, she could be flying in the air if it weren't for the sound of galloping hoofbeats on the ground. There was only the power of the horse and her. The absence of distressing thoughts calmed her.

As they neared the other side of the pasture, she tugged the reins gently and Mandrake began to slow. They entered the woods at a canter. Lindsay rode him along a trail to the front pasture, the highest point on her property, and stopped to look around at the treetops of her woods in the valley below her. She loved this place—its seclusion, its smells, the wild animals, the abundance of everything she found peaceful and good in life.

She walked Mandrake back to the stable, passing ancient fence posts and terracing from years past, built by WPA workers during the Great Depression in the 1930s to control erosion—perhaps some of the same workers who helped excavate the Indian site in Macon with her grandfather. She brushed down Mandrake, checked his hooves for stones, and made sure he was cooled down before giving him his food and water.

She undressed and took a quick shower. The telephone was ringing as she stepped out onto the mat, and she ran into her bedroom and grabbed the phone before the answering machine picked up.

Chapter 21

"**L**INDSAY?" SAID THE voice on the other end. "Lindsay, is that you?"

"Yes, who is this?"

"This is Anne."

Lindsay frowned. "Anne. Hi." She tried to sound glad to hear from her father's cousin.

"I won't beat around the bush. I'm calling about the Indian relics."

"Yes?"

"We've been hearing up here that you and your brother sold them. Me, Steven, and others I won't name think you had no right. The relics belong to the family."

"First, neither Sinjin nor I have sold any artifacts. It's bad enough to hear those accusations from strangers. I don't like hearing them from family. Second, they do not belong to the family. When they are found, it will be between the State of Kentucky and the Native Americans in the area to decide ownership."

The line was silent a moment. "That's about what Steven said you'd say," Anne said.

"I'm glad he understands," Lindsay said.

"I'm not saying he agrees. Those Indian relics are the property of the people whose land they were found on. I know what your daddy says about him owning the land, but the fact is, Mother has lived there for years and she has rights."

"Anne, the artifacts were only stored there, possibly illegally. They were not dug up there. They were probably dug up several places around the state of Kentucky."

"So you say."

Lindsay sighed. "Anne, I don't really know what to say to you. I don't have the artifacts. If I did have them, I would hand them over to the University of Kentucky to sort out. That's all there is to it."

"A half-million dollars is a lot of money. You can't tell me you would just hand that over. I think you and St. John's sold them. We'll be watching."

"A half-million dollars!" exclaimed Lindsay. "What are you talking about? The artifacts aren't worth nearly that much."

"That's not what the papers say."

"Well, the papers are wrong. This is really getting out of hand." Damn, Lindsay thought, with stories like that, all the sites around will have to double their security. There will be pothunters coming out of the woodwork. "Anne, what did you hope to accomplish by calling me?"

"I wanted to reason with you. Get you to share."

"There's nothing to share. Does Maggie know you're calling?"

"Now, don't you go worrying Mother with all of this. She's not been well."

In other words, no, thought Lindsay, Maggie doesn't know. "She's gotten ill since I talked to her last?" said Lindsay. "I'll have to give her a get well call."

"Now, don't you be worrying her."

"Anne, I call and talk to your mother regularly. She'll think something's wrong if I don't call. She knows I'll call if she's not feeling well."

"She doesn't want anyone to know," said Anne.

"Look, Anne, I'm sorry to be having this conversation with you, especially since we haven't spoken in a while. I wish you would believe me about the artifacts, but since you don't, I can't help it." Lindsay thought she heard some-one talking in the background, coaching Anne. Probably Steven, she thought.

"Our daddy talked about a stash of Indian treasure, Steven remembers. You don't know that it don't belong to Daddy."

Lindsay was silent a moment, trying to think of the right way to word her question so as not to scare Anne off. "Oh, Anne, come on," she said. "That's hard to believe. You've never mentioned anything about a cache of artifacts before."

"It's true."

Lindsay heard some shuffling, then another voice came over the phone. "Don't you be calling us a liar, Lindsay Chamberlain."

"Hello, Steven." Lindsay didn't mention that they rang her specifically to call her a liar. "I'm not saying you're lying, just that I've never heard anything about your father having any stash of artifacts."

"Well, he did. You forget, Dad worked on digs, too, back in the thirties. He talked about the Indian treasure sometime in the late forties when times were hard for us. He said if they got too hard, he knew about a stash of Indian treasure he could sell," Steven said.

"How do you know these are the same ones?"

"Don't be ridiculous. How many stashes of Indian trea-sure do you think there are in the family?"

"Does Maggie know about them?"

"Stop bringing Mom into this. No, she doesn't. Dad never talked to her about money."

"Do you know any people named Creasey? Hank Roy Creasey or Henry Ray Creasey?"

"No, never heard of them."

"You ever hear of a Lonnie Cross?" asked Lindsay.

"What? Lonnie Cross? You talking about my uncle Lonnie?"

"I guess. Who exactly was he?" Lindsay asked.

"He was Dad's youngest brother, actually half-brother. Dad's daddy got killed, and Mamaw married one of the Cross boys. Lonnie got killed himself in a mine cave-in. Why? He got something to do with this?"

"I saw his name in a newspaper article that the artifacts were wrapped in. I wondered if he was related."

"See? See? I told you. That's proof. Don't you go destroying that piece of paper, Lindsay Chamberlain. Me and Anne heard you say you have it."

Lindsay visualized the two of them with their faces together on each side of the receiver. "I won't. I'll send you a copy if you like," she told him.

"Yes, you do that," he said.

"Look, Steven," began Lindsay.

"I think I ought to tell you," interrupted Steven, "Anne and me are talking to a lawyer."

"Fine," Lindsay said, rubbing her forehead. "I think that's the best thing for all of us. We'll let an objective third party sort it out."

"I was hoping we could come to an agreement. Keep it in the family like," he said.

"I'll tell you what I told Anne. I don't have the artifacts, and I don't know where they are, and if I did, they'd be sent off to the University of Kentucky."

"We're talking about a lot of money. That would mean a lot to our grandchildren," Steven said.

Don't do this to me, Lindsay thought. Don't act like I'm cheating my—she wrinkled her brow—my second cousins once removed out of an education. Lindsay decided to plead helplessness. "It's out of my hands now. If the artifacts are found, they won't even come back to me. You and your lawyer will have to take it up with the authorities."

"We'll do that. And we'll be watching to see if you come into any money."

Don't hold your breath, thought Lindsay as she said good-bye to Steven.

"I wish I'd blown the darn things up," she said aloud. That thought stuck in her mind: blown the darn things up. She shivered and realized she was still wet from her shower. As she dried off, that thought returned: blown the darn things up. It reminded her of the explosion at the mine where Henry Ray Creasey was supposed to have died. Lonnie Cross died in the same cave-in. Lonnie Cross was the half-brother of Billy MacRae, her great-aunt Maggie's husband. Anne and Steven MacRae's uncle, thought Lindsay. She had never heard anyone in her family mention this, but all families tend to hide their skeletons.

Lindsay's grandfather gave Billy MacRae a job at Ocmulgee in the thirties. Okay, she thought. That's a chain of clues. Hank Roy, Henry Ray. Hank is a nickname for Henry. Henry Ray, Hank Roy. Same initials: H. R. What if Hank Roy Creasey and Henry Ray Creasey were the same person? What if Henry Ray Creasey didn't die in the explosion but survived with a badly broken right leg? What if he changed his name and came to work on a dig with her grandfather?

She put on a nightgown and robe and sat on the bed thinking. What was it she was trying to come up with? What was that sudden cognition that a minute before had zipped through her brain too fast for her to catch it? Maybe the artifacts were supposed to be in the mine? Hidden? She shook her head. It had left her, if there had been anything there in the first place. But she was close, she felt it. Keep the chain going, she thought. First, establish that Hank Roy Creasey and Henry Ray Creasey were the same person.

There were too many mysteries to solve, past and present. Lindsay stretched out on her bed and closed her eyes. She heard the roar of a fire, jerked awake, and ran downstairs. Sinjin and Sally had returned from Macon and built a fire in the fireplace.

"What are you doing?" Lindsay asked. "It's seventy degrees outside. It's too hot for a fire." But they ignored her.

Sally was dressed in her *Rocky Horror Picture Show* costume and was sitting on the arm of Lindsay's favorite chair, legs crossed, swinging one leg back and forth and showing off an ankle bracelet. Sinjin wore vintage 1940s clothes. Sitting in the chair was Edward G. Robinson with an unlit cigar. Sinjin held out his hand and a match appeared. He flicked it with his thumbnail, it flared, and he lit the cigar. Now, it was no longer Sally but Gerri Chapman who sat on the arm of the chair with her arm around Edward G. Robinson's shoulder. Robinson took a puff from his cigar and looked at Lindsay. "You should have it all figured out, by now," he told her.

Gerri laughed.

Sinjin turned to say something to her, but an expression of horror came over his face. All their faces took on terrified expressions.

"What . . ." Lindsay said, and started to turn, when she heard a loud bang and felt something hot strike the back of her head, causing her to fall forward. "I'm all right," she whispered, feeling the rug under her fingers. "I can move, they must have just grazed me."

She looked about her, but everyone was gone. She stood and raised her hand put to the back of her head, then gazed at a smear of blood that wet her fingertips. "It doesn't feel like much more than a scratch," she said. She went to her small downstairs bathroom and looked in the mirror. One of her eyes was sagging, the other was completely dilated. "No, God, no," she thought. "I'm in trouble."

Lindsay's eyes snapped open. She was lying on her bed. A dream. Just a dream, but the fear clung to her like wet clothes.

"Lindsay?" There was a rap on her door. "Are you awake?"

It was Sinjin.

"Yes." She got up and looked in the mirror before opening the door. She looked normal, but her heart was still pounding.

"I see you got a new vehicle," Sinjin said. "I like it."

"I picked it up today. I like it too. How did your trip to Macon go?" she asked.

"It went well. I'm sorry I got back so late. Sally and I stopped for dinner. I brought you something in case you haven't eaten." He paused. "Are you all right?"

"Yes. Just a bad dream."

"I woke you. I'm sorry."

"I just fell asleep. I wasn't in bed."

Lindsay ran a brush through her hair and joined Sinjin downstairs. He had brought her fried shrimp, fries, and hushpuppies, which he was heating in the oven. Lindsay didn't know she was hungry until she smelled the aroma of the warming seafood. She handed him the articles Derrick had sent and sat down at the table to eat.

"How's Sally?" she asked, really wanting to know how he and Sally were getting along.

"Fine. Her ex-boyfriend's trying to get back into her life."

"Brian came by and apologized to me for Gerri's behavior," said Lindsay. "What does Sally think about him?"

"Right now, she's pretty mad, but who knows? Maybe later on. . . ." He let the sentence trail off as he bent to open the oven and began shoveling food onto a plate that he set in front of Lindsay.

Lindsay wanted to ask him how he felt, but the words never got past her lips. She didn't know why. Perhaps she didn't want to be a matchmaker, in case things didn't work out. She dipped a fry in ketchup and popped it into her mouth.

"Sally gave me a tour of Ocmulgee National Monument," he said. "Impressive. I liked the earth lodge."

"I guess Sally told you that it was probably not an underground structure after all."

"Yes, but I'm afraid some of the subtleties of archaeology are lost on me."

Lindsay laughed as she reached up and pushed her hair back from her face. She started to reply to Sinjin when she saw the blood on her hand. She stood, knocking over her chair, and a small, almost whispered scream escaped her lips.

"Lindsay, it's ketchup!" said Sinjin. "I started to mention it when you put your hand to your head."

"Ketchup?"

"Yes." He stood and took her arm to guide her back to the table. "Lindsay, you're wound pretty tight. You want to tell me what's wrong?"

"Nothing, it's silly. Just a dream."

"What dream?"

"Nothing," she said a little too sharply. Lindsay looked at her sleeve. She had dragged it through the ketchup. "Damn." She took off her robe. "I guess it got in my hair, too." She went to her room, changed into a nightshirt, and blotted flecks of ketchup from her hair with a wet cloth.

"You all right?" Sinjin asked when she returned.

"I'm fine," she said. "What did you and Sally find in Macon, anything?"

"Yes, we did. They do have some records of the people who worked there. We found a reference to the date when that Creasey fellow arrived at the site. He was on a 1935 roll but not on the ones for the following years. We copied a list of the people who were working there with him. I'm not sure what good it will do us, but here it is," he said, laying a stack of copies on the table. "Papaw and Billy are listed."

"That's interesting. We knew Papaw was there, but not sure about Maggie's husband. Anyone else we know?"

Sinjin laughed. "I doubt we know any of them."

She thought for a moment. "Look for the names Dodd, Timmons, and Stillman. They were in the mine when it

exploded. Two of them died. Maybe their relatives followed Creasey."

"You think the mine explosion is connected to Creasey's
death, then?"

"I think there's a good possibility. Creasey was supposed to have died in the mine, but he shows up in Macon
under another name, then gets himself stabbed and packed
in a crate."

"What?"

"Didn't I tell you?"

"No."

Lindsay told him about the newspaper articles and the
phone call from Anne and Steven. "Look at the picture,"
she said.

Sinjin examined the copy of the newspaper article for a
minute. "It sure looks like the same man, doesn't it? Or a
very close relative." Sinjin stroked his jaw. "Are you thinking that maybe it was this Creasey fellow who caused the
mine explosion, and a relative of one of the dead men
wanted revenge?"

"It makes sense," said Lindsay.

"Yes, and it still leads right back to our family," he
reminded her. "Billy could have followed him there to
avenge the death of his brother Lonnie."

"None of the other names are on the list?" she asked.

"No."

"What about Warfield?"

Sinjin looked at the list and shook his head. "Was he
another one killed in the mine?"

"She. And no, she was killed earlier." Lindsay pulled the
article from the pile and handed it to him.

"Another twist," he said, reading the article. "Do you
think the artifacts taken in these thefts could be the ones
that showed up in Papaw's shed?"

"It's a possibility."

"You've made a lot of progress," said Sinjin. He put the paper down and looked across the table at Lindsay. "Now, tell me what's going on with you."

"What do you mean?" she asked.

"You know what I mean. You're all stressed out."

"I'm just tired."

"What was that business a while ago with the ketchup?" he asked.

"I told you, I'm just tired."

"You've been tired before."

"Sinjin, I'm fine. I can handle a little stress."

"What about you falling in the well?"

"What about it?" she asked.

"It's not like you to be so careless. You could have been killed."

"Kerwin didn't fill it back in. He should have."

"You should have realized the possibility and been on the lookout. You're an archaeologist. You grew up playing and fishing in the woods."

"Sinjin, I don't know how many times I have to tell you. I'm fine. I know myself. I'm in control."

"Look, Lindsay, I couldn't help but notice your new well and the filtration system. It looks like the engineering section of the Starship *Enterprise* in your well house."

"My old well went dry and I had to have a new one dug. It's deep, almost four hundred feet, but the water's full of minerals and has to be filtered."

"It must have been expensive," he said.

"It was. What are you getting at?" she asked, narrowing her eyes at him.

"It must be a burden on your income. I know you just finished a major renovation of your house. And the Explorer—did you trade in your car to lower your monthly payments?"

"I'm handling it," she said, holding her chin up.

"If you need . . ."

"No, I don't."

"You have to be worried about your job."

"Of course. Yes, I'm worried about my job, and I have to clear my name before I can even begin to apply for a position anywhere else. No one is going to hire an archaeologist suspected of stealing artifacts. And I won't be able to get a job doing forensic work, either. I'd have no credibility on the witness stand."

"Then why are we trying to find out who killed this fellow sixty years ago? Why are you spending time on the Foster murder? Why aren't we spending that time hunting the artifacts?"

"I don't know where the artifacts are. I don't know where to look for them." She hesitated, not sure whether she should mention this to Sinjin in his current mood. "And I'm worried about what Will Patterson is up to. I feel I need to keep a hand in."

"What are you talking about?"

Lindsay had no choice but to tell Sinjin about her visit with Will. When she finished, Sinjin was incredulous. "You mean he's been sending you possible killers for you to evaluate?"

"Sort of."

"Sort of? He has. Lindsay, what's wrong with you? It's not like you to allow yourself to be manipulated."

"I'm not being manipulated," she said, staring hard at Sinjin.

"It looks like it to me," he said.

"I have everything under control."

"You just said that, and I see how you have everything under control. On top of everything else, I think you're still feeling the effects of your getting lost in that cave last year.

That had to be the most stressful time in your life—lost and struggling for your life in a place where one mistake could be deadly. You're about to fall off the edge."

"I'm not."

"You having headaches? You find yourself buying lots of antacid?" Lindsay said nothing. "Look, Lindsay, I have a high-stress job. I know the symptoms that tell me when I need a break. I see those symptoms in you. I'm going tomorrow and tell Patterson to lay off you. You aren't a detective."

"No, you're not. I can take care of my own life. I don't interfere in yours."

"Yes, you do."

Lindsay had a retort ready, but she saw the smile playing around his lips. She smiled too. "Okay. I did, once, and then only because it affected me, too." She frowned. "Sinjin, I'm afraid of what Patterson might do. I have no proof, nothing other than a feeling, but I'm afraid he's planning on, well, killing whoever killed Shirley Foster."

"What? Good grief, Lindsay. You have to turn this over to the police."

"I don't know for sure. All I have to go on is a fleeting glimpse of an expression on his face. I can't go and slander the man based on that. But I can't allow him to kill somebody, either."

"*You* can't allow? Lindsay, are you listening to me? You aren't in control of any of this. Other people are. I'll repeat what I said before: Drop everything but the artifacts, because that's the problem you need to solve to get your reputation back. Put your full attention on that."

Lindsay could see his point. If she weren't so tired, she might agree with him. "But I feel like if I don't hold everything together, it will all collapse," she said.

Sinjin reached out and took her hand. "It might all collapse—or not—despite what you do. Would it help some of the stress if I gave you a loan?"

"No, thank you. I really prefer to take care of my own finances."

"All right," he said.

Lindsay stood up. "I'm going to bed."

"I'll clean up down here and lock the doors," he said. "You need a good night's sleep. We'll talk in the morning."

Lindsay lay awake in bed, tears spilling from her eyes and running down into her ears. She wiped them with a tissue. I'm fine, she said to herself. I'll figure this out. In her mind she looked at the index cards she had made. She had left the Suspect cards for the missing artifacts blank. Who did she suspect? Einer. Why? He was in the lab the day after the artifacts were unpacked. Is that all? He visited the rare book room. That was nothing.

You've focused on him because you don't like him, she told herself. But he may be the one who sicced Kaufman on me. Irene said it was an associate dean, but there are other associate deans. It didn't have to be Einer. How would anyone else know about the artifacts that had been brought from Kentucky? From one of the students? Frank said that Einer didn't know about the artifacts, that he hadn't told him about them. Lindsay tried to remember what was said when Frank and Einer walked in after the skeleton fell out of the crate. Nothing about the artifacts. She specifically recalled that she had not wanted to mention them to anyone, but she hadn't told Sally or Brandon not to mention the artifacts. Anybody could have known about them. She sniffed and reached for another Kleenex and blew her nose.

Lindsay had flirted with the idea of Brandon as a suspect. Why? He was near Nancy Hart Hall when she was locked in. Very weak. He had photographs of the artifacts. He could have used the photographs to find their value, if he didn't already know. Anything else? He frequently asked about the artifacts and how her search for them was coming. But so did everyone who knew they were missing. Brandon was her student and it was natural to be concerned, but the last person she ever wanted to accuse was one of her students. She tried to shove Brandon to the back of her mind but without success. He had easy access to her letter opener. She didn't like that thought. She shoved him to the back of her mind again.

Anyone else? Kaufman? He wouldn't draw suspicion if he parked behind Baldwin at night. That would be true of any of the campus police. She didn't like that idea, either. The campus police at UGA were among the best. But what about Kaufman? He was dogging her. That's why she wanted him to be a suspect. Not a very good reason.

Sid the lawyer and Kathy, Sinjin's ex-girlfriend. Sid was on campus. Kathy lied—no matter that she later recanted. But Kathy might be the mother of her niece or nephew, and Sid would be Kathy's husband. She didn't like them as suspects, either. And it would be a stretch to connect them with the other thefts.

Lindsay had nothing. She wasn't much of a detective. Frank was right. There was more evidence pointing to her than to anyone else. Maybe I have multiple-personality disorder, she thought. Nope, no missing time to account for. I suppose I'm in the clear. So is Sinjin. He would never have done this and gotten her in so much trouble.

There were her other relatives. No. They wouldn't have called her, demanding that she return the artifacts. Maybe they were just being clever. No, they aren't that clever. Maybe Steven and Anne's children did it and didn't tell them. Another long shot. She turned over, closed her eyes, and tried to go to sleep, but thoughts kept racing through her mind. If she could just get them to make sense.

Kaufman had wanted to get a search warrant for my place, she thought. He couldn't because the judge he went to didn't think there was sufficient probable cause. If an administrator told Kaufman that he'd had his eye on me for a while, why couldn't Kaufman have used the administrator's testimony to get a warrant? Because the administrator didn't want him to. It was one thing to sic Kaufman on me with that reason; it was quite another thing to take that reason and make it public. It wouldn't have withstood the scrutiny. Why had he—or she—told Kaufman that lie in the first place? To make me less credible? To keep Kaufman busy going in the wrong direction?

And what about the artifacts in Sinjin's Jeep? It would have been easy enough to put them there. He kept the top down most of the time. Why hadn't artifacts been planted at her place, she wondered? They didn't know where she lived? That was possible. Living deep in the woods the way she did, anyone would need directions to find her place. There were no real street addresses like in town. But Tom Foster had found her. It could be done. Her home wasn't a secret. They would have to be sure no one was at home. With Sinjin visiting and her irregular schedule, that would be tricky. Where would they put them? Both her house and the well house were usually locked when no one was home. They would have to break in, and that would look suspicious. The only other building was her stable, and to get to it they would have to cross paths with Mandrake.

Horses are both curious and territorial. When any stranger came near Mandrake's fence, he pranced up with his neck bowed, his tail flagged, and pawed the ground. If they tried to come inside his fence, he would rear, stomp, and snort. If a stranger actually made it inside the fence with him, Mandrake would chase him. The horse probably wouldn't hurt him, but he could sure scare him to death.

She saw the strobe of headlights cross her window and heard car doors slam, then a knock at the front door. Who could it be at this time of night? she wondered, putting on a robe. Downstairs, Sinjin, in the sweatpants he slept in, had pulled on a T-shirt and already answered the door. Lindsay recognized Captain Grant, head of the university police. With him was a young female officer. Their faces were grim.

"Dr. Chamberlain. Could we come in and talk with you?"

"Certainly." She and Sinjin moved aside so they could enter.

Lindsay led them into her living room. She and Sinjin stood together, facing the two law enforcement officers. "When was the last time you saw Detective Kaufman?"

"Kaufman? Down at the Public Safety Building, with Frank Carter. Day before yesterday, I think? I'm sure it's recorded somewhere. Why?"

"His body was found this evening. He'd been stabbed," said Grant, eyeing her closely.

Lindsay opened her mouth, stunned. "With my letter opener, no doubt," she said.

Chapter 22

LINDSAY HAD TO admit to herself as she sat in her living room under the intense gaze of the two university police officers that the comment about the letter opener was about the stupidest thing she could have said.

"Exactly why did you say he was stabbed with your letter opener?" Captain Grant asked. He was a man Lindsay knew and had worked with in the past. She was reasonably sure he didn't think she had murdered Kaufman, but these days she was never completely sure of anything.

Sinjin sat down on the couch by Lindsay, taking her hand in his. The two officers sat down in chairs opposite. It was a moment before Lindsay answered. The man was dead, and a moment ago she had sounded flippant. She hadn't meant to.

"It has my name on it, and whoever is doing this seems to want to direct the attention of the police toward me."

"Someone has a grudge against you, you think? Do you know who?"

Lindsay shook her head. "Not necessarily a grudge. It may only be that I'm a convenient scapegoat. I know Kaufman was married. Did he have children?"

"Two teenagers," said the woman, introduced by Grant as Officer Sharon Meyers. "Twins."

Officer Meyers was young and athletic-looking. She had short blonde hair and green eyes which glittered at the moment as if she were holding back tears.

"I'm sorry. I'll do what I can to help you find the murderer," Lindsay said.

"Where were you this evening between seven and nine?" asked Grant.

"Here. I left work about 6:45. I talked to a faculty member, Trey Marcus, for about fifteen minutes before I left. I drove home, stopping at the Ford dealership up the road from here, and talked to Jake Gilroy. When I got home, I opened my mail and I rode my horse. I have my dirty riding clothes from riding bareback. I know that's not proof, but it does support what I'm telling you. After that, I took a shower. All that took about an hour and a half. Two of my cousins called, and I talked to them about a half hour. It was long distance, and I imagine it will show up on telephone records along with the exact time. I fell asleep on the bed until Sinjin got home."

"It looks as though we can verify most of that," Grant said. His attention turned to Sinjin. "Do you mind telling us where you were?"

"Not at all. I went to Macon this morning with a friend, Sally Flynn. We were there most of the day and got home about ten this evening."

Grant's cell phone rang. He answered it and listened to the caller. "Interesting," he said, and punched the disconnect button.

"Kaufman was shot and the letter opener placed in the wound. Whoever it was couldn't possibly have hoped to fool us. It was obviously done to pull your chain, Dr. Chamberlain."

"Detective Kaufman must have discovered who was stealing the artifacts," said Lindsay. "That would be the only reason to try to connect me."

"You argued with Kaufman several times," said Officer Meyers. "Can you tell us what that was about?"

Lindsay eyed her a moment. She didn't know if Meyers

was unwilling to let go of her as a suspect, or if she was trying to get a handle on how Kaufman was thinking about the investigation.

"He had focused in on me for the theft of the artifacts without, I believe, enough justification. He appeared not to be looking anywhere else for a solution. He was antagonistic. I reacted to his manner."

"You didn't know that he wasn't being thorough in his investigation. He had his methods of interviewing people and he got results." The way Officer Meyers's chin was thrust forward, Lindsay assumed she was being defensive and not informative.

Lindsay deliberately concentrated on keeping her voice even and cordial. A fellow policeman had been murdered. She knew that produced an angry hurt in the entire force. But Lindsay was tired of people painting a target on her and shooting at it.

"I understand, and had his interaction with me been only between me and him, that would have been fine, but it was also in the papers, and he interviewed me in the presence of my department head. All this has compromised my position at the university. I'm having to fight to keep my job, and I haven't done anything. Sacrificing my job and reputation for his investigative methods was rather callous, I think."

"Kaufman can't be held responsible for the press," said Grant mildly. "We can't stop them."

"I'm aware of that, but knowing that the press would be on it, he should not have been so insistent on my guilt."

"You just overreacted," said Officer Meyers. "He was no more focused on you than on anyone else."

This wasn't an argument Lindsay could win, she knew that, but she plunged ahead anyway. She was angry at Kaufman for getting himself killed. "You're wrong," she said. "Everyone knew he was investigating me: the newspapers, my department, you. But you don't know who else he was investigating, do you?" It was a guess on Lindsay's part, but she thought she was right. "Why is that?" Neither answered her and she continued. "Someone was manipulating him, giving him false information to cloud the case. I think he caught on, and that may be the reason for what happened to him this evening. I've been told it was a senior administrator, an associate dean."

Grant looked surprised. "You don't suspect an associate dean of murder, do you?"

"I don't suspect anyone. I don't have enough information. But I do suspect an associate dean of directing Kaufman toward me. Irene Varnadore, sheriff of Dover County, knows Kaufman and his wife. She may be able to help."

Lindsay wanted to ask them questions, but she knew they wouldn't answer her. She was a suspect.

"May I see your riding clothes?" asked Officer Meyers.

"Sure." Lindsay led her upstairs to her bedroom. She opened the clothes hamper. Her riding clothes were fortunately on top. She pulled out her jeans and showed Meyers the seat and legs. There was a distinct pattern of dust and horse hair on the seat. No matter how well she brushed Mandrake, riding bareback always got her jeans dirty.

"I saw your horse. He's really beautiful. Reminds me of the Black Stallion. He looks like a valuable horse," said Meyers, taking a sudden turn toward friendliness. Lindsay was surprised her jeans were that convincing.

"Thanks. He's a gift from my mother. She raises Arabians. I'm really sorry about Detective Kaufman. Sheriff Varnadore thought a lot of him, and he was very kind to my graduate assistant, Sally Flynn, when she was attacked. This is a terrible thing, and I'll be glad to help in any way I can."

"Thank you. He'll be missed." As Lindsay led her down the stairs, Meyers tried to make light conversation. "I noticed your Land Rover as we drove up. How does it drive?"

"It's not a Rover, it's a Ford Explorer, and it drives well."

"Oh, well, it was dark."

They reached the landing, and Officer Meyers told Captain Grant about the riding clothes. He nodded to Lindsay and Sinjin, and they left.

"Just when you think things can't get worse," said Sinjin.

Lindsay stopped by Jake Gilroy's Ford dealership on the way into work and signed all the paperwork. It always surprised her how much was involved in buying a car—more than buying her property. If Jake had gotten a call from the campus police, he didn't indicate it. Lindsay was relieved. The press she had been getting lately was bad enough, but having the police going around to people she knew and checking her alibi was embarrassing.

Captain Grant did phone her mid-morning and told her that her alibi had checked out. Lindsay thanked him for calling.

"Do you have any leads?" she asked.

"Not really. Kaufman usually kept meticulous notes, but he didn't tell anyone where he was going last night."

"It must have been a spur-of-the-moment thing, and he must have not expected any trouble," said Lindsay. "Otherwise, he would have told someone or had backup."

"It would seem so. He did record in his case file the name of the person who told him that he should investigate you. We're going to talk to him."

"Is that information you can share with me?"

"No."

"Well, thank you for calling. I appreciate it."

So, thought Lindsay, at least I know it's a him. She picked up the phone and called Will Patterson at his office. She was glad to hear that he sounded sober. He hadn't yet fallen off the wagon.

"I was wondering if you could do me a favor?" she asked. It was the least he could do, she thought, for all the aggravation he had caused her.

"Sure thing," he said. "What do you need?"

She told him about Detective Kaufman and about the missing artifacts. "The campus police can't give me any information about the circumstances of his death, or any other leads they have," she said. "Do you have any contacts who might give you that information?"

"Hmm, maybe not directly. I don't do much university work that involves the campus cops, but I may know a few people who know a few other people."

Lindsay told him what she knew about Kaufman's death, including her alibi and the letter opener. "His death has to be related to the artifacts. Why else put the letter opener at the scene?" Will agreed with her.

"I think Kaufman discovered who was stealing artifacts on campus and maybe even what they were doing with them," Lindsay added.

"I'll find out what I can and get back to you. It shouldn't take too long."

Lindsay thanked him and hung up the phone. A thought struck her. She picked up the receiver and dialed Patterson's number again. "Do you think you could find out if he called anyone right before he left the office?"

"Well, maybe, if it was long distance."

Lindsay shook her head as she spoke to him. "He would have made it from his office on campus. All campus calls that go off campus are logged electronically, even if they're local."

"Really? I didn't know that."

"Most people don't," she said.

"Who would have that information?"

"BellSouth initially, then the business manager of each department gets a printout once a month, I think. But I'm sure the police would be looking for that information first thing. Maybe your sources will know."

"They might. I'll check. That's interesting to know about the phone calls."

Lindsay could imagine him tucking it away for future reference. She said good-bye again and dialed Sheriff Varnadore. "Irene, I just wanted to say I'm sorry about your friend, Detective Kaufman. Friends are hard to lose."

"Thanks. It was such a shock. Jesse called me late last night with the news."

"I told the campus police to talk to you because you knew him. They came to see me last night."

"Really? Did they suspect you?"

"It seems that whoever did it left something of mine at the scene." Lindsay told her about the letter opener. "Fortunately, I could account for myself."

"I heard that he was shot."

"He was. The murderer put the letter opener in the wound," Lindsay told her, then belatedly wondered if that was an item the university police were keeping to themselves. She mentioned as much to Irene.

"Somebody hates you in a big way," the sheriff said.

"Maybe. I don't like thinking that there's someone out there who hates me that much. Perhaps they just wanted to confuse things."

"If the letter opener was evidence in another case, I wonder what the perp was doing with it?" Irene mused. "Kaufman must have had it with him."

"I don't understand it either," Lindsay said. "I just wanted to give you my condolences." Irene thanked her and they hung up.

Lindsay hated to think what the papers would say today. Probably something like: "Lindsay Chamberlain, soon to be former Archaeology faculty member, has been questioned in the death of the campus detective who wanted to arrest her for stealing antiquities." Lindsay put her face in her hands and thought about Kaufman's family. Whatever she was going through, they were going through something so much worse.

• • •

Sinjin came to her office bearing turkey sandwiches, three bean salad, potato chips, and Cokes for lunch.

"You want to eat in the cemetery?" he asked.

"Let's go to Memorial Park. I'll drive you in my new Explorer."

It was a windy, cloudless day, cool enough for a jacket. They chose a picnic table next to the duck pond and she brushed leaves and twigs from the concrete bench and sat down. She had to anchor the napkins with her drink can to keep them from blowing away. Five geese waddled up from the pond, and she threw pieces of her bread crust to them. The geese all jumped for the bread, honking noisily.

Sinjin watched her silently for a few moments. "How you doing?" he asked finally.

"Fine. You don't need to look at me like I have a terminal illness." She paused. "I'm sorry, I shouldn't have said that."

"That's all right. I like your new truck."

"I like it, too. The moon roof is kind of fun. Captain Grant called and told me my alibi checked out."

Sinjin smiled at her. "At least that's one thing you don't have to worry about." He took a bite of his sandwich. "I had a long talk with Maggie this morning. I didn't mention anything about the artifacts. I told her that looking at all those old photographs and newspaper articles had gotten us interested in our family history."

"Did you find out anything from her?"

He pushed his salad around the Styrofoam bowl with his fork, and several seconds went by before he answered. "Yes, I did. We'll probably never know exactly what happened, but I think I can make a good guess."

"Are you serious?" Lindsay said. "You've figured it out?"

Sinjin nodded. Lindsay wanted to ask him if their grandfather had done it, but she couldn't bring herself to say the words.

"I asked Maggie if she remembered Billy's brother, Lonnie. Of course, she did. She had never heard of Creasey, by the way." Sinjin took a large envelope from inside his jacket and selected a photograph from among several inside. It was of their grandfather and a younger couple with their arms around each other's waist. "This is Lonnie Cross." He pointed to the young man.

Lindsay picked up the picture and examined it. "He looks like Billy." She laid it down on the table.

"And this," Sinjin pointed to the young woman, "is Rebecca Warfield."

Lindsay's jaw dropped. "You mean the one . . ."

"Yes, the archaeology graduate student who was killed during the theft of the artifacts. She was engaged to Billy's brother, Lonnie Cross."

Chapter 23

"**B**ILLY'S YOUNGER BROTHER was engaged to the archaeology student who was killed?" Lindsay whispered.

"Maggie said Lonnie nearly went crazy when she was killed. Vowed to find who did it. Here's what I think happened."

Lindsay set her sandwich aside and listened to her brother.

"It was the middle of the depression, and times were hard for everyone. You said Creasey's bones showed signs that he'd worked hard all his life." Lindsay nodded and Sinjin continued. "He apparently had turned to petty thievery to make ends meet, according to the article. Stealing Indian artifacts was an easy occupation for him to move into. I don't imagine it was a crime that had a high priority with the authorities. That is, until he broke into a lab at the University of Kentucky and unexpectedly ran into a student working late. He must have panicked and hit her on the head with the first object at his fingertips, which happened to be a grinding stone, and it killed her."

Lindsay shivered as a gust of wind blew through the park.

"Lonnie Cross," Sinjin went on, "started looking for his fiancée's murderer. I don't imagine it was too hard to get a lead on who was dealing in Indian artifacts. It may not have been as much a secret back then, when collecting was more acceptable. He got a line on Creasey.

"Creasey may have hidden the artifacts in the mine he worked in, maybe in one of the played-out shafts. Lonnie Cross got a job in the mine, found out about the stash, and confronted Creasey. Something happened, and there was an explosion. Perhaps Creasey planned it to get rid of Lonnie Cross. Whatever the motive, Lonnie and three other men died in the explosion and cave-in."

"The article said that Lonnie Cross was suspected of causing the cave-in," Lindsay said.

"The survivor gets to write history." Sinjin stopped and took a bite of sandwich and a sip of drink. "Creasey was hurt pretty bad, from your description of his bones, but I don't think he died. He knew he was in trouble, that someone might find out the truth, that someone might follow in Lonnie Cross's footsteps. So, I think Creasey went to his people after he got out of the hospital and had his family send an obituary to the newspaper. I don't imagine that was too hard. Newspapers don't require a death certificate. Creasey changed his name slightly and headed south.

"But that bit of trickery didn't fool Billy, and Billy followed him. Maggie said that Billy was beside himself when his little brother, Lonnie, died. He almost beat up a detective who suggested that Lonnie had caused the explosion. Maggie said she was glad when Billy wanted to go to Georgia and work with Papaw. She thought it would be good for him to get away. I think Billy caught up with Creasey at the archaeology dig in Macon and killed him, to avenge his brother's murder. One other bit of evidence: Billy was a tall man, as tall as Papaw, and he was left-handed."

Lindsay absorbed everything Sinjin told her, turning it over in her mind, comparing it with the facts she knew. She could find no fault with his analysis, but that didn't mean it was true. "What were the crates doing in Papaw's shed?" she asked.

"I think Papaw helped Billy cover up Creasey's death."

"Why would he do that?"

"When you thought Sid and Kathy had stolen the artifacts, you were willing to sacrifice those items if it would keep peace in the family. You thought Kathy was carrying my baby, and you didn't want anything to stand in the way of me having a relationship with my child. As dedicated as you are to archaeology, you were willing to sacrifice the artifacts, if necessary, for your family. I think Papaw did the same thing. Maggie was his favorite sister. She was married to Billy. It would have killed her to have Billy arrested for murder and sent to jail. He hid the body and the artifacts in a safe place that only he knew. I don't think even Billy knew where they were. Billy knew they were hidden somewhere, he even alluded to his son of their existence, but I'll bet he didn't know where Papaw hid them."

"There's no proof to support your scenario. Papaw could have killed Creasey," Lindsay said.

"I don't think he did. I think Papaw would have turned Creasey over to the authorities when he found out about the stolen artifacts. Billy's motive was much stronger. Creasey had killed Billy's brother and his brother's fiancée. And Billy had a temper. He may have confronted Creasey, and they may have gotten in a fight. We'll never know exactly how it happened. But you knew Papaw. He didn't have a temper, and I don't think he did it. There was Creasey, a possible murderer and thief, and there was Papaw, the respectable archaeologist. Papaw wouldn't have been afraid to own up to it."

"Unless it was deliberate murder," said Lindsay. She wanted Sinjin to come up with some definitive piece of information or logic that said her grandfather hadn't done it.

"He wouldn't have committed murder. He would have turned Creasey over to the sheriff. I'm certain of it." Sinjin reached out and took Lindsay's hand. "Papaw was proud of his work in archaeology and proud of you. He would have thought a lot about the legacy he was leaving to his son. He was worried on the day of your graduation what legacy he was leaving you. I think that's what he was thinking about in that picture."

"I want to believe that's what happened," Lindsay said. "I wish we could know for sure."

"Sometimes you don't get to know for sure," he said.

"What are we going to do about it?" she asked.

"What's to do? The authorities have the same information we have. More, they have the skeleton. If they're interested and think of it, they can ask if the family has any old photographs and go through the same process you did. We have no evidence. We're just guessing."

"It will always look like Papaw killed that man and stole the artifacts."

"Yes, and I don't know what we can do about that without accusing Maggie's dead husband of murder."

"You did a good job," Lindsay said. "Looks like you have a little bit of detective in you, too."

He smiled. "Runs in the family, I guess. Besides, you did all the work."

Lindsay had only one voice mail waiting for her when she returned to her office from lunch—Will Patterson. She dialed his number.

"You found out something, Will?" she asked.

"Yeah, quite a lot, actually. Kaufman was found in his car on Chase Street at 9:30 last night by a couple who saw it in a ditch. They called the police. The police think he was killed someplace else, then the killer put his body in the car and drove the car to where it was found. They don't have a medical examiner's report yet, but, as you said, they do know he was shot and that your letter opener was added later."

"I don't suppose you discovered if he called anyone before he left his office?"

"Yes, I found that out, too" Will said. "Kaufman called

Chris Pryor at home. Chris wasn't there. He then called Chris's shop from his car phone. The police talked to Chris, and he told them that Kaufman wanted to know how much his parents were paying you to find his sister's killer. He told them that as far as he knew, I was the detective his parents hired, and Kaufman should ask me what your fee is."

"Why did Kaufman want to know that, I wonder?" Lindsay asked.

"Chris told the police he didn't know," Will replied.

"Anything else?"

"I found out who was pointing Kaufman to you. It was in his notes." Will paused.

Lindsay gripped the phone. "Who?"

"Ellis Einer. Know him?"

"Yes, I know him. I thought he was the one. Damn him! I suspect that he had something to do with the artifact theft, but I have no evidence, just a hunch."

"I'll keep my ears open," Will said. "If I hear about anything else, I'll give you a call."

"Ellis Einer," Lindsay said out loud after hanging up the phone. "That son of a . . ." She rose from her chair, grabbed her purse and jacket, and stormed out the door. Walking across the old part of campus was something she usually enjoyed—the old buildings, huge ancient trees, green lawns. Now, however, she saw nothing of the beauty as she crossed in front of the library and made her way down the grassy quadrangle to the Administration Building situated next to the famous arch, the symbolic front door to campus.

Lindsay stopped inside the building's lobby only long enough to look for Ellis Einer's office number in the directory. The assistant dean's office was at the end of the hallway on the first floor. She marched through the glass doors and told the secretary she wanted to see Einer.

"Do you have an appointment?" the secretary asked.

Lindsay had to tell herself that this woman was not at

fault. She forced herself to speak calmly. "No, but what I have to see him about is important." A man came out of Einer's office at that moment and Lindsay saw Einer sitting at his desk as the door closed. "Oh, I see he's free," she said, and before the gatekeeper could close the drawbridge, Lindsay dashed into his office.

"Dr. Chamberlain, this is a surprise," Einer said, smiling broadly. "What can I do for you? Please sit down."

Lindsay remained standing. "You can tell me why you told Detective Kaufman that for a long time you have suspected me of stealing antiquities."

"I don't know what you're talking about." All traces of his smile disappeared.

"Murder brings things out in the open, Dr. Einer. Don't deny it, I know it is true. What I don't know is why."

Einer said nothing for a moment. Lindsay could see him fighting to keep his temper. "I knew that there were some thefts," he began slowly. "You have been living beyond your means, and . . ."

"What? Exactly why do you think that?"

"I know you have a $100,000 Arabian horse and a $55,000 Land Rover, and you are a nontenured assistant professor who has been on the faculty only a couple of years. I know what you make. You can't afford those luxuries."

"Dr. Einer, you have no idea what I can or can't afford. How do you know about my horse?"

"My daughter has an internship with your vet. She was quite impressed with your stallion and mentioned it to me."

"Did she also tell you that my mother raises Arabians and she gave me the horse?" Einer said nothing. "And you don't know what I paid for my Rover or anything about my finances. How dare you use that flimsy evidence to justify telling Kaufman that I'm a thief."

"Dr. Chamberlain. I suggest that you keep your voice down."

"I suggest you do some serious repair work on my reputation."

"Perhaps it would be better if you leave."

"You know what I think?" said Lindsay. "I think you're the one stealing the artifacts, and you accused me in order to misdirect Kaufman."

Einer leapt up from his plush leather chair. "How dare you . . ." he sputtered.

"You use the rare book room where items are missing, you know about the artifacts stored at Nancy Hart where items are missing—you've complained enough about the space—and you knew about the artifacts that my brother brought from Kentucky."

"All that is rather weak, don't you think?" He relaxed, folding his arms, smiling at Lindsay. "Besides, I knew nothing about the Kentucky artifacts prior to their disappearance. You certainly didn't tell me about them, and if you ask Dr. Carter, he'll tell you he didn't tell me. I can't very well steal something I know nothing about. And I would watch very carefully whom you accuse of theft, Dr. Chamberlain. Your position at this university is very precarious."

"You've made sure of that." Lindsay turned and marched out of his office and came face to face with Captain Grant and Officer Sharon Meyers. Obviously, they had heard everything—as did everyone else in the office suite.

"Dr. Chamberlain," Grant said. "This is a surprise."

"How did you find out who Kaufman was talking to?" asked Officer Meyers.

"I have sources," Lindsay said. "And why did you think I drove a Land Rover?"

Before Officer Meyers could answer, Einer came out of his office, his hand outstretched to Captain Grant, grinning broadly again. "I'm glad you came by," he said, a little too loudly, Lindsay thought.

"Watch him closely. Kaufman may have caught on to

him," Lindsay said to Grant and Meyers. She turned to see Einer give her a malevolent look.

Lindsay returned to her office, sat in her chair, and stared at her grandfather's trowel sitting on the bookshelf, thinking that she should feel panicked about what she had just done. But she didn't. She felt relieved that the helplessness she had been feeling for days had lifted. Which astronaut said, "If you have only ten seconds to catastrophe, you spend nine seconds thinking and then you act, no matter what that act is"? Maybe it wasn't an astronaut, maybe it was Mr. Spock. Whoever it was, Lindsay believed they were right.

Frank burst in without knocking. "Lindsay, what in the world were you thinking? Do you know who I've been talking to?"

"Ellis Einer, no doubt."

"Yes, Ellis Einer. Lindsay, have you gone crazy? You know, don't you, that there is no way they are going to renew your contract after this? Just what were you trying to do?"

"Shake him up."

"Well, you succeeded."

"Good, did he confess?"

"Don't be flip, Lindsay. This is your career."

"Yes, I know it's my career, and I'm not going to sit back and watch while Einer tries to destroy it. He's been sitting up there in his plush office whispering in Kaufman's ear, lying, slandering me, making me a grand larceny suspect, and I've been helpless up until now, because I didn't know who was telling lies about me. Now that I know, I'm not going to sit around and wait to see if things just happen to work out in my favor."

"You think the answer was to go to his office and accuse him?"

Lindsay stared at Frank for a moment. "Yes, I do. Do you know why he said he did it?" Lindsay answered before

Frank could say anything. "He said it's because he thinks I'm living beyond my income."

Frank opened his mouth and closed it. He sat down. "So, he admitted accusing you?"

"Yes, he admitted it. I told you before that I thought Einer was the one talking to Kaufman. I had a friend confirm it from police records before I went to Einer's office. Frank, the only reason he accused me was to make sure the investigation for the missing artifacts went astray. As far as I know, he had nothing against me personally. I think my brother and I were simply convenient."

"But how did he know about the Kentucky artifacts?"

"He was here when the skeleton fell out of the crate."

"Yes, but there were no artifacts visible then," Frank said. "I didn't tell him about them. It's not something I wanted him to know about. He's always bitched about the amount of storage space we use. Do you think one of the students could have told him about them?"

"I don't know. I don't think so. I don't know who would have. Sally and I asked around, and I really don't believe any of the students have talked with Einer. They don't even know who he is."

"Lindsay, the artifacts were stolen less than two days after they arrived. Their presence here wasn't common knowledge. Perhaps that's why Einer thought it was you. That, and the fact that some of the artifacts were found in your brother's Jeep."

"Those were planted, Frank." Frank sighed, and Lindsay wondered if he really believed Sinjin had stolen them after all.

"Maybe he didn't know that, Lindsay. Maybe that and your seeming to spend money beyond your means really did make him suspicious."

"He told Kaufman that he'd suspected me for a long time. I assume he was talking about the thefts from the museum about a year ago."

"That is strange," Frank conceded. He brushed his black hair from his face and wrinkled his brow. "Still, going to the Administration Building and publicly accusing Einer. I just don't know."

"The way it was, all he had to do was sit tight. It would all blow over. There wasn't enough evidence to arrest me, so his conscience would be clear about that, but the police still had me and Sinjin as their prime suspects, and they wouldn't look anywhere else, certainly not at him. I had to shake him up."

Frank couldn't seem to come up with a counterargument, but Lindsay could see he clearly didn't think her solution was the right one, either. "What do you think this will gain you?"

Lindsay had to admit to herself that she wasn't sure— but not to Frank. "I want to direct some of the police's attention toward him, and I want to make him nervous. He'll be more apt to make a mistake."

"Lindsay, you're sounding like an old detective movie. Why don't you give the police your suspicions and let them take care of it?"

"Because they don't care about me like I do. My career crisis is not a crisis to them."

"Be careful. As bad as things seem now, they can get worse if you persist in pushing Einer."

"Maybe. And maybe they'll get better." They were both quiet a moment, and Lindsay cooled down a bit. "Trey tells me that Francisco Lewis is coming to town," she said.

"Yes. I'm hoping we'll all know a lot more about the future of the department by the time he leaves."

"Is this impending change the reason none of the non-tenured faculty have gotten the letters renewing our contracts?"

"I think so, but I don't know for sure. I've called Administration, but I can't get an answer."

Frank left with a final warning, which Lindsay planned to ignore. Whether it was just adrenaline or the act of taking initiative, she felt better. She wasn't planning to let Einer off the hook, at least until she got a better answer from him.

But she was stumped about what to do next. A rash act would only take her so far. It was time to devise a more thoughtful plan. She really didn't know anything about Einer, other than the usual academic information. She knew his doctorate was in physics, but he had been an administrator for most of his career. Who could she ask about him, she wondered? The Pryors knew him. They were the ones who sent Einer to her in the first place. She doubted they would talk to her about him, but maybe Chris would. She pulled an Athens phone book from her drawer and looked for the number of the Glass Imagerie.

As Lindsay waited for the clerk to get Chris to the phone, she considered several ways to ask him about Einer and rejected them all, opting for the straightforward approach. She expected him to politely tell her he didn't know anything, and that would be it. She heard rustling as he picked up the phone.

"This is Chris, what can I do for you?"

"Chris, this is Lindsay Chamberlain. I know this is unusual, but I was wondering if you can tell me anything about Ellis Einer? I know he's a family friend and I would-n't blame you if you went to him with this—" She hurried on before he could answer. "But you are the only person I know to ask, and it is important to me."

"Well, sure. He's my parents' friend, mainly. They play bridge together." He hesitated. "I'll tell you what I can. How about over dinner? Maybe you can meet me at the Last Resort this evening?"

"Yes. Thank you, Chris. I appreciate this."

"I don't know what I can do, but it'll be nice to have dinner with you."

Chapter 24

LINDSAY FOUND CHRIS waiting for her outside the entrance to the Last Resort Cafe. "Thank you for meeting with me," she said.

"No problem. I've been looking forward to it all afternoon." Chris wore jeans and a navy windbreaker and looked more comfortable than the last time she had talked with him. "I appreciate what you did for me and my family."

"I only did what Will hired me to do."

"Nevertheless, finding Shirl has given the whole family some closure to a very painful period."

They entered the restaurant and seated themselves at a corner table. The waitress came with menus and water. Lindsay ordered only a salad. The sense of relief brought about by her action had not yet reached her stomach. It was still tied in knots. Chris ordered a sandwich and a beer.

"I saw your mother at the cemetery beside Baldwin yesterday," Lindsay said.

"She and Dad've been pretty upset. Tom told them about Monica and Jeffery being adopted. They don't understand why Shirley went to all that trouble to hide it." He shook his head. "I could hardly remind them of the disapproving comments they made about our cousin who was adopted."

"I haven't seen an announcement of a funeral service for Shirley," Lindsay said as considerately as she could. "As difficult as funerals are, they do help reach closure."

Chris frowned. "Mom and Dad have been trying to get Tom to allow them to hire another forensic expert to examine Shirl's bones. They're arguing over that now."

That surprised Lindsay, but she said nothing.

"That's my fault, I'm afraid. Mom and Dad were upset over some of your findings, and I told them that if they weren't satisfied, they should get another opinion. Right now they're trying to convince themselves that Tom made up the adoption story in order to stop them from pushing for a new forensic examination. I don't think Mother believes that, but Dad does."

"Perhaps a second opinion would be a good idea for them. Another forensic anthropologist will find the same thing I did."

"I suppose you're wondering why I don't just tell them the whole story about the adoption." Chris signaled the waitress for a second beer.

"It's none of my business."

"I've tried a couple of times but I have neither the courage to hurt them nor the desire to go through their questions of why I hadn't told them before and why Shirley had confided in me and not them."

"I can understand that. You were put in an awkward position," Lindsay said.

"Do you think this guy—Ferris—did it?" Chris asked.

"I don't know. There's no real proof either way. I don't think he'll be convicted on the evidence the sheriff has now."

"I wish it were all over. Having Shirley's remains helps, but I just want it to be over."

"This must be really terrible for you," Lindsay said. "I shouldn't be bothering you."

"No, I didn't mean that." He smiled at her, then reached out and touched her hand, gently brushing the back of it with his fingertips. "I really meant it when I said I've been looking forward to this. Please, ask your questions."

Lindsay smiled back. "OK. Do you know if Einer has an interest in antiques? I know his degree is in physics, but have you heard him talk about antiquities or anything like that, or does he have any in his house?"

"The only thing I've ever heard him talk about with my dad is politics. They are of like minds. I've been to his home for dinner, and he does have antique furniture in his house. But you mentioned antiquities. You mean like Greek or Chinese vases?"

"Something like that. Or Native American artifacts?"

"No, I haven't seen anything like that in his house or heard him express any interest. Except I know he's complained to Dad about the amount of space the university uses to store Indian artifacts."

"Yeah, we've heard that, too."

Chris smiled. "I don't think he likes things like that. He's more of a hard-science kind of guy, I think. If you don't mind my asking, just why do you want to know these things? Thinking of buying him a gift?"

Lindsay shook her head. "Hardly. He, well . . . look, I know he's your friend."

"He's Mom and Dad's friend. Like I said, he's a science guy. I'm an art guy. I've never figured why they put Arts and Sciences together in the same college. They should be separate—a College of Arts and a College of Sciences."

"And a College of Humanities?"

"Yeah, that, too. Keep all those science people from complaining about all us arts and humanities people. So, what's the story on your interest in Einer?"

"Have you read the papers lately?"

"What about, in particular?"

"About me."

"Yes, I've seen a few articles," he said. "Must be tough."

"Especially since I haven't yet received my contract renewal for next year."

"Because of the articles? Most of the stuff I've read is just speculation."

"There are a lot of changes going on involving my department, and that's part of the reason for the delay. But the accusations—or speculations—haven't done my prospects any good at all."

"I'm sorry to hear that. Where does Ellis figure into this?"

The waitress brought their food and Lindsay waited until she left before she continued. "He's the one accusing me."

Chris raised his eyebrows. "Why?"

"He says it's because he thinks I'm spending money beyond my means. I believe it's to throw the trail off himself or someone else he is trying to protect."

"I find that hard to believe." Chris didn't look cross or cool, but sympathetic—and skeptical.

"Everyone finds it hard to believe, but there is no other reason for him to cast blame on me. The police are looking only at me. If I don't get to the bottom of this, no one will, and I'll be the one to suffer. The artifacts haven't shown up anywhere, except those that were planted to cast suspicion on me. I'm hoping they're hidden somewhere until they can be moved. Let's suppose for a moment that Einer is behind the thefts. Do you know if he has a place he might store stolen antiquities—a mini-warehouse, a summer house? How about a basement?"

Chris shook his head. "I don't know the answer to that. He does have a basement, but his wife and daughter live in the house. They would run across a cache of stolen goods, don't you think? Unless you believe they're in on it with him."

He thought she was paranoid. Lindsay shook her head. "No. I doubt it. I know I'm grasping at straws, but the artifacts are somewhere. For a while they were stored on campus."

"Perhaps they still are. There are a lot of possibilities on campus, and the university owns property all over the state. If it's true and Ellis is the one, then he conceivably could have access to any number of storage sites anywhere in the state of Georgia."

Lindsay sighed. "You're right. I didn't think of that. I suppose it's hopeless."

Chris reached across the table and took her hand. "Nothing's hopeless. I tell you what, Mom and Dad are playing bridge over at his house tomorrow evening. I'll tag along and have a look around. He does have a garage apartment they sometimes rent out to students."

Lindsay shook her head. "No. If I'm right and Einer is the one, then he may also be a murderer."

"What?" He let go of her hand.

"I'm sorry, I shouldn't have said that."

"Since you have, what are you talking about?"

"Did you read about the campus policeman who was murdered?"

"Yes."

"He was looking for the artifacts, and he was the one Einer was telling that I was a suspect. I believe his death had something to do with the missing artifacts."

"I don't believe Einer would do that. He's a bit disagreeable, but murder?"

"I know. I have a hard time visualizing it, too, but if it is true, you don't need to be caught snooping around."

Chris smiled. "He won't do anything while my parents are there."

"You're making fun of me."

"A little."

"I know I must sound like a paranoid lunatic."

He smiled, looked away, then back at her, still smiling, as if she were funny instead of crazy. "A very charming paranoid lunatic. Seriously. I see your reasoning. It's just that I can't believe he'd commit murder." Chris took her hand again and rubbed a thumb across the back of it. "I'll do what I can. After all, I owe you."

"For what?"

"I'm sorry for putting the idea in my folks' heads about hiring another forensic expert. In view of what's going on in your life right now, you don't need your credibility questioned any further."

"No, you were right about a second opinion. Anything that will give them some peace. And you don't owe me anything."

Chris squeezed her hand gently and let it go. They ate and talked about the exhibition Chris was putting together. "It's called 'Me and My Sister.' It will be mostly my work and hers. I thought it might help Mom and Dad, and me, too. Shirley gave me a lot of support and believed in me when no one else did. I'm doing well, and I owe much of it to her and her faith in me."

After dinner, Chris walked Lindsay to her Explorer, parked two cars down from his. "Maybe we can do this again," he said.

"Maybe we can. You've been very nice about this," said Lindsay.

Like Irene, Chris was very different away from the people who pushed his buttons. He looked at Lindsay for a moment, then kissed her cheek.

Back in her office with the door closed, Lindsay laid her head on her arms on her desk. She was almost never sleepy during the day but now felt like she could sleep through the whole mess and not wake up until it was over. The sudden ringing of the phone made her jump. She picked up the receiver as if it were a snake.

"Lindsay, this is Anne."

Lindsay rubbed her forehead. "What do you want, Anne?"

"Steven and I have proof."

"Proof of what?"

"Proof that the Indian relics belong to us. Your father, Edward, gave us the proof. I don't think he knew it, though." She had a slight chuckle in her voice.

"What's your proof?"

"When your father opened one of the crates, he found Dad's knife. It had his name carved on the bone handle as pretty as you please. Your dad gave it to Mom. We just now found out about it."

Lindsay sat up straight. "Knife?"

"His big hunting knife."

"How big?"

"What?"

"Was it as long as, say, a ruler?"

"Yes. What does that have to do with anything? You aren't going to sidetrack me, Lindsay."

As Anne spoke, Lindsay opened her desk drawer and pulled out the Kentucky newspaper and spread it open on her desk. She looked closely at a stain that she'd seen on it the first time she looked through the paper, but hadn't paid much conscious attention to. She had thought it was a smudge. Now she saw the pattern of the stain, two dark shapes side by side. The left shape was more or less rectangular, the right shape was like an arrowhead, and the bottom edge of each faded away. It was a pattern she'd seen before, the pattern made when someone takes a bloody knife in his hand and wipes the blade with a cloth, or in this case, a newspaper. An arrowhead on the right indicates the person held the knife in the right hand; an arrowhead on the left means the knife was held in the left. This stain had been made by a person holding the paper in the right hand and the knife in the left. This was a left-handed person.

Uncle Billy's knife was in the crate, Uncle Billy was left-handed. She wondered if that particular newspaper, the one with Creasey's false obituary, was used on purpose, as a clue, or perhaps as irony. Oh, Anne, she thought.

"You listening to me, Lindsay?"

"Yes, I'm sorry, Anne. I was just surprised."

"We thought you would be." Anne sounded very satisfied. "He's right here. You talk to him, he'll tell you."

"Who?" asked Lindsay. "Dad?"

"No, Lindsay Chamberlain. Dodd . . . Malcolm Dodd. He's the rest of the proof. Are you listening?"

The gravelly voice of an old man came on the phone. "Miss Chamberlain?" he said.

"Yes. Are you the Malcolm Dodd who brought Henry Creasey out of the mine after the explosion?"

"Yes, ma'am, I am. That was a long time ago. I'm eighty-five now; I was about twenty or twenty-one at the time. How'd you know about that?"

"I've been reading about it in old newspapers."

"That was a bad thing. A lot of good men was killed in that explosion."

"Did you know Henry Creasey well?" asked Lindsay.

"Not real well. Him and his people kept to themselves mostly. I worked with him on some things. That's what Steven and Anne want me to talk to you about."

Lindsay relaxed in her chair as he began his story.

"That was back during the Great Depression. Everybody was poor then. Me and my brothers went squirrel hunting every Sunday when we wasn't working in the mines. Mama would go out with my sisters and pick wild plants. There's plenty of wild food you can eat." Lindsay heard someone urging him on in the background. "I'm getting to it," he said to them.

"Take your time," Lindsay said.

"Thank you, ma'am. Anyways, we was poor, but Creasey and his people was what you called dirt poor. Henry told me that he used to eat a handful of clay every morning before he come to work in the mines so's his stomach wouldn't hurt from hunger. We'd sell anything back then. Me and Willard—that's my brother—used to go to where the drunks hung out and we'd collect their bottles. We'd sell 'em to the bootleggers for a nickel a bottle, sometimes the same bottle over and over. Henry found out about how to look for Indian relics. You'd go to where there was an Indian burial ground, take a rod and push it into the ground. It had a certain feel when it hit some bone or a pot, then we'd dig it up."

"I'm familiar with the practice," Lindsay said.

"Well, he found that there'd be people who'd pay pretty good money for these relics. So, that's what we'd do on Sundays, me and Henry, when we wasn't in the mines." Dodd stopped talking a moment.

"Go on, tell her," Lindsay heard Steven say.

"Well, we found out it was a lot less work if we let the archaeologists dig the stuff up first, and then, well, we'd, uh, take it from them. I had a hard time with that, so I didn't go with him much, but Henry got real good at it. He gathered a whole lot of relics and hid them in the played out part of the mine we was workin'. He was going to sell the lot of them when the accident happened and he got bad hurt."

"How did the explosion happen?"

"I don't know. Henry said it was Lonnie Cross what did it, but I knowed Lonnie and he wouldn't do nothing like that. Some said it was Henry did it, but I don't know. He got hurt hisself, and he knowed about dynamite; that was his job."

"The newspaper said he died."

"I know it said that, but they was wrong. He didn't. He may have put it in the papers hisself. He was always dodging something. I saw him when he was mostly mended. He said he got work with the CCC down in Macon, Georgia, to the place where archaeologists was diggin'. He was going

to meet somebody who was going to buy his relics for a lot
of money."

"Do you know who that person was?"

"He told me it was Billy MacRae. He said Billy had a
brother-in-law who was an archaeologist and they'd pay
good money to get the relics back. The idea was that Henry
would sell them to Billy and Billy would sell them to the
archaeologist. They'd both make money off it. Henry
thought it was funny, selling the relics back to the people
he'd stole them from in the first place."

"So, Henry Creasey met Billy MacRae in Macon?"

"I reckoned that he did. I didn't hear from him again
after that."

Lindsay heard shuffling noises, like the phone was
being transferred to someone else. "You heard him, Lindsay," said Steven. "You heard him say that our father
bought those Indian treasures."

"I also heard him say that he was going to sell them to
his brother-in-law—which was Papaw," Lindsay said.

"If he'd done that, your papaw would've put them in the
university, wouldn't he? No, Daddy bought the relics and
stored them in the shed where they stayed for these sixty-
odd years. Those are our Indian treasures, Lindsay Chamberlain, and me and Anne want them or the money."

"Well it's a moot point at the moment, Steven, because I
don't know where they are. When they turn up you can take
your proofs to the state and deal with them. The artifacts
aren't mine to turn over to you."

"This is proof, Lindsay. Daddy's knife was there with
them. You heard Malcom Dodd's testimony. That's proof."

Lindsay sighed. "It might be, Steven, but I'm not the one
you need to talk to. I have no authority over them whatsoever.
Go to your lawyer and ask him to take it up with the state."

"Then you admit it's proof," Steven persisted.

"It's proof of something," Lindsay said. She heard the telephone change hands again.

"Maybe we'll take it to the newspapers," said Anne. "Get public opinion on our side. It's a good story. They'll print it."

"Anne," said Lindsay, "have you forgotten about the skeleton found with the artifacts?"

"What about it?" she said.

"You don't think the newspapers'll be interested in that?"

"Just one of the burials. That's what the newspapers say."

"What?"

"I have it right here. It says that maybe the skeleton is an Indian burial that was wrapped in old clothes to protect the bones."

Lindsay groaned. That was the story Sinjin gave Maggie. She must have given it to a reporter. "It's not an Indian burial."

"So you say. It's right here in the newspaper."

"How did you find Malcolm Dodd?" Lindsay asked.

"Me and Steven took out an ad in the papers. You asked Steven if he knew anyone by the name of Creasey, and we figured it was important. We asked if anybody knowed a Creasey or a MacRae back during the depression that had something to do with Indian relics. There'd be something in it for them if they came forward. Mr. Dodd answered. You aren't the only smart member of the family, Lindsay Chamberlain."

Lindsay smiled. "No, apparently not. That was very clever, Anne."

Lindsay could almost see Anne's satisfied countenance as she hung up the phone. Lindsay drummed her fingers on her desk. "Well, Papaw, I suppose that's it," she said to the photograph of her grandfather. "I've done my best. If Steven and Anne go to the newspapers, at least it may come out that you wanted to buy back the artifacts for the university."

Lindsay replaced the Kentucky newspaper in the box with the other old papers in which the artifacts had been wrapped and taped the box closed. She wrote a note to the authorities in Kentucky where the skeleton was shipped, explaining where the newspapers came from and that they might hold evidence related to the identity of the skeleton. They will just have to figure it out, she thought to herself.

She made a label and took the box up to the main office and asked the secretaries to let it go out with the next mail. Then she went home, putting the skeleton out of her mind and concentrating on where the artifacts might be located.

She drove home the back way. It was more scenic than the main route and there were fewer cars on the road. It took longer, but she preferred it. Asking Chris about Einer was a long shot. She wasn't sure she had learned anything useful from the meeting, at least nothing she hadn't already known about him. She knew he wouldn't keep the artifacts on his property. If he had them and they were still in town, they were probably somewhere on campus. However, as Chris had pointed out, the university owned a lot of buildings all over the state. The artifacts could be sitting in any one of them, labeled with something like Fredrickson Foundation. Or he could have sold them to a private collector, in which case she would probably never discover their location.

What a mess Creasey created all those years ago. What a mess her grandfather had left her with. Were the stolen artifacts connected with the death of Kaufman? And what was Kaufman doing with her letter opener? It should have been in the property room along with the box of artifacts. The box of artifacts—Lindsay wondered if it was missing also. The police would know, but they wouldn't tell her. What would Kaufman have been doing with them? Could he have been in on it? Lindsay wondered, not for the first time. That would be an avenue of investigation she would just have to set aside for a while. Now that Kaufman was dead, she couldn't accuse him and expect any cooperation from the police.

Sinjin was at home when she arrived. "I thought you were going out with Sally," she said, settling on the couch and kicking off her shoes.

"I took her home early so she could study for a test."

"You got my message, didn't you?"

"Yes. How did your dinner with Chris go?"

"It was nice. I didn't find out any information, but I had a good time. He's really a nice guy."

"Sally told me about your conversation with that guy Einer. It's all over the department."

"I'm sure it is. I thought he needed shaking up."

"From what I hear, you did a good job of that."

"Well, I still haven't solved anything, but maybe he'll get nervous and do something rash."

"That's what I'm afraid of," said Sinjin. "Something rash might be something dangerous."

"I got another call from Anne and Steven today," Lindsay said, changing the subject. She related the conversation to him. "It looks like your hypothesis was correct. Billy did it with a knife in the cornfield. He probably lured Creasey down to Macon to meet with him with the promise of buying the artifacts. Since Lonnie was his half brother and they didn't have the same name, Creasey probably wasn't suspicious. Maybe they got in a fight or maybe Billy just took his revenge. Anyway, it's done. I sent the newspapers to the authorities in Kentucky. They have all the evidence I have, if they choose to pursue it."

"Poor Anne and Steven," Sinjin said. "I'm sure they didn't know what they were really telling you." He grinned and shook his head. "So, that story I gave Maggie got in the papers and now it's back to us."

"I suppose I'd better call Dad and let him sort the thing out. Maybe he can reason with Anne and Steven."

"Lindsay, I got a call today. There's a fire in California," Sinjin said.

"You have to go?"

"Not yet, but I may. I'm afraid to leave you, with everything up in the air like this."

"Sinjin, I've lived quite a while by myself. I'll be fine. I'm sure you've stayed longer than you intended, and I appreciate it."

"I know, but you've had a lot of close calls."

"Yes, I agree. I think you'll just have to give up your job and move in here with me. We can both look for jobs at the same institution so you can watch over me at work, too."

Sinjin grinned. "How about a little TV tonight? Get your mind off of everything?"

"I could use a relaxing evening."

Lindsay popped a couple of bags of popcorn into the microwave, and they settled in the living room in front of the television. Sinjin flipped through the channels with the remote.

"You know, there is a *TV Guide* around somewhere," she said.

"This way's much better." He grinned and settled on the movie *Quest for Fire*. "Have you seen this?" he asked.

"Yes, but I don't mind watching it again. I like it."

"You sure? What's it about?"

"It's kind of a primitive picaresque story about a tribe from about eighty thousand years ago. They have fire, but they have to keep it going, because they don't know how to make it. When it's put out in an attack, three members of the tribe set off to steal fire from a more advanced tribe. It's about the adventures they have hunting for fire. You know, they learn about life from their adventures, that kind of thing. I think you'll get a kick out of it."

"It sounds like your kind of movie," he said, returning with two bowls of popcorn.

Lindsay smiled, her legs crossed under her and her popcorn in her lap, and watched the movie. About halfway through the show, Lindsay looked at her brother.

"Sinjin, if you wanted to make someone burst into flames, how would you do it?"

"I thought we were going to forget about that for a while."

"The movie reminded me of it. You know: quest for fire. Aren't there chemicals besides napalm that would cause the same effect as the witnesses described?"

"Yes, there are, but if they're used, they leave traces of residue. Why don't you wait for the complete chemical analysis of the remains?"

"The Pryors are having another forensics expert analyze the bones. My reputation is being attacked from all sides. I need to do this."

"Why are they having someone else look at them?"

"They don't like some of my findings, I suppose."

"Surely a second opinion's not a big deal?"

"No. Another expert should find the same things I found."

"There are other things you can use," said Sinjin, "and some of them are pretty mean. But the problem is, you need something more than a kitchen to mix the chemicals."

"We have a university with labs all over campus," Lindsay said. "Do you always have to have an outside ignition source to set them off?"

"Pretty much, but the source can be subtle. Something organic."

"Really? People are organic, you know," Lindsay reminded him.

"But you'd still have to throw the substance on them. I don't know of anything that would work the way the witnesses said. They were mistaken. Now let's watch the movie."

They watched in silence a while, Lindsay forgetting about her problems.

"Was it really like that eighty thousand years ago?" Sinjin asked.

"Could've been. Shirley Foster wrote in an article that there was more color in ancient history than we portray. Of course, eighty thousand years ago was way before textiles."

"Jeez, Lindsay, give it a rest," he said.

"Yeah, you're right." They fell silent again and watched the movie.

"Does she go through the whole movie naked?" Sinjin asked, gesturing at a young woman on the screen.

"Pretty much." Lindsay grinned. An image flashed through her mind, from somewhere in the depth of her subconscious, she supposed, but didn't know exactly where. "Why was Hercules tearing off his clothes?" she asked.

"Hercules? Did I miss something?"

"You know, in the statue. Why was he tearing off his clothes?"

"What statue?"

"You know, it shows a bearded, muscular Hercules in a ragged tunic trying to get it off."

"I have no idea," Sinjin said. "Why are you asking?"

"Wasn't it poisoned or something?"

"I don't know what you're talking about," said Sinjin.

"I seem to remember something about Hercules' cloak being poisoned with, what was it, dragon's blood or something?"

"Where are we going with this?" Sinjin asked.

"Blood. Dragon's blood," Lindsay said almost to herself.

"Do I need to call a doctor?"

Lindsay threw a piece of popcorn at him. "In an article Shirley Foster wrote, she mentioned a dye named dragon's blood." She reached for the phone book on the end table, looked up a number, and dialed.

"Kenneth, this is Lindsay."

"What do you want?" he said.

"I have a question."

"Go to the library. Do you know how long I spent with the sheriff because of you?"

"Come on, Kenneth, you'll be getting rid of me soon enough. Indulge me."

"True," he said. Lindsay thought he sounded happy. "What's your question?"

"Do you know what dragon's blood is?"

"Are we talking about realgar?" Kerwin asked.

"I don't know, are we? Is it an ancient red dye?"

"Yes," he said.

"What is it, exactly?"

"It's a compound of arsenic."

"Arsenic?"

"Yes. Why do you want to know?"

"I was just reading about dyes."

"This isn't about Shirley Foster, is it? Is this some kind of trick?" Kerwin said, his voice full of suspicion.

Kenneth Kerwin's voice sounded sinister when he was wary. Lindsay imagined him grabbing Shirley and kissing her. She thought of the song Will Patterson said described Shirley. "She's frequently kind and suddenly cruel." Lindsay bet Shirley would have laughed at Kerwin rather than becoming angry. Did he follow her to the Foster farm, hide in the woods, and become infuriated when he saw what he thought to be an assignation with a much younger man? And then what? Take the napalm or whatever he just happened to have in his trunk and throw it on her? Or take gasoline and throw it on her, then somehow ignite it? But Lindsay could not see Kerwin lurking in the woods and doing all that. Also, this was a premeditated murder, not a spur of the moment one.

"No," Lindsay said, "It's not a trick. I just wanted to

know. Was Hercules' cloak poisoned with dragon's blood?"

"No. The blood of a centaur, if memory serves. Now please call the library if you have any more questions."

She hung up the phone and turned to Sinjin. "Dragon's blood is an arsenic-based red dye used in prehistoric textiles," she said. "Shirley probably used it, because she was into re-creating old dyes and fabrics by original processes."

"And?"

"And the medical examiner said there was arsenic in her remains."

"At least now you're making some sense," Sinjin agreed, "but that only means she was wearing fabric she made. So, what does that have to do with anything?"

"Could Shirley's death have been an accident? Could the dye in her clothes have ignited somehow?"

"Arsenic doesn't have the properties that the witness described," he said. "I can see maybe the arsenic becoming absorbed through her skin and killing her eventually, if she wore the clothes all the time, but the arsenic wouldn't catch on fire."

"Maybe if it were mixed with something or . . ." Lindsay threw up her hands. "I don't know. I feel so close. Edward G. Robinson said I'm close and I should have it figured out by now."

Sinjin turned down the volume on the television. "Just when did he say this?"

"In a dream."

"Edward G. Robinson came to you in a dream and told you that you're close to solving the death of the Foster woman?"

"No, he didn't come to me in a dream. I dreamed about him, and he said that I have all the pieces and I should have solved it by now—or something like that."

"And you put some kind of faith in this?"

"Not in that. In the brain. It likes to organize facts. It

puts like concepts together and often stores them in the same place. That's why sometimes when you go to bed with a problem, you find the solution in the morning. Anyway, while it's working on things, those things sometimes come out in dreams. It's simply the brain organizing things. At least my brain works that way, and I doubt if my brain is unique."

"Oh, I think your brain probably is very unique."

Lindsay stood. "I'm going to get a beer. You want one?"

"Sure."

She started toward the kitchen. "You know, maybe someone treated her clothes to make them so they would catch fire, or maybe she was trying out a new dye. I'll have to find out how Hercules was killed."

"I guess then you need to look for someone who knows mythology and is a chemist."

Lindsay walked into the kitchen and came back out almost immediately, staring at Sinjin wide-eyed.

"What?" he asked.

"Gloria Rankin, the girl hit by the bus, who was coming to see me the day she died, was a classicist and a chemist."

Chapter 25

"**T**HAT'S SOME COINCIDENCE," Sinjin said after a moment.

Lindsay came back and sat down opposite him, leaned forward, and placed her hands on her knees. "That was where I saw the statue of Hercules tearing off his clothes. It was in Park Hall, where Gloria Rankin had an office. There were some journal articles with them, one of them authored by Gloria Rankin." Lindsay tried to remember the title. "I think it was a review of *Trachiniae* by Sophocles. Isn't that about Hercules?"

Sinjin shrugged. "Look, I agree it's interesting that she has a background in chemistry and mythology. But I'm not sure how this ties in with Shirley Foster's death. You think this Rankin girl was coming to confess?"

"Maybe. Or maybe she knew who did it."

"But why come to you so long after the death? Why didn't she go to the authorities when it happened?" Sinjin asked.

"Maybe she didn't know what she knew until the body was found and the newspaper reported that the body was partially burned. I don't know, something about the description must have clicked with her. This doesn't look good for Luke Ferris," Lindsay said. "He was driving the bus that hit Gloria. He was with Shirley when she died. Maybe he got the idea from Gloria's article of a way to start a spectacular fire. Maybe Gloria remembered his interest and was coming to tell me."

"Still, why you and not the authorities?" Sinjin asked.

"Maybe Gloria wasn't sure. Maybe Luke was a boy-friend and she didn't want to get him into trouble if it was nothing, and she decided to check it out with me first." Lindsay shook her head. "But he was on a regular route with the bus. I don't know how he could time it so that he arrived at the place she was crossing the street at just the right moment."

"You have another problem, too," Sinjin said. "I don't know of a process to treat fabric that would give the results reported by the witnesses to Shirley's death, and you still have the problem of how it could have been ignited. Neither Shirley Foster nor her clothing spontaneously combusted."

Lindsay stood up again. "I don't know. Maybe I could talk to her office mate again . . ." She started into the kitchen again, then paused. "When I was in Gloria's office, I saw her thesis on the shelf. It had a very catchy title. Something like *The Source of Medea's Sorcery.*"

"Isn't that the chick who killed her kids to get even with her husband? What does that have to do with this?"

"She did something else, too." She put her hand to her head as if she could massage the information out. "You know, I never really liked the classics all that much, and now I wish I'd paid more attention." Lindsay looked at Sinjin, half a smile on her lips. "She gave her rival a cloak that caught fire when she put it on."

Sinjin cocked an eyebrow. "Okay, I'll admit, that's inter-esting. It's more than interesting—but Medea and Hercules are just myths."

"Myths often have some basis in fact. The important thing here is the subject of Gloria Rankin's thesis, *the source of Medea's sorcery.* I think Gloria figured it out. Her master's was in chemistry, and she combined that with her interest in the classics." Lindsay folded her arms. "I'll bet there is some connection between Gloria's murder and Shirley's. I'll bet it was the same person. I need to find out what her thesis said." She looked at her watch. "Too late to get to the library. I'll go first thing tomorrow and check out her thesis. Wait, no. I'll have to go to Park Hall. As I recall her master's was from the University of Chicago. Our library won't have her thesis."

"There still has to be a way to ignite the clothes," Sinjin said. "You know, Lindsay, as nice as this all sounds, it seems like you're working your way to some elaborate murder weapon. Why not just shoot her—unless the goal was to watch the conflagration that resulted and her death was just the by-product? Luke Ferris was a firebug, and I still think he had something to do with it."

"Maybe. And maybe it was an accident. Maybe Shirley had been trying out new dyeing techniques and stumbled onto something deadly by accident." Sinjin was shaking his head as she spoke, but once Lindsay got her train of thought traveling at full steam, it had a lot of inertia behind it. "Maybe Shirley was trying to make Medea's cloak. That would be something a textile historian with an interest in the classics might like to experiment with. Maybe she just grabbed the wrong jacket that night." Lindsay hesitated a moment.

"You don't even know what the myth of Medea is," Sinjin pointed out. "You need to verify that before you start building a scenario around it."

"There's Luke's dream," she said.

"Not a dream again."

"I told you, sometimes dreams are just the brain organizing itself. Luke's been having a recurring dream about hitting Gloria with the bus. When he gets out to see about her, he is Hercules trying to lift the bus off her." Sinjin raised his eyebrows. "Yes," Lindsay said. "Another coincidence.

His therapist believes he's trying to deal with the guilt of not being able to save her—which does make sense and may be part of it. Brains put like concepts together. Hercules is strong and could save her, but why him and not Batman or a Power Ranger?"

"Okay, why?" Sinjin asked. "'Cause Batman's the coolest."

Lindsay rolled her eyes. "The medical examiner said that Gloria didn't die immediately. Luke reached her first. What if she spoke to him and mentioned the name Hercules?"

"And that's why he dreams of Hercules and not Batman? Maybe, but this is getting to be a stretch."

Lindsay shook her head. "No, it isn't. In his dream Luke wore a red cape. 'Red' again. Gloria may have mentioned something about red, too. Maybe the arsenic that makes the red color is part of the formula. Hercules had a poisoned cape. Suppose she knew that and it was on her mind?"

"That still doesn't help Luke."

"It might. Why would he tell about the dream? He would feel uneasy just mentioning the name Hercules if he had read Gloria's stuff and tried it out. Maybe Gloria was going to tell me she thought the whole thing was a tragic accident on Shirley's part. First, I have to establish whether Shirley knew Gloria. But that shouldn't be hard."

"You're looking for a coat that ignites, not one that poisons," Sinjin reminded her. "However, I would like to see Gloria Rankin's formula. I'll go with you tomorrow."

Lindsay felt good when she arrived at work—optimistic. So when she found the letter on her desk and ripped it open, she was unprepared for the contents.

"Dear Dr. Chamberlain," it read. "Unfortunately, we have decided not to renew your contract for the coming year." Lindsay read no farther. She wadded up the paper and threw it across her office. She bit her lip, determined not to let the tears that were already starting to sting her eyes spill over. She would bite through her lower lip if necessary, but she wouldn't let anyone see her cry.

Sinjin stood leaning against the wall by the door, watching her. "What is it?"

"Pink slip," she managed to say.

"Oh, Lindsay," he said, starting to come to her. Lindsay stood up, her body stiff and her chin out. He stopped.

"Probably Einer's handiwork. I'm sure he's furious about my visit yesterday. I'll bet all the other untenured faculty got renewals today. Separating me out would be his style. I have to take some student records to the main office. When I come back, we'll go to Park Hall."

"You all right?"

Lindsay looked him in the eye. "I'm fine."

She scooped up a couple of folders from her desk and walked upstairs to the office. Most everyone must have known, because they all were reluctant to meet her eyes. Trey was there. He greeted her sheepishly, looking guilty. His contract must have been renewed, she thought. She gave the file folders to Edwina, who smiled sweetly at her. Lindsay smiled back and went into Frank's office.

"Lindsay, sit down," he said.

She closed the door behind her and sat in the chair by his desk.

"Einer called me this morning, gloating, so I knew what the letter said before it was brought over. I put it on your desk rather than in your box." Frank's blue eyes were kind. "I'm going to talk to the dean," he said.

"I don't think it will do any good, but I appreciate your willingness to try."

"Lindsay, if you hadn't . . ." He didn't finish.

"Frank, it wouldn't have made a bit of difference. I'm glad he acted out of spite. It makes things easier for me."

"What do you mean?" He looked wary.

"I hope you don't think I'm just going to go home and lick my wounds."

"No, Lindsay, I would never think that."

She rose to leave. "Don't worry about me. I'll land on my feet."

Lindsay and Sinjin walked to Park Hall. They crossed the street where the faded *X*'s marked the place where Gloria Rankin had lain, had passed LeConte, and had walked across to Park.

"What are you going to do about your job?" asked Sinjin.

"I don't know. I told Frank I'm not going to take it lying down, but in reality there's not a lot I can do."

"What are you going to do about a new job?"

"I've been toying with the idea of being a full-time consultant. Maybe become a garage archaeologist."

"Garage archaeologist?"

"Work out of my home. You know, respond to a few bids on salvage archaeology jobs."

"Will that pay the bills?"

"I don't know. I don't really want to move, but I may have to. We'll see."

Lindsay went straight to Gloria's old office and knocked on the door. Theodora was there reading an article; in fact she looked like she hadn't moved since Lindsay's last visit. She didn't look glad to see Lindsay.

"I would like to take a look at Gloria Rankin's thesis. Would you mind?"

Theodora shrugged. "Go ahead."

Lindsay took the thesis from the bookshelf and sat at Gloria's desk. Sinjin pulled up a chair and sat beside her. She flipped to the abstract. The thesis combined Gloria's interests in chemistry and classics. Lindsay looked at the review of literature first.

"She mentions Shirley Foster," Sinjin said.

Lindsay whispered so she wouldn't disturb Theodora. "Shirley is prominent in her field. If Gloria wrote about textiles at all, she would have to mention Shirley's work. It doesn't mean she knew her."

Gloria's literature review described two legends whose primary characters suffer very similar deaths. One was the legend of Hercules, the other of Glauce, the Corinthian princess who met her death at the hands of the sorceress Medea.

"His cloak wasn't poisoned," whispered Lindsay. "It caught fire."

According to the account by Sophocles, wrote Gloria, Hercules shot the centaur Nesus with an arrow dipped in the poisonous blood of the Hydra. Seeking revenge, the clever dying centaur Nesus told Hercules's wife how to make a love potion by collecting some of the centaur's blood and mixing it with oil. The potion was to be kept in a sealed jar. If Hercules ever were to fall in love with anyone besides his wife, she was to weave him a cloak and treat it with the potion. Once the cloak was treated, she must keep it in a box and allow neither sun nor heat nor water nor anyone but Hercules to touch it.

The potion was not a love potion at all, of course, but a deadly concoction. And as these legends often go, Hercules did fall for another woman, and his wife sent him the magic cloak that supposedly would bring him back to her. To the great surprise and dismay of everyone, except the centaur's spirit, when Hercules put on the cloak sent to him by his wife, his perspiration caused it to burst into flames, burning his skin and boiling his blood. He tried to rip off the cloak, but by this time it had become part of his flesh. He jumped into water, but then the fire burned even hotter. Finally, Hercules could no longer take the pain, and he lay down on a burning altar. There he was consumed and his spirit rose to Olympus.

"Never trust a dying centaur," Sinjin said.

The death of Hercules, wrote Gloria, was almost identical to the fate of Glauce as described by Euripides. Jason, husband of Medea, fell in love with Glauce. Medea treated a gown with a potion that was like liquid fire. She sent the gown to Glauce in an airtight container. When Glauce put on the gown, she immediately burst into flames. The gown clung to her skin, and she sought water from a fountain, but the flames grew hotter, killing Glauce and eventually burning down the palace.

One scholar identified critical similarities of the events in the two myths. A garment treated with a potion had to be sealed in a container that kept it from water, heat, and air. The garment was to be given only to the one for whom it was intended, and only they could touch it. When donned, the garment burst into flames, melted into the skin, and water caused the flame to burn hotter. She also identified chemicals she believed were used.

"Jeez," said Sinjin, "that does sound exactly like what happened to Shirley Foster."

Lindsay flipped to the methodology chapter, which went on to describe Gloria's experiments with different substances suggested by Mayor and chemicals she added herself, all of which, she said, were used in the dyeing and cleaning of ancient fabrics. When describing her results, Gloria stated that she would list the chemicals involved in the process but would not reveal the critical amounts, nor would she reveal the exact steps in treating the fabric.

"That means whoever used her formula probably knew her and got the formula from her," Lindsay said. "They didn't get it from her thesis." Lindsay moved her finger down the pages, looking for the list of substances that Gloria finally came up with. "Here." She pointed to the list of the major ingredients. "Mainly sulfur, quicklime, and bitumen. Interesting, Lila Poole talked about fire and brimstone.

Isn't brimstone sulfur? I wonder if that's what she smelled."

Sinjin stared at the page a long moment. "It might work. Add water and you could get spontaneous combustion from the quicklime," he whispered. "More water would make it worse. As it burned, you'd create sulfuric acid, which would dissolve human tissue. The petroleum would add fuel and give the substance clinging properties. You could make something mean with that. I'm glad she didn't publish the exact process in her thesis. Who would know the exact process? Wouldn't her committee have to?"

"Yes," Lindsay said, "they would have to know that she really did the work before they would sign off. This is a master's thesis, so there are probably three faculty members on her committee. But she could have told anyone she trusted, and they might have told other people." She paused. "So, water would ignite something like this?"

"Possibly, but I think you'd need a heat source to set it off, something like the heat from the sun, or a campfire, or a fireplace. Then the water would act as a catalyst and make the fire hot and uncontrollable."

"Wouldn't the fabric smell suspicious after being treated with those chemicals?" Lindsay asked.

"Yes, but it could have smelled like cleaning fluid or mothballs. Both are derived from hydrocarbons, which is what bitumen is. This is similar to the problem you get with storing oily rags in the basement, only you never know when oily rags are going to spontaneously combust. Gloria figured out how to make it quicker and perhaps more controlled. But she still needed an ignition source."

"Smart girl," Lindsay said.

"Yeah, but apparently it was the death of her."

"If it weren't for Gloria's death, I'd think Shirley's death might have been an accident that she brought on herself. I believe that if she read this thesis, she would want to try these formulas. It's the kind of thing she would do. I wonder if Gloria's death could have been just an accident. The bruise was very small, and the umbrella is just suggestive."

"What are you going to do with this information?" asked Sinjin.

"Give it to the medical examiner. Maybe he can run tests for these particular chemicals in Shirley's remains," she said.

Lindsay looked up and Theodora was staring at them. Lindsay grinned at her. "Thanks for letting us look at the thesis."

"Sure," she said, not taking her eyes off them.

"I think that's all I need. I won't trouble you again."

"Good." She watched them put the thesis back on the shelf and go out the door.

"I think we may have upset her," said Sinjin.

"Yeah, I think so."

Students were gathered outside Lindsay's office when she returned: Sally, Brandon, Liza, Bobbie, Bethany, and Robin.

"We heard," Brandon said.

"It's not fair," added Bethany.

"You are going to protest, aren't you?" Bobbie asked.

"We're going to write a letter to the dean," Sally said.

"I appreciate your support, I really do. I won't take it lying down, but don't expect them to change their minds. Bureaucrats don't often do that."

"This is just spite," Bobbie said. "Surely the administration won't let it happen."

"It was the dean himself and not Einer who signed the letter," said Lindsay. "There is more to it than just spite."

They all turned just as Gerri Chapman rounded the corner. She stopped abruptly, frozen by the hostile stares. "I'll come back," she said.

"No," said Lindsay, gesturing toward her open door.

"Please, I want to talk to you." The students stepped aside, giving her a path, but not a wide one. Gerri looked as if she were running a gauntlet. She almost jumped inside when she reached the door. "Excuse us," said Lindsay as she closed the door.

Inside, Gerri looked even more uncomfortable. Lindsay had a good six inches in height on her. "Listen," said Gerri, running a hand through her auburn curls, "I know what you are going to say."

"Did you take my letter opener?"

"What?" Gerri stared at Lindsay open-mouthed.

"When you were in my office the other day, did you take my silver letter opener?"

"Letter opener? What are you talking about? No, of course not. Is that what you brought me in here for?"

"Do you know Ellis Einer?"

"No, should I?"

"Who is Lewis's backer on campus? It's not Einer?"

"No, it's the dean—and the vice president of the university. The vice president and 'Cisco were at Oxford together. I don't know any Einer."

Gerri looked as if she were telling the truth. Either she was a good actress, or she was genuinely baffled by Lindsay's questions.

"And what are you doing down here? Come to measure my windows for curtains?"

"I know you must feel bitter," Gerri said.

"Bitter? No. Mostly puzzled, but I'm working it out," Lindsay said.

"I just came to tell you that we can give you a lot of consulting work," said Gerri.

"Consulting work? You're kidding, right?"

"No. I have no ill will toward you. With everything that's going on, I know it will take you a while to find another job."

"What do you know about what's going on?"

"I know about the cloud you're under because of the missing artifacts."

"You wouldn't, by any chance, have been making those clouds, would you?"

"No, I'm trying to be friends. I know this is hard for you. I'm trying to make it easier."

"It's quite a coincidence that I start having all these troubles when you show up here after my job. I hope you see how that would make me suspicious."

"Is that what you think? Is that what they think?" Gerri gestured toward the door.

"I'm asking. I imagine others will, too," Lindsay said.

"I know I can sometimes be a bitch, but I would never deal in artifacts. Never. I'll admit to maybe using your bad luck just a little. I mean, I guess Brian talked to you, but I didn't instigate any of it."

Lindsay stared at her, arms folded. "If you did, I'll find out about it."

"I didn't. Look, I didn't come down here to gloat or anything. I came to offer you work."

Lindsay smiled. "When you have work to offer, we can talk. Until then, Pancho, this won't be over until it's over." Lindsay opened the door for her. The students were still waiting outside. Lindsay smiled and winked at them as Gerri passed.

"Sinjin's taking me to lunch," Sally told her after the students went back to their work. "Why don't you come with us?"

"Thanks, but no. I'm not hungry, and I have a few things to do."

"All the students are on your side."

"That means a lot to me." Lindsay wanted to hug Sally.

"Gerri's such a jerk," Sally said.

"She's certainly a woman who's not afraid of going after what she wants, that's for sure."

Lindsay sat at her desk and keyed into her word processor all the information she had learned from Gloria Rankin's thesis relevant to Shirley Foster's death. She printed out two copies and addressed two envelopes: one to Sheriff Irene Varnadore and one to Medical Examiner Eddie Peck. Next, she reached for the phone to dial Will Patterson's office. If she could make him consider the possibility that Shirley's death was an accident, it might take his mind off Tom Foster and Luke Ferris, at least long enough for the authorities to find the murderer. It struck her, as her hand rested on the phone, that this method of murder didn't seem like something the volatile Tom Foster would do. She could see Tom shooting Shirley or strangling her but not anything as melodramatic as reenacting an ancient myth.

The murderer was someone who really hated Shirley Foster, like Medea and Nesus hated their enemies. This was someone with a different mindset from the suspects Lindsay knew. Even if Irene Varnadore were jealous of Shirley, Lindsay couldn't see Irene doing this. And what connection could Irene have had with Gloria Rankin? Maybe it was an accident, after all. Maybe Gloria wasn't murdered and neither was Shirley. But who buried Shirley and why? Tom Foster? Had he found her dead and decided to just not report the body so that he could use her money? That was possible. It made more sense. Tom loved Shirley and would have buried her carefully, but he seemed genuinely surprised when Lindsay found the bones. Could he have been acting? Lindsay dialed Will's office.

"Patterson. What can I do for you?"

"Will, this is Lindsay Chamberlain."

"Lindsay. Need some more information?"

"Yes, something a little different this time. Do you know if Shirley Foster knew Gloria Rankin?"

"Gloria Rankin? Where have I heard that name before?"

"She was the student hit and killed by a bus a couple of weeks ago."

"That's right, by that kid, Luke Ferris. Why do you want to know if Shirley knew her?"

"I've come across information suggesting that perhaps Shirley's death was an accident. Can I come by and talk with you, say in fifteen minutes?"

"Sure. I'm in my office all day today. An accident? Yeah, please come by."

Lindsay took the letters to the main office to be picked up by the postman, and set out for downtown Athens by way of the sidewalk on Jackson Street. Downtown was only a few blocks from Baldwin Hall, an easy walk. The day was clear and cool, and flowers were blooming all over campus. Walking would give her a chance to think, to wade through all the permutations of possible events in Shirley Foster's last days and try to weed some of them out. Lindsay ignored the hordes of students changing classes and waiting for and leaving buses. She could just as easily have been alone.

She passed Personnel Services and grimaced. She might soon be using their services to look for a job unless she could think of a way to get hers back. And despite telling Frank and her students that she would fight for it, she knew it was virtually impossible to change a decision by the administration. Someone would have to admit they were wrong. Unless she could remove the cloud from her name, she would have a hard time finding another job as good as the one she had here. Maybe she could hire Will to follow Einer. Perhaps Einer would lead them to the artifacts—if they hadn't already been sold on the black market. She hadn't really investigated the illegal collector's market. That would be an enormous undertaking. It all seemed impossible. However, Will could find out for her what information the campus police had about the missing artifacts; that would be a start. Surely, Kaufman had collected some information. Of course he had—why else had he been killed?

The wind gusted and Lindsay pulled the front of her denim jacket together. She glanced across the street back at the old building where the Georgia Museum of Art used to be housed. The people at the museum must have some information on the thefts that occurred there a couple of years ago. She made a mental note to talk with them after she talked to Will.

"Hey, babe, need a ride?" Lindsay arched her eyebrow and turned, ready to give a sharp retort to the guy in the car that had pulled up beside her. When she saw it was Chris Pryor, she grinned. "Sorry, couldn't resist," he said. "I just went to your office looking for you."

"I'm on my way to an appointment."

"I have a surprise for you," he said.

"What?" She leaned over to talk through the open window of his car. Chris was dressed in jeans and a navy blue heavy T-shirt and smelled like Safari. He definitely was better away from his parents. Lindsay imagined that had probably been true of Shirley as well.

"If you could make a wish right now," he said, "what would you wish for—besides world peace and an end to hunger?"

"That's easy, the artifacts."

"I love this. I have always wanted to grant a beautiful woman her heart's desire. But I'm warning you, it's going to cost you at least a month of dates."

"You're kidding! You found them? I don't believe it. Where?"

Traffic was backing up in the street behind Chris's car. Someone beeped a horn for him to move on.

"I'm blocking traffic," he said. "Get in and I'll tell you all about it."

She got in the car. Chris frowned. "Unfortunately, you

were right about Einer, and I have to confess, I didn't really believe you."

"You found them at his house?" asked Lindsay.

"No." Chris pulled away from the curb and turned the corner toward Thomas Street. "By the way, I left a message for an Officer Sharon Meyers of the campus police to meet us. They said she's working on the case. Is that all right?"

"Yes. Sure. Where are the artifacts?"

Chris sighed. "I hope they're at my glass factory. If they aren't, I'll have called the police and got your hopes up for nothing."

"Your factory?" Lindsay asked. "I don't understand."

Chris headed out North Avenue. "After we talked last night, I called Brooke Einer, Ellis's daughter. She just got her vet degree. We used to date. We're still pretty good friends. I thought I'd just kind of ask about her father and antiques, that kind of thing, nothing too heavy. I remembered that a week or so ago she had asked if she could store some boxes in the old glass factory. She knew I didn't use it very much. I store everything in my gallery downtown, and I only use the old factory when I'm doing some glassblowing or etching. I told her sure. I thought she was moving her things, you know, getting her own apartment or something. Anyway, last night when I asked her about it, she said it had really been for her father. She had given him the key."

"Einer stored the artifacts at your factory?" Lindsay was having trouble seeing how all the parts fit together.

"I asked myself, Why in the world would he want to use my space, when he has so much to choose from on campus, unless he thought campus was too hot?"

"Is his daughter in it with him, do you think?"

Chris shook his head. "I don't think so. To tell you the truth, I don't think he would trust her. I like Brooke, but she's a bit of a gossip."

Lindsay had to agree with that. "She wouldn't tell her

father that you asked her about the space, would she?"

"I don't know. That would be short notice to move everything, though."

"I was thinking of Detective Kaufman. His death, I believe, had something to do with the artifact theft."

"I didn't think of that. Okay, here's what we'll do. We can see the parking area from the road. If anyone's there, we'll just drive by. Otherwise, we'll go in and wait for the police."

Chris's old glass factory was about five miles out of town. He explained to Lindsay on the way that the factory used to belong to Tom Foster. Shirley and Tom had given it to him as a Christmas gift during better times, after Tom had built his new plant.

"Nice gift," Lindsay commented.

"I'll say. I renovated it for my use. I'm planning some more work on it. I'm doing well enough to hire someone to run my gallery downtown, and I can get back to making glass sculpture, which is what I really like best."

The factory was a windowless cement-block building with a metal roof. From the front, Lindsay could see only one door. Just around the corner, on the right side of the building, Chris told her, was a larger garage door leading to the storage room. "That's where the artifacts are, if they're there," he said. There was no sign of anyone in the parking lot, so he drove up to the front entrance.

"I gave Brooke my key to the storage room," he said as he unlocked the front door. "It has a separate lock, and I'm not sure I have another key. We may have to break in."

They walked into a small entrance that probably had once been a reception area. Now it was an empty room with brown paneled walls and a green carpet with brighter color in the places where the furniture had sat.

Chris led Lindsay through a door and switched on the light. This room was an office with an oak desk in one corner and a large tan leather sofa along one wall. An oval glass-topped coffee table sat in front of the sofa. The light wood-grain paneling was of a more expensive style than that covering the walls of the reception area. The floor was done in emerald green and black tiles, with a design that looked almost like gemstones.

"Nice office," Lindsay said.

Chris tried the door to the storage room. It was locked. He opened a couple of drawers in the desk. "I may have some extra keys somewhere," he said. "I'll go look. Make yourself at home. There's a bathroom in the corner." He left by the door opposite the one they had entered.

Lindsay sat down on the leather sofa, then rose and walked around the office restlessly. There was a picture on the wall next to the desk. It was of Chris and Shirley standing in front of their parents' house. They favored each other. There was a phone on the desk. She thought she had better call Will Patterson and tell him she would be late. She picked up the receiver. There was no dial tone. She put the phone back in its cradle, exhaled impatiently, and looked at the photograph again. They were both smiling, looking happy. Chris must have been, what, about twenty-six or twenty-seven when it was taken? Nice, old white house, she thought. Bleak House, their father had named it. Lindsay wasn't much of a Dickens fan. His stories were too bleak. She smiled to herself. She had liked *A Tale of Two Cities*. *Bleak House*. One of the characters in *Bleak House* died of spontaneous combustion. Creepy coincidence.

Like an old movie showing in her mind, she saw Stewart Pryor come into his den when she and Sinjin had visited them, wearing his smoking jacket. Lindsay told him it was beautiful. "It is, isn't it. Shirley made it," he said. "She wove the fabric herself. She made several for me—different ones for special occasions." He patted his pockets and found them empty. He walked to the mantel, took several matches from a crystal jar, and slipped them into his jacket pocket. The movie switched reels and Fred MacMurray was giving Edward G. Robinson yet another match from his pocket, asking why he didn't carry his own. "I tried that," Robinson said, "and the damn things kept exploding in my pocket." Then Lindsay heard Stewart Pryor say, "Shirley made me a beautiful Christmas jacket. Dyed it herself to get a special color of red. It was on display at the museum. Some damn fool lost it."

Lindsay heard a gasp, then realized that it was her own voice. She spun around and came face to face with Chris. His charming smile was gone. "I was with Will when you called. I knew you were on your way to figuring it out when you called and asked if Shirley knew Gloria Rankin."

Chapter 26

"**T**HE POLICE AREN'T coming, are they?" Lindsay said.

Chris laughed. "No."

"You're a really good liar," she said, willing her eyes to look at him and not at the door she wanted to run to.

"Yes, I am. For a lie to be convincing, you have to add a little truth here and there to give it credibility."

Bolt, said something in Lindsay's brain, and she ran for the door they had entered. She made it, but it was locked. She turned around, ready to defend herself, but he hadn't moved. He didn't need to. He knew she couldn't get out.

"That's why it was so hard to find out who killed Shirley. She wasn't the target, was she?" Lindsay remembered the police dragging Shirley's car from the lake, and the soggy disintegrating gift box that was in the trunk. "Shirley must have been returning her father's smoking jacket, the red Christmas one, dyed with dragon's blood. But it was cold waiting for Will at the lake that night, and she put it on. You had intended to kill your father."

"At least toast him a little," Chris said. His calm demeanor frightened Lindsay all the more.

"What had you planned? That he would be sitting in front of the fireplace sometime during the Christmas season, maybe talking to Shirley, and suddenly a spark from the fire, his pipe, or maybe a spilled drink, and he'd spontaneously combust?"

"That was the plan. A little ill-conceived, I know. I wanted him to die like Mr. Crook in *Bleak House*. It seemed fitting."

"You must hate your father."

"Of course I hate him. He made me miserable all my life, and Shirley, too. We could never do anything to suit him. He just wouldn't leave me alone."

"But you killed Shirley instead, by mistake."

Chris wavered visibly. "Yes. That was the last thing I wanted. I loved my sister."

"But you were willing to allow her to watch her father go up in flames?"

"No, I didn't intend it that way. Shirl was supposed to be out of town during the two weeks before Christmas. I was going to arrange for him to get the jacket back while she was out of town. She wouldn't have been there. Anyway, I was never sure I would go through with it. I liked the irony and the justice of it. I liked carrying it out to the extent of treating the jacket, and having that magic coat in a box was like some secret power."

"Using his own petroleum products in the formula," said Lindsay. "I imagine that was satisfying, too."

"And handy," he said.

"You buried Shirley, didn't you?" Lindsay said.

"Yes. The hardest thing I ever did." His eyes seemed to mist over, but it may have been the light.

"And took the money?"

"Yes. That was easy." He seemed to recover. He looked confident again.

Shirley was his weak spot. Maybe there was a way she could use it.

"How did you find her?"

"I knew she was meeting Will. She confided in me—we

were close. I discovered the box was missing from the office here. She must have found it and taken it. She probably figured I'd picked it up from the museum and forgotten to take it home. It scared me at first, but then I thought, what irony—Shirley would deliver the magic jacket *for* me. I wouldn't even be connected. And I could always steal it again before Dad wore it if I had second thoughts. Then she didn't return from the lake. I went out there, but I was too late. I never dreamed Shirl would put it on. You're right. It must have been cold out there by the lake and she had forgotten her own jacket." He was silent for several moments, staring past Lindsay back to that moment by the lake. He blinked, then turned his attention back to Lindsay.

She searched for something else to say to keep him talking. "Luke Ferris will probably go to jail for her murder, and he tried to save her."

"Life's tough sometimes."

Lindsay glanced at the coffee table and noticed the handcuffs. When she looked back at him, Chris held a gun.

"So," said Lindsay, "you left Will's office and came looking for me. Lucky for you I walked."

"If I hadn't run across you, I'd have waited near his office and enticed you away with promise of the artifacts."

Lindsay glanced at the storage room door. "The whole story about Brooke Einer was a ruse to get me out here. The artifacts aren't there."

"Oh, they're there."

Lindsay looked back, open-mouthed. "You took them?"

Chris smiled a pleased-with-himself smile. "I'm afraid so."

"Einer had nothing to do with them?"

"Oh, yes. We have a nice little business together. I have the contacts; he has the access." He picked up the handcuffs and opened them.

"Put these on. You can cuff yourself in front. But put

them on tight. I don't want you slipping out of them."

"No."

"I'll just knock you out and do it myself, if you don't. I know you probably won't believe me, but I like you and I hate doing this. I even had this fantasy—well, I won't tell you about it. It was nothing kinky or anything like that, just nice."

Lindsay put the handcuffs on her wrists. "What are you going to do to me?"

"First, I want you to write a letter. I'll let you compose it in your own style."

"A suicide note?"

"No, it's a letter to a prospective antiquities buyer. I have a letter for you to use as a model." He fished in the pocket of his jeans. "I must have left it in the car."

Lindsay needed to stall for time, time to think of an escape plan. She should be getting good at it by now. No one knew where they were, but Will was expecting her. Maybe by some miracle he'd get suspicious because Chris left in a rush—he must have—when she called. When she didn't show up, maybe he'd start thinking. Thinking what? That the two things were connected? A long shot, but she needed hope almost as much as she needed a good plan. Unless Will was in on it, too. That thought made her sick.

"So, Einer is in on it. Who else? It won't hurt to satisfy my curiosity."

"No, it won't. Just me and Einer."

"Not any of my students?"

"No."

"And not Will Patterson?"

Chris shook his head. "No, not Will."

"Did you lock me in the basement of Nancy Hart?"

"No. Einer did that. That was a close call. It scared him. He was coming to move boxes of artifacts, and there you were in the room. Now, I'm going to my car, and I'll be back in a jiffy. You'll be safe in here. There's nothing for you to get into, and the doors will be locked. Don't try to use the phone. I disconnected it a minute ago."

He left Lindsay in the room alone. As soon as the door was shut, she flew over to the desk and opened the drawers, looking for anything. There was nothing in the top drawer but antique and art catalogs and some packages of salt and pepper from a takeout place. She tried another drawer. Nothing whatsoever of use. She opened the bottom drawer and found a squirt gun. Why couldn't it have been a real one? She also found a wig, camisole, white lace garter belt, and hose.

"What?" she murmured. Then she got it. Dr. Frank N. Furter, of course. Chris was the one who attacked Sally. Lindsay dropped the items as if they were snakes. Her handcuffs clanked against the drawer. Handcuffs. They were probably Kaufman's. She thought she might throw up.

The rattle of the doorknob made her slam the drawer shut and sit up in the chair. When Chris entered, she realized how hard she had been wishing it was someone else. He handed her a letter and a pen, opened one of the drawers of the desk, pulled out a blank piece of paper, and laid it in front of her.

"Write one similar to this one."

"What does it say?"

"It says you know of this gentleman's interest in acquiring rare Indian artifacts, and you have some to sell. List enclosed. Address it to Palmer Brewster."

"One of your business associates?"

Chris chuckled. "Hardly. I wouldn't name one of my own contacts. No, he's more of a competitor. Your letter will identify him to the authorities at the same time that it implicates you in the illicit trade. Kind of clever, don't you think?"

"Brilliant," Lindsay said sarcastically. "Then what are you going to do?"

"Just one step at a time. Take all the time you need. I probably would." The expression on his face was sympathetic. Lindsay wanted to slap him. His gaze shifted to the bottom drawer. Part of the wig was sticking out of it. "I see you've been going through the drawers."

"You're the one who attacked my graduate assistant."

"I was at the Tate Center with a friend—Brooke, if you want to know. I saw your student, and I wanted to send you a message you would take seriously."

"These are Detective Kaufman's handcuffs, I assume. He came to see you with a box of artifacts, didn't he? That's what that call to you was about the night he was killed. He checked the artifact box out of the property room, probably just wanted your advice. Did he see something he shouldn't have?"

"That getup, actually." Chris pointed the gun at the drawer. "He was working on the assault case, too. He put two and two together rather quickly—I'm an art dealer with a silly costume who sells to collectors, someone in a silly costume threatened your student to stop your investigation into stolen artifacts. Dad was always trying to get me to think quickly and act decisively. That's what I did. I shot Kaufman. I had to."

Keep him talking, thought Lindsay. Please, let somebody be looking for me. "And you put my letter opener in the gunshot wound. Are you the one who stole the letter opener from my office?"

"Yes. I saw it. It had your name on it. Einer thought it was a good idea to try and blame the theft of the artifacts on you and your brother. The Classics Department and the library would notice their missing antiquities sooner or later, so would the Archaeology Department. You were a made-to-order suspect. You had access; you were in all the right places."

"Gloria figured it out and was coming to tell me. That was a chancy thing, pushing her in front of a bus with her umbrella," Lindsay said.

"You did have it all put together, didn't you? I didn't set out to be a serial killer, but it does get easier. Now, if your curiosity is satisfied, you had better get to writing."

"One more thing. Why, after all the years of living with your parents, did you feel you had to kill your father? You were on your own, you had your own business. You were doing okay, weren't you? I know you borrowed money, but . . ."

"Yeah, I was doing better than okay. But you're right, it was the loan. Can't you figure it out?"

"I know your dad was trying to buy your loan."

Chris waved his hand, encouraging her. "And? Go on."

Lindsay remembered Stewart Pryor bragging about how he could manage money. "If he bought out your loan, he could foreclose and become the owner of your business," Lindsay said. "And he would find out about your trade in antiquities. You've been laundering your illegal income through your gallery."

Chris's voice was cold and somber. "Damn, you are good. I knew you had all the pieces." Then he exhaled, his shoulders slumped, and his mood changed. "He couldn't leave me alone. I had my own business, and he just wouldn't let me be. He and Mom were such control freaks. Einer and I had a good thing going. I was having to work hard borrowing money to cover for the fact that I had plenty. I like nice things. If I bought a nice car or something, I had to listen to a lecture from Mom and Dad about managing my money and my responsibility to my creditors. But I was handling everything. Dad had this hair up his butt about taking over my loan. He would have had his hands all over my business, and I couldn't have that. He'd find out, and worse than that, Shirley would find out. I had the money, but if I went ahead and paid off the loan from Mom, there would be questions about where I got the cash. In my business, I can't have questions." He turned to go. "Write the letter."

"You don't have to kill me." Lindsay tried hard not to let

her voice crack. "If you were with Will when I called, he must have told you that I said Shirley's death could have been an accident. You can move the artifacts, and it would all be my word against yours." She wanted to say she wouldn't tell, but he wouldn't believe her.

"Nice try, but no. Mom and Dad would always look at me funny, wondering if I killed Shirley. I can't have that. They can't ever know. Since she's been gone, Dad's stopped nagging me. Both of them have been depending on me. I'm not going back to the way things were—to worse than they were. I can't do that."

"Then do me a favor."

"What's that?" He was getting impatient. Lindsay didn't want that.

"Write an anonymous letter to my brother. Tell him the truth about me being dead. Please don't leave him wondering."

He stopped dead still, silent for several seconds. Lindsay could see his indecision, if she just knew how to keep it going. Why hadn't she become a psychologist?

"I will." He turned and left Lindsay alone to write the letter.

When the door was closed, she searched the drawers again. Nothing helpful. She had a germ of an idea about the squirt gun. She took it and a couple of packages of salt to the bathroom and filled the toy with hot water, put the salt in, shook it, and put it in her jacket pocket.

She tried soaping her hands and slipping the handcuffs off. But they wouldn't come off, no matter how she tried bending her thumbs or pulling on the cuffs. She stopped and listened. She heard Chris knocking around in the adjoining room where she guessed he worked with the glass, and wondered what he was doing. She gave the bathroom a quick look as she was drying her hands. Nothing useful there.

Lindsay suddenly had another idea. Two ideas. She felt

good. She took the tank cover off the toilet, carried it into the office, and stood it up against the end of the desk. She took the Frank N. Furter clothes from the drawer and laid them on the end of the coffee table. She picked up the toilet tank lid and, with as controlled a motion as she could manage in the handcuffs, brought it down on the cloth covered end of the table.

The sound of the breaking glass was muffled, but it still seemed loud to her ears. She stopped a moment and listened, hearing only the whooshing sounds from the other room. *What's he doing? This is a glass factory. He's firing up the furnace. Oh, damn. Oh, damn. Please let me get out of this.*

Lindsay moved quickly. She set the tank lid down by the couch and picked up a shard of glass with the camisole—it was a long piece with razor-sharp edges and a needle point. She used it to cut out three strips of leather from the sofa. She wound the largest around the broader end of the glass several times and tied it securely with the other two strips, forming a handle. *I'm not an archaeologist for nothing,* she said to herself, giving her glass knife a quick examination. It looked dangerous.

She was implementing two ideas. It felt good. The squirt gun was a real long shot, but the knife might work. She was about an inch taller than Chris and in good shape. He was physically fit and would be a lot stronger. *That's the advantage of testosterone,* but he wasn't expecting her to mount a defense. She had toyed with the idea of writing a coded letter with the first words of each sentence making a secret message, but unless puzzle master Will Shortz got a look at the letter, no one would ever figure it out. *No, she wasn't going to die,* and she certainly wasn't going to climb into the furnace. He probably planned to shoot her and burn her body. She had to concentrate on breathing so she could keep her wits about her.

Lindsay looked around the room again. Was there anything else she could use to her advantage? The doors needed to be blocked. The door leading to the furnace room opened inward and so did the storage-room door, but the one they had entered when they arrived opened away from the office.

Lindsay shoved the costume fabric into the cracks under the doors to the furnace room and storage room to try to jam them. She shoved the desk across the floor and against the storage-room door. It was not heavy enough to keep Chris out, but it and the clothes acting as a wedge would slow him down and maybe give her a chance to strike. She dragged the glass-topped table over to the front door, stood it on end, and leaned it against the door. Maybe when he opened the door, the table would fall on him and the sharp edges of the broken glass would injure him enough to stop him.

The couch was heavy. She pushed it across in front of the furnace-room door. She stood by the end of the sofa and held her knife tight in her grasp, listening to the swooshing sounds of the furnace.

Chapter 27

LINDSAY HEARD CHRIS'S footsteps coming toward the room. She held her breath. He put his key in the lock and pushed on the door.

"What?" she heard him say. "Cute, Lindsay, but this just delays things. I can wait you out."

He pushed. The sofa moved. Lindsay shoved back. She held the glass knife firmly in her hand. Stick your fingers in, she thought. He didn't. Instead, she heard him walk away. She listened and thought she heard him behind the wall where the couch had stood. That would mean he's going into the storage room, she thought. He could probably push that door and get through, and he could certainly get through the front door unless a miracle happened and the glass table fell on him.

She turned the knob. He hadn't locked the furnace-room door after trying it. Accident or trap? She moved the sofa and quickly pulled out the fabric jamming the door. She heard the storage-room door rattle. She slipped into the furnace room. She couldn't lock the door behind her, they all needed keys to lock and unlock. Damn.

The room with the glass furnace was huge. On the opposite wall she could see flames through the door of the furnace. Beside the furnace sat a huge sink. On another wall was a fume hood, and beside it was an emergency shower. She ran to the fume hood, turned it on, and looked in the cabinet underneath. Empty, except for tubes of calcium gluconate gel, used to treat skin exposed to hydrofluoric acid, the acid used to etch glass. Her plan might yet succeed. She grabbed one of the tubes and threw it into the emergency shower, where it landed against the wall just as she heard him coming.

"There you are," he said, "I thought I could flush you out." He had the gun at his side. She had put the knife in her jacket pocket and hoped it didn't show. She held the squirt gun. "I see you found my squirt gun." He grinned. "I guess you have to make do." She leveled the gun at him. "Have we gone a little nuts?" He raised his hands as if to surrender. "If it makes you feel better, I'll play."

Lindsay watched his gun hand, then looked him in the eye, wondering which would tell her when he was about to shoot.

"I have a riddle I would like you to consider," she said.

"Sure. Shoot. Perhaps I shouldn't have said that." He grinned again.

Lindsay squirted the hot water on his neck and chest, watching a large dark spot appear on his navy shirt. He looked at it briefly and smiled. "Feel better?"

"The riddle is, what chemical do geologists, palynologists, and glass etchers all use that is a local anesthetic?" He looked puzzled for a moment, noticed the fume hood fan running, and wrinkled his brow. Lindsay gestured her head toward the shower where the gel lay. His eyes widened. "You don't have much time," she said. "If you shoot me, there will be no one to get help."

She saw his gun hand move, and she jumped aside just as he shot. He screamed as he ran to the shower and pulled the chain. He snatched the gel off the floor and pulled off his shirt. Lindsay ran to the storage room, closing the door behind her. The room was stacked, filled up high with boxes. She could still hear him screaming as she ran to the loading dock door and pulled on it. It was locked. Everything was locked. Chris stopped screaming. She knocked over a huge row of boxes in front of the two interior doors and hid behind another stack of boxes, holding the knife tightly in both hands, barely breathing.

She heard him trying to open the door. "That was good," he yelled through the crack in the door. "I had the gel rubbed on my chest before I remembered that I'm out of hydrofluoric acid. You fooled me as well as scaring me shitless. Now let's stop all this and get it over with."

She said nothing. She heard the boxes sliding as he pushed his way in. She listened to his footsteps, glad she was wearing running shoes.

"This is silly," he said. "Just come out. This must be as nerve-wracking for you as it is for me."

He was getting close, but she was afraid to move. If he saw her, he'd just shoot and get it over with, as he put it, and forget about her writing the incriminating letter. She crouched. From her vantage point, she could see the keys he had left hanging in the lock of the office door when he had tried to open it before. She needed those keys to get out. If she had not blocked the way, she could make a dash, grab the keys, and run into the office and out the door. She might make it. He might not be a good shot. But the door was blocked, and he would have a clear shot if she tried to go that way. He would be coming around her row of boxes in a moment, so Lindsay eased herself around another row, away from the keys. Damn.

The room was getting hot, from the furnace, she supposed. Sweat trickled between her breasts and down her back and stung her underarms. Fear made her nauseated. She stayed still. He was coming down the row where she had been. He wasn't saying anything now. He was just going to hunt until he found her. She held on to her knife. The keys were out of her range of vision now. Desperately, she tried to think of a plan, but none came to her. She waited. It occurred to her that if she could find something to throw, maybe she could misdirect him. There was nothing she could see on the floor that she could use. It probably only worked in the movies anyway.

There was only one row of boxes between him and her and no place else for Lindsay to go. She acted. She shoved the stack of boxes, knocking him off balance. He fired the gun as she shoved the knife into his lower back. He screamed and dropped the gun, but she couldn't see where it fell. Chris staggered, looking for the gun and gripping the leather-wrapped knife handle sticking out of his back with his left hand. Lindsay ran for the door, grabbed the keys, and ran for the only open door, which led into the furnace room. There was an ear-shattering bang, and a bullet whizzed past her arm and sent chips of concrete flying from the block wall. She didn't stop. She ran into the office and tried to unlock the door into the reception area. She tried one key after another. Damn, there were too many of them.

"Stop. Stop, or I'll shoot." Chris's voice sounded desperate.

She turned her head and saw him holding the gun on her. She must have missed everything vital, but he didn't look good. He was sweating, breathing heavily, and he was in pain. Lindsay had no doubt he would behave like any wounded animal. Gone were the talking and any feelings of guilt. There was only the anger that comes with pain and frustration. The light switch was next to her hand. She turned off the light and dove behind the desk as he fired the gun three times. She stumbled on something on the floor and he turned and fired twice more into the desk. That was six bullets, or was it seven? She had no idea how many bullets the gun held. She felt along the floor. It was the toilet tank lid she had tripped over. She eased her fingers around it awkwardly, trying not to jangle the handcuffs against it. As careful as she tried to be, the cuffs clinked against the lid. She jumped out of the way as another shot was fired in her direction. She heard Chris walking toward the door. He was going for the light. She grabbed the tank lid and swung it at the sound. It connected with some part of his body. He yelled and she heard the gun clatter to the floor. She swung again. She heard him drop.

Holding the lid, Lindsay eased over to the wall and slid along it until she came to the door. She flipped on the light switch. Chris lay on the floor, blood trickling from a gash on the side of his face. She looked for the gun on the floor, but it wasn't in sight. It apparently had slid under the desk or the sofa.

The keys were still in the door and she began trying them again, watching Chris closely. He groaned and moved slightly. Give it up, she told him silently.

Finally, a key turned in the lock. She opened the door, closed and locked it behind her, and flew out the front door, colliding with Sinjin.

"Lindsay, are you all right?" He looked at the handcuffs. "What in the hell is going on? We heard shots from the road."

"Oh, Sinjin." She leaned against his chest. "I have never been so glad to see anyone in my life."

"Where's Chris?" Will Patterson called, coming from the parking lot.

"He's in the office. I knocked him out." Will started for the door. "Be careful, he has a gun and has already killed three people. He's pretty desperate. I heard the gun fall, but he may have come to and found it."

"I'll be careful."

Lindsay turned back to Sinjin. "How did you find me?"

"Sally and I brought lunch back to her office. She had an old *Red and Black* on her desk with an article in it about Gloria Rankin being hit by the bus. Gloria's picture was in it, and I recognized her from the picture on the mantel in the Pryors' house—the one you said Kerwin was in. Gloria Rankin was with Chris in that picture. Apparently, she had been his girlfriend. It kind of worried me. Then we found out no one knew where you were. Will called your office while we were there. He said that you called him asking about Gloria Rankin and were supposed to come over, but you never showed up. I asked Will about Chris and Gloria. He said he didn't know about them, but he said Chris had been in his office and left right after you called. We put it all together and both got worried. Chris wasn't at his shop and the clerk didn't know where he was. Will knew about this factory. It was his idea to come here."

"I'm glad you did."

The sound of a gunshot cracked through the air and Lindsay ducked. "Oh, God, if he shot Will, he'll be coming out here with a gun and he'll kill us. We've got to get help."

"It's Will," said Sinjin, pointing as the private detective emerged from the door.

"He found his gun," Will said, putting his own back in his shoulder holster. "We called the police from the car phone on the way over. They'll be here any minute."

"Chris?" asked Lindsay.

Will shook his head.

Lindsay felt sorry for Chris's parents. Two children dead.

Lindsay couldn't get out of the handcuffs until the police came. She told them her story. They had a hard time understanding exactly what Chris did to his sister and why, but they had no trouble with the fortune in antiquities stored in his glassworks, among which were the Kentucky artifacts. They accepted Will's explanation that he had shot Chris in self-defense. Apparently, the evidence bore his story out, but Lindsay couldn't help but wonder.

Sinjin took Lindsay home, and she went to bed. "Call

Dad," she told him. "Explain everything to him about the skeleton, Papaw, Billy, the whole thing. Let him handle Anne, Steven, and everybody else."

"Sure. Get some sleep, baby sister."

When Lindsay awoke, Sinjin was packing. "The fire in California is worse. I have to go."

"But I just woke up, I was hoping . . . this is too soon."

"I'll be back," he told her. "I've got to fly out there. Sally is taking me to the airport. I hope you don't mind. She's driving my Jeep back here."

"So, you'll be back as soon as the fire's out?"

"Yes, and I'm taking you out on the town when I get back. And this time we're going to have fun, and nobody's going to die."

Lindsay grinned. "You and Sally are getting along pretty well, huh?"

He smiled back. "Not bad." He stopped packing and took her by the shoulders. "I hate to leave you here. You need a keeper. I swear, Lindsay, your life is far more perilous than mine."

"I know it must seem that way."

"*Seem* nothing, it *is*. Do you want me to enumerate the close calls you've had just since I've been here?"

"But that's only since you've been here. It's not like that all the time."

"I'm glad to hear it. I don't want anything to happen to you, baby sister."

After Sinjin and Sally left for the airport, Lindsay went to her office to get the file she had been putting together for her tenure application. She took it to Mary Catherine Dellinger, an archaeology buff who had worked on several digs with Lindsay. She was also a lawyer who had taken on the university in four major cases and won all of them.

Mary Catherine's seventy-year-old hands showed mild

arthritis around the knuckles, but they were sure and steady as she turned the pages in Lindsay's folder. Her nails—long, shiny, and strong, were painted a peach color that matched the suit she wore. She listened without interruption as Lindsay told her the whole story. Her white hair was in its usual French twist without a strand out of place. Lindsay didn't believe she had ever seen it any other way. Mary Catherine fixed her dark blue eyes on Lindsay and asked, "What do you want me to do?"

"I want you to write the university a really scary letter."

Mary Catherine smiled. "With this and everything else you've told me, I can scare their pants off. What would you consider a remedy?"

"My job and tenure."

"No money?"

"I'd rather have job security."

"All right then, we'll start with five million and work down to job security." She smiled, showing even white teeth.

Lindsay left Mary Catherine's downtown office and went to Will's. She half expected him not to be there, but he was, filling out some paperwork.

"Lindsay," he said, ushering her in and motioning to the red leather chair in the room filled with Shirley's ghosts. "I'm glad you came by. I wanted to thank you for solving the mystery of what happened to Shirley. It wasn't pretty, but there is a kind of peace in knowing. Irene's dropped the charges against the Ferris kid. I guess you know."

"Yes, Irene called and left a message on my machine. I need to call her back."

"There's something I want you to know. I really did shoot Chris in self-defense. That's the truth."

"I thought you did."

That wasn't exactly the truth, and Will shook his head. "I know you wondered about it, and frankly, I don't know what I would have done if he hadn't had the gun ready to shoot me."

"I imagine his parents are taking this very hard."

Will shrugged. "My association with them is finished."

"What are you going to do now?"

"I don't know."

Lindsay sat there, saying nothing, and for an awkward moment they stared at each other. Lindsay took a deep breath and said what was on her mind. "Don't go anywhere you can't return from."

"What a delicate way of putting it."

"You've thought about it, I'm sure. I just, well, I . . ." She stopped, embarrassed, not knowing what to say exactly. "You're the person who knew Shirley best, the way she really was, not the person she showed to her parents or to anyone else. If you aren't here, she's truly gone."

"You're kind, Lindsay Chamberlain. I'll keep that in mind. Things are better. I didn't think closure was possible, but maybe it is. If I figure out how to buy that detective agency in Atlanta, can I put you on as a consultant?"

"Sure. I might be needing work if I can't get my job back." He raised his eyebrows, and Lindsay explained the situation to him.

"That's gotta be tough. They're outta their minds if they don't keep you."

"Some would say they are frequently out of their minds." She stood. "Maybe we can have dinner sometime."

"Maybe so. I like you."

It took only two days for the Dean of Arts and Sciences to summon Lindsay to his office. The dean and the university's counsel wanted her to come without her attorney. Lindsay called Mary Catherine.

"Oh, I think it will be fine," Mary Catherine assured her. "Don't you worry. What they will probably offer you is your job, the tenure you asked for, and in exchange, you don't sue. Will that suit you?"

"Yes."

"Good. You can show me the contract before you sign it, but I think things will be fine."

She was right. First, the dean and counsel distanced themselves from Einer's remarks to Kaufman about her. Then they defended his actions, saying it was reasonable for him to look for someone in a position to know about artifacts, who also appeared to be living beyond her means, but they regretted the inconvenience it had caused.

Cut to the chase, Lindsay wanted to shout at them. Instead, she listened quietly, vowing that if they said anything else in defense of Einer, she would walk out and turn the whole thing over to Mary Catherine. If they were aware of the accusations she had made to the police about Einer and the police telling her that, in the absence of corroborating evidence of his duplicity, it was her word against his, the dean and the university's lawyer didn't say so. They did, however, offer her her job with tenure. Lindsay read the contract in their presence.

"This appears to be satisfactory. I'll let Mary Catherine read it, and if she also finds it satisfactory, I'll sign." She stood, they shook hands, and she left. On the way out of the building she met Ellis Einer. He walked by as if he had no idea who she was.

"We're all really glad you got your job back," said Sally, "but I think you should have stuck it to them."

"I got what I wanted." Lindsay sat leaning back in her chair with her feet up on her desk.

"But Einer got away with it," Sally said. "That's not fair."

"More or less, he got away with it. But his reputation's damaged. I'm sure many of the people he works with believe he's behind the thefts. Sometimes, all you get is the satisfaction of being right."

"But what about Gerri Chapman and Francisco Lewis?"

"I assume Lewis is still coming. He can't fire me, but there's nothing to prevent him from assigning me a janitor's closet for office space. We'll just have to see what happens when he gets here."

"Are you worried?" asked Sally.

Lindsay smiled. "No. I'll deal with problems if they arise. This political stuff is just part of university life."

Sally still frowned. "Isn't anything secure?"

"Just family, friendship, and personal integrity," Lindsay said.

Sally went to her desk, shaking her head. But the smile still played around Lindsay's lips. All in all, things were pretty good. So what if she had learned some things about her grandfather she would have preferred not to know. The new relationship with her brother was something she had yearned for for a long time. And Derrick—yes, things looked pretty there good.

Her telephone rang and Lindsay looked at it, wondering if she should pick up the receiver.

"Chamberlain, this is Trey. Can you come up to my office? There's something I want you to see. Bring Sally if she's there."

"Sure. We'll be right there."

Brandon and Bobbie were in Trey's office when Lindsay and Sally arrived. The three of them were grinning like Cheshire cats.

"What's up?" asked Lindsay.

"You remember that paper I've been working on about the Southern Cult hand-eye motif?" Brandon asked.

"Yes," said Lindsay, wondering why they were all grinning at her.

"You remember how we took pictures of the Kentucky artifacts, and I took a lot of pictures of the mica cutout of the hand-eye?"

"Yes, as long as I live, I'll never forget them."

They all laughed.

"Well," said Brandon—apparently this was his show, and Lindsay felt a pang of guilt for suspecting him of having anything to do with the thefts—"Dr. Marcus has been helping me and Bobbie scan the photographs. We were going through them and we found this one."

They watched as Lindsay and Sally took the eight-by-ten photograph and examined it. The date and time in digital lettering, entered automatically by the camera, were in the left-hand corner. The photo was so clear she could see the texture of Sally's hand as she held the shiny mica cutout. Brandon was a good photographer.

She looked at Brandon, Bobbie, and Trey. They were still watching her closely, waiting. She looked back at the picture—the mirror-smooth mica, the hand, the etching of the eye in the center of the palm. Like an illusion that at first you can't see but then becomes clear, Lindsay saw it and grinned. There, on the day the artifacts were unpacked and their value discussed, the day before Ellis Einer came to Lindsay's office, the glossy mica hand with the all-seeing eye showed the reflection of Ellis Einer's face as he stood in the doorway leading to the archaeology lab, his eyes aglow at the sight of the Indian treasure.

More praise for
DRESSED TO DIE

Beverly Connor knows how to mix anthropology
with a mystery that ultimately educates the reader
while keeping them on an exciting edge.
—Harriet Klausner, Painted Rock Reviews

From the very first page of *Dressed to Die*, Chamberlain's cool head and rational hypotheses about the
densely packed plot keep the reader in suspense
amid the rising tension. Her stability and potent feminine intuition give suspicion a good name.
—*Daily Press/Banner Herald*, Athens, Ga.

"Delightful." **—*Northwest Arkansas Times*, Fayetteville**

"A highly charged, tightly plotted, and well-paced
mystery. . . . The forensic techniques are as fascinating as the political dynamics of the University of
Georgia.

—*I Love a Mystery*